THE
LAST
BOOKANEER

Also by Matthew Pearl

The Dante Club
The Poe Shadow
The Last Dickens
The Technologists

THE
LAST
BOOKANEER

MATTHEW PEARL

Harvill *Secker*

LONDON

1 3 5 7 9 10 8 6 4 2

Harvill Secker, an imprint of Vintage,
20 Vauxhall Bridge Road,
London SW1V 2SA

Harvill Secker is part of the Penguin Random House
group of companies whose addresses can be found at
global.penguinrandomhouse.com.

Penguin
Random House
UK

First published by Harvill Secker in 2015

www.vintage-books.co.uk

A CIP catalogue record for this book is available from the British Library

ISBN 9781846556197 (hardback)
ISBN 9781846556203 (trade paperback)
ISBN 9781448113071 (ebook)

Printed and bound in Great Britain by Clays Ltd, St Ives plc

Penguin Random House is committed to a sustainable future
for our business, our readers and our planet. This book is made
from Forest Stewardship Council® certified paper.

MIX
Paper from
responsible sources
FSC
www.fsc.org   FSC® C018179

For my children

THE
LAST
BOOKANEER

I

CLOVER

Some books are to be tasted, others are to be swallowed,
and some few to be chewed and digested.
Francis Bacon

No, I suppose you never heard of such a creature.
E. C. Fergins

Back in my salad days laboring for the New York Central and Hudson River Railroad Company, I would always keep an eye out to see if he would enter our car before the hour of departure.

"Expecting some pretty lass, are we?" the cook, grumbling with sarcasm, would ask me as I was scrubbing a table or polishing silverware to a blinding shine.

The man I would look for was given no more attention inside the cars than the bootblack or the traveling baker balancing his bread tray over his long arms. I suppose most people probably never looked at him long enough to take in his appearance. Middle-aged, middle-height, shaped like a plum, he had white metal-rim spectacles and a sharp nose and chin. His substantial and intelligent mouth was always busily readying itself for a smile, a song, or a whistle, or a shape of surprise. He would maneuver his bulky cart down the aisle of the train, a striped umbrella and his soft felt hat tucked above the top shelf of books. Reaching our dining car, he would push his bright green cart to me. Both of us had found the only man on the train who appreciated the other.

"My favorite customer," he would cheer me on; then, leaning so far over his cart it might tip over: "What catches your fancy today, Mr. Clover?"

My fellow dining car waiters liked to read novels about poor boys who become rich, or rich men who were secretly criminals. They turned the pages so rapidly the words were scenery, like the fields and farms that passed our windows for long stretches at a time. I was looking for something else in books. I could not really say what, but I think I can say why: a notion started in my own brain was probably wrong, but an answer read in a work of literature would be right. That was my conviction at nineteen, and only in later years would I come to trust myself over a book.

Despite Mr. Fergins's kind words, I did not really qualify as a customer. My pockets were so empty I was the only one living in New York City who did not fear thieves. But the generous old bookseller would leave me a book of my choice before continuing through the cars. If the tables were cleaned and set early, I could read until I felt the floorboards shake underfoot with the rumble of the engine. Then I'd hurry to return the borrowed volume while helping to carry his cart off the train. As he stood on the platform when the train began to run, Mr. Fergins waved his handkerchief as if he were seeing off his son.

In the village where I was born we did not have the variety of books that is only made possible by a bookstore or a circulating library. The local minister would give my mother books for me to read—black, thick, drab volumes meant to educate in menial or spiritual ways. Literature? I hardly even knew the word. My eyes were opened by an old, weathered copy of Milton I found when I was thirteen and the minister invited me to use his library. The poem was religious, but there was something new about it. The stories that I had heard so often in sermons were transformed by the poetry. They were made flesh and bone. It seemed I felt the tingling breath of Lucifer on the back of my neck, the light touch of Eve grazing against my arm, the expulsion not only of our first parents but of all the provincial boredom of my life. I cannot recall what questions I asked about *Paradise Lost*, but it must have been clear to him I was interested in the poetry over doctrine, because the book disappeared. Five years later, when I accepted the first job that brought me away from country life, I think I knew however much I tried I would never truly feel at home in mammoth, steam-filled Manhattan, with its incessant gallop, but the books consoled me. They were everywhere you looked, in the front of shop windows, displayed on tables along the sidewalks, in brand-new public libraries as big as castles. Even inside train cars.

Mr. Fergins may have been uninteresting to others. A relic of a time much slower than 1891; to them, he was as ordinary as his clothes. But they could not see the real man: amiable and unassuming, humble; there was a meaningful quality to his reticence, something unspoken. He endured the usual rudeness and impatience faced by salesmen. Perhaps this explained his patience toward me. Just as he would never dismiss the tastes of the waiters who wanted their fill of "sensation books," he never questioned my worthiness for steeper paths. Books could function in two different ways, he told me one time. "They can lull us as would a dream, or they could change us, atom by atom, until we are closer to God. One way is passive, the other animating—both worthy."

"I am just a railway waiter," I said once while lifting his cart down from the train. "No book in the world will change that."

He gave such a friendly, all-consuming laugh that I found myself laughing without wanting to, my heart sinking to the bottom of my chest as my eyes fell to the tulips painted on the cart. I suppose I'd hoped he'd argue.

"Forgive me, my young Mr. Clover. I laugh only at your formula. Literature will not change our profession or the quality of hats on our heads, heaven forbid—by change, I mean another thing entirely." He fiddled with his white spectacles. "Another thing . . ."

BUT HE DID NOT FINISH SPEAKING before the engine began to run and drowned him out.

Being a railway waiter means standing in place while the world moves around you. Because of us, instead of noticing that they had trapped themselves inside the belly of one of the most remarkable mechanical inventions of modern times, moving at speeds never before achieved, travelers could pretend that they were sitting in a dining room similar to their own. One evening around seven o'clock, on a popular route, our dining car teemed with people. There were frequently men and women of distinguished character, wealthy, well known, respected. On this occasion, there was a table on the far end of the car attracting stares that turned into stage whispers. I was too busy with my passengers to pay attention until Rapp, the waiter assigned to the table, grabbed my elbow. His skin was darker than mine, and he had greasy hair and a slight mustache waxed into crude points at each end, in imitation of our head cook.

He said: "You're a bookworm, Clover."

"What about it?" I was in no mood for his teasing.

"No offense. Sensitive one, you are. Just that I've noticed that grim half-breed face of yours perks up when you're talking to that queer peddler."

Rapp was just as much a half-breed as I was, as were all the railway waiters back then, but I was more annoyed by how he spoke about my friend. "Mr. Fergins is no peddler."

"Rambles through the cars hawking books, don't he? Ain't that a peddler? Besides, that ain't what I wanted to say. Thought you'd fancy a look."

He gestured with a nod toward the table. There was a passenger, back facing me, his hair worn long with strands of white and silver. He sat at a forward angle over his meal of boiled leg of mutton with Parisienne potatoes as though he were driving a team of horses.

"Mark Twain—Twain, the writer. Don't you even know about the things you know about?"

I had never seen an author in the flesh. I had never *considered* seeing an author in the flesh long enough to think what I would do.

Rapp's half of the car remained busy, but my tables had begun to clear, and the chief cook called me over to help. After I was charged with a smoking tray of food for one of my tables, the cook opened the ice chest in the floor and pulled out a bottle of wine. It was for table sixteen.

I took a few deep breaths and crossed to Rapp's side, where I turned to face one of my favorite authors, a half-dozen witty and clever sayings at the tip of my tongue. From under a wig of silver hair, a frightful old woman looked back up at me, flicking her long tongue over the white blur of her false teeth. "Heavens, what are you standing there for?" exclaimed the lady. "You can see I'm thirsty, boy. What kind of waiter are you?"

My hands moist with hot sweat, the bottle slipped through my fingers. Shattered glass and splattered wine: the greatest fear of the railway waiter. All the occupants of the dining car were gaping at me and it seemed every last one joined Rapp's laughter.

I could not bring myself to tell Mr. Fergins what had happened. A few days later, he was rolling his books through our cars and calling out his newest titles. I still felt the sharp sting of humiliation. Even minor embarrassment lingered a long time with me. I fell off a horse when I was seven years old, and some mornings in New York City, waking on my hard cot in a closet-like room, the shrill laughter of my former playmates rang in my ears.

The bookseller must have heard something of the practical joke, because he spoke to me in such a way that he might have been visiting my sickbed.

"There is no keeping a secret on a train," I said, my eyes falling to my hands.

He tried an innocent smile, then frowned at himself for giving himself away. "Come. Any man could drop something on a moving train."

"One of the other waiters played a dirty trick. Said Mark Twain was in the dining car, and I believed it. I stupidly believed it."

"No, but Twain wouldn't be traveling that route this time of year," he began, then stopped himself, excusing the strange digression by clearing his throat. "Mr. Clover, you believed your unworthy associate's statement because you are an honest man, and you expect honesty reflected back from the world. I have been known to be the same way."

"The worst part, Mr. Fergins, was not Rapp's joke. It was how I felt when I saw it was not really him." As I finished the statement, I realized with shame that there were tears in my eyes.

"You are always better off to read a book, anyway, than to meet the person behind it."

"Why?" I asked of the peculiar reassurance. By the time he held out his handkerchief I had forgotten my own question.

"Do you know why you are so upset?"

"I don't, sir," I admitted.

"Let us think about it. Maybe it will come to you."

"No. I haven't a clue why I have turned into such a baby over a silly prank, some broken glass, and an author who was never there to begin with. New York City is too hard, just as Reverend Millens warned."

"Millens?"

"My father," I explained, telling the bookseller more in two words than I would ever reveal to the other waiters or the fellows in my tenement. "Well, I never knew he was, until I was thirteen. His church helped bring my mother to the village when she was a girl during the war, and then she assisted him in the work of arranging for others to come there. We could not be in his congregation, of course, but he would leave me books when I was a boy and, later, would let me pick them for myself. Sometimes I could hear his sermons from inside the library, which was above the chapel. When I told him I wanted to leave, he warned me the city would be too much for me, that it would be hard enough for a white man."

"New York is hard for everybody; that is what makes it what it is. You know, Mr. Clover, when most people read a book, they take from its story happiness and strife, good and evil, morality and sin, so on and so on. That is not what is most important. It is always in the parts that we cannot fully understand—the holes in a story, the piece missing—where the real truth of the thing lurks."

I shrugged, not seeing the point.

"There may come a day when you will understand what you are grieving today. Then the story you just told about Mr. Rapp's loathsome prank will have another meaning, and be more important to you than an actual encounter with a so-called genius. Then you will think back and say, 'Mr. Fergins was a true friend.'"

He seemed to guess I was most concerned at the moment about whether he would judge me for crying; he patted my arm reassuringly, which helped, and I sat back and listened to his wonderful descriptions of the latest books, as if he were offering up new and better lives. He even read me part of Coleridge's "The Rime of the Ancient Mariner," with all its stormy rhythms. *We were the first that ever burst*—as I listened, I felt as though his words were the winds and they were driving us on—*into that silent sea.* In later years, this would be one of my happiest memories of my time as a railroad man.

New York City was so expensive that on only six or seven dollars a week (depending on gratuities) my chief amusement besides reading had to be to walk the island from end to end and watch. Watch the wealthy families stepping up into extravagant four-horse chariots, watch the vendors in the crowded quarters of hardworking Chinese or Germans. Everyone, the wealthiest or poorest, seemed to be in a hurry, but not I, not when I was away from the railroad. My mother's cousin had a stable for police horses, so I saw him once every few months, but mostly he would have me help tend to the horses. From time to time I would encounter the bookseller in the city. I was so accustomed to seeing Mr. Fergins on his rounds through our train, I marveled the first time I saw the man with the roar of the city around him—but there he was, bent over his green cart, pushing it through the streets as though he had done so for all eternity. On one particular day, I was passing through the uneven streets of the lower portion of the city, studded with mansions of bygone eras that had turned into warehouses as the wealthy were building estates closer to the park. It was growing late, the brick buildings tinted a peaceful orange by the sun, when he appeared, struggling over the dents and breaks in the sidewalk. I rushed to help.

"My poor legs rejoice for you, young Clover," he said, his face wet and pink with effort. "I purchased this cart from a florist—that is why there are tulips painted on one side—and sometimes I think of what it would be like filled with bouquets. Nothing in the world—not a ton of bricks—feels as heavy as books being moved." He pointed our way into a boardinghouse. It was a modest wooden structure near the slow, dark river that separated New York from New Jersey. Well-dressed and well-bred gentlemen boarders occupied the sitting room. Pushing the cart into Mr. Fergins's chambers on the ground floor, the umbrella tumbled from the top shelf.

As I retrieved it, I noticed it was misshapen, with the general form of a banana, and there was a stain on the striped fabric of the umbrella, a dark red, perhaps rust. The bookseller seemed embarrassed by its condition and tucked it back into the cart. "Always rolling off . . ." he apologized.

I was amazed by the sheer number of volumes of all kinds of bindings, colors, and sizes wherever my eyes traveled. Every conceivable space on any table or shelf and much of the floor was claimed by piles about the height of a tall man's knee, with a wobbly wooden ladder that could be wheeled around. Mr. Fergins, his energy restored, mounted this with an athletic step that propelled him to the tops of the highest peaks. There were strong fumes of oil, too, though not nearly enough light to read the titles of the books without putting your face against them.

"Now I see how you can boast such a wide selection in your cart."

"Oh, no. These are not books that I sell on the train cars or in the street, dear boy. I have a pair of storage rooms two streets away for inventory."

"Oh?"

"These are books and folios I collected, starting long before I had my own stall in Hoxton Square in London. Much of it was purchased from the stock of bankrupt publishing firms, private libraries, auctions, sometimes junk dealers who were too ignorant about books to know what they had in front of them. Go on, do look around for yourself. These books have witnessed life and death."

I laughed at the grave proclamation until I saw he was contemplative and serious. I made my way through the great maze of books, careful not to brush any binding with my coat. Interspersed with the familiar names of literary greats lurked mundane, interchangeable titles such as *Manual of Bibliography, Bibliographers' Manual,* and *American Bibliography.* There was a shelf of humorously titled books such as *Drowsy's Recollections of Nothing* and *History of the Middling Ages* that were not books at all, but rather imitation volumes Mr. Fergins had purchased from a public auction at the country home of the late Charles Dickens, who commissioned the false books to conceal a door in his library. I stopped to examine some books resting above these.

"Have you ever read it?"

I was looking at about half a dozen books with the same title: editions of Mary Shelley's *Frankenstein.*

"Read *Frankenstein*? No, sir. Reverend Millens would have barred it from coming near his library. I have never seen it with my own eyes, actually. Is it a proper book?"

"After Sir Walter Scott read it, he wept, for he knew that even *he,* the finest writer in the history of Scotland, could never write a romance as original as a twenty-one-year-old girl had done. Does that answer your question?"

I was not sure it had. "Scott I'd borrow from a friend and smuggle it inside my house. That and Stevenson."

"There is nothing as lovely as a borrowed book. Those two Scottish geniuses' books share a particular quality—I mean Scott and Stevenson. When you begin to read them, you feel like a boy again, and when you close the book you've turned into a better man." Mr. Fergins went on, smiling and extending his arms wide, as though to embrace the room: "Now that you have made a closer inspection, what do you think is the single most valuable book in here?"

I told him I could not guess.

"Try." The warmth of the room made his forehead bead with sweat and his spectacles slip down the bridge to the pointy tip of his nose.

He seemed so pleased at the idea of me picking out a book. Not wanting my ignorance to shine through, I took my time to weigh my choices, then I selected a large volume bound in heavy black calf leather.

"Excellent. That is one of the first folios of Shakespeare, but it is sadly incomplete. You see?" He brought it to a desk—where there was just enough free space between stacks of books to open the big volume—and showed me that pages were missing before pointing out other imperfections that remained invisible to me after he described them. "I purchased this for just two hundred shillings from the estate of a deceased lawyer in London some four years ago, and it is worth at least three hundred and fifty. Can you believe that? More remarkable than any original edition of Shakespeare is the fact that today for a shilling you can buy a fantastic modern edition of Shakespeare's greatest plays. No, this is not one of my gems, but it is a clever guess, Mr. Clover. Now, hand me that one, if you please—yes, the second shelf down, two-thirds of the way across, the one that looks like a scared kitten who has been dragged from a river by its scruff."

It was a small, worm-eaten thing. He waited for my assessment.

"It appears to me to be a collection of poems," I said. "It is in tatters, I'm sorry to report, Mr. Fergins. It is missing a title page, which I suppose ruins the ability to resell it. And on top of that, it has been defaced—there is writing in pencil on many of the pages." Words had been circled, underlined, drawn over with arrows into the margins, where there were illegible markings.

"Good, good. That is a volume of John Donne's poetry. It is not a first edition, nor a rare one, and the thing presents no particular features of bibliographical interest. Yet, in my estimation, that would be worth in today's market more than a thousand dollars."

"Why?"

"Because this copy belonged to Samuel Taylor Coleridge. Those marks you noticed written in pencil are the notes Coleridge made on

Donne's poems. Imagine! It is the real power of a book—not what is on the page, but what happens when a reader takes the pages in, makes it part of himself. That is the definition of literature. It reminds one of the quote from Francis Bacon about books."

I did not know the quote, never having read Bacon. But I was too timid to ask that or much else as he paraded me through the rest of his temple of books and excitedly showed me his favorites. He taught me what "signatures" could be used to identify a first edition, and how to most efficiently compare editions of the same books for changes and imperfections. He showed me books that other collectors or sellers had tried to repair only to further injure the edges of the papers, a problem, he explained, that booksellers referred to colorfully by saying the book had been "bled." He discussed prices of the books, contrasting what he paid with the actual or current value. I was flattered because his tone suggested I, too, could learn a trade in books if I desired. But it was disorienting to hear these names—Shakespeare, Wordsworth, Scott, my own sacred Milton—coupled with the crude sounds of numbers. "Now, if you remember only two things from my lessons, promise me it will be these: do not follow the latest fashions of Parisian collectors, and never pass up the chance to buy a book of English poetry dated before 1700."

"I promise, Mr. Fergins."

Through all of this, a small but persistent clicking sound could be heard, then another simultaneous clicking over the first. The bookseller let out one of his sudden laughs. Imagine an old wolf howling for the last time before lying down to die, and there you have his memorable style of laugh. "You are looking around for a clock, I take it. No, there are many things that have become dearer to me since the day I left London, young Mr. Clover, but time is not among them. In fact, I have no use for it outside the timetable for your railroad. The sound you are hearing comes from inside there."

He led me to a large glass case and pried open its iron cover. The floor of the case was filled with pine and buttonwood leaves. On top of this soft bedding were elaborately constructed compartments with strips and squares of various materials—leather, cloth, paper. There were two ventilation windows on the sides of the case, and a petroleum lamp burning hot, with a saucer of water over it that created a mist you had to squint through. I stepped back, startled by an unexpected movement. The case was filled with an assortment of translucent worms. He told me a professor of one of the city colleges had loaned him all of it in order to observe the creatures inside. Then he handed me a magnifying glass to look through.

"What are they?"

"Bookworms. Well, that name itself has always been wrong. There is no *actual* species called a bookworm. We who have an interest in books imagine these pests all fit into one type of category because it grants them unified purpose. We prefer a villain we can't see to at least have a name. They are not even worms, actually, but the larvae that become certain types of insects. There are types of moth and deathwatch beetle, for instance, that feed in the larval stage on all the materials used to make a book—glue, cloth, paper, leather. Take *Anobium bibliothecarum*. They produce the clicking you heard. These little creatures range from one twenty-fifth to one quarter of an inch and bore holes from cover to cover. Once they grow into adults, they have no use for these sorts of food. Think of it. They are raised on our books, then must leave them behind forever. The mouths of these little fellows are the most terrible things you've ever seen—all teeth and muscle. Observe for yourself through the lens. But make sure none get out—imagine the Judgment Day that could come of that, in this little room of all places on earth."

He showed me sketches he had made of each type of larva and indicated which ones the book hunter should most fear.

RAIN WOKE THE CITY after a cool and still night the one other time I chanced to meet the bookseller in the streets. Walking through City Hall Park, I noticed my friend among the sea of faces. I had to look twice, because he was without his book cart, because he held up that poor umbrella of his, and lastly because he was partially blocked from view by a man in a heavy wool coat and a beaver hat. I had previously supposed Mr. Fergins was fifty-odd years old, as a sort of average of his saggy eyelids, his elastic mouth, his delicate porcelain skin, his sturdy head and limp body, each of which, on its own, suggested a slightly different age. This time, his posture seemed more bent than I had noticed before, and as the raindrops rolled off the warped wings of the umbrella, onto his shoulders and hat, and filled his lenses with drops of water, he grew older before my eyes. The two men were standing midway up the white marble steps to the magnificent courthouse.

I hailed my acquaintance once he was alone but he did not hear; as he climbed toward the massive columns I called again. He turned to look for the source. For a moment, an uncharacteristic sternness came over him.

"Mr. Clover," he said to me, his customary cheer creeping in. The other man had just departed, marching down the steps. I wondered if he could have been a lawyer discussing some sort of trouble. Even with his easy smile in place, the bookseller seemed pensive.

"I could help push your cart today. I needn't report to the station for hours."

He tucked the umbrella under his arm and was rubbing his gloved hands together for warmth. "Believe it or not, I've left my cart behind in my rooms today. I must look like a mermaid absent her fish tail without it. I fear I must excuse myself, for I need to go in the court-house. Pray come if you like, Mr. Clover."

I knew the invitation was probably made out of politeness, but having only ever seen the outside of the building, I accepted anyway.

We walked through the gallery in front and down the corridor, where there was some commotion at the entrance to one of the rooms. A throng of people jostled each other and talked loudly, reminding me of the time I had visited the horse races outside the city between trains. The big double doors to the room had just been opened and the crowd flowed inside.

"What's going on in there?" I asked.

Mr. Fergins peered up at the clock above the end of the hall. "Ten minutes to spare. Very well. Let us enter the madness."

The room was filling with men and some brave women, most in fine clothes and holding expensive hats in their hands or under their arms, away from the crush of bodies. The bookseller's hands and umbrella were more effective tools for clearing a path than I could have guessed. The room suddenly seemed to hold its breath, then exhaled with even greater excitement. I positioned myself at a height to see the source. A prisoner had just been brought in at the front of the chamber. He had irons around his wrists and a bailiff steered him toward the front table. There was a man near us, evidently a physiognomist, who stood on a bench and dictated observations to an assistant: "Head and brow, showing an excess of animal passions . . . Jaw and high cheeks, a force of nature . . . In profile, a fearful intellectual capacity is revealed in the front lobes—have you gotten that down?"

Turning away, I suddenly felt a hand on my head.

"Nice, quite nice," I heard.

"Pardon me!" I cried out, brushing the intruding fingers off.

The physiognomist pulled back. "Very sorry there, boy." Then, to his assistant, he said in a quieter voice, "take this down. As previously observed in my notes of their race, the present mulatto contains features of the Caucasian in the cerebral area, explaining the greater capacity for intellectual growth over the common Negro."

"See here—" Fergins began, getting between us, but the eager scientist had already pranced away to try to get closer to the prisoner.

There were jeers and mutterings, and soon rough epithets tossed from all sides of the crowd. "Scoundrel" and "traitor" could be made out; then, louder, "Pirate!" This last word was taken up by other voices in the room.

The man in question, in the brief intervals in which I had an unobstructed view, appeared unmoved by the near riot. He was tall, a full wave of dark hair on his uncovered head, with handsome features, a grim half smile that never showed his teeth, and a slightly crooked jaw that might have been broken. I could not help but feel a touch of admiration for his imperviousness to the noisy hostility. I moved closer to the front of the room, pulling Mr. Fergins along, even as I began to sense hesitation seize him. Then, as the prisoner passed near us on his way to the dock, his eyes locked on—*me*.

No, I realized almost at once, he stared over my shoulder at my companion. The prisoner stopped. He opened his mouth to speak and the room fell hush. Then the words pulsed and popped from his mouth like the sounds of a drum. Words I could not understand at all. It was a language I had not heard even while strolling the docks of New York City—which to me meant it was not a language.

Ooot-malla malla-malla-malla ma!

The articulate gibberish of Babel, as my father used to say in his sermons on the signs of the devil's language. That was how it sounded to me. As the prisoner spoke, the color of blood filled his face, while all color simultaneously drained from the bookseller's cheeks. The audience seemed to take the man's burst of nonsense as taunting toward them. The jeers increased. I wrapped an arm around Mr. Fergins, using my other arm to battle our way back to the gallery and then to the staircase.

He was walking ahead of me as I peppered him with questions about what we had seen and what had happened. "Ah, here we are," was all Mr. Fergins said. We had climbed one floor up and now reached a door, painted crimson, that ended a long corridor. The bookseller rapped the point of his umbrella high on the door, and when the door was opened, with an abrupt farewell he left me standing alone. I waited as long as I could but he never returned.

The next few occasions Mr. Fergins passed through our cars I was busy, or he was, and there was no time to discuss the strange turn of events at the courthouse. Another week passed. Then there came an occasion when engine problems disabled a train on our track, and the waiters sat around in the fashion of the leisurely class, wrinkling our fine liveries, alongside the darker-skinned dishwashers and porters. The bookseller, whose grin was wider than usual as his books were snatched at a brisk pace by stranded travelers, brought over an armful of volumes he said he had chosen for me, to which I replied, "No time today, Mr. Fergins."

His mouth formed a long *o* and his large brown eyes appeared sad beneath the thick lenses I now noticed were etched with elaborate scratches. I asked him to take a table with me in the empty car.

"Excuse my rudeness, Mr. Fergins. But you left me standing there in the courthouse, and you ignored my questions."

"Quite right!" he said, shaking his head. "You are right about everything. My only excuse is that I was unusually distracted that day. What shall I answer for you?"

"Who was that prisoner we saw being brought into the courtroom?"

He seemed startled by the question. His shoulders relaxed, but he did not speak for another moment until he asked, urgently: "Have you ever heard of a bookaneer?"

I shrugged at the queer word, then shook my head.

"No, I suppose you never heard of such a creature."

A passenger knocked into the book cart and the slender umbrella tumbled down. Mr. Fergins seemed so proud when he caught it that he might as well have stopped a baby's fall. As though to explain his pride, he added one of his peculiar asides: "This homely thing saved my life, you know."

"The umbrella?" I replied with a quizzical stare.

"Did you know, Mr. Clover, that there are more patents filed by people set on improving umbrellas than for any other object? Yet they hardly ever change."

"What has been pricking my curiosity was that you seemed to understand what the prisoner said—that mixed-up balderdash he called to you."

"I?" His howl-laugh started and then broke apart into smaller, self-conscious giggles.

"Yes."

"Who am I? Whatever makes you think that? Youthful imagination. I sell books and try to make people happier doing it: that's my life in a nutshell. Let me show you a new novel from London."

"I know what I saw," I insisted, blocking his hand as he reached for the cart. "He was looking right at you when he began to speak in that strange tongue, and whatever he said troubled you. Mr. Fergins, I was there!"

The bookseller sighed, the bottom of his spectacles fogging for a moment, then clearing again to reveal pained eyes. "That was the first day of the man's trial. I had been asked by the judge, because of long years of examining handwriting and the qualities of paper and ink, and so on, to review some documents related to the case. It is rather a tedious service, but I felt I should agree to the request. I suppose that man you saw is rather cross with anyone who might be asked to assist against him. He is a dangerous sort. I do not know the words he spoke, but I hardly like to think of what he is capable of."

"Why is he so hated? Did he commit treason? Murder?"

"Murder!"

"Something infamous, I'm sure. Why else would all those people come just to leer at him?"

"No, he is not a murderer, not of men, at least—of books."

"*Books*, Mr. Fergins?" I responded, too incredulous to complete my thought. "You don't mean . . . A book cannot be . . ."

"The details of this narrative, in which I played a small part, will throw sufficient light on the subject, Mr. Clover, and should you suffer me to tell the story, you may well come to see what I think you have suspected these past months, that books are not dead things."

That was how the last case of the bookaneers, the existence of which is known by so few, the specifics by none who walk the earth, came to be told to me.

II

FERGINS

Robbery of a publisher—I said that if he regarded that as a crime it was because his education was limited.

M ARK T WAIN

You meet all kinds in the black arts—I mean printing.

A PRINTER'S DEVIL AT THE C ROWN

If you should ever meet people who tell you they know something about the bookaneers, be skeptical. They probably deal in myths and fables. That most people have never heard of the bookaneers and never will stems from the bookaneer's unique position in that long, twisty, and mostly invisible chain of actors that links author to reader. It will be the bookaneers' collective fate to have appeared and disappeared with only traces left in our atmosphere, like so many meteors. The story I have to tell is about a particular bookaneer of the most extraordinary skill—the last true representative, some might say, of that name and tribe. My account is true in all particulars, because I was there.

The story has no beginning—I mean no single obvious starting point—but stories ought to try to begin somewhere. London will do, then. My bookstall in Hoxton Square was near the corner of Bowling

Green Lane. I grew it, cultivated it, and—excuse my sentimentality—
loved it for years to the exclusion of almost everything else. My stall
backed onto a fence, the iron spokes of which were clothed with moss
in every variety and shade of green and brown from two hundred years
of growth. A church bell tolled periodically from one end of the street,
a fire engine clanged from the other, and my books were situated com-
fortably between these sounds of spiritual succor and earthly warning.

Around people who enjoy books, the bashful disposition of my
youth grew into a sociable one. Strangers talking over piles of books do
not remain strangers for long. Had I never learned to like books, I
would have become the dullest sort of hermit. When I was younger
than you, Mr. Clover, I set myself for the law, persuaded that a profession in which books were carried about and consulted at all times
would have to be agreeable. But the harder I tried, the more that discipline's endless doctrines made my head ache. I quit with no plan in
sight.

I've never been able to bear asking for help when I need it most, and
I needed it then. What a spot to be in, with no prospects and no sympathetic family member. Fortunately there was a bookshop. Every
young man's story should have a bookshop. This one was not far from
where I was boarded. I spent so much of my time inside—hiding, I
suppose, from my friends and my parents' friends, from my landlord,
from having to justify my decisions and, high heaven forbid, make new
ones—I might well have been counted as an employee. Soon enough I
was. Stemmes, the book collector who owned the place, probably felt
he had no choice but to invite me to apprentice. For more than three
years I slept in a windowless chamber beneath the shop. I packed
crates, pushed brooms, and tried to avoid falling from old shop ladders
while wielding my duster, but I also learned about book values and
imperfections, about which auctions to attend and how to win the best
volumes, about how to search for the right book for a customer and,

when necessary, the right customer for a book. I enjoyed every minute of the work. Well, that is not quite right. I disliked being closed up in dark rooms all day and growing unused to sunlight while trying to please a gloomy, stubborn man who would spout maxims such as "exaggeration is the octopus of the English language," which I assumed must mean *something*. When I learned that an outdoor bookstall in a leafy square was shuttered, I gathered every cent I had in this world and purchased the municipal license, its shelves, and its stock.

My natural gifts for salesmanship may have been lacking, but they grew with the delight I had in my humble enterprise. I kept five sets of stacking compartments of shelves, with my chair in the middle, and an inventory tailored to the enduring loyalists who came by several times a week. Unlike other bookstall keepers, I never chased anyone away for wanting to read a chapter or two under the shelter of my awning on a hot or rainy day. In fact, readers too poor to make a purchase had been known to come to my stall every afternoon for two weeks until a novel was finished.

My parents never recovered from my dropping out of the law. Once, I overheard them speaking in their garden, my mother remarking to my father that at least I had my books—I will never forget how these words sounded in her voice. "At least he has his books," as though without them I was nothing. They always blamed my reading, you know, for my having fewer friends than my brother and for my weak eyes, never thinking that because I had weak eyes and because I was shy, having a book at the ready rescued me.

I should mention that in the course of having the bookstall, I met a few handsome women now and again who were as interesting as they were affable. And my thoughts turned to starting a family whenever I would see Veronica and Emily, my beautiful little nieces, who lived in the country and kept me on my toes during my visits. But books are jealous mistresses. As soon as I was back in London my time was consumed to the point that the pursuit of anything more than cordial friendships was always cut short. Before long, I had lost my youth and my patience for indulging others. Books were everything in life; books were better than wine.

Yes, you could say I had all I ever hoped for. Before the age of thirty, I was blissfully self-sufficient, earning enough to live on and attracting notice for skills that carried special value in our trade. For example, I was unusually adept at deciphering handwriting that was deemed illegible scrawl by others, even though my own eyesight was never better than mediocre, and that only by being glued to spectacles. My abilities were useful in identifying markings made inside books by previous sellers or readers and by authors themselves on proofs or in rare first editions. I could imitate a particular person's handwriting, as well, so that samples of the style and appearance could be mailed outside of London to potential buyers instead of waiting for photographic reproductions. I always had a penchant for remembering what I read, and for reading a wide range of subjects in literature and history alike, which allowed me to date proof sheets or other materials discovered unbound and waiting to be priced. It helped that I spent long days at my stall dipping into every sort of book imaginable in between serving customers. The worthy bookseller must know not only the details of Spencer's childhood but also the history of papyrus in ancient Egypt.

Most readers mistakenly believe books are creations of an author, fixed things handed down from high into their waiting hands. That is far from true. Think of the most interesting, the most alarming and brilliant choice made by a writer in literature; now consider that equally interesting, alarming, and brilliant maneuvers were made by people you will never hear about in order for that work to see the light of day. The path is never without obstructions, even more so when the publication proves influential or controversial. After years of keeping my stall, I grew more conscious of such hindrances. I noticed other shadows over the literary kingdom I had been too naive to see, and had occasion to encounter some of the denizens of these shadowlands: shameless autograph hunters and forgers, collectors who tried passing off third editions as firsts, publishers who gave false discounts and fabricated advertising costs, customs officials who sought graft on expensive editions imported from abroad. There is a verse I write in my notebook from memory once a year: "Though an angel should write, still 'tis devils must print, and you can't think what havoc these demons sometimes choose to make." Thomas Moore meant the printers' devils, the name for those men with the thankless and tedious tasks of dwelling in a printing press. But the devil has taken many forms in our trade.

Among the various mischief makers and profiteers who have besieged books from time immemorial, there arose the bookaneers. Their origins go back to the first American laws to govern copyrights. That legislation, passed in 1790 by high-minded and arrogant legislators (the usual politicians, in other words), deliberately left works of foreign authors unprotected, which caused other countries to retaliate by withdrawing protection for American works. This opened doors to various kinds of pirates and black markets, European literature plundered by Americans and vice versa. Publishers did their best to shut those doors—at first. But you will find in life that greed for profits is too strong for even good men to resist.

In the new era—not just to publish, but to publish first and cheaply—the publishers had to find individuals with particular sets of skills who could obtain manuscripts and proof sheets through persuasion, bribery, extortion, and, at times, outright theft, then transport them from one country to another. After a while, the publishers and these covert agents expanded beyond trying to secure foreign books; assignments were handed out to spy on rival publishing houses and execute any errands that had to be accomplished out of view.

In short: a bookaneer is a person capable of doing all that must be done in the universe of books that publishers, authors, and readers can have no part in—*must* have no part in. Bookaneers would not call themselves thieves, but they would resort to almost any means to profit from an unprotected book. Take the pocket Webster's from the bottom of my cart and open to "B"—it would go right there, between "book" and "bookish." No, you will not find "bookaneer" in any dictionary, but pay attention and we will fill one in.

You wonder, no doubt, how from my modest perch as a keeper of a stall and a hunter of books I would have any view at all of such a shadowy crevice in the literary universe. I admit to feeding a special fascination with the subject from the first time I became aware of it. When an acquaintance would point out one of these bookaneers to me at a social club or hotel tavern around the city, a bolt of excitement would shoot through me. It was not the same sort of thrill as one's first glimpse of a long-read author—in that case, a personal encounter usually renders the subject more human, but in the case of the bookaneers, who were by nature secretive and remote, an encounter inspires a rather opposite effect. Of course, my own dealings with bookaneers were rare and brief, and I would never have anticipated that was about to change.

"I HAVE A BOOK for you."

Those words reached my ears while I was pulling a wagon down a bumpy sidewalk from a storage room to my bookstall. I remember it as a hot and muggy afternoon. I protected the books from the humidity and sun with a light blanket. The man who addressed me had a confident gait and a wide build that commanded attention. I shielded my eyes from the bright sun for a better look. He had a bushel of red hair shooting out from under a formal hat, dancing eyes, and a thick but well-combed mustache.

A glance told me the book in his hand was not mine, for I make it a point to know every one of my volumes on sight. "Not one of my collection, but I thank you nonetheless."

"I have *this* book"—the red-haired fellow said more slowly, revealing a wide gap between his front teeth on both the bottom and top, then held it close to me with both his hands—"for *you*, Mr. Fergins."

With that, he let the book drop spine-first to the sidewalk, where it tumbled into the street. I hurried to pick it up before it could be trampled or knocked into the gutter. By the time I stood again, he was gone. I could not help but wonder if this stranger had known that I would never under any circumstances leave a book—even the ugliest, most neglected tome—abandoned in the street. I cleaned off the cover with my handkerchief. Inscribed on it in small lettering was the title *Develin's Leister.*

Sometimes a customer would inquire whether I might sell a book on consignment, and I agreed whenever I could. I would subtract a small commission from a sale, and the whole transaction contributed to the reputation of the bookstall. But if this really was a request for a consignment account, never had I received a proposition so vague. After deliberation, I decided to add the book to my shelves and see what happened. When the stall opened the next day, there was a businessman whom I had never seen before, unmemorable in every way except for a small purple flower over his buttonhole, who browsed quietly for a few minutes before he purchased three books—including the one dropped by the flame-haired stranger, which I had placed on a low shelf beside two other volumes of similar color. I was somehow unsurprised by this strange turn in the strange circumstance. When I went to put the money handed over by the businessman in my strongbox, there was a five-pound note folded in my hand. I trembled with . . . confusion, amazement, excitement. My fingers, my hands, my entire body, were electrified.

You want to know more about the book that caused all of this disturbance. I'd put my palm to Gutenberg's Bible that I never opened it. Right away I recognized that odd title: *Develin's Leister*. The old farmers of England, trading tall tales, would often tease each other, "You picked that story up in *Develin's Leister!*" The legend goes that Develin had been some poor farmer who was always promising to write a book but, like most people who talk too much of writing one, never wrote a word of it. Nobody ever determined where the title of the book came from or exactly what it meant, but the book itself never existed—it was pure myth, an emblem of all the books in the world that would never be written, which is a great deal.

I could see that the volume given to me by the stranger was not an old one. There was a metal clasp, attached to a strong strip of leather, as was customary in bygone eras for large volumes of devotion. But the grain of the leather was recent. The book, in all ways, was a chimera. More than that, there was an implicit threat in the tone of the stranger's words to me, at least in my ears, forbidding me to open it.

Not long after all this transpired, my former employer Stemmes was forced by ill health to close his shop on the Strand and retire to the seaside. When a bookshop in a city of culture such as London stops its operations, it is viewed by the wider community as a failure of mankind—a sign that books are no longer being read, or only the wrong sort of books, that literature's finally dead, or in a temporary state of decay, that bookshops will one day disappear altogether and be replaced by mail order, that eventually books themselves would be finally and fully buried by that awful foe, so much cheaper and easier to carry: newspapers. But for those of us in the trade, it was about saying farewell to a friend.

A celebration for Stemmes was held at a lively, somewhat seedy tavern. In addition to the honoree's good friends, fellow collectors, and booksellers, there were some newspaper and magazine men as well as representatives of the less respectable publishing classes using the occasion as a stage for debauchery. A rotund young man, hardly sixteen, whose face was pocked and freckled, squeezed himself into a seat next to me. He already smelled strongly of alcohol and his manners betrayed a general vulgarity.

"Pardon my thick legs, sirs, pardon!"

Trapped by this creature, I looked to the other side of me, but the nearest person, an Irish illustrator of my acquaintance, was engaged in a rant with another man against the newest school of painters in London. I whistled a song to suggest I was content to be by myself with my pint, but hints were not this young man's forte. He told me he was a printer's devil—a fact I also might have guessed by the inky smears up and down his fingers, knuckles, and hands. The freckles I had noticed on his face were actually splatters of ink, maybe from that day, maybe from a year's worth of toil.

I moved again to change my orientation, but the devil nudged my ribs hard with his elbow. "Any great men here, fellow? I'd give a shilling to see Tennyson or Browning in person before they die."

"I shall let you know if I see them."

"Literary men must drink to write. Believe me, I know. Oh, I'd never write a word myself if I can help it. But I watch. Do I. You meet all kinds in the black arts—I mean printing. All kinds! From the meanest machine men who run the press, to the great bookaneers. The authors rarely venture down into the bowels of the presses, but I'm sent to them oftenly enough when I'm asked to collect proofs—you'd think I was the tax collector, you would, to see their faces fall when I show up at their doorsteps asking if they've finished their chapters—"

I stopped him. "You have actually met a bookaneer before?"

"Why, man, nearly the whole class of them have passed before my eyes one time or another since I started in this line as a mere boy of twelve. Even Belial, one time."

"By heavens! What was he like?"

"The greatest one I ever seen," he went on, ignoring the question and enjoying the fact he had hooked his fish, "the chief of them, is a fellow named Whiskey Bill. You've heard of him?"

I said I had.

"It's said he near invented the profession single-handedly. Surely he's too humble to admit it. He is not to be crossed, or quarreled with— of course that goes without saying when it comes to those hardened book pirates. The publishers who try to empty the pockets of readers quake at the sound of Bill's name more than any other. But he rewards his friends richly and opens paths for them."

"What do you mean 'paths'?"

"Paths to great fortune and glory." He added, somewhat hastily, "they say."

"What does the man look like?"

"What should the man look like?"

Before I could object to the absurdity of the question, he pushed his chair out and hurry-scurried away. Disappointed that the exchange had ended almost as soon as it became interesting, I then felt his noxious breath return on my neck.

"A head of fire," he said.

I spun around. As my eyes followed this imp strutting across the tavern on his way to the piano, they landed on another figure—the redheaded man who had dropped the mysterious book at my feet in the street. He was taking his high hat down from a hook, and as he fixed it on his head, Whiskey Bill—for I realized who he was at one fell swoop—tipped it in my direction, meeting my eye and offering that condescending, satisfied, double-gap-toothed smile that would become so familiar.

I had an urge to follow after him as he ascended the stairs, and a competing urge to run out the back door. But I did not budge. However distant my own life was from the bookaneers, I correctly surmised that any attempt to question him would run counter to what had just transpired. Whiskey Bill was ready to tell me who he was on his terms. It could not come from his own lips, and I knew enough to understand that nothing ought to come from mine. I remained seated for a long time, contemplating the peculiar situation and my position as an accomplice to a prominent bookaneer. I might have been filled with more qualms than I was, but the fact was, the longer I thought of it the more thrilled I was for it. The secrecy and potential danger—at least as I imagined the life I was entering—was enormously gratifying. I realized in an instant, as though struck in the face, that I did not have everything I wanted and hoped for—that I wanted this, wanted to be inducted into this realm. I actually prayed to God that night not to make a misstep that would strip the chance.

Apparently pleased by what had already passed at my bookstall, and my discretion at the Crown, Whiskey Bill began delivering books at irregular intervals. He never came to my stall. He'd pass me the package in a crowded street or sidewalk, on an omnibus or a ferry, with no explanation of how he'd found me and no conversation beyond the most basic greeting. Then a customer, different each time, always a stranger to me, would purchase the volume at my bookstall, leaving a too-large sum of money in my hands and never waiting for change.

My general interest in the bookaneers had given me some advance knowledge about Whiskey Bill. Despite what the printer's devil proclaimed to me, Bill was not the greatest example of his field; in fact, had there ever been a Professor Agassiz to work out a classification of the literary pirates, Bill would have been placed in the second tier, forever trying to push up his rankings. Then at the bottom rung were the so-called barnacles, those who had some experience in bookaneering but no patience, resorting to careless thefts and inevitably spending time in and out of jails; as the name suggests, these were parasites of the trade, acting on intelligence purloined from better and more successful practitioners.

The legends of bookaneers' deeds passed around Pfaff's Cave in the old days would inevitably include dramatic circumstances and intrigue, breathless chases through streets and buildings, confrontations with celebrated authors and battles of will with ruthless printers of wealth and power. As usual the truth is a source of disappointment. The commonplace bookaneer usually did little more than sit in dingy taverns to negotiate sundry transactions, act as a courier avoiding customs, and submit poems and stories plagiarized from an obscure magazine to other obscure magazines under false names, with the ambition of pilfering a few dollars here and shillings there. No heavily armed authors waiting in ambush, no sudden betrayals by trusted associates, no hidden passageways aiding an escape.

But if so many representatives of the craft were drudges and Jeremy Diddlers, a small and unofficial guild of professional, expert bookaneers rose to the pinnacle of greatness. They moved frequently between both sides of the Atlantic. I believe I could count the ones operating at a given time on one hand. They grew beyond the control of the publishers, who came to fear as much as rely on them. Each was a king.

These men—and one particular woman of note—were not mere publishers' clerks moonlighting as amateur thieves or spies. They spoke and wrote dozens of languages, were as well read in literature as any professor or man of letters, could identify the handwriting and style, even the stray pen marks, of thousands of authors and book illustrators through the small lens of an opera glass. Little wonder the rest of their brethren looked at them with equal parts awe and bitterness. They have been called audacious criminals, but this is not entirely accurate— the greatest bookaneers stepped into a void and helped control the chaos caused by the broken copyright laws and the maelstrom of greed that rumbles just beneath the surface world of books.

My prevailing interest in the tales of the bookaneers ripened into outright fascination once I became a footnote in Whiskey Bill's operations. I filled my notebooks with any scrap of gossip and partial anecdote related to them. I myself might have composed a treatise, *On the Classification of Bookaneers.* But despite my thirst for a fuller knowledge of their practices, I confess I still could not bring myself to open any of the mysterious volumes Bill delivered to me. I knew just enough to know they were no ordinary books. They were bound by hand, usually in thick brown leather, with the metal clasp and a different title each time of a book that did not exist. I felt his eyes always upon me and imagined that if I did unclasp one of the volumes, even in the privacy of my own chambers, my connection with this secret world would vanish there and then. I would rotate the thing in my hand, squeeze the leather, and conjure possibilities. Proof sheets of a highly touted novel not yet published. Manuscript pages missing for a hundred years from an unfinished masterwork. A decoy meant to trap a rival publishing spy.

Cast a look at my little cart. Some fancy the book a quaint, tame object, and it is not difficult to understand why. But take a longer look, Mr. Clover. Recall that when the first presses produced copies of the Bible, the scribes who had to spend years at a time on the same work, just as it had been done for centuries, streamed out from the monasteries with quills raised in the air, decrying the work of the devil. When one of the pioneering tradesmen printed certain words in red ink to emphasize them, it was proof that he had used his own blood. That was why the printers' assistants began to be called "devils." Soon printers were threatened with burning, and some were indeed put into the fire along with their equipment. From the beginning, the creation of the modern book was viewed as the work of Satan—an attempt to usurp the word of God.

No tameness there, and those were just the opening battles. In my boardinghouse, you took note of my copies of Mary Shelley's astounding and wild novel written when she was still more girl than woman. When *Frankenstein* was published, it was considered terrible and disgusting, a waking nightmare, yet it defied all intellectual hysterics by entrancing millions of unsuspecting readers. The book took on a life and importance of its own, not unlike how the creature does in that novel. Not unlike the bookaneers growing into a powerful monster nobody in the trade knew how to domesticate.

Since the advent of the modern industry, there are no parties in the book world who are innocent of commodification, commercialization, and competition, for even the high-minded authors who come to it young and starry-eyed compromise with reality; the readers remain relatively unaffected and pure, though their money must change hands. To a bookaneer, the past, present, and future of literature was all fair game. To the fervent imagination of a bookseller and collector like myself, there was no end to what treasure and mystery might be pressed between two boards.

Perhaps it was not only superstition, not only the pure pleasure of guessing that stayed my hand from the simple act of opening Bill's books. I now must wonder if I feared how what I'd find inside would change my life.

I BRIMMED WITH a new feeling of self-confidence about my place among other bookmen, and I gleefully frequented the best London social clubs and coffeehouses that served the literary and artistic circles. In these settings I was to encounter most of the reputable bookaneers of a generation. These were heady days, long before Molasses became mixed up in a case of murder, before the Berne copyright negotiations, when there was plenty of business for everyone. The trust

Whiskey Bill had shown in me led other bookaneers to transfer books anonymously through my busy bookstall, as well as hire me for assignments that matched my talents for handwriting identification. I could never know when I was being tested or not, and always made certain to perform my tasks in a timely and straightforward manner, indulging only in necessary questions. It was in this way that I came to have a minor but useful part in the world of the most surreptitious of bookmen. It was in this way that I crossed into the sphere of Pen Davenport.

Davenport was one of the three most infamous bookaneers in the world—the immortals, you might call them. An American by birth but long a citizen of the world with no home in particular, Davenport could often be observed keeping society among the London litterateurs. Then there was Kitten, a French lady who was considered the most determined and skillful of the set. You can still see a striking image of her on the third floor of the British Museum, in a painting of a green-cloaked damsel, for which she was used as a model by one of the great Bohemian painters of the past decades. The third bookaneer who was equally celebrated, Belial, an Englishman whose real name until recently was unknown, was rarely seen in public. He was always on a bookaneering mission, as far as anyone could tell. Davenport commanded interest and attention, but if you looked *at* Davenport you would look *for* Belial, and that gave the absent one of the pair a unique power.

Neither Belial, Kitten, nor Davenport were among the bookaneers who had employed my services. It was rather peevish of me to be discouraged by this. I confess that. I had been admitted into the world of the bookaneers by chance, and now all I wished, more than any earthly object, was to observe the absolute best. What is that Arab proverb old Mr. Stemmes would sometimes repeat? Beware the camel's nose—for its whole body will soon follow. You have the gist. I had never been greedy, but in this instance I could not restrain myself. Though Belial might as well have been the invisible man, and Kitten was too intimidating to approach, I decided that the next time I happened to see Pen Davenport I would come right out and tell him my desire.

I must have been invigorated by the breeze one brisk spring evening, because I thought I'd try some places where he might be, and found my way to the district of Covent Garden. When I entered the dark Italianate rooms of the Garrick Club, the clocks inside were chiming midnight while the noise and bustle of men was fresh and unflagging. Here was a place that made the thought of ever sleeping seem foolish. I hoped that listening to the after-theater conversations I might overhear some gossip related to the bookaneers, and more specifically a hint of a recent sighting of Davenport around London, though for all I knew he was on a remote mission and far from English soil.

I was flattered when the unassuming usher bowed and told me to follow him. "We have a place waiting for you."

How highly my new associations with the bookaneers had elevated my social status. Here in New York, culture is only occasionally more powerful than money, but in London, wealth will never be even a close second.

The Garrick was crammed with expensive collections of books and a range of paintings, modern and old, some of which the museums would consider too strange or obscene to display. Just as the wall space was split between art and literature, so was the roll of members and guests who frequented the place, these authors and artists also joined by many of the great actors of the theater. There were so many performers in wigs and false mustaches and heavy powders, you assumed everyone was in disguise even if they were not, and you felt that same feeling as in the best theaters of the day. Magical beings and not ordinary humans must reign here. There was one band of happy mummies and ghouls, raising glasses for a toast to a successful show. As I was conducted through a long passage off the main dining room, I prepared to ask the usher if there had been any interesting visitors that evening, when we stopped at the entrance of the smoking room.

The usher stepped to the side and I saw him. Pen Davenport was at a table in the center, the air around him a swirl of bitter tobacco scents—from musk to mustard. I glanced back over my shoulder. The usher had vanished into the dining room.

"I understand you have been looking for me."

My jaw actually dropped.

Drowsy, thoughtful eyes the color of emeralds glanced up from beneath long lashes. His voice was quiet enough that I had to lean an ear toward him. Above him was a painting of David Garrick, the legendary actor whose name inspired the club's, dressed as Macbeth and contemplating a dagger; to the left of the speaker, an elegant statuette of Thackeray.

I clapped my mouth closed. "Pardon?"

"Then you haven't been searching for me?"

I was so amazed I could hardly reply. Before the Garrick I had paused at a few taverns and clubs of literary bent where, my previous notes reminded me, I had seen Davenport in the past, but I had not given any indication of my purpose.

I found my tongue. "I looked for you this evening, yes, but have not uttered your name to another living soul."

"You did not have to. In the past four hours you visited the Beefsteak, the Green Room, the Canary House, the Hogarth, and now the Garrick, and did little else but whistle to yourself and hide behind your spectacles. I know who you are. You have performed trifling assignments for some middling bookaneers, and outside of that fact I would wager your life is rather plain. White-rim spectacles are only worn by a man who keeps clean. So if you are doing something unusual, it is surely connected to *our* profession, not yours. If two of the five places had been different, if you went to the Crown or Stone Tavern on your tour of London club life, even if only one of the five had been a favorite haunt of some other bookaneer, of Molasses's or that redheaded lout Whiskey Bill's, for instance, then it would have been less obvious you searched for me."

"But how did you know where I've been? Were you . . ." I swallowed my next word.

"I have not had you followed," he said, guessing my question. "I'm afraid, bookseller, you will never be important enough to follow." It is difficult to accurately describe how Davenport could speak with sincerity but without much inflection; only he could manage pronouncing "you will never be important" not as an insult, but as an impersonal observation.

"No, of course I couldn't. I didn't mean—"

"I maintain multiple sets of eyes across the city wherever there are literary characters. The clubs, the drinking dens, the coffeehouses, the circulating libraries, the printers' shops and their warehouses. I am informed of visitors' routines, and breaks in those routines. Unlike some of my more grandiose challengers who fancy they are too distinguished to be viewed by fellow men, I make myself just visible enough to know when someone wishes to find me. Now, if you please." He flicked his hand for me to take a seat.

Shaking off my nerves, I lowered myself into the chair opposite, almost slipping down the big leather cushion onto the floor. There was a sample of the club's famous gin punch waiting for me on the table. I could not stop myself from staring at the man.

"When they dreamed of turning iron and metal into gold, they called it alchemy. The much more far-fetched dream of turning bound sheafs of plain paper into fortunes, they call publishing," he mused with an arch expression on his face. Though I was nearly a decade his senior, at twenty-six years old he commanded a conversation in a way I never had. "Usually when a man seeks my company," the bookaneer continued, "I expect him to do some of the talking."

"Of course, Mr. Davenport." He held out a cigar to me. "No, thank you; tobacco rather irritates my—"

"Hold it, at least. I will not be seen in the smoking room of the Garrick with a nonsmoker."

I complied. "That's sensible."

"It is a doomed calling, you know."

"What?"

"Bookselling. Your problem is the educational system. It's become too good. Aristocrats enjoy spending as much money as possible on books. The greater portion of the population that learns to read, the more they will revolt against having to pay to do so. Now, your business."

I explained how recently I had been given the unexpected chance to be of some service to some in his field, and that I thought, perhaps, that if he should ever need assistance similar to that which I had performed from time to time for his fellow bookaneers—not that he would, being so accomplished—but in the odd event, the unexpected and unlikely occasion, the rare spot that he did find that he did, I thought to leave him my card.

"Oh. You are finished?"

"Well, I—Sorry."

"Do you know how many of the great bookaneers have passed through this room over the years?"

"No."

"They were individuals who rose, usually without the name of a college or a family, to hold as much sway as rich publishers and esteemed authors, more so in some cases, in determining the public's access to books. If they did wrong sometimes, well, so have the publishers—so have books themselves, which have started wars and have ended them, have saved lives and vanquished them without mercy. I understand you are a sort of encyclopedia when it comes to knowledge about our trade. I wonder if you noticed how I rate among the bookaneers—"

"Oh, the very top of the pile, I'd say! Pen Davenport? A master. Right up alongside Belial."

Later, I would understand that Davenport was not to be read all at once, like a broadside, but unfolded gradually, as the pages of a long, multivolume set of books. I had made two mistakes in a single breath. I had interrupted his monologue, without intending to, and I had said Belial.

His deep annoyance showed itself only by the downward slope of his brow and the pursing of his fine mouth. He punished me with three long beats of silence before his face relaxed. "Belial," he began in a grumbling voice. "Belial would eat your heart if given the chance. Tell me this, bookseller. Imagine Belial sitting beside me right now, and he offered you a place helping him, and I offered the same. You must accept one or the other, for we two are men of opposite principles."

"How do you mean?"

"I am a man who respects the supremacy of books; he is one who seeks to gain supremacy from them. Which man would you accept?"

"Why, I suppose whoever needed my help more."

I took his elaborately crumpled chin and his hunched shoulders to mean I had insulted him. "If you noticed how I rate among the bookaneers, if you possessed that modicum of knowledge, you would know that the reason I am first-rate is that I need no help. Certainly not the help of a man who believes I would do anything in the style as a ruffian such as *Whiskey Bill*."

"My apologies." I gave my spectacles a good polish and then took another quick glance around the room. "I am sorry I do not know what bookaneers have been in this place through history, Mr. Davenport. But I can tell you that Edgar Boehm said he made that statuette behind you in only two sittings with William Thackeray in 1860, but in fact he completed it only after the novelist's death. One of those four seemingly identical—seemingly, I say—early editions of Shakespeare on that oval table in the far corner is a forgery, and I would venture to guess a misprint on the title page of the third novel from the left on the shelf to the right of you has led the librarian of this club to believe it is a much older volume than it is."

"Listen to me, bookseller. I am going to ask you something, and if you can answer, I may give you a chance."

Hope returned to me, and hearing the beating of my heart in my ears reminded me how much I craved what he held out. I prepared myself, took a deep breath, nodded.

"Understand, Mr. Fergins, that when a man does work for me, he works for no one else."

"What is the question?"

"It is a simple and easy one—too easy. Whiskey Bill transferred a number of books over the past year and a half through your bookstall into other hands. What were in those books?"

I felt my racing heart skip. "I cannot answer."

"You do not remember or—" He broke off. He studied me through a series of slow blinks, then nodded. "No. You are loyal to the man."

I smiled and shook my head no. "I cannot answer, Mr. Davenport, simply because I do not know. You see, I never opened them." I placed the unlit cigar down in front of him and began to gather myself to leave.

"Wait a minute."

I paused at the threshold of the smoking room. I wasn't even certain he was still addressing me. When I turned around, he was concentrating on his cigar for a while before he put it out and spoke again.

"Congratulations. You gave the one right answer, bookseller."

"Did I?"

His hands were folded in his lap, the fingertips on one hand tapping the tips of his other hand as he considered me and waited for me to say something sensible.

I almost broke down laughing. *Pen Davenport* had congratulated me, and Thackeray and Macbeth were witnesses.

III

It is no exaggeration to say the publishing trade nearly ran aground a few years after I began to assist Pen Davenport. Several times, as a matter of fact. The greatest change for the community—and the terrible threat to the continued livelihood of the bookaneers—was the attempt to enact an international agreement on copyright. This movement, wide awake after a dormancy, tipped the trade into a state of uncertainty that disrupted every level of the profession, from the papermakers and compilers to the millionaire publishers. Meanwhile, printers and binders perfected methods to make books more cheaply and quicker than ever imagined. Book prices fell into disarray. Bookselling was no longer a trade for a rational man, as I discovered while keeping the dire accounts of my bookstall. You might wonder, as I continue my story, whether I was wise to put my bookselling business at further risk through my unorthodox associations. There were times when the added income from Davenport's assignments were all that stood between the operating or shuttering of my much loved bookstall.

I have mentioned that it was the lack of copyright protection for foreign works on both sides of the Atlantic Ocean that gave birth to the modern bookaneers. To shine the bright light of the law over the publishing field would all but obliterate their profession. Indeed, there came a time when the United States—a nation where it seems even lawmakers detest laws—finally agreed in principle to an international treaty. Authors celebrated the news and visited Congress to shake hands, but the gloom was palpable for those who were accustomed to keeping order in the hidden corners of the trade.

About a decade into my association with Davenport, some older bookaneers passed away or retired. The formidable queen bee of the group, the deceptively named Kitten, was gone, though her indelible mark never went away, especially from the methods and emotions of Davenport. Many of the lesser bookaneers moved on to simpler work, and the parasitic barnacles scrambled for whatever scraps remained. But here was something strange: it was the first-rate bookaneers, those who had been most nimble in their techniques and had shown the greatest abilities and foresight in their line of work, who blinded themselves to the inevitable downfall of the profession. The very best of the remaining bookaneers, it seemed, were set to sink with the ship because they could not fathom dry land.

The literary taverns around London sat gloomy and idle, often half-empty, filled with faint echoes of golden times. Fewer and fewer assignments reached me from Davenport. With my business troubles mounting, I was forced to sell some of the rarest editions in my personal collection. Visiting Paris for this purpose, I found its book community mired in a similar malaise, and witnessed or heard about the same affliction in New York, Boston, Philadelphia, as well as Berlin, Barcelona, Vienna, Zurich, Rome, and all the centers of publishing.

That brings us to approximately a year ago, in the fall of 1890. One quiet morning back at my stall, I was contemplating the dispiriting numbers of my ledgers. In the grip of such hard times I could not afford a single loss to my stock. Any bookstall owner will tell you that being in business outdoors means books disappear. It might be the wealthiest gentleman in the neighborhood who, peeping into a book of history, remembers an appointment and, without thinking, walks away with the unpaid-for volume. There were others, mostly urchins of the street, who would try to grab a book to sell somewhere else for small change. I kept one of those great, big theological tomes at a table in front of my chair, which I could drop onto an offender. I also employed a young boy of my own to stand guard and watch for books that "grow legs." Lastly, I kept the books on my shelves spread out just enough that I could see out every side of the stall from where I sat.

My little guard had gone on an errand for me when I spied through one of these slits a boy of ten or eleven strutting by, walking his fingers along the spines of the books. He slowed his step. I knew what was about to happen. I leapt up armed with my *Jones's Theology* but he had already begun running off at the speed of a thunderbolt. By the time I started to give chase, I was too breathless from the exertion even to yell "thief," and the little Oliver Twist was far gone into the crowds.

To my surprise, I did not find anything missing. I counted my inventory once more. There was, as it turned out, one book more than there should have been. I recognized the size, shape, the clasp, the grain of the plain brown leather, and most of all the name of a nonexistent book, in this case *Concerning the Three Impostors,* by Emperor Frederick II. It had to be—it *was* one of Whiskey Bill's, so long absent from my sight. I looked around, as though the bookaneer might be standing there tipping his dandyish high hat to me as he had done from the stairwell at the Crown, which by this point had long ago closed its doors. Exhilarated by the chance to do what I never dared, I carefully opened the metal latch, threw aside the leather strap, and with great ceremony turned to the title page, then turned to the next page, then the next, the next, then skipped ten, twenty, forty-five pages ahead, thirty pages back. The pages were blank.

Running my hand through the book again, I noticed the back cover was thicker than the front. I had come across some examples of binding from the fifteenth and sixteenth centuries in which church relics were kept in a sort of cupboard inside the leather. It could be a crucifix or perhaps a tooth. Old Stemmes told me he once found a human toe, though I presume he was inebriated and had dropped a piece of sausage there. Now, the book I held in my hands at the moment was not from another century, but I suspected it might share the same design, and I carefully peeled back the compartment, where there was a sealed letter.

Closing my stall an hour and a half early, I hurried to the far side of the square and hailed a cab to Dover Street. It was a long drive between two parts of the city; unlike New York, which ends abruptly when it pleases, London stretches out obnoxiously in every direction. I entered a tall and narrow building awkwardly combining the grammar of French and Greek architecture into a monstrosity of pillars, arches, gables, and friezes; this was one of the new "private" hotels where an inhabitant was not bothered by being forced to pass through any of the public rooms. There was also no elevator, and climbing the four steep flights took the wind out of me for the second time that day. After four pulls of the bell Davenport appeared, weary from interrupted sleep. It was three o'clock in the afternoon.

"You have brought breakfast, I assume, Fergins," he said in a croak, turning his back and leading me in. "The other day when I went down to the dining room, there were two American girls—at separate ends of the room—with their elbows on the tables. I found it amusing, but I could hardly enjoy my food listening to all the English ladies grind their teeth over it."

His rooms were in the usual disarray, piles of newspapers, magazines, and only a few books scattered here and there. Shelves were mostly empty. Davenport almost never kept a book, unless he was especially amused or repulsed by it. There were some etchings and landscapes on the wall, but most had been turned around so that the plain brown backs of the frames faced out; these the bookaneer felt were gaudy or in some other ways lacking in style. He would usually change hotels every time he returned from a mission away, or every four or five weeks if he remained in London, but he had stayed put here for two months despite complaining about it. I stopped to lean against the wall of his sitting room, trying to smile through my panting. "I might, I just might have a lead—well, I have something I trust you'll find intriguing, anyway." I put my hand to my coat. "But first, my dear Davenport, how are you? You are not unwell, I hope?"

"Wait a minute."

He washed and rubbed the sleep out of his eyes. The forty-four-year-old face still appeared boyish from a distance but a closer inspection revealed weathered skin, creased faintly like well-worn cotton.

He hated pleasantries, but my question was real. I had been worried about the bookaneer, about the states of lethargy and dark moods of solitude I would find him in.

"Unwell and as well as ever. Have you come all that way to ask me that?"

"No. It's Whiskey Bill."

He shrugged. "He retired, or whatever you might call stopping something nobody else cares if you do."

I removed the volume of blank pages from my coat and explained how it had come to be at my stall, and how I found the letter hidden in the leather cupboard inside the back cover. My narrative did not get a rise out of him and he waved the letter away when I held it out. "Don't you even want to see it, my dear Davenport?"

"Read it to me."

"The letter is marked P. D. on the front. I suppose you agree it must be meant for you, and that we are quite justified in unsealing it."

He was just as uninterested in the ethics of the matter.

I opened the letter, making certain to show that I had not previously tampered with it. I gave an involuntary laugh.

"What do you howl about, Fergins?"

"It *is* for you." I tried not to be melodramatic in my reading, but the anticipation and the strong wording probably lent a theatrical edge to my voice.

> *Friday, 17th October 1890. My dear Pen. I write to you with days remaining to me before I die. You must see me, sooner, not later. Your life depends on what I have to tell you.*

I gasped. "It is signed 'Whiskey Bill.'"

But when I looked up from the extraordinary letter I found Davenport fully absorbed in watching the oblong circles of his cigar smoke dissipate into the stale air of his room. I was about to say something to try to break his trancelike state when he responded.

"If he says he is dying, that settles the question. Whiskey Bill is not dying, and if he were, he would not tell anyone about it until it was too late to enjoy."

"Penrose Davenport! I'm surprised, very surprised at your callousness." I wagged a finger at him.

"You think me heartless," he remarked, turning his whole body toward me for the answer. I just realized I haven't fully described Davenport physically. This is a knotty task. Davenport appeared markedly different depending on the hour, the day, the lighting, the season, his mood. His abundant sand-colored hair was usually uncombed and styled only by the whim of the breeze, raindrops, or the degree of humidity, but the times he applied powder and oil to it suddenly his head took on a fixed and rather unnatural geometric slope. He always smelled of hair lotion, even though he used it so rarely. He was not much taller than I am, but he held himself straighter and with more poise so that a few inches would have been added to an onlooker's estimation of his height. The man's weight fluctuated, sometimes day to day, at least so it seemed; his cheeks and belly could seem quite bloated or alarmingly slender. Even his voice, so long divorced from the influence of any particular land as much as it was by favored cigars, floated in and out of vague accents. All of this constituted a kind of natural disguise, with the effect that men who had met him or seen him before would show no recognition in their next encounter. He was handsome in a rather cold way. There were no expressions fashioned on his face for the comfort of others. He grinned and smirked but rarely smiled. His oval eyes did as they pleased and held no gaze out of courtesy. If there was a fly on the wall, it was likely he was more interested in it than in looking at you while you poured out your heart. When he did direct himself to you fully, as he did at the moment he asked me if I thought him heartless, it had an almost dizzying effect.

"No, no," I replied in a gentler voice. "Of course not. You are not heartless. Callous, dear fellow. Merely callous. What good would it do the man to falsely claim he is sick?"

"Arrange for a visit to the asylum, Fergins. You think Bill was once your friend. You are grateful to him. Your face shows you grieve, but do not waste your compassion. He was not your friend and, worse still, he is *not* dying."

I took up the letter again. Davenport had noticed in a single glance, seeing the page upside down, what I had missed altogether in my exhilaration at the message. The paper was stamped with the mark of a lunatic asylum.

IT IS MY SINCERE HOPE you never see inside the asylum in Caterham. It is a massive colony of buildings located on an elevation. The rear structure was dimly lit, mostly by tallow candles, and the narrow stone corridors were lined with stacks of dirty aprons and barrels overfilled with animal bones. The place suffered from both too much and too little ventilation; doors were tied so they would not slam from the wind, and despite windows that were nailed shut, gusts of bone-chilling air came over and around us, mixing with the awful human odors.

Dried, shriveled wreaths and holly still on the walls had been meant to add cheer two or three Christmases ago by some well-meaning attendant. We could hear keening wails and shouts from the day room. Despair mingled with rage and confusion. As we were conducted through these passages, I found myself whistling a child's lullaby to soothe myself.

"We divide the idiots from the lunatics the best we can manage," explained the attendant guiding us, who seemed inexplicably cheerful, "but the boundary between the poor creatures is not always a clear one."

At that moment, a pair of rats, each the size of a child's boot, crossed at our feet. We soon came to another rat about the same size, this one dead.

"I ought to remove that before anyone eats it."

"Eats a rat?" I asked.

"Stay," the attendant requested. As I tried to determine whether he was addressing me or the rat, our guide lifted the dead creature by the tail with an almost tender motion. "Poor creature," came his mournful whisper.

Our destination was a small stone chamber with a square window in the middle of the door. Whiskey Bill, the energetic masculine figure with a heavy red mustache, had transformed from the last time I saw him. He was another being altogether from the man who first surprised me on the street twenty-one years earlier. Entirely bald—in fact, other than his eyebrows, his face and head seemed hairless—his skin now sagged over his eyes and his pupils were cloudy. He wore the drab asylum-issued coat of thin gray material. At least there was his familiar smile showing off the big spaces between his teeth, but his coughing and retching disrupted his greeting. A Bible completed the impression of a deathbed.

Davenport waited until the attendant left us before he began the conversation. "You do not expect me to believe you have gone mad." His tone was less hostile than his original reaction to the letter. Mistrust is in the bookaneer's blood. If a bookaneer were to let his guard down even for a moment, a mission could be lost. In the history of the bookaneers, as far as I have understood it, no one bookaneer could ever really tolerate another, with one chief exception that I will speak of soon. That is why I never took Davenport's suspicions of Whiskey Bill to reflect real animus against the man.

Bill craned his neck to confirm that the attendant had exited. Then he winked. "You are the fellow, Pen. I recently found myself as poor as Job's turkey, and if the authorities here believe you insane they give you all your meals and a bed. Ain't this a rather adequate place for an idiot asylum? They let me work in the gardens. The inhabitants of the female division are just on the other side of an awful low hedge. Some very fine specimens there, Pen!"

Davenport arched an eyebrow. "You speak of the insane women."

"Perhaps some are like me, and merely in financial embarrassment and looking for help. Who knows but perhaps I shall marry one of them. Never marrying has been a regret. Do you know in London one person in every nine hundred is thought to be insane?"

"Knowing that figure should disqualify you from being one of them. You are always enthusiastic at the wrong time, Bill."

"Pen," Bill continued, moving his body up and down. "Press down on the mattress. This bed is not half-uncomfortable. Did they tell you this ward has its own aviary? There is only one condition. Every day and a half or so I must do something rather outré so that the doctors do not declare me cured before I am ready. I see the old bookseller found you," Bill said, turning toward me with a tight nod. "He was meant to serve a role as a go-between only."

"I could wait outside," I offered.

"I always said a bookseller is one-quarter philosopher, one-quarter philanthropist, and . . ." He made a silent calculation. ". . . two-quarters pure rogue. You are a disloyal sort," he said to me—still in a sadly weak warble compared with the voice as I remembered it, despite his rising emotion. "Disloyal as a Jacobite!"

"You should thank Fergins for convincing me to see you," Davenport said. "Nor is he treacherous or disloyal for ceasing your arrangement; he merely valued his skills enough to work for the best of our line. I've made a wager with Fergins. If you really are dying, I shall owe him a pair of gloves."

"Yes," I chimed in. Davenport had a tendency to invent small moments that had not happened even when they did not serve a purpose. I had learned to accept them as real. "Calf leather, I hope, if I win, Davenport. But I pray you are not too unwell, Bill," I added.

"Now I would thank you to explain what we are doing here," Davenport said, stepping over my sympathy. "We wasted time enough on the train here. What is this nonsense about my life depending on speaking with you? The only reason I allowed Fergins to drag me out here is that I am curious to see what trick you are planning."

"No trick! We have been flying at each other's throats for so many years, Pen, but Lord knows I've always been honest about hating you. You'll admit that. You are the fellow. You are the fellow."

"You have said."

"Be patient with an old man."

"An old devil."

Bill's eyes widened and brightened. "Maybe so, Pen! I need to tell you some things, so take a seat and listen. Please. If you want the bookseller, let the old goat stay. He was always harmless as a butterfly."

Davenport rolled up his sleeves as if he were about to operate, and carried a stool close to the head of the bed. I took another stool by the foot of the bed.

"Thank you. Pen, I have seen firsthand what a scoundrel you become when someone questions your way of thinking, but you always were a gentleman at heart. There is a new mission, one of phenomenal importance and, potentially, profit."

"Is this about your Poe obsession? It is the way of the commonplace bookaneer to go in for a Holy Grail."

"No!" Bill cried, coughing with exasperation as he tried to expel his words. "It's not that. Something . . . bigger—Stevenson."

Stevenson. As in Robert Louis. One of the most popular living writers in the world. The author known for *Strange Case of Dr. Jekyll and Mr. Hyde, Treasure Island,* and *Kidnapped,* whose work was demanded by readers around the world. We looked at each other. I knew Davenport's mind was moving at great speed, though he did not look interested.

"One of the more capricious but gifted writers ever to set pen to paper. He is sailing the Pacific by private means to improve his health," Davenport said. "They say he will return to Scotland when he feels restored, but nobody knows how long it will be."

"He is never to return," Bill said with somber finality.

"Are you implying Stevenson died while at sea?" Davenport asked.

"What do you know about the island of Upolu?" Bill asked.

"I concentrate on the literary world. I do not know much about distant lands of illiterates. Fergins likes to know a little about everything."

"Upolu is one of the three primary Samoan islands," I said, "formed by a volcano and still in its shadow. Samoa is also known as the Navigator Islands, because of the abilities of its natives to command the sea without any of our modern equipment. Upolu is its capital of government and commerce."

"I ask again. Is Stevenson dead?"

"No—not dead yet, Pen."

"Then has he been taken by savages?"

"Worse! He remains by his own will. From what I have learned, he alighted at the island of Upolu and decided never to leave. Stevenson, or the shade of Stevenson, lives in seclusion there, an exile from all civilized people and things. Do you realize what it all means? How close we are?"

"Close to what?" Davenport asked, and he made the slightest gesture to me, at which I removed a pencil and my notebook.

"Glory, dear Pen! These writers take the essence of every person around them, turn them into books and stories without permission or even a simple thank-you, and want all the credit and glory for themselves. We are the only ones who can stand in the way, who can take that glory right from their pockets. God as my witness, I've taken some for myself these long years. The intelligence I have been able to collect informs me Stevenson is finishing the most important book of his life. But he is a bag of bones now, unlikely to survive much longer, and if his illnesses do not claim him first, the island will. The place is a hell on earth, with roasting temperatures and consumed with deadly quarrels among the pagan tribes. Between the spears of the natives and the intervention of heavily armed foreign governments, plus the mischief of tropical disease, no white man is safe. The novel, this masterpiece, will perish out there—but if one were able to bring it back to civilization . . . I know when you want something you go at things like one o'clock, no matter how lackadaisical you seem to others. You are the one to do it, Pen!"

"Have at it yourself when you decide to leave this palace."

"You see I am no longer in any condition to do anything of the sort. I have spent my fortune and my health hunting for Poe's lost novel, alas, which is never to see the light of day. If you can retrieve Stevenson's book, my dear Pen, you will yield a terrific fortune. You can bring the publishers and their damned monopolies to their knees begging you for it."

"Even if any of what you say is true, you must know I would not give you the satisfaction of following a lead brought by you, Whiskey Bill."

Bill looked him up and down. "I used to know you as having a grander sense of destiny, of our profession. A man who sought to transcend mere errands parceled out by the gluttonous publishers. A man not quite so . . . calculating in everything."

"Fergins."

I began to collect our coats and hats. Then I noticed Davenport had tilted his head back and was looking at the ceiling. Knowing what he was thinking, I spoke softly to him: "Samoa. Warlike tribes, dangerous climate. Too risky, treasure or not, my dear Davenport."

Whiskey Bill scowled at me, then stretched his hand out to the other bookaneer, though he could not reach him. "This will be the final gift to posterity, to the world at large, from our work. I *am* dying," Bill said in a quieter voice filled with pain. "You are the only one who can do this. My ambitions must vanish—but I need not vanish from history. When the yarn is told, I will be spoken of as the man to have passed the mission along to you, and that will be something. I will have played a part. That will be—it will have to be enough. Your permanence in the legends of the bookaneers—your *life* as it exists beyond these earthly skins—depends upon this chance, Pen Davenport. I know you long for such a laurel. I know that like me, you do not yet feel our calling completed."

"You know nothing about me." There was an unusual tremor in his voice.

"To the devil with laurels, then. With the copyright treaty about to go into effect on the first of July, Pen, how many missions are still left for you? The end comes. Why, it would be the most lucrative pursuit since the discovery of Shelley's lost novelette. Do you know how much money you would walk away with if you managed to do this?"

I had already started calculating this in my notebook—factoring in Stevenson's last three contracts, the scarcity of major successes over the last twelve to eighteen months, and the unique value to the public of an author's last work. "Twenty thousand pounds, at least," I said. When I met Davenport's glare, I felt my cheeks flush with color and I looked down at my hands.

Bill, heartened by my mistake, straightened himself on his pillows. "Talk of a true 'treasure island.'" His bearing now grew funereal. "In making myself your enemy, Pen, I believe I have served almost in a role similar to a friend—goading and encouraging you to do more."

"There are no friends in our line of work," Davenport said.

"No," Bill said, his eyes darting over my face before continuing. "Then perhaps you would say I have served as something of a mentor to you."

"I've had only one."

"You have been afraid of the bigger missions since she's been gone. You loved her. We *all* loved her, you know, in our own ways."

Davenport rose to his feet and drew back as though to slap the man's face. I was about to try to catch him when he extended his hand down toward the bed. They shook.

"I have nothing more to say," said Davenport. "I trust I will meet you in the field again one day, Whiskey Bill. Godspeed."

"That day, I will finally best you."

I must have apologized a dozen times for having persuaded Davenport to take that trip to the asylum—I could hardly remember if it really had been a matter of my convincing him, but that was how he saw it and so it was fact. A few days passed. He had some business back at the Garrick Club and I received a message to go there. I found him in the same smoking room where we first met. He was sitting next to a well-known German printer, who excused himself to the card room.

"Your notebook, Fergins," he said.

He snatched it out of my hands. Turning the pages furiously, he found the notes I took at Caterham. He held it out to a spot where there was a little more light than smoke.

"I do apologize for talking you into that awful place. You were right, I shouldn't have bothered you. I should have torn up Bill's letter when I received it—and burned it in the fire, too."

"Try not to speak for a minute." He hummed to himself. "Did you think there was any truth to what Whiskey Bill tried to sell us?"

"That nonsense about Samoa, you mean?" The fact was, I would have preferred Davenport drop the whole matter. I did not like the glimmer I had noticed in his eye at the talk of Samoa. But I had to be honest. "Something in his voice—well, I could not help but think that at least some of it rang true."

Davenport showed my comment the respect of a slow nod. "It was a ruse, a trap to send me on a wild goose chase far from here. The very fact that you believe it shows how well planned it was. The question remains this: Why would he want to do that? I want you to make inquiries into Stevenson so we can prove Bill's deceit. Meanwhile, I need fresh reports on Ruskin, Swinburne, Hardy, Tennyson, any author of esteem living or passing through London this season. Do you understand?"

"Then you do not believe what he said? Any of it?"

"Look around us." Pen gestured around the room at the plush leather furniture and the large portraits hanging in rows around the walls. "*Here* is the environment of a man of literary eminence such as Robert Louis Stevenson. Somewhere that feels just dangerous enough to excite the imagination, but is actually as safe as could be. That is what a writer craves, and that's why when it's time for writers to die, they die in their beds."

"Perhaps Stevenson is the exception."

"I told you, Whiskey Bill is neither insane nor dying. Everything that Judas-haired swindler says to us is a lie. He is using the fact we cannot prove where Stevenson is while he is out at sea in order to catch us in his web. Count on the fact that it will not work. But he might try again through other means, and I will be prepared. I suspect he wants to lure me out of London, at which point he'll leave the asylum and claim some prize for himself that is right under our noses, maybe having to do with Stevenson, maybe another litterateur of value with Stevenson a red herring to draw us away. The more elaborate his scheme, the more profit hidden behind it. I believe once we know why Bill dangled this before us, a lucrative mission will be revealed."

He added something else to my assignment: "Watch Bill's activity in the asylum as closely as possible. When Bill is discharged, we'll know something is about to happen. For now, he speaks of seeing aviaries in this asylum so they will believe he's hallucinating, but when the time comes he will start speaking rationally enough. I will be ready, count on that."

I informed Davenport's spies around the Liverpool ports and the London railway and coaches that money was available for information about any communication from the South Seas, in particular the Samoan islands, regarding literary visitors. I also wrote to ports in Scotland and Ireland providing incentives for the same. It had long been my responsibility to stay informed about the movements of every important literary man and woman on three or four continents, to know when they tended to visit their publishers; when and where they went on holidays. Ask me where Lewis Carroll takes tea on Tuesdays, I can tell you; wonder where Miss Rossetti markets every other Monday, I'll answer. I pumped all our wells of intelligence in literary circles.

Meanwhile, I volunteered my services at Caterham to pass out old, unwanted books from my inventory to the patients at the asylum. In Whiskey Bill's room I explained to him that our visit had inspired great sympathy for the lunatics; the bald-headed bookaneer laughed, Davenport's tactic naturally transparent and unsurprising. But he did not try to interrogate me or coax me into revealing anything else. The best times to observe Bill were when he was napping or otherwise engaged. I also found several occasions to review the doctors' notes and records, though I was yet to uncover any meaningful clues.

In addition to the Bible, he kept a few books of French writers nearby. He told me that he had hoped to go to Paris one more time, and to die there instead of in England, since the climate was better.

"I am glad you found a rather kindred soul in our dear Pen," Bill said to me during one of my visits. I was seated by his bed, waiting for him to make another move on the chessboard I had brought for him.

I nodded halfheartedly and didn't correct him, but I was certain Davenport would never describe us as kindred souls.

"I cannot begrudge a man to do what he must, no, no, not even a lowly bookseller. You were a good fence, but there were plenty of others just like you. No grudges, not in this life!"

"Check."

"He is too good for his own good, that Pen. If he does not succeed, he resents everyone else, and if he succeeds, he resents himself. Any one of us would have bowed to dear Kitten and followed at her skirts. But she chose him. *Him.* No, no grudges, but I'll never forgive old Pen for that." His words had begun to run together a little. My eyes traveled over his face and the frame of his body, which had steadily shrunk from the meager rations that were served to the patients. The whites of his eyes were veined with red. "And he gathered them together into a place called Armageddon."

"Rook to knight's third square?" I asked, tracing the suggested move with my finger.

"Do you realize why he chose you all those years back, Fergins?"

I looked at him again. "You're confused, Bill. I courted Davenport."

He pushed his tongue through the gap in his teeth and smiled. "I am not as confused as you think. Do you believe it? That Pen Davenport would engage the services of a stranger who happened to call on him unannounced? He had been waiting for you."

This idea astonished me. "Who am I?"

"People in the book world always hated the bookaneers because our operations forced them to be honest with themselves about what the whole thing really is—that literature and money were two edges of a single sword. Bookmen of all stripes like to cling to the idea they have a nobler calling than most. But we were instrumental in bringing books to the masses. You were known to adore the idea of a bookaneer. To idolize us. You were never plagued with any conscience against it, like so many others had, which meant you could be safely used."

I remained unconvinced that Davenport could have arrived at such conclusions about me by watching me—or having me watched—at my bookstall. But I did not press Bill about it. Besides, while his smile remained frozen, his eyelids had started to droop. I felt another wave of sadness come over me, seeing him this way. "He is not your friend . . . he is not dying." Davenport's words repeated in my ear, warning me against sentiment. But sentiment is hard to deny to a man in a sickbed. Close your eyes, Mr. Clover, and if you wait long enough it will seem like we are moving at a fast pace, because your brain *knows* we are sitting on a train, even though we remain idly waiting on that broken train's repair. To know, intellectually, there is no movement, should be sufficient, but a man's brain is stubborn when what is happening in life is different than what was expected. Do you see what I mean?

—*I can understand, Mr. Fergins, how you would be sympathetic to Whiskey Bill as the first of the bookaneers who trusted you. That would have meant the world to me if I were you. But I wonder about something else. Would it matter?*

Would what matter, Mr. Clover?

—*Sorry, my question wasn't clear. What Whiskey Bill hinted about Pen Davenport. That Mr. Davenport chose you, rather than you choosing him. Would it make a difference if it were true, Mr. Fergins?*

Maybe. Maybe in some ways it would make a difference. Who knows?

—*What did Mr. Davenport say when you asked him if it was true?*

Asked him! Could my modest abilities of description give you such an improper portrait of the man? No, Davenport would never answer such a question. It would not happen once in a thousand times that he would tell you something about himself when asked—maybe once in a million times, or twice in a million times a million times. He could tell you something about himself on his own, but never if you asked, though he would ask you anything he pleased.

At the asylum, I found myself gratified by the surprised and thankful exclamations of the patients who accepted books from my cart; some broke down in tears to have a new book to read for the first time in years. Certainly, some of the inmates were coarse or lacked conversational skills, and two different men, plus one woman, confessed to having been Jack the Ripper. But I now better understood the peculiar cheerfulness I had seen from the attendant who had taken us around on our first visit. Passing through a place of misery even briefly will infect your soul, but doing something to help, even if it was a small token, gave a feeling of resignation and an unexpected contentment.

One rainy afternoon, while doing my rounds through the institution, an attendant brought a message received for me at the front office. It did not surprise me that I had been located there, since the lunatic asylum had become something of a second home. I tipped the attendant as though we were standing in a gold-trimmed hotel instead of this den of misery.

When I unfolded the paper, I had to catch my breath. It was a reply from one of Davenport's informants I had contacted. Belial had been sighted sailing for the South Seas. One of the patients nearby began to weep. I put away my cart and started down a hall to the other side of the building to search for some privacy so I might concentrate and plan. I had to get word to Davenport, and quickly.

Then I heard someone call out, startling me. The words came again—*stop thief!* It was more of a screech, actually. I looked up and saw a rainbow-colored parrot in flight. It was the bird who was yelling "stop thief," again and again. There were innumerable other birds among verdant surroundings—canaries, macaws, goldfinches. I had wandered through a curtain into an aviary.

Confusion swirled in my mind. Before exiting the building, I decided to peek in on the bookaneer, knowing it was time for his nap. Looking through the layers of dust on the small window that the attendants used to check on a patient, I could see his sunken cheeks and ghastly hairless head above the blankets. He seemed to be muttering something in his sleep. Quietly, I opened the door and crept in.

I leaned forward, close enough to take in his putrid breath. "The beast," he seemed to say. "The beast."

My hand hovered over his shoulder, tempted to shake him, but he sat bolt upright before I had the chance.

Bill shouted at the top of his voice, a mad glint in his eye: "Beware the beast, Penrose Davenport, beware the beast! The beast! The beast!"

The attendant rushed to control him but he kept shouting it until the agitated lunatics of the ward caught on to the cry and raised it to a fever pitch.

The beast!

The beast!

The beast!

The words rang out and shook the walls and floors from all sides; even some of the birds in the aviary joined the chant and screeched: "Beast!"

As attendants arrived to subdue Bill, he began laughing and spitting wildly. Two men held him under his armpits while one gripped his legs. I watched the once potent bookaneer carried off like a hare to the cookhouse. I followed as far as I could, as though there was something I might do. Even after they had disappeared into another wing of the building, I still could not bring myself to exit the grounds. I pushed my cart for a second round of deliveries. After an hour or so wrestling with my fidgety thoughts, I saw two somber attendants go back into Bill's room. I hurried after them with my book cart to disguise my purpose. They left the door open. They were stripping away the bedclothes and collecting the personal belongings in a box. There were now two pieces of news to turn Davenport's plans upside down: First, Whiskey Bill was dead; second, Belial had a head start on the mission of a lifetime.

IV

It had not been a performance, and the ruse Davenport was so certain about never existed. Whiskey Bill had served a mission in a silver bowl on a silver platter. Do not mistake the conclusions I drew as criticism of Davenport's intuition or his methods. On the contrary. To be brilliant is not a matter of being right more often than the next fellow; yes, that may be part of the pedestrian definition. It is in large part a matter of holding firm to convictions as long as possible, but not a moment longer. The brilliant man must trust he is right even when adrift alone with his convictions, and few people have the stomach for it. There are millions of average women and men who will refuse to take positions at the most important moments in their lives—moments that would have changed the course of their existences—for fear of being proven wrong. Fear is the impassable gulf between the ordinary and the remarkable. Between all of us and Pen Davenport.

Davenport was no fool. He embraced reality when it came for him, and then blamed others. "This is what should have happened," was a phrase frequently spoken by him. You would not have heard from him even an admission as mild as: "Well, now you see, Fergins, I suppose Whiskey Bill was not sending us on a wild goose chase while pretending to be dying, after all. He really was dying and the mission was genuine. To think, there was an aviary in that asylum, just as he told us!"

"This is what should have happened, my dear Fergins," he said a week after Bill's death from heart congestion. "That damned asylum should have transferred Bill to a proper hospital. We could all see he was losing a bit of his mind, very well, but the poor fellow's body was falling apart and those white-coated fools were blind enough not to see it. Now"—he waved his hands in the air in the way of a professor who has forgotten his line of thought—"it is too late."

"Wholeheartedly agreed, Davenport," was how I would usually respond to these vague nods to his errors.

There was nothing to gain by dwelling on another bookaneer's sad demise. There was plenty of work ahead. I had to follow our informant's initial lead about Belial's South Seas trip by tracking down the probable dates and vessel of that man's passage out of England (Davenport was at least three weeks behind his rival, as far as I could determine). I was able to confirm sightings of the shadowy bookaneer consistent with preparations for such a voyage, but Belial's exact day and means of departure remained murky and unprovable—as frustratingly invisible as the legendary bookaneer himself. Meanwhile, I gathered together every known detail of Stevenson's singular life to add to my existing knowledge of the man.

Sickly as a child, Stevenson surprised his very pessimistic and industrious family by surviving long enough to study engineering, following the family profession on his father's side, before growing tired of it and switching to law, which did not last much longer. Literature beckoned—"literature beckoned," of course, that is the predictable turn to everyone but a budding author. Leaving Edinburgh and soon Scotland altogether to seek a climate salutary to his fragile health and to be closer to Bohemian and artistic friends, in Paris he fell in with an American woman, more than ten years his senior, called Fanny Osbourne. She was already married and had two children, a boy and a girl, and would soon enough be divorced and married again, this time to Stevenson.

By then he was writing at a furious pace about his colorful travels, and soon his giant imagination pressed him into writing novels. Of course, many writers who have written articles, poems, essays, or criticism sooner or later decide to try their hands at a novel, and fail at it, not realizing how much life must be contained in the form. But Stevenson was different. Remarkable novels flowed from his pen. Novels that nobody expected and novels that built worlds. Novels made him a fortune. Stevenson's writing was unique and easily identifiable, and yet it was difficult for a reader to imagine the storyteller himself. Here is another way to put it: the reader wants to rescue E. A. Poe; he wants to be a friend to Longfellow; wants Dickens to be *his* friend, Sir Walter Scott to be his wealthy uncle; but would be satisfied simply to lay eyes on R. L. Stevenson. He excited as much curiosity about himself as any novelist had in half a century, one of the secrets to the immense interest in his books, no matter their subjects. His rather picturesque and wild life only added to this. The gangly writer and his unusual family spent time in San Francisco, New York, and back in Scotland and England before setting sail for the South Seas.

Poor health spurred Stevenson's most recent odyssey, and along the way something made him decide not to go back.

I arranged for Davenport's passage on the first ship launching for the South Seas, which happened to be a British man-of-war; the bookaneer had been touched by blind good fortune, for the frigate would be the only ship to sail out of Liverpool for the South Seas with room for passengers for another four months. Three months to the day after the death of Whiskey Bill, the day this mission was born, Davenport stepped aboard the warship and wondered aloud whether he ought to have brought a hat with a wider brim to keep the sun out of his eyes; I kept my umbrella above him for shade.

I had prepared whatever useful materials I could find on Samoa for the bookaneer: maps, cyclopedia extracts, pamphlets, travelogues. The travel books were written by gentlemen adventurers with forgettable initials before creaky surnames, and they might as well have all been written by the same fellow, so plain and uninformative were their contents. The dozen or so rather obscure books written as detailed studies of the island nation were out-of-date and often inaccurate. No matter. As far as I could tell, Davenport barely glanced over the materials I provided for him. This surprised and concerned me, for he usually prepared thoroughly. As he studied the clouds, I gave a careful glance to each sailor who walked by, on their way between fixing ropes and ladders and sails, as though each boy in his blue tunic and white trousers could harbor a design against Davenport.

It was hard to fathom what was in the bookaneer's mind as I helped carry his belongings and two large casks of freshwater aboard. His face maintained its inscrutability. I ought to note that the bookaneer had grown a beard; the tangled, shapeless thing did nothing to age his youthful face, instead making him appear like one of the young actors who would come to the Garrick with false whiskers glued over their pretty cheeks. Then again, he always managed to appear rather slovenly before an important mission, for which he would later snap into fine form. I wish I could convey something of his inner thoughts, but I could not glean anything definite from him. I'll do my imitation of Homer, who will stop to describe his heroes suiting up in armor in order to suggest, however indirectly, their states of mind. On the day he began the most fateful mission in the history of the bookaneers, this was the modern armor of our far-famed Pen Davenport: a narrow shoe-tie neckcloth tucked snugly into a crimson velvet waistcoat, where his thumbs were hooked on opposite loops; his dark checked overcoat of the inverness style, with a cape hanging elbow length. In place of a brazen helmet such as the sort the blind bard of Chios dwelled upon, our journeyer had an old-fashioned smoking cap that covered the tops of his ears.

Wishing him Godspeed, I began to exit when he asked me two questions.

"Do you think, Fergins, that Belial has already completed the mission? That I will be doing nothing more than wasting my strength sailing across the world?"

"I have had every scout and spy I trust listening for news, and I believe we would have heard of it. Remember, two ships in the past four months have wrecked on their way to the South Seas. It's just as likely Belial never made it there, or was waylaid."

He nodded, reassured by my optimism, if not by the report of nautical trends, but I wanted to be comprehensive. He invited me for a quick farewell drink.

I fixed two glasses of champagne. He was slouching to one side at the small table that constituted the only other furniture in the berth beside the bureau. I sat diagonally across, on the edge of the bed.

"What is it you fear so much about my trip, my dear Fergins?" Davenport asked, swirling the golden liquid in his glass before losing his interest and putting it down.

"Did I say I do?"

"Then you do not?"

I shook the glass side to side until more bubbles rose toward me. I had promised myself not to admit my trepidation, but I never was one who could duck a direct question, certainly not one from Davenport. "There is something about this endeavor that fills me with dread, I confess it. *Something . . .*"

"I have had my share of difficult missions."

"Of course you're right. And on the other hand . . ."

"No other hands today, Fergins. To the point."

I said what I had been burning to say all along. "The great Robert Louis Stevenson, ailing and helpless, isolated on a remote island with no law and order, writing what is likely to be his final novel: a bull's-eye, a bookaneer's ultimate prize."

"You think it all too perfect."

"Too perfect not to contain peril."

"But of course you think so."

"What do you mean?"

"Fergins, you are a Londoner! That is why you think like that. Which is very different than to say you are an Englishman, by the way," he mused. "The Englishman is too superstitious to question good fortune, the Londoner too intellectual to accept it."

"And the American?"

"The American," he said, smiling at the accusatory tone of my response. "The American expects the good fortune." He studied his slightly overgrown and sharp fingernails, then smoothed his beard with one of them. "Do you know what Kitten would have done?"

My voice dried up at the usually forbidden topic.

"If she'd learned of this mission," he continued, his emerald eyes clouded. "Do you know what she would have done? She would have recited to me all the reasons I should not go and I would have been convinced with all my heart to stay away from the blasted thing. Then when she returned with Stevenson's manuscript grasped to her bosom like a newborn babe, she would have raised a little eyebrow, so that it tugged her face ever so slightly, and said, 'Davenport, you failed the test.'" He raised his glass. "To Kitten."

Curious as it might sound, over the course of several years between the day my assistance to Davenport began and the time Kitten disappeared, I cannot remember speaking to the fascinating woman more than a half-dozen times. I had encountered her. I would be walking with Davenport late at night as he gave me instructions for an assignment, for instance, and we would part ways at the lighted window of a tavern or hotel, where I could see her inside, bathing indifferently in attention while waiting for him. Or there she would appear at the corner ahead of us, rising up and down on her toes, a coat wrapped around her and a colorful scarf hugging her head so that she was nothing more than a face, and Davenport would bid me an abrupt good-bye as he hurried to her side.

Yes, I *did* see her during that period. I was confident that I knew what she was to Davenport and presumed to understand what he was to her, but I could not claim to know her. This is important to understand, Mr. Clover: nobody spent more time with Davenport than the two of us, but to each other we remained almost strangers until—until it was too late. As for Davenport, he only ever talked about what he wanted to talk about and usually he did not want to talk about her. Most of what I knew about Kitten came from my long study of the field. It was believed she was born in France but as a young woman traveled widely, chasing opportunity. Rumors persist about what she did during those years. She was a grave robber in Egypt, an opium trader in Hong Kong, a bravo (or assassin) in Berlin, depending on who tells you.

The next thing heard about her was during an extended time in America in the war that broke your country to pieces. Her role as a spy for both sides is recorded in two history books, one titled *Spies of the Rebellion* and another privately printed called *Natural Traitors*, which devotes half a chapter to a woman known then as Jane Grimm. During wartime, when American book publishing was as splintered as the rest of the country, this thirty-year-old Frenchwoman had occasion to smuggle the proof sheets of valuable books from the Southern states to Northern publishers, and vice versa, marking the beginning of a long career that would bring her great profit by utilizing her diverse set of skills as thief, smuggler, and trickster.

She had been known by a variety of names at different times and places, and like many who spend life operating in the shadows, she could have been forgiven for forgetting the one she was born with. Her name among the bookaneers was a bit of an affectionate jest among those who knew, despite her size, how really ferocious she was, like a kitten with a spool of thread.

Those two words of Davenport's in his toast—to Kitten—ended any debate. I met the side of his glass with mine and prayed I would see my companion again.

A TOLLING BELL from the deck alerted visitors to return to land.

I put my glass back on the bureau of Davenport's stateroom. "I should leave you to it."

"This mission is delicate, Fergins. Unusually so. If my subject were to somehow learn of the purpose of my presence, or be given any reason for extra caution, the mission could be compromised rapidly—and more precariously—than perhaps any other I've had. I will be on a primitive island, with infrequent chances to leave and little means of communication with the outside world."

"You know, Davenport, that I am entirely discreet about our dealings."

"The very reason I am reluctant to convey any doubt. I suppose I mean to urge you to reinforce even your usual discretion and make a fortress of your knowledge."

"Without question," I said solemnly, then thought I ought to add something more formal. "I vow to you before God I shall never say a word of it."

"You always understood me, Fergins." This was Davenport's way of saying many things ordinary men would have uttered in plainer words: *Thank you,* or *Stay in good health,* or *I will miss your company, my friend.*

After exiting the berth and taking the long passage to the stairs, a new worry struck and slowed me down. He had sounded hesitant and seemed to be swatting at his own doubts. He had spoken as if we might not meet again. This is what I realized only at that moment: Davenport, for once, shared my dread and sense of danger. As the bell tolled on, I knew I had but a few minutes. I had to convince him to come off the ship with me, to forget this whole affair. Then I noticed something strange. A large fly, following in front of me wherever I turned. Then another black spot swirled right before my eyes, rising and dropping, becoming bigger, splitting into two. Black spots filled my vision; dryness plugged my throat. My knees trembled and buckled and I dropped down, gasping. I knew my earlier instincts were right, the trepidation, the fear that there were enemies hiding among us on this frigate. I tried to stand again and call out to Davenport to save himself but my legs were jelly.

I CANNOT REMEMBER what visions I beheld while unconscious. I am vain enough to wish for something a little profound, if not Descartes' dreams of a new sort of science then at least ones with entertaining portent, such as young Mrs. Shelley's vision of the awful being that she would animate into Frankenstein's creature, or Robert Louis Stevenson's own nightmare of a respectable man who transformed into a disreputable criminal—perhaps my visions even contained something prescient about what was about to come in the Stevenson affair. A glimpse, perhaps, of a tall, thin white man presiding over a band of natives, death hanging over the scene. There is only one thing I do recall clearly: her face. I saw her. Kitten, whom Davenport had spoken of just a short time before black spots were multiplying before my eyes and contamination flowing through my veins. His musings about her must have invited her into my unconscious brain. I remember that I did not see her as you would see a portrait or a sculpture, fixed and final, or even as a memory, indistinct. I saw her as you would someone sitting where you sit across from me—on a train like this, with no one else to look at, no obstructions, the rest of the world receding.

Kitten, you ought to know, was a thing of beauty. I choose the word with the care a poet might, for the *thing* that made her irresistible was vague. The modern lady is encouraged by etiquette books and trivial magazines to seek what I call the ideal of inoffensive expressionlessness. Smile a small, refined smile as to not appear ungraceful; powder the cheeks and brow to appear flushed, but not artificial; choose dress shapes to make short seem taller, tall seem shorter, wide to seem slimmer and slim to appear rounder, and say or do nothing conspicuous when it can be helped. It all seems rather foolish to a fatal bachelor such as myself, whose romantic impulses were left behind in the uncut pages of my youth, but to a cub such as yourself, the ways of women will remain for some years too shrouded in mystery to judge.

Kitten did not subscribe to society's usual dictates to women, except, of course, when she assumed a role for the purposes of bookaneering. Her personal wardrobe lacked the frills and feathers prized by ladies, had long sleeves, and was not tailored to be especially well fitting. She clothed herself in manly shades of brown, black, and gray. Her eyes, one gazing in a slightly different place than the other, were foreboding, of a blue color so fine as to be almost transparent—more intimidating than charming—and her pale pink mouth and smooth brow seemed ready to contract into a frown, as though she were listening to the beginning of a joke she would not find funny. She had a tendency to fold her arms under her ample bosom or clamp them at her hips in gestures of pointed impatience. Her voice was coarse, grating even. She might have qualified as plain or even dull if judged by our common standards. Without possessing the trappings of conventional prettiness, wherever she went there were men obsessed with her and women jealous. With age, the dark strands of hair were woven with silver while her face creased with the sorts of lines other women labored to hide, and her power over men doubled—tripled. There was a vulnerability, though; despite her exterior there were times, from a distance, when I saw her break down into tears and need Davenport's company. As I've said, it is difficult to define her allure and, I'd propose, impossible to ever replicate it. It is too often overlooked in this age of magazines how attractive it is for a woman not to care a dime what men think of her.

I've mentioned my own interactions with Kitten were quite limited, but there were a few times, not long before her notorious final mission, when she spoke to me. These occasions were so rare that I remember each of them well, even when nothing important passed between us. Once, I was standing on the crowded Oramin bridge, in Berlin, when I heard my name called out in that unmistakable voice: hoarse, commanding, seductive, disorienting.

Under other circumstances I would have been tickled merely to have Kitten address me. "Perhaps this is a time for more discretion," I whispered to her, thinking other bookaneers and competing parties could be in earshot.

"The vaults were empty, after all that fuss," she said. "Do not look surprised, Mr. Fergins. I know why you're in Germany and what you've come to help your master find. But the stereotype plates Pen wanted have been moved to a catacomb under an old circulating library up north."

I studied her as I tried to discern whether it was possible she was trying to trick me, or whether Davenport had been working with her in this mission, in defiance of his own rules of bookaneering, and why she was telling this to me. "How did you know to find me here? How did you know where I would be?"

"I didn't *know*. But I know Pen's mind more than you could ever know, Mr. Fergins, and I supposed this is where he would set a rendezvous. I guessed it would be easier to find you than to find him." I nodded, accepting her vaguely belittling but true statement, worthy of Davenport. She went on: "Give him this; it tells him where he can find me. Since I cannot stay in Berlin after tonight, I will trade him my information in exchange for a reasonable part of the takings of the mission. Do just as I say. You will find I do not like to give instructions twice."

She was nearing fifty then and, as I've said, had become more striking than ever. Her self-possession, her composure, her poise, her alluring boredom, her selfish resolve, her secrets, all of it came out in every movement and every word she spoke. She handed me a piece of paper, gesturing for me to look at it. It was blank. I knew it was written in invisible ink. It was not a very elaborate method of hiding something, but Davenport would know he was the first to read it.

More than you could ever know—those were the words that teased me; in later years, as things began to go downhill in the Samoan mission, you could say they haunted me. It was Kitten, so there was more than one meaning possible. Did she mean that I would never be able to know how well she understood Davenport, or that I could never understand him the way she did? Either way, my heart was sinking with their weight. That night, after sprinkling a little lemon juice on the note in order to reveal the message, Davenport left me at the hotel and was not back until the next morning. I supposed he retrieved the information he needed from Kitten to complete the mission and then remained with her for the night. Davenport was insistent that his relationship with Kitten was kept separate from professional dealings, and that, with few necessary exceptions, the best bookaneers never worked together. I would not question him, of course, because to question him about anything was fruitless, but it mystified me how he could pretend their labors and emotions were not already mixed. I knew many bookaneers believed that would be the bookaneer's downfall (his, not hers).

There were a few more conversations I had with the famous female bookaneer when we happened upon each other over the course of day-to-day routines, and these were sometimes cordial but never very friendly. She would always say at least one thing that made me uncomfortable. One time there was a comment she made about liking to imagine what people thought about when they saw her with a younger man such as Davenport. "They must ask themselves," she said, "what it is about me that he cannot resist." When something more significant finally passed between us it would once again be on the Continent, this time in darkness.

Now, in the vision that appeared to me onboard the *Colossus*, her face was stern but not without a hint of the grand humor for which she was loved and hated. Those eyes. You and I have talked much of reading. Well, these eyes are the eyes of a reader, eyes that do not just take words in, but confront and challenge their worthiness—the eyes of a queen or empress who has known nothing but control over other people. Her black hair was curly and loose, made to seem darker because her complexion was light. Her mouth was little and curved, giving a reminder of what it withheld (kind words, kisses, smiles) from all—all but one.

Time was rushing and time was crawling—again like being on a speeding train. The next thing I can remember after the eeriness of a dead woman's (living) face was the moment my eyes began to unlock themselves, the lids heavy and unkind. Human eyes, even my poor examples, are remarkable instruments. In utter darkness they moved back and forth valiantly as though something could be gleaned; the blind man's eyes do the same tired dance. I was in a small, dark, close place that smelled of wood. My thoughts at once turned to a coffin. There was the sound of crashing waves. I tried to scream, but I could call up no sound, and in my head I could only hear the clanging words of Poe writing of being buried alive: *Fearful indeed the suspicion—but more fearful the doom!*

Though I still could see nothing, it felt as though the wooden compartment I was inside was settling into the water. I pounded my fists against a wood plank and shouted. Then the horrible guilt settled on me: swim lessons. I had hated the water as a child, and instead of using the lessons in the lake to develop my skills, as my brother did, I would stay where it was shallow enough to stand and pretend to swim. Now the sins of my youth, like the young chicken, came home to roost. I tried to put myself in the best position to imitate swimming.

Light suddenly poured in from above.

"Fergins!"

I looked up to see Davenport. The bookaneer, standing over me, looked confused, as though I had just woken him up. He rubbed his eyes with his thumb and forefinger as he glanced around.

"Davenport!" I exclaimed, my voice sounding raspy, with a note of horror stuck in it. I had been rolling around madly on the floor.

"Do you know—" He interrupted himself with a soft chuckle. "Do you know what you look like? Fergins"—more low laughter directed at me—"what are you doing?"

"Swimming. Well, preparing to," I said with as much dignity as possible.

"Now you look like you've seen a ghost—or, no, that you are a ghost yourself. You know, those books you've given me suggest the Samoan people believe in a wide variety of ghosts and demons living around them at all times. It's a fascinating way to view the world. That with each death, the world grows more populous."

He opened the shutter on the window and a little more light crept into the berth. The same chamber, I realized with a jolt, where I had poured champagne.

"Wait a minute," he went on, taking my spectacles from their case, which was on the table.

"That is very kind, thank you, but . . ." I shook my head, dizzy and lost for words. "What happened?"

"I found you on the edge of the stairs—facedown, Fergins. Quite worrisome."

"Davenport, we must act quickly. You are in danger. I believe I was poisoned!"

He did not seem moved one way or the other. "Sedated."

"Do you mean . . . ? Please know I mean no offense by this question, Davenport, but do I understand correctly that you did this to me? You brought me to your berth and mixed some kind of drugs into the champagne?" He hadn't even a sip from his own glass, I remembered.

He appeared, if not offended, irritated by my statement. "This is *your* berth. I had arranged for it in advance with Ormond, the very fine old English skipper of this *Colossus*. Mine is just across the corridor. Smaller and less well appointed, but adequate."

"Why would you do it, Davenport?"

"Let us take some fresh air to talk about it."

We went above and took some chairs up on the deck. Sailors occasionally passed on some errand in their uniforms, which were far less starchy than I remembered upon boarding. We were out at sea and the winds were strong and the snow-white sails full and magnificent. Davenport crossed his legs and looked over at me, as though he were back in the Garrick Club in '71 waiting for my part of our first conversation.

"Davenport!" I repeated. "Aren't you even going to explain?"

"I needed you to come with me to Samoa," he said with his usual absence of emphasis, his hands crossed over his lap. "Think of the position I was in. You increasingly dislike long ocean voyages as you've gotten older. You grow nauseated and turn green. Even ten years ago your sea legs were wobbling. Remember the time you had to retrieve me from southern Italy and the schooner nearly capsized?"

"I recall something about it."

"And I am not blind, my dear Fergins. I could see that your concerns about my mission flowed deeper than the treacherous passage, as you admitted. Would you have come with me halfway across the world this time?"

"You never asked me."

"Oh, you would have readily agreed to it. Then, at the last moment, you would have confessed that you could not keep your resolve and would have apologized profusely before quickly disembarking and trying to take me with you."

"Not so." I tried to stay strong in my protest even though my voice must have confessed that he was right.

"Cheer up. You've passed the first day and a half of the voyage in tranquility and you shall be better able to manage because some of your senses will remain numbed for another few days." He gestured up to the darkness gathering in the distance. Even the ocean looked black where an awning of clouds was sweeping in ahead. "Old Ormond says we are sailing into a storm, but then this far out at sea they are forever trading one storm for another."

"Why?"

"I cannot say. Particles of vapor attracting each other."

"I mean: Why do you need *me*? Indeed, I have often felt myself no more than a nuisance when I have traveled with you. How in the world can I be of help to you in Samoa, of all places?"

He leaned forward, seemingly giving this question more studious thought than the subject of my sedation. "At the start of July, when the new laws of copyright go into effect, my time as a bookaneer reaches an end. Well, there may be an odd job here or there, but mostly it will be finished except for the lowest scum of our profession, the barnacles who can hardly even be called bookaneers. We have not discussed that fated hour much, you and I, and I should just as soon keep it that way. Except for this: I want you to write a record of my last mission."

"A book?"

"Heavens no! I should as soon be shot for adding to the world's bloated library. When did it occur to people to start writing books about what they like for supper? Not for posterity's sake either, as Bill was babbling on about. I do not give a whit for any of that. I simply want to remember what it was like. For myself, I mean. When I am old and forgetful."

"You wish me to chronicle what happens in Samoa, then? That is why I am here on this ship?"

"Not just what happens this time. My history as a bookaneer. Perhaps some ruminations on the trade."

The proposal did not entirely surprise me. Davenport disliked talking about himself but really liked other people talking about him.

"I have always wished you would discuss more openly . . ." I began. He glanced at me with a bored frown, impatient, as usual, for my answer. "It will be my honor, Davenport."

As our discussions went on through supper, somehow my hesitation to come on the mission—a pure hypothetical, given the fact that he had never asked—became painted as a grave error on my part, and I must have apologized three or four times for the inconvenience of his taking extreme measures. "Why, if I were you, I would have lashed my arms and legs to the mast," I offered. Questions occurred to me at regular intervals. "Where are my notebooks?" "Do I have enough to dress myself in?" "What about my bookstall?"

One of the trunks I had helped to carry onboard, it turned out, was filled with my belongings. As for the bookstall, Davenport, who had devised his plan to bring me several weeks earlier, had arranged for a temporary overseer, a mutual acquaintance called Frank Johnson.

"Oh," I said, "he is a reliable sort." Johnson was a former doctor who had given up his original profession to enter the book trade and for years was a competitor to my original mentor, Stemmes. He was a good bookseller, an honest businessman, and a big, friendly man, if slightly supercilious. He often boasted that he was related to Dr. Samuel Johnson and would only admit he was not if the other person knew enough to laugh at the ridiculous assertion. When I saw him, he would address me as "brother bookseller."

"He retired two years ago from the trade but has been terribly bored, so he will relish being surrounded by your books on a temporary basis. I made it clear I expect him to live up to your standards."

I could not help but feel flattered that Davenport, who could not be bothered to pay his hotel bills or eat a proper meal on most days, had made elaborate arrangements on my behalf. Being an associate of Pen Davenport, you alternated between wanting to run away and not being able to resist the chance to see what might happen next.

IT IS NO PLEASURE CRUISE, sailing aboard a man-of-war, but the luxury steamship companies are not in the business of sailing for distant lands known for headhunters and cannibals. Frigates had better accommodations than dirty, crowded merchant vessels, at least. When the gunships had berths to spare, passengers brought extra income to defray unforeseen costs, besides breaking up the monotony for the officers. The *Colossus* had been called to the South Pacific to the island nations where the British government had interests to protect and oversee, including the several islands that comprised the small nation of Samoa.

To see the passengers is not so different from what you must see, Mr. Clover, in this restaurant car of the railroad: each person is trying to escape from somewhere or trying to find something they think they have lost. There were about a dozen fellow passengers onboard with us, including an Australian merchant named Lionel Hines. We dined with him at the captain's table several times. His head and stomach were large in relation to the rest of his body, his eyes like a squirrel's, his speaking voice loud and intense. The protruding position of his bottom jaw made his teeth seem clenched, and the shape of his mouth seemed made to vent anger. You will see I have cause for the thoroughly harsh opinion of him.

"What exactly is it you are going to do on the islands?"

He asked this question at supper with some of the officers. He was looking at me, so I opened my mouth ready to answer, but Davenport's voice interrupted before I spoke.

"We travel on business, Mr. Hines."

Davenport, sitting to my left, had put a period to the exchange in only six words, because he knew that no man of business wanted an obligation to give details of his purpose, and for Hines to press us would violate that unspoken rule. *Business* was a word that stopped conversation. Hines grumbled slightly, his teeth back to their clench.

This man was particularly displeased with me, though I identified no logical reason for animus. I am believed overly garrulous by many—oh, I know how a peddler is seen by other people. We talk and talk until money changes hands for our wares and then we shut up and move on. But we do not talk in order to sell, contrary to what people believe; we talk because to sell, to convince, to persuade, is a life of loneliness, whether the goods are books, gold watches, or flowers. In any case, Captain Ormond, with his clay pipe always fixed in his mouth, and his officers seemed to enjoy my company, laughing at my anecdotes about some of the colorful characters who would come to my stall in London. I make no personal claims as raconteur. But they were hearing only complaints from the mouth of Hines, and little of anything out of Davenport, who stayed in his tiny berth for four or five hours at a time. There were no female passengers aboard. Many of the other passengers were even more seasick than I was. I was the best option for amusement, in other words, in a place with little competition.

There was a small chamber belowdecks the crew called a library. It had three benches, a broken table, no librarian, no shelves, and no more than twenty inexpensive books kept in an old trunk, half of which were related to sailing or marine matters. Even the semblance of a library was a siren song calling me to it, and as storms overtook the craft and we were forced to spend most of the time between decks it became my usual station. I would put the books out on the table and benches to organize them, even though they would be tossed around again by the waves once they were back in the trunk. This is how Hines found me occupied on an afternoon when the ship was pulled hard by the waves in every direction.

"Rough go of it, isn't it?" I greeted him. "They say it helps to keep the eyes away from the water."

He paced back and forth. "Well?"

"Pardon, Mr. Hines?" I had a Walter Scott book in my hand and could not imagine what he was expecting me to say. "Is there something I can help you with, Mr. Hines? I would be happy to help you choose a book."

"'Mr. Hines! Mr. Hines!'" he echoed mockingly. "Do you know what it is that so irks a man like me about a bookworm like you?"

I felt the blood drain from my face and said I did not.

"You look like you're reading even when there is no book in your hands. A shadow falls in circles around your eyes even when you do not wear your dapper little eyeglasses. Savvy?"

"Spectacles. If my eyesight were a bit better, perhaps eyeglasses would suffice. But I confess I do not understand—"

"You read instead of going to church; you forsake God."

"I did find church rather repetitive in my childhood, for it was like reading the same book again and again, and back then I was reading one or two books every day. But see here! I have never forsaken God, and have lived by righteous principles."

"You think you're better than the rest of us. Better than a man like me without a formal education. Is that what you think about while you hide yourself behind your precious books?"

He was leaning into me and shouting as he revealed his anger, and my answers did nothing to assuage him. I could smell liquor on his clothes and breath, an indication of how he was coping with the increased time belowdecks. I stretched my arm out toward the nearest bell to call for a steward, but it was just past my reach. His hand came toward my face and I prepared to be struck. Instead he snatched off my spectacles.

Here you go, Mr. Clover, take a look at the world through my spectacles. Everything blurs, doesn't it? Thank you—now, don't drop them! Mr. Clover, you see how much hard work they do for me, and what happens when I am deprived of their help. Everything blurred together. I stumbled to my feet and backed away to try to see better. I could make out enough to determine that Hines had put my spectacles over his own face, stretching the metal roughly to fit over his ears. He was using a nasal pitch to imitate my voice. I could hear another man enter the chamber from behind me and I burned with greater shame at having a witness. When I became a bookseller, I sometimes think it was to ensure, however little money I earned, I would not have to encounter men like Hines.

The second man was an utter kaleidoscope of warm colors from where I stood.

"This is between me and your book-obsessed friend. You stay clear," warned Hines.

"Fergins. Mr. Hines," he finally greeted us. It was Davenport.

When he fell quiet I could hear his calm breathing as he was assessing the scene.

Hines threw my spectacles back at me as though to remove evidence of taking them. I put them on and blinked a few times to gain my bearings.

"Just a little conversation between men, I say," Hines went on. "No, I stand corrected. Not between men. Between man and bookworm. Savvy?"

"You do not like that my friend is in the book trade."

"It's nothing to me what he is," groused the merchant, slipping into a more civilized tone. "I simply do not appreciate being condescended to by men who think they are better than me because they carry the leathery odor of *books* on their skin."

"I tend to agree with you," Davenport said, situating himself on one of the benches with a lit cigar and handing a cigar to the Australian.

"Do you?"

"A man must never think reading a book makes him special. Speaking of that, what book is it that inside your coat?"

Hines played dumb but Davenport never could countenance liars, or dumb liars, and went on without mercy: "There is a certain way a man carries himself with a book on one side, and the outline through the material of an inexpensive coat is a distinctive one. I noticed when you first came down the stairs into the captain's room our first evening. Yours is a thin volume, and a small edition, no doubt, perhaps poetry. I've found the man who carries a book in his coat pocket relies upon it with passion and a dependence as a captain of a ship does upon a compass on a moonless night. A book that changed your life."

"What nonsense you speak!"

"Show me," ordered Davenport.

We both waited. The motion of the ship rocked us left and then right. There was nothing more the man could say. The wrath on his face drifted into submission. Hines reached into his coat and slowly pulled out a slender book, just as Davenport described. The bookaneer passed it to me.

"*Leaves of Grass*, by Walt Whitman," I said, rotating it in my hands. "The pages have been cut with a careful touch. The leaves have been turned many times but none torn. This book has been wonderfully treasured."

Hines stood with his head hung low. "I should thank you for my property back."

Davenport put down his cigar and took the book from me. He leaned his face close to the merchant's. "Books inspire a man to embrace the world or flee it. They start wars and end them. They make the men and women who write and publish them vast fortunes, and nearly as quickly can drive them into madness and despair. Stay away from what you do not fathom from now on, and we will like each other better."

He reached into Hines's coat and slipped the book inside. Hines did not look at either of us. He walked over to the table and drew his arm across it with a grunt, sending books flying to the floor, before exiting.

I began to try to thank Davenport but he spoke over me.

"Excellent," he said to himself. "An excellent development." His voice was almost pleased (giddy, really, for Davenport).

I was confused. "How did you even know I needed help down here?"

"Help?" He seemed to be considering my meaning. "I was listening to the pleasing sounds of the storm from the passageway, imagining what horrible screams one would hear if a ship scuttled, when I saw Hines with a marching step and a rather pitiful look of rage on his face on the move in this direction. Knowing you have been spending time in here as a sort of sailing librarian, and having taken note of his amusing dislike for you, I presumed there was the possibility of a confrontation."

"You were precisely right. Well, I do appreciate your help," I reiterated, a little less sure.

He still seemed perplexed by my sentiment. "Did you not see it, Fergins?"

"See what?"

"When I remarked that books could start wars, his eyes fell like a rock, however unconsciously, on *this*."

He pointed to a copy of Robert Louis Stevenson's *Treasure Island*, a standard in the library of any ship where there were young men among the sailors. In fact, a book that had made more than its share of sailors.

"*Treasure Island*?" I asked.

"Not the book, but the name of the author drew his unconscious thoughts," Davenport noted with an air of satisfaction. "I have suspected that Hines, as a merchant with dealings in Samoa for some years, would have some knowledge of what Stevenson is involved in there. Of course, I do not want to draw attention to our interest by asking direct questions. But now he has begun to reveal his impression of Stevenson's role on the island, and to add knowledge that I believe will make my mission successful."

"You came into the library to see if the man would reveal something about Stevenson?"

"Indeed. And very much worth the effort."

He gave a proud nod, rising to his feet. As I sat frozen with astonishment, he started to walk toward the door but stopped when his eyes landed on a book, one of the volumes knocked down by Hines and now sliding across the slanting floor. His bottom lip quivered slightly and he closed his eyes before he stepped around the book and continued out.

V

I suspect you have never heard of a French novel called *The Castle in the Forest*. How a copy of it came to lead a life at sea in the frigate's library, I will not venture to guess any more than I would the provenance of the rest of the trunk's hodgepodge. There was a time long ago when the author of that title, Elizabeth Barnard, was very popular, particularly in France, where she lived, and an era when each of her books would have been translated into English and many other languages. Now her name, like those of her novels, is all but forgotten, not only by a young man your age, my dear Mr. Clover, but by most people. There is no great mystery to what happened to Mrs. Barnard, for it happens to so many authors. People imagine that literature is the collection of books that we read as a nation or society, but, for just a moment, picture it as something alive instead, a new organism. Not a pretty or delicate thing, either. A grotesque, cold-blooded beast, as big as the biggest whale and growing. Give it seven or eight heads while we're at it, and it feeds on a book in each loathsome mouth simultaneously. Each book requires whatever blood and tears an author has, but to the beast of literature it is merely one sliver of a meal to swallow down, and upon ingesting it that particular head of this beast licks all its shiny red lips, as if to call out, "Next!" If the same author provides another meal quickly enough, then the beast has been pleased; if not, the beast swallows the unlucky author whole instead and waits in rage for the next one. The hydra-headed abomination savors female authors in particular—Mrs. Shelley and Harriet Beecher Stowe could never satisfy its appetites after their respective masterpieces had been consumed. The moral is this: authors do not create literature; they are consumed by it. As a bookseller, I am often asked if I didn't dream of being an author, but I should rather think it is the author who learns to dream of becoming a bookseller. I do not seek the mantle of genius. I am an appreciator, an observer, a preposition, and content in that, and that is me in a nutshell.

Back to Pen Davenport's ambivalent emotion upon laying eyes—for what was probably the first time in years—upon that book sliding across the library floor of the man-of-war. I believe his reaction relates directly to an early time in his career as a bookaneer, and it is worth a brief digression to shed some light on it. Mrs. Barnard moved from her native England to the beautiful rural environs of France after marrying a French potter. She had already published a few forgettable pieces of magazine poetry in England under her industrious maiden name, Werker. While in their tiny village in France and while her husband shaped clay, she spent her hours writing prose alone in their quiet cabin. There were heroines, and magic, and sorcery, and devious monsters disguised as suitors. These may sound like trifles to a young man who prefers Socrates over Horatio Alger. But there is a truism that if women who live in the countryside enjoy a book, then that book could sell anywhere, and Barnard soon was writing novel after novel, with her novels keeping the presses in Paris humming around the clock. Success plagued her with overly enthusiastic admirers as well as ruthless critics punishing her for popularity. After five books, she proclaimed that she would never put pen to paper again. As quietly as they had come, she and her husband moved away, some said to Ireland and others to Bath, for a life of peace. A few years later, news of her death reached the Continent.

It was about a month after the newspapers reported her death that a young man in rustic clothes was walking into the offices of Mrs. Barnard's publisher in Paris. He explained that he was hired to remove some crates left abandoned in a shed on the property formerly belonging to the potter and his novelist wife, and was given permission to keep what he liked. He came upon a bundle of papers and, preparing to burn it, noticed the page on top. *A Tomb*—so it said—a romance by Elizabeth Louise Barnard. The publisher on the other side of the desk from this visitor had many years of experience and a deep suspicion of forgeries. He never knew Mrs. Barnard personally, as she had been reclusive even before her abrupt departure, but he knew her work intimately. To his utter joy, after examining the mysterious pages, he had no doubt they were authentic. Since the family of the deceased had given this young laborer permission to keep whatever he wished, he owned the manuscript. The lad had lucked into a golden goose.

To the publisher's amazement, the visitor refused to sell. "No. If she wanted to have it published, wouldn't she have done it herself?" young Pen Davenport moralized in French.

Davenport made himself scarce but left enough traces to be found and sent for. He knew the publisher's head would burst thinking of the money he could make from a posthumous Elizabeth Barnard book.

The publisher soon arranged to have him return to Paris. "Good day," the publisher greeted him, with a big smile this time.

"I must tell you, sir, that I haven't changed my mind. Indeed, I have not even brought the manuscript I suppose you're still after."

The man recovered after a moment of disappointment and took the young laborer on a tour of the offices. He brought him to a vault. There was not money inside but stereotype plates and woodcuts from which their books were made. He meant to persuade the naive lad by demonstrating the importance of the trade of publishing, one can suppose, by placing the objects in his hands. The young and morally upright man did not waver. However, after a long day being regaled by the publisher at Paris's finest coffee shops and wine taverns, the visitor finally relented, agreeing to a small fortune in exchange for retrieving and handing over the manuscript. The publisher happily parted with the sum. He could barely contain himself. After all, whatever he was paying this simple country boy was far less than he would have had to pay Mrs. Barnard herself, who had been a very hardheaded woman.

A few weeks after purchasing the manuscript from the laborer, he received a letter from England. It purported to be written by Mrs. Barnard, assuring him that she was very much alive, that the rumors of her death in the papers were so foolish she had not even responded to them, and that she had heard about his plans to publish a new book by her while she was visiting London. She had written no book called *A Tomb*, she protested, and in fact everything she had ever written had been published and she did not seek to enlarge the list.

The publisher trembled at the thought of losing the money he had given to the laborer and the far greater sums spent preparing the publication. Childishly, he hid the letter and then incinerated it in the boiler. He did his best to forget it. Until one day a woman appeared in their offices. She was short with thick black curly hair and a glowing white complexion, smelling of oranges and mint, with a small mouth.

"Good afternoon. I am Elizabeth Barnard, and I understand you are publishing a book under my name that I did not write."

The publisher was speechless, no doubt burning up at the thought of the lad who had somehow tricked him. *Him*, of all people.

"Mrs. Barnard. Thank goodness you are among the living!"

She waited, her expressive brow wrinkling.

"We must have been duped," he went on.

"By whom?"

"I do not know. A confidence man! A Jeremy Diddler!"

She replied after a thoughtful pause. "Did you not receive my letter in time to stop publication of the hideous thing being called a book?"

"No, I suppose . . . No. A letter? I never received it," he stammered and sputtered, turning red as a beet.

She took both his hands in her own and turned his palms upward, stroking each with her thumb. "An odd thing—it is an odd thing. I have a messenger who swears he delivered it into these hands."

It is said by some he actually got on his knees and begged her mercy, but it hardly matters if that detail is true or fanciful. Rather than endure a lawsuit, he paid her an exorbitant sum and agreed to publish an announcement that *A Tomb* was a forgery.

This French publisher, who died a few years later, his demise perhaps hastened by the cruelty of this episode, was said to be a very big, strong-limbed gentleman. The lady bringing him to his knees was barely five feet tall. Even I have not been able to confirm whether Davenport and Kitten, who of course presented herself as Mrs. Barnard (who really was under the ground, in an out-of-the-way burial yard outside Bath), had coordinated their efforts, or Davenport had made his move forging the document and Kitten made hers on top of it. In any case, the tale of their mutual success became one of the most renowned in the annals of the bookaneers, and, by many accounts, was the true beginning of their love affair.

THERE WAS an interesting development with our uninteresting and despicable fellow passenger, Hines. Once Davenport had humiliated him during our confrontation in the ship's library, he was as docile as a lamb toward the bookaneer. I had been as kind as could be to the man—kinder with every barb and insult thrown my way—yet he still only scorned me, while Davenport had wrung his neck, figuratively speaking, and in doing so rendered him tame. More important, he continued to be a useful source of information about Samoa, however unpleasant his delivery.

"You bachelors might look to pick a girl in Samoa to bring home and marry," he said crassly to us, "if you wouldn't mind your darling wife showing her bosom to every man she meets."

"Pardon me?" replied Davenport.

The merchant's face shook with laughter. "A joke, good fellow. I like to have some fun with new visitors. Those brown women on the islands never cover themselves up above the waist, you know. But they're still embarrassed if you happen to see one of them without the little clothes they wear!"

"How do you know that?" Davenport could not resist asking, stopping Hines's laughter cold.

"All I'm saying"—he screwed his face into a serious one—"is that they're happy to have a white man to marry, so they don't end up carrying their husband's bloody, brown head home from a battlefield. Many whites marry the prettiest natives or half-castes they see when they're in the South Seas. It's all well and good to bring them back with you—just don't bring a white woman to the islands. It is all too primitive; being in a place like that kills a civilized woman."

Another time, while playing euchre with the first officer and another passenger in the smoking parlor, the merchant chimed in, "It is important always to remember one thing about savages: they are far more frightened of us than we ought to be of them. Savvy? It will feel as though you are dealing with people who are deaf and dumb, or just beasts, but they can be persuaded to understand our ways. You probably heard the story of the gunboat *Adler*."

Davenport and I said we had not.

"German warship," continued Hines, leaning back on the cool wooden bench and stretching his legs out, though there was hardly room for all of us in the small space around the table. He was pleased to assume the role of expert. "The Germans sent it to anchor at the Samoan harbor of Apia to enforce their government's preferences in the last battle for the rule of the islands three years ago, which was between two of its chieftains—Mataafa, who the natives had chosen as king, and Tamasese, the savage who had made a deal with the Germans to rule how they wished him to. Its guns pointed at the coast, there the hulking vessel waited to be defied. It could eradicate a whole village with a single shot. Then a hurricane ripped it from its spot and brought the ship down at the top of the reef where it remains—a complete wreck."

"Nature keeps to its own plans."

"And probably prevented war between the Americans and Germans. Listen closely—here is what is most remarkable. The natives formed lines of men to rush into the beating surf and try to save the lives of the German sailors who, only hours before, were prepared to fire on their villages. You see, the savages are simple and good fellows, on the whole, who bow down to the needs of the white men when it comes to it."

"What happened after the storm?" I asked.

"The Germans kept their position having the most sway on the Samoan island. The consul ordered three more warships to take the *Adler*'s place, while the Americans and British each carry one of theirs at a time, like the *Colossus*, and bring them in and out as they see fit."

In addition to learning more about the current German stranglehold over the Samoan people, we picked up from the merchant and some of the experienced sailors a few useful Samoan words, adding to those we had gathered from the dry pages of our books. Davenport was also using the time to observe Hines and the other passengers and make certain none were there for the same reasons as we were.

—*Very sorry to interrupt.*

Pray interrupt when you like, for this tale is for you to hear, Mr. Clover, not me to tell.

—*Well, as I understood it, Mr. Fergins, by the time of your ocean passage, the laws on copyright were already set to change, isn't that so?*

That's right. The international copyright treaties were signed at Berne and the underground market for books was about to fall under the jurisdiction of courts in just a few months from the time I speak about, in the beginning of that July.

—*You said there were hardly any bookaneers remaining, since everyone knew the profession was doomed. Why would Mr. Davenport worry there would be another one in his midst without him knowing?*

Even in this extinction period for bookaneers, Davenport simply could not quash his suspicious nature. After all, *he* was pretending to have a purpose other than his real one, and so could the Australian, or anyone else we met up until the time Davenport held Stevenson's novel in his hands. You wonder if he wouldn't know another bookaneer by sight. True enough, in most cases. However, any person can be a bookaneer without even realizing it.

So Davenport contrived a reason to suggest an invitation into the merchant's berth, and after a few moments, he had taken the inventory he needed. Especially of the books (of which there were just three, two on etiquette and manners, and one called *The Thorough Business Man*), but also ancillary objects, with an eye toward any of the following: spyglasses, especially smaller ones that could be hidden in a pocket; professional pens, erasers, and other writing instruments that could be used to alter or forge manuscript pages; pens (or cuff links or buttons or similarly inconspicuous items) just slightly too large—by a few millimeters around—that were actually hollow hiding places for purloined papers (a bookaneer could fold a standard piece of paper to the size of a five-cent coin without damaging it); cords that could replace telegraph wires and appear to be operational but actually hinder communication. A bookaneer's arsenal. This man did not have any of these.

"You—bookworm," Hines hailed me one evening at the captain's table.

"Did you say something, Hines?" His comments were so often rude or simply random this had become my first reply to anything he said.

"You know me, busy enough with important ledgers and the rest, don't have any more space in my brain for your fine books, friend," he said, believing, I suppose, that saying the word *friend* would make me forget his abuse. "You in particular may have some trouble on the island." A silk handkerchief, engraved with his full name, would often be drawn, readied for a sneeze or to dry his brow, only to be crumpled from one hand to the other and back, unused.

"What do you mean, Hines? What kind of trouble?" I asked.

"Books, friend! Savvy? You will have trouble finding books. They do not exist in Samoa."

"What do you mean?"

"The natives just tell their stories to each other, like chattering birds. As I understand it, they appoint certain men to be memorizers— legend keepers—who are in charge of remembering their race's simplistic tales and passing them on. You might be interested to know that there is one white scribbler living on Upolu, though, up on a mountainside in Apia. R. L. Stevenson—you must have heard of the fellow."

"I heard a rumor about him sailing the South Seas," said Davenport, knowing that ignorance would risk more attention than partial knowledge. "What's a man like Mr. Stevenson doing in a place that has no books?"

Hines hunched forward slightly. "Meddling."

The mystery had been building in our minds since first hearing Whiskey Bill's description. Why had Stevenson left behind the rest of the world to remain on an island desolate of any trace of culture? I was burning to ask Hines more questions about what he knew of Stevenson's life on the island, but Davenport wisely returned to his meal and I followed his example.

Our lack of interest had its intended effect. Once he had attention, the merchant wanted to keep it. "Remember the map of Upolu I showed you in my stateroom?" he continued. "Stevenson has a large plot of land he calls Vailima, four hundred acres in all, where he has built quite an impressive mansion."

"What does it mean, Hines?" I asked. "The name of his property, I mean."

"'Five streams.' Stevenson's place is high up, right at the edge of a volcano, with some waterfalls, and you can only see the place from out in the ocean. Anywhere else on the island, that vast property of his is invisible to the human eye. He is an island on an island."

The only other time Stevenson came up in conversation during the voyage was another occasion at the captain's table, a meal with Captain Ormond present. Ormond was a hardened sailor who, when asked the date, would answer only, "Eighteen hundred and war." Of course, dates and times meant little to men at sea who lived by latitude and wind direction, the reds of sunrise and oranges of sunset.

"Stevenson, yes, then there's Mr. Stevenson," the captain of the *Colossus* said with apparent admiration. He had been talking about some of the earnest missionaries, the lazy beachcombers, and other white inhabitants to be found on the islands.

Hines, who had been seasick and in a fouler-than-usual mood despite passive weather, grumbled to himself, then asked what the captain thought of the man.

"Splendid! I never met him, though," Ormond said, taking a smoke from his weathered clay pipe. "He was holed up in that plantation of his during the other times I have been stationed at the Apia port. Nor have I read but one or two of his stories and can't say I remember those awfully well other than the fact that they were terribly entertaining."

"I must say though I do not pretend I could write a novel I would also never read one, and for the same reasons. But if you are not some rabid reader, Captain Ormond, then what is it about him that makes you smile like a child sucking on candy?" Hines asked irritably.

Ormond's admirable face and brittle lips became very serious, even macabre. He put his pipe down. "Because, Mr. Hines, maybe that is what it takes in these parts of the world. A man with a novelist's romantic imagination, to save those islands from the dark times that the rest of us bring them."

Hines finished chewing and frowned. "Well, I've seen that odd scarecrow Stevenson from time to time riding on his ugly horse in Apia, with his even odder wife. How a man with arms that thin could even write books is a fact beyond my understanding."

LAND!

Fiction writers have employed their inventive powers to imagine life on other planets, with the strange beings living there among sometimes dreary, sometimes fantastic landscapes. These wordsmiths go to too much trouble. Visit the far reaches of our own earth and you will experience what it is to enter another world. From a distance the islands of the South Seas greet the eye with the most magnificent majesty. Then, steering closer, the land that hours earlier looked lush and dark green becomes rocky and frowning, before turning bright and colorful and welcoming again as you glide along the coast. Conflicting impressions rushed through me as we closed in on the Samoan islands, still small dots of color in the blue horizon. I felt bursts of excitement, of peace; of sanctuary, of peril; of familiarity, of mystery; of being home, of being as far from it as I could ever be.

I asked one of the officers how we would know which island was Upolu. He said I would know it when I saw it.

The staggering sun beat down on the shiny white decks. To my right, Davenport leaned far out over the railing, sending a few seabirds fluttering away. He was once again clean-shaven and looked ten years younger because of it. He was looking over the horizon when the islands came into view about eight miles out and gradually grew in size. He set a cigar between his teeth and tried to light one soggy match after another before giving up. Then he turned away.

"Don't you want to see the islands for yourself?" I asked, astonished that after nearly a month at sea he would have such fleeting interest. He had come above deck only a few minutes ago.

"I just did," he said, on his way back belowdecks. "Wake me when we get to port, Fergins," he called back after me.

To Davenport this apathy was an exercise in self-discipline. In order to concentrate on his mission alone he refused to play a part in the inevitable excitement of reaching a new shore, when every detail of whatever you can make out assumes the shape of a revelation. But I relished the moment, and could understand what the officer meant about knowing Upolu on sight. At the center of the island, a giant volcano jutted up to the heavens, with other mountain ranges spread across the rest of the island. It was unusual, beautiful, and rough. First we heard, then saw a silver waterfall crashing down from hundreds of feet above. There were four warships along the coast, one with American and three with German colors. As we glided closer, there could be seen the wrecked hulk of the German warship Hines had told us about, circled by loud gulls and swept over by a frustrated white surf avenging itself in rust. About one mile away, a pilot boat awaited us, bobbing up and down on the great foamy breakers, which is when I went to rouse the still-indifferent Davenport. After we laid anchor at the harbor, we were met by a fleet of long, narrow canoes, each occupied by one white man at the stern and muscular brown-skinned rowers lining the sides. More Samoans waited at the shore, holding up jewelry made of shells, as well as chickens and mats, presumably for sale or trade.

Books comparing the various races of savages in the South Seas are filled with praise for the Samoans. They tend to be as tall as Europeans, their skin a combination of red and brown that is less jarring to the eye of certain whites than the midnight black skin and wild, frizzy hair of the inhabitants of some nearby islands. Native Samoans often wear mustaches but consider smooth chins cultivated. The peculiar tattoos that cover much of the skin of both sexes suggest the appearance of being fully clothed even though they never are. The sight of the native women with uncovered breasts was shocking not only to me, but even to my much more cosmopolitan companion. Still, the fact that Samoans are not cannibals tends to curry great favor with foreigners. Even putting aside not eating us, they are among the friendliest people you could meet. Their smiles are sincere, their eyes open and honest, their attitudes light and well-meaning.

One of the first things I noticed as we moved closer was that the natural colors on the island were almost impossibly varied, sparkling and bold, starting with the fish rushing away from our path beneath our canoe. The natives were wrapped in a multitude of colors, too, with wildflowers and cloths, and their smooth skin shimmering in the sun with tattoos, sweat, ocean water, and coconut oil. The air was clean and thin, with a mixed floral scent that was strong everywhere.

After climbing a ladder down the side of the frigate, Davenport and I joined a few other passengers in one of the canoes. The white man in our craft introduced himself as representing the English consulate. As Hines had informed us, the capital of Apia, situated at the harbor, had been gobbled up and divided over the years among the three foreign powers—Great Britain, America, and Germany—arranged in proximity to their respective consulates and array of warships. There were also churches of several denominations, from which the missionaries operated. This busy area was called "the beach," and that was where all white settlers and visitors congregated for their safety. Only a fool would think to lodge elsewhere. We were fools, but I did not know it yet.

I have stood in a full suit in the sultry climate of Castile watching where a government censor was carrying a crate of books while awaiting Davenport's instructions; have lined my hat with writing paper to deflect the sun of Siena in the middle of August, while wearing a long black cloak to conceal a smuggled fourteenth-century book. But tropical heat is oppressive in a unique way. It consumes you entirely. It seems to enter the skin and eyes, to crawl under the hair and nails; it becomes part of you and takes your breath. I'd learn there are only two Samoan seasons: hot and dry, and hot and rainy.

The Englishman wore what we would discover was the typical uniform of white men in the South Seas, which was a thin suit of white linen and a large straw hat. He was a pleasant, gray-haired man whose skin had become a faint bronze from the tropical sun. Mine, as bad luck would have it, would turn splotchy and itchy during our time on the island. The consul passed the back of his hand across his brow, as though he were the one doing the rowing rather than the natives, who sang—or chanted—as they pulled us toward the shore. "Apologies for the heat; can't do much for it but bathe and drink 'ava—that is like their wine. The brown folk like sun, anyway."

"How do you like being on the island?" Davenport asked.

"We do some good for the people here. Oh, you'll come across some complaints—maybe you have already from the navy men. I hear the King of Tonga is talking about drafting a constitution so no foreign powers knock on their door. But most of the islands around here would be lucky indeed to have as much interest from more advanced governments as Samoa does."

"Even from the Germans?" asked Davenport.

He cleared his throat, also clearing away Davenport's question. "Do you fellows need any advice on lodging at the beach during your stay?"

"No," was Davenport's answer. "We have that settled."

I was as surprised as the consul appeared to be.

"We do need transportation to the interior, where we will be staying," Davenport continued.

"I can help arrange that," said the man, after a rather curious expression had crossed his face.

He told us there were hardly any coaches or buggies on the island because they simply did not fit on the roads. Supplies and belongings had to be tied in bundles to the horses or stored in saddlebags. When we reached the beach, which curved into a half-moon shape, we hired two horses for ourselves and a guide on horseback to lead us. During our ride, Davenport told me that he had already rented a cottage.

"From whom? We have spoken to nobody else since landing."

"Hines."

Hines, that hateful enemy of mine from the frigate, turned out to own a significant amount of land in Samoa. After riding almost an hour across uneven terrain through lush, monotonous jungle, we reached the "cottage," a simple but sturdy oval hut with two rooms, a verandah that ranged three sides of the structure, and an iron roof that caused a ruckus with the alighting birds or raindrops. Out there we were entirely alone with the exception of a sunny native, Cipaou, whose service came with the lease.

"You will find the Samoan boy honest and even hardworking," Hines told us when he called on the cottage on the second day. "Though, like all the natives, he can behave like a child, and may decide one day he is done with his labor for you, and move away to the opposite side of the island without remembering to collect wages!"

I had tried to ask Davenport why he would have accepted an arrangement with such a loathsome man as Hines. I was certain he gave us as remote a location as possible to spite me. But the bookaneer had become all but silent—discourteous, even—since we'd reached the harbor, and made it perfectly clear he was not about to give me any explanation, at least not a meaningful one.

Our morning ritual began the day after our arrival. We took our horses out along a narrow stream until reaching a group of trees heavy with bananas and coconuts. Occasionally we could spot a Samoan boy or two in the distance across the stream, sometimes tending a herd of a few dozen cows. The boys, like our own man Cipaou, seemed strong and agile and wore colorful kilts, called lavalavas, made of island bamboo and whatever other materials they had learned to obtain from tree bark. Davenport would indicate to Cipaou what he wanted, at which point Cipaou would pull himself up on the tree with terrific strength and use a large blade to slash down the selected fruit. We would then store these in our baskets.

On the fourth morning, I woke with a momentary confusion about where I was. Sleeping on a pile of soft mats on the floor, in the style of the natives, did not help my patience, nor did Samoa's stifling humidity. I stumbled across the room and opened the door because leaving it open every few hours was the best way to give the cockroaches, spiders, and death's-head moths egress, since they found ways inside regardless. Davenport was lying facedown on the floor on two of the other mats, which served not only as our beds but also as our dining surface, our writing desks, and, well, the entirety of our furniture.

"Davenport," I called softly, tapping his shoulder.

I had to nudge him twice more before he lifted his head. "The boy is here?"

"Not yet. I wanted to talk before Cipaou arrives."

He pushed himself up on his elbows and worked against a tiger's yawn. "Talk then, Fergins."

I was interrupted by Cipaou's whistle, announcing that he was waiting on our verandah. A half hour earlier than the day before, but then
again, the natives did not have watches or clocks. Whites often return
to Europe or America from Samoa and say the natives do not know
how to work. This is not so. They do their work, and well. They merely
do not work on a schedule and see no reason to.

"Ready the horses, if you will," Davenport called out to the servant,
who knew a little English. "What is it you wanted to say, Fergins?"

"I was only thinking. We have bananas to feed the whole British
consulate of Samoa, Davenport. Yet we hardly stray from our strip of
land and have only been in the village of Apia twice since our arrival,
without making any inquiries either time about Stevenson or learning
anything about anything. Perhaps if you send me on an errand to the
village today, I can see what I can gather."

"Maybe you believe I have contracted island fever."

I changed my approach. "Davenport, you were the one who wished
me to observe this mission with great attention, in order to record your
methods. Right?"

He would admit nothing of the kind, but did give me a more satis-
fying reply. "If we seek out Stevenson and he learns we did, then he is
far more likely to scrutinize us and our purpose. A white man secluded
in a land like this must keep a suspicious and careful outlook to protect
himself—an island on an island, as Hines described Stevenson. That is
why we must have him find us instead of the other way."

"But how would he find us? Why would he bother? We have hardly
seen another human being since our arrival, besides our dear Cipaou,
have barely talked to those we have seen, and this blasted cottage Hines
stuck us in is nowhere near Stevenson's house."

He acknowledged my facts to be true and, raising his puckish eyes,
seemed about to say more when Cipaou whistled again. "Wait a minute
while I dress," he said to me, "then I will finish explaining myself." But

he never did finish; whether forgetting or never intending to, I could not say. We spent the afternoon strolling the clearings of the forest, slicing coconuts and storing the milk before helping Cipaou prepare a fire for dinner, which would consist of pink crayfish caught from our stream. That was the closest thing we had to meat. I nearly choked to death trying to get it down. I was too exhausted at the end of the day to make any further complaint.

The next morning we were in the same fields when there was a distant sound, the sound of galloping. Having isolated ourselves, and having passed the time by listening to Cipaou's stories of thieves, evil ghosts, and runaway cannibals populating the island, the very idea of other beings now caused me alarm. Even Cipaou seemed to have his ears pinned back.

"What is it?" I asked.

"Peace, Fergins," Davenport said, then: "Cipaou, good fellow, do not worry, all is well. Continue without us, if you please; we will catch up soon." Cipaou reluctantly left us alone. Davenport now turned to me and said, "I expected three or four horses, and from the sound of it, there are only two."

"You expected?"

He gave a brief grin.

On the opposite side of the stream that ran along our property, two riders were approaching. One wide-shouldered man who had coffee-colored skin cut a strong figure; he was thin-lipped and steady, his head wrapped up in a red and white bandanna. As he came closer, I was surprised to notice that he appeared Chinese, for his garments were a strange mix of European and native Samoan, with a white shirt and a long loincloth made of tree bark. The second rider was gaunt and tall, with long, dark hair straggling out from under the brim of an old yachting cap. His mustache hung in low waves, matching his flowing hair. He was, in short, as odd-looking and long-limbed as his bony, odd-looking horse.

It was Robert Louis Stevenson. Unlike other authors, who looked nothing in person like the faces that were claimed as their likenesses for the purpose of promotion, his face was instantly distinctive as his frontispiece portrait. His years of illness made him appear far older than forty. He rode a piebald horse of white with patterns of light brown spots and a shaggy mane; the creature, who had a face like a donkey's, seemed old and his legs a little bowed, his back bent. The Chinese rider waited for Stevenson to step down from his horse before he did the same. Time seemed to slow as the novelist positioned two thick branches across the stream as a temporary bridge.

While I had pictured this to myself, there was something more incredible about the sight of the famous author, the invalid in exile, than I had anticipated. First, there was his physical appearance. His head. You have never seen eyes so far apart in your life. Unusual eyes, too. They appeared as though they were carrying some just-seen secret and were busy scanning for another. The sheer width of the man's brow was remarkable. If Samoa really had been another planet, we surely would have assumed this was the king of its life forms.

These were the words spoken by Stevenson after he crossed over to our side of the stream: "Do either of you know today's date?"

"The seventh, I believe," offered Davenport.

"Month?"

I answered March.

"Well! I thought it might be April. Thank you. Americans?"

"Yes," said Davenport. "That is, I am. My friend, Mr. Fergins, is a thorough Englishman."

The man extended a long, unsteady arm to me and then to Davenport. His fingers and big palm were cold to the touch. It was startling in the hot, moist tropics. His eyes and hands had the nervous movement of sickness.

"Tusitala is what I am called here. John Chinaman is over there"—he pointed over his shoulder with his thumb—"and, of course, Jack."

I looked for the other member of their party, until I realized he meant the bowlegged horse.

The novelist continued. "What brings you gentlemen to Upolu?"

"A book, actually," Davenport said enthusiastically. "I am hoping to write a book about traveling the South Seas. The ones I've encountered have been lacking. Life, customs, and so on."

"It is hard to reach the truth in these islands," Stevenson said cryptically.

"You must appreciate the place to be here."

"After being through most of the South Seas, I can tell you this is my favorite island."

"Is it?"

"Without a doubt," said Stevenson cheerfully, glancing at his companion for affirmation. "Hawaii is nice, yes. This is better. It is far more . . . savage. There is more of the savage in me than Honolulu can satisfy."

We both replied with polite laughter, but Stevenson did not join in, nor did his implacable companion. On past missions when I accompanied Davenport, I would spend most of my time doing research on his behalf in libraries and museums, delivering or receiving messages, transporting books, and making his sleeping arrangements. I was usually at a distance from the heart of things. Now I kept my eyes on Davenport for hints on how I should behave, while through it all the quick glances of Stevenson's silent Chinese companion traced our slightest movements. The murky brown orbs of the novelist, meanwhile, betrayed no sign of any particular feeling toward us—neither friendship nor suspicion, and certainly no great curiosity.

The whole conversation must have been only three or four minutes, with brief exchanges about the plant life and the roads, or lack of them, and about the land near the cottage, before Stevenson and his companion took their leave and crossed the stream. "Death on a pale horse," the novelist called out of himself, with a grim laugh, when he returned to his saddle.

We rode behind Cipaou in silence on the way back to the cottage, though I was bursting to speak. Reaching our destination, I immediately retrieved my notebook and flipped through it.

"Here!" I said, stretching out the word.

"What?"

"You said to me shipboard, Davenport, during our discussions of the history of the profession—I shall quote you, my friend, so you do not allege that my memory grows faulty with old age. Yes, the sixth rule of the trade: 'The bookaneer avoids, whenever possible, in crafting a disguised identity, the appearance of any interest in publishing or books in order to leave their subjects unsuspecting of their intentions.'"

"I must have said something to that effect."

"You told Stevenson you're an author."

"If you think I violate my own law, you misunderstood. I was telling you how typical bookaneers behave, but, in that instance, they would be decidedly wrong. Those bookaneers believe they are being inconspicuous. But the writer is a peculiar breed. A man or woman whose very profession and trade is built upon the elevation of his or her own ego as capable of a task most others are not. An author is an author because people cannot do what he does, not because they do not want to."

"Did you ever want that? To become an author, I mean," I said. When Davenport did not like a question, or did not want to answer, he pretended he did not hear it. Given that as the only response, I reverted to the earlier subject: "Stevenson—or Talofa, or whatever it was he called himself—parted from us without an invitation or suggestion of any reunion. If you presented yourself as a politician, a dignitary, a missionary, a merchant, even a census taker—surely you could contrive some reason to enter his home and start to gain the intelligence you will need to see the mission through. I'm afraid to say, Davenport, that your claim to be a writer failed to excite any feeling in him at all."

"Tusitala."

"What?"

"He is called Tusitala," said the bookaneer. "Talofa is a Samoan greeting, meaning, more or less, 'love to you.' Their tongue has a charming ring to it, doesn't it?"

"And what does Tusitala mean?"

"Ask the question a few times around the village, my dear Fergins, and we'll soon earn a reputation for having a singular interest in Stevenson. We'll learn in time."

"Never mind the language lessons, Davenport."

"Fergins, to one author, another author is a comrade, a threat, and a shadowy reflection all at once. If we had been making ourselves conspicuous around the very few shops and offices of Apia, Stevenson would likely have no use for us, but because we have remained quiet and removed, away from the village, he shall feel the need to know more of me, mark my words. Remember that one of his earliest publications was a book about traveling through Belgium and France, so to learn of a man writing a travelogue will give him an itch of nostalgia for a simpler time—a time when his life was ahead of him, a time before illness and the weight of family problems had led him into this exile. In any event, it fits with my having a companion who is a bookseller, and I would not have wanted to force upon you a new name and identity."

"Something else that confounds me," I said after considering how the whole explanation somehow turned out to rely on doing me a good turn. "How did you know Stevenson would come to us out there today in the first place? You said you were expecting it. I do not see how that is possible."

"You were right when you said yesterday that our land is quite far from Vailima—that is, from the novelist's *house*. But you were overlooking the fact that the property of Vailima encompasses more than four hundred acres. When we were out at sea and Hines—whose presence was far more useful to us than you realized—showed me on a map the properties he owned on the island, I could see that this one bordered at the very tip the far reaches of Stevenson's land, hundreds of acres away from the novelist's library though it might be. It was a speck on the map, but it was just what I needed."

"That is why we were out riding that same path every day?" I asked, laughing with the realization that all the time heaping bananas had not been wasted along with the bananas themselves.

"On our first day riding the grounds, I noticed some cows—fat cows—at the stream that bordered our property and ran into Stevenson's. I had learned from the pages of your books on the South Pacific that cows are rare in Samoa and are sequestered so that they are not stolen. Cows are creatures of habit who prefer no disruption to their routines. I suspected these cows were accustomed to complete quiet in their little corner of the universe, and so our little ride each morning began to annoy them and send them farther away. I also suspected that once Stevenson's servants noticed that this was happening around the same time each morning, they would alert their master, who would take them to inspect the cause sooner or later, and of course find no threat to the cows—but would find us, and in the process would introduce himself. I thought the servants who had seen us would be riding with him, which was why I expected to hear the sounds of more horses approaching. But Stevenson is evidently a man who takes matters into his own hands—a thing to remember."

"What do we do now?"

"We wait again," said Davenport with some pleasure.

Two days of routine came and went before a houseboy (as they were called even though they were really young men), who was dressed in the same lavalava as the outside boys, but with a fine white livery uniform on top that made me long for English civilization, arrived with a simple note written on a piece of stationery.

FROM THE FIELDS OF VAILIMA

Please do us the honor of your
company tomorrow afternoon,
for tea and cookies.

VI

———◦○◦———

Davenport became entirely stoic whenever I would become excited, as happened over the invitation to Vailima.

"We have entrance into the man's house, where his manuscript will
be at arm's length."

"Nothing is so simple, Fergins," Davenport said. "For one thing,
Belial is still not accounted for. He could be out there circling us. Circling Vailima, waiting to knock the whole thing on its head. We must
have our eyes open at all times to avoid his traps."

I took in the possibility. I thought about the last time I had seen
Kitten, and the word *Belial* sent a fresh chill through me. "I fear I am
at a disadvantage," I said, trying to hide what I was really thinking
about. "With all your history with the man, I never had a chance to see
him in person, and now that I think it over you've never assigned me to
gather information on him. There are times over the years I wondered
if the man was a figment."

"I never assigned you anything on Belial because there is no information to gather. Not really. No one knows where he lives or where he
goes when he is not bookaneering. He talks of a wife incessantly,
though I've never seen her. If she exists, I shall never stop pitying her.
He might as well be a figment. Am I understood?"

"Pardon?"

"It's something he always says. 'Am I understood?' He could be telling you that it is noontime, and still finish the sentence with, 'am I understood?'"

I thought about Davenport often saying, "Wait a minute," with no regard to how long the so-called minute would actually be, but I nodded. "What exactly does he look like?"

"Like no other."

"There must be some way to describe him."

"He looks . . . to be honest . . ." It was rare to find Davenport lost for words and he seemed annoyed by the fact. "I have it, Fergins. He looks like one of those ancient Greek sculptures of a god, just before the Romans knocked off its arms and nose."

There you have Davenport truly believing he was answering a question.

I thought I had this somewhere on me. Here, Mr. Clover, while I drink my water, I present evidence for my statement about the bookaneers' practices. See where I have underlined.

The Bookaneer's Rules . . . Collected and Transcribed by E. C. Fergins from Penrose Davenport

. . . The bookaneer does not tell his stories.

. . . The bookaneer should refrain from and avoid sharing information with other bookaneers.

. . . Missions should never be undertaken or altered for the sole or chief purpose of competing with or sabotaging another bookaneer.

. . . The identities of parties engaging the bookaneer's services should be protected for all time.

. . . Similarly, the bookaneer is never to reveal his identity to the Subject of a mission even after a mission has ended.

. . . The bookaneer avoids, whenever possible, the appearance of any interest in publishing or books in order to leave their Subjects ignorant of his intentions.

. . . If the bookaneer requires assistance on a mission, the assistant must never question anything that may occur.

. . . The bookaneer should never work for or cooperate directly with an author, as to leave their respective interests uncontaminated.

As you think of these during my tale, keep in mind that Davenport liked to make qualifications about these commandments. To return to our visit to Vailima. I could hardly sleep that night thinking of what it might be like. Ceremonious and formal, maybe, or warm and raucous. When the hour finally came the next day for our call, we rode up a long, steep mountain road—"road" on Upolu being anything less dense and impassable than an uncut jungle—that ended at a vast clearing. Palm trees swayed back and forth in clusters along the property. There were servants spread out in every direction. Two at the entrance gate. A party of rugged servants working the grounds with hatchets tucked into the bands and belts. House servants standing stock-still with rifles around the shoulders of their white liveries, staring coldly out at us. It reminded me of what the other whites had told us—Hines and the man from the English consulate—that no part of the island except for the beach was truly safe. That no white man in his right mind would leave the beach, yet here was Stevenson's house. And here we were.

Mount Vaea, the volcanic center of the island, was a giant above us, climbing into the thick white and silver clouds and throwing deep shadows. Vailima was as high up on Upolu as could be. In fact, if you looked back, as Dante warns never to do with the threat of returning to the beginning, all you could see beyond the green slopes was the unbroken expanse of ocean.

Before we could reach the threshold of the house, a large and muscular man, one of the house servants, blocked our way and demanded something of us in Samoan. "Solosolo! Solosolo!" he was repeating.

"What do we do?" I asked Davenport when no solution to the standoff presented itself.

"Handkerchief," called a voice from one of the many windows just below the terra-cotta roof. "It means 'handkerchief.'"

This did not in itself clarify the demand.

"Solosolo. Show them!" continued the disembodied voice.

Davenport and I glanced at each other. "Solosolo," the bookaneer said with amusement, removing his wrinkled silk handkerchief from the pocket of his shirt. He unfolded it and held it up, then turned it to show the other side. I did the same with mine. The big man in front of us studied them with the careful eyes of a museum-goer, then waved us ahead through the door.

Fanny Stevenson, who must have been the voice we had heard from above, was racing down the stairs as we entered. "We cannot be too cautious," she explained of the handkerchief ceremony. "Louis becomes ill so easily, we must ensure nobody having a cold comes near him. Please, follow me, sit down with us."

Do not wait to hear the impressions of Robert Louis Stevenson I gathered from this visit, because we never saw him. Davenport had been wrong about inciting Stevenson's compulsion to investigate the new "author." It was Fanny, an American, who had heard from her husband of a new British citizen on Upolu, and had insisted on sending for me. For *me*. Davenport was nothing more than an afterthought.

She asked me an array of questions, many political, about England and Scotland and the latest news from abroad. She hardly said a word to Davenport, whose annoyance would have been obvious only to me.

Fanny's adult daughter and son, Belle and Lloyd, sat obligingly across from us in the large hall. The walls were a calm shade of blue, reminding me of the ocean on a clear, windless day. Though the place was impressive, the dust and flies still gathered in the air here as they did in the most humble hut on the island. The three Stevensons presented a picture of a very purposeless family. Each one meticulously rolled his and her own cigarette, but other than that seemed content to wait around. From somewhere in the house, there was the high whistle of a wind instrument.

"Louis says if a man does not roll his smoke oneself, it is not worth smoking," pointed out Lloyd to illuminate his fastidious cigarette-making procedure. He leaned far back in his chair and glanced languidly at us as he finished, admiring the result before resting it in his lips. I was so consumed by the fact we were in the Stevensons' home, I hardly recall what initial opinion I formed of Lloyd that day. He was tall and slender like his stepfather, but sturdier, with a face more juvenile than his twenty-two years, and had a way of shrugging his shoulder that could dismiss entire philosophies of existence. "But you know Louis," he added, as though we did. "He has his rules for life."

Belle chuckled. She was much shorter than her brother, with a dark tint to her pretty skin that seemed better suited to island life. "Example. He believes women should be allowed to divorce, but men shouldn't. Thank goodness, or I might still be chained to that worthless drunkard."

"If there had not been the possibility of divorce, you would not have married Joe at all," Lloyd said; then, in my general direction: "My sister is attracted by the possibility of trouble, you know, Mr. Fergus."

"Well," she insisted, "I now have my higher calling here in Samoa."

"It's Fergins, actually—" I interjected.

"Calling? I was not aware you had found a higher calling," needled her brother.

She ignored him, and with a slight fluttering of her eyes, turned to Davenport. "Oh, do you like it?"

Davenport had stood and was examining the large hearth. This was at one end of the hall, opposite a rickety piano.

"It is handsome, Miss Strong," said Davenport. "But I would think a fireplace would have limited utility in the tropical climate."

"Useless thing," Belle Strong confirmed with a dash of disgust, her finger pointed at the hearth, though her dark eyes lingered on Davenport. "As a point of fact, you gentlemen are sitting in the first and only room in all Samoa to have a fireplace. Only Louis dares use it in this never-ending heat. It is rather a spectacle for the natives around here. Your missionaries can teach them all they want about Jesus Christ, but the silly creatures will still stick their heads inside and try to understand whether this is something good or it is from the devil."

"Louis declared he would not live in a house without a fireplace," added Fanny, chortling and then shaking her head at the thought. The novelist's wife, like her daughter, was short with dark hair and big, sparkling eyes. They could have been sisters, and in some way Fanny would be the more intriguing of the two. She wore a native-style dress that would be called a nightgown in London or New York, shapeless and decorated with tobacco and spots of grass that were the only evidence so far of any members of the family ever leaving the house. She left me with the impression of Bluebeard's wife after being brought into the light. Her infectious smiles were followed each time with heavy sighs. "It almost bankrupted us, costing more than one thousand dollars to build, so I suppose his threat nearly came true. Mr. Fergins," she said, turning back to me with an almost desperate air, "what do you really believe about how Louis would be received were he to ever go back to Great Britain?"

I could see how important it was to her that I give an encouraging answer.

"With a hero's welcome. King Arthur coming home from Avalon. Great writers move us all closer to God. And there are very few great writers left in the world, Mrs. Stevenson."

(Fanny, she chided me. I protested. She insisted.)

"Those who remain," I went on, "like your husband, are really walking treasures, Fanny. Imagine Wordsworth and Dickens come back to life to walk the streets and shake hands with their readers. It would be as if you brought the English language itself to life."

There was never a suggestion of Stevenson receiving us that day, nor on the next visit a few days later. Fanny was just as bored with her fellow American and preoccupied with interviewing me about her husband's literary reputation. We only caught a glimpse of Belle and Lloyd this time before they went off on a picnic with some of the domestics, then we had tea with Fanny, until a servant came to whisper something to her that caused her to furrow her brow before excusing herself with a quick march out of the room.

I could see Davenport growing more irritated that even time to ourselves in the house could not be very productive. To gain entrance into the life of an author who lived alone was usually a rare opportunity for a bookaneer—it reminds me of when Davenport managed to be invited in by Miss Dickinson, for instance, to be part of her eccentric household in Amherst in the summer of '78—but to be in Vailima was to be an insect under glass. One of the servants, whose Samoan name had been anglicized from Sala to Charlie, was particularly prone to being right at our heels as we wandered around, amusing himself by translating Samoan words into English and vice versa, in a deep, excitable voice. "Loi: Ants!"

"How have you learned so much English?" I asked him, careful not to step on the long line of ants to which he was pointing.

"My master gives me lessons," Charlie said, tucking a smile under his carefully groomed mustache. His hair was dyed a soft orange, but his mustache was dark black, making him seem an amalgam of several men. Along with his earthy necklaces, he wore a wooden crucifix.

"You do your master proud," Davenport said. Then, struck with an idea, he added, "I mean to say, you do Tusitala proud."

"Tusitala: Teller of tales!" translated Charlie.

Davenport threw a grin in my direction. "Teller of tales," he echoed.

Not long after, the halls were pierced with a strange howling noise. There was a pause, then it rang out again.

"What is that?" I asked after noticing Charlie was reluctant to speak.

He whispered to us with a very different tone, one of trepidation: "*Tusitala.*"

The awful noise—which reached our ears once more—was kind of like how I'd imagine the war whoop of your nation's backwoods Indians. Servants ran from all directions and entered from outside, chasing the sound.

"I'm very sorry for him," Charlie mumbled. "He does not know what is in store."

"Who doesn't?" Davenport asked.

The attendant's eyes widened with fright. "Whoever did wrong to Tusitala."

Charlie joined the stream of servants and we both followed. The natives had collected inside a small, dimly lit room entered through the library, a chamber we would later hear referred to as the master's den or sanctum. Each took his or her place sitting on the floor, forming a semicircle around a narrow bed. Charlie threw a look back that cautioned us not to come closer, so we remained in the library.

Leaning my body toward the French doors, I could see arms, long and gaunt as oars, of the man who was sitting up in bed, wrapped in what appeared to be shawls and blankets, and propped up by pillows. Though his face was obscured from view, I knew at once it was him. That is one thing about Stevenson. Even a fingertip of his was unmistakable. In a pitch-dark room, one would surely *feel* his presence before ever seeing him.

I could also see the profile of Fanny standing by the bed, guarding him like some enchanted dragon beside a medieval king.

Stevenson began a prayer in English, his voice sonorous, commanding. "Our God, look down upon us and shine into our hearts. Help us to be far from falsehood so that each of us may stand before thy face in his integrity."

The rest of the bizarre session was conducted in the native tongue. Each servant came up to the bed and placed his or her hand on a Bible, which Stevenson gripped with his long fingers, then repeated the very serious and absurd oath stated by their master.

We found Charlie later that day, and he translated the refrain best he could remember: "This is the Holy Bible here that I am touching. Behold me, O God! If I knew who it was that took away the pig or the place to which the stolen pig was taken, or have heard anything relating to the pig, and shall not declare the same—be made an end of by God this life of mine!"

Even before we knew what the words meant, I could make out enough to know that the ritual ensnared a bowlegged young man who trembled and stammered when it came to his turn to recite. After a brief exchange, the bowleg confessed to having eaten the missing pig in question.

"Fiaali'i," Stevenson intoned after the culprit groveled for forgiveness, the master now switching to English, "your wish to eat was greater than your wish to be a gentleman. You have shown a bad heart and your sin is a great one, not for the pig—I hope you know the damn pig counts as naught—but because you have been false to your Vailima family. It is easy to say that you are sorry, that you wish you were dead: but that is no answer. We have lost far more than food meant for Lloyd's birthday. We have lost our trust in you, which used to be so great, our confidence in your loyalty. See how many bad things have resulted from your first sin? You have hurt all our hearts here, not because of the pig, but because we are ashamed and mortified before the world. I am not your father. I am not your chief. The belly is your chief!"

Lloyd Osbourne would make an offhand remark during our stay in Samoa, capped by the philosophical shrug of his, that I cannot help but recall as I think of that scene we witnessed. "This, Fergus," he said to me of Vailima, "is the only place where you will ever see Samoans run."

IT WAS A BURNING HOT DAY on our next call to Vailima. Sitting in the great hall felt like being inside a volcano. A little native girl was fanning one side of Belle's face with a beautiful span of crimson feathers, while Belle fanned her other cheek with a Japanese-style fan. She mentioned to us that her stepfather had been out on the grounds before our arrival but now, yet again, had retreated to the seclusion of his sanctum. I could see Davenport was trying his best to appear unmoved by our continuing bad luck. The more time went on without developing some kind of relationship with Stevenson, the harder it would be to invent excuses to keep calling on them, and I knew he worried that our invitations would run dry before he had a chance to ingratiate himself with the writer.

"It is a hard and unexciting life. Most times the only people there are to talk to around here are the domestics," Belle complained, her plump pink lips puckered. "And they hardly speak English."

"New faces must be a welcome sight, then," Davenport ventured, perhaps hoping she would be our way of ensuring the continuation of our visits.

She looked him up and down, studying him with as much interest and doubt as when she had first met us. "Sometimes," she said with so little inflection, it might have come from Davenport himself.

Fanny was bent over the spotless but dusty fireplace smoking a cigarette. I still had to swallow down my horror at the sight of the wife of one of the world's greatest novelists smoking in a public room.

"Unexciting?" I wriggled into the conversation. "It seems there is no lack of excitement here, Miss Strong."

"Yes," she answered, taking a long puff from a cigarette. "For instance, when I found my husband had taken his opium and his native wife to the other side of the island. The ape, the disgusting ape, the foppish little drunken ape."

"I see," I surrendered.

"If you brought Austin home from school, you would be less lonely. A boy should be with his mother."

"Even when the mother is as miserable as I am?" Belle replied to Fanny, then I swear the two women blew smoke at each other.

"Mrs. Stevenson," Davenport said, "how long did it take to build this fine home?"

"Oh, quite long."

It was like that between Davenport and Fanny Stevenson. He tried to nurture conversation with her, but she gave him nothing in return.

She never told him to call her Fanny. Belle soon felt so warm she would not say more than a word or two at a time. After rolling his own cigarette, which I knew he despised, and smoking a little, Davenport looked over at the piano and said something horrifying.

"My dear Fergins," he began without looking my way, "why not play a song for us?"

"What?"

"I'm sure the ladies would appreciate a distraction from the heat," he said. "Mr. Fergins is often asked to play at parties and such. Go on now, Fergins."

"Please do, Mr. Fergins," Fanny encouraged me.

"It took eleven of the brown boys eight hours to carry that awful heavy thing up here on poles," Belle added, always the first to describe any difficulty. "Of course, nobody here plays except me, and I am simply terrible. You must, Mr. Fergins."

Lloyd patted me on the back and helped me up. I stood there.

"We're waiting," Davenport said.

"What would I play?" I asked, barely concealing my misery.

"The latest from London," came the ridiculous answer from the bookaneer.

I had perhaps been asked to play at a party once or twice in my life, so *often* was a considerable hyperbole, and my answer when asked would have been a resounding no. I had not played a note in more than two years. I walked over to the old piano, cased in black ivory, and sat on the bench. I tell you I was so troubled by the idea of playing in front of this room of languid, sweaty Bohemians that I closed my eyes as I played. The keys were cold and stiff against my unwilling fingers and I felt myself wanting to melt atom by atom and disappear into the tropical air.

When I stopped, there was some discordant clapping. This sent a flood of fresh humiliation through me.

"More, Mr. Fergins," said Fanny with a big, loose grin. She was my advocate in all things.

"I mustn't," I said, stepping away from the bench to make it final.

Then I heard the slower clapping of a newcomer.

"Excellent. Better than a dig in the eye with a sharp stick, anyway." Stevenson was looking at me with those all-seeing wide-set eyes from the entrance into the room. "The new men. I remember you. Have you not been served a drink? Even our houseboys are wilting today. I will get it for you myself. A lemon drink, or something stronger?"

I could only bring myself to repeat, "Lemon drink?" He took my question as an answer and returned a few minutes later.

The novelist wore a remarkable costume: a tight-fitting flannel shirt revealing his excessively thin and long arms, and white flannel trousers, which were rolled up and tucked into one brown wool sock and one purple, which had holes, revealing the pale flesh of the bottom of his feet when he walked across the room.

"How about we start a fire?" he asked as he brought me the drink, and handed another to Davenport.

"Too hot," came the retort from wife and stepdaughter.

"Yes," said Stevenson, his face falling with disappointment. "Today is probably too hot. Mr. . . . ."

"Fergins," Davenport answered for me.

"Yes, that's right. Englishman. Mr. Fergins, pray humor us with some more music. Something classic this time."

I can hardly explain the effect of a direct command from this otherworldly man, but there I was, planting my backside again right on the piano bench, where I had sworn to myself mere moments before I would never return were my life dependent on it, my fingers fumbling into position as I tried to remember a Strauss waltz I was once taught by a piano master in exchange for a rare copy of Longfellow's first published volume. Stevenson kept time with the song by picking at one end of his mustache with his finger and thumb, swinging a limp cigarette caught between his lips.

STEVENSON DID NOT STAY in the room very long that morning, but before he exited he bid us to come again soon. Davenport was as pleased on our ride home as a child with a new toy.

"I never knew you played piano, Fergins."

"That is because I absolutely do not, or at least certainly not well enough to play for anyone but my nieces, who are by now better than I am at eight and ten years old. If you didn't know, why on earth did you ask me to play?"

"Because I had a line of thought, while we were sitting there languishing in the stillness and heat in that big room. They have wallowed in the South Seas for a few years. They are musically inclined enough to have a piano, not an everyday object on this island, and I have heard a kind of flute in the house that I suspected might be played by Stevenson—since I heard it in the presence of each other family member. Not played well, mind you. Nor did you have to play anything well—and you did not—as long as it was something new. New for them, I mean, having been gone for so long. I thought that in a place like this, novelty might be enough. I do not play a note, and supposed a thorough English gentleman like yourself might. You should be proud, Fergins!"

"Humiliated," I said quietly. "That's what I should be. Am."

"Oh?" Davenport replied as though the point were irrelevant.

Of course, my concern for my own dignity *was* irrelevant here. We had been brought back to Stevenson's attention, which meant the real campaign to find the manuscript could begin. Davenport was so pleased with me that he volunteered an answer to a question from days before. "You had asked me whether I ever wanted to be a writer. . . ." But I do not want to forget my place in the story, so remind me to return to that.

We would learn that as easily as Fanny Stevenson alternated between smiles and sighs, Robert Louis Stevenson alternated between reclusive and public periods, and it seemed around this time he had entered one of his more public moods. When we next went to Vailima, we came upon the novelist and John Chinaman—as the attendant was called whom we met with Stevenson at the stream—clearing an area of tangled brush at the entrance to the property. As before, John followed Stevenson several paces behind, watching without actually helping. Stevenson was covered in mud and dust and carrying his own tools.

When we reached the front verandah, Stevenson let out one of his war whoops, this time serving to call his family and natives over to see to us. Despite the fact that the Vailima servants saw the man every day, they gaped at the gaunt, earth-encrusted, long-legged novelist when he passed, as though he were one of the island's gods.

"It is time for 'ava," he said to us with a grin.

We sat crossed-legged in a semicircle on the large front verandah, joined by Fanny and Belle.

I discovered now why Fanny Stevenson was so keen on having an English bookseller in her company. She seemed to think I could convince him to return to civilization.

"Oh, Mr. Fergins has been telling me with what reverence you would be greeted in London or Edinburgh," she said as the servants passed out lemonade and cookies. "He knows the sympathies of the public as well as anyone. Tell him, Mr. Fergins."

"Well, in a manner of speaking, I oughtn't try to claim—"

"Tell him exactly what you told me, Mr. Fergins."

I repeated my assessment—King Arthur and Avalon, Dickens and Wordsworth, the English language come alive.

Stevenson seemed unaffected. "Barkis worries what the politicians think of me being here, with the British consulate on the island always wrestled into submission by the Germans, who have the most firepower and money," he said without looking at me. "Barkis," he called, repeating his curious pet address for his wife. Nobody ever bothered to explain it to us, so I assume it was inspired by Dickens's famous line "Barkis is willing," now applied to Fanny's rather amazing willingness to follow the writer to the ends of the earth. "Barkis, my dear fellow, do not concern yourself with politicians. I once thought meanly of the plumber, but how he shines beside today's politician."

"It was merely an informed speculation on Mr. Fergins's part. A welcome one, if you ask me, Louis."

"Tusitala," he said, not to correct his wife but to instruct us. He turned to Davenport. "Did my wife tell you that she dislikes Americans?"

"Not yet, but I'd like to hear why," Davenport said.

"She thinks Americans and Australians are dangerous when they go to foreign lands because they care only about conquest and do not mind what the public will think of their actions. Frankly, I lost my only chance for the public to love me unconditionally by not dying. What do you have to say to that, Mr."—Fergins, his wife reminded him—"Mr. Bookseller?"

I wilted under Stevenson's sidelong gaze. "Well, but, in truth . . . I daresay . . . regarding any speculation on my part . . ." I never properly began or ended.

Stevenson clapped his hands together as several bowls of different sizes were brought over. One of these bowls, filled with the roots of a native plant, was carried by a very pretty girl. Her ample bosom was draped with six or seven necklaces of beads, stones, and small animal teeth hanging down; around her neck was a rather beautiful collar made from whale teeth. The exposure of so much skin, like anything else on a primitive island, began to seem normal after a while. Her black hair was oiled tightly over her ears and in three buns around her head, with a few strands falling freely along with a display of flowers down her neck. Her cheeks were round, while her eyes were close together and sharp, suggesting simultaneously a childish angelic nature and a touch of craftiness. Behind her stood a middle-aged dwarf, perhaps three or three and a half feet tall, with long arms and a watchful glance at the whole party.

The scantily clad girl began to chew a piece of the plant root, then added another piece of the root, chewing vigorously, though keeping her lips closed. She added another piece and one more, until I was astounded she could fit anything more in her mouth. She was carefully shifting the already chewed-up roots into her cheeks until finally there was no more room. She spit the masticated roots into the bowl, poured water from another bowl, and then mixed the concoction together. The first serving was poured into a carved coconut shell and passed to Stevenson, who drank it in one draught.

"Here is the 'ava," said our host in an apparent part of the ritual. "Now let it be shared!"

After the shell was filled again, Stevenson passed it to me. "'Ava is a great tradition here," he assured me. "The honor of making it is to go to the most beautiful maiden in the village, or, in our case, here at Vailima. Do not worry, she rinses her mouth quite thoroughly first."

I must have blanched visibly at the thought of drinking the spit-up brew because all at once I saw the following happen: Stevenson laughed, Belle nodded knowingly, the silent dwarf squinted, and Fanny raised impatient eyes.

"You grow accustomed to this life," Belle said, more a warning than an assurance.

"In some places in Samoa, a visitor would be imprisoned for refusing 'ava," Stevenson added, enjoying my discomfort, perhaps revenge for complimenting his literary status too highly.

"To tradition," I said, raising the shell to my lips. The mixture had a strong odor of sand and oil and looked like soapy water. It had a pungent, unpleasant taste. I hoped I would not grow accustomed to it.

Davenport took the next portion that was poured. With his eyes on the girl's face, he drank the vile liquid down without pause. She cast her head down as each drinker took a turn, though I noticed her gaze kept drifting to Davenport's.

"Compliments, Tusitala," he said.

"A pleasure," Stevenson said. "You see that I have gone into far lands to die, and here will I stay until buried—unless, of course, we can manage one more visit to Italy; I always wanted to return there one day. But I imagine the reality is obvious to outsiders like you gentlemen. The word is out, and my doom is written."

Fanny squirmed at this declaration, one repeated on a regular basis, to judge by its delivery. Stevenson did not appear to be suffering, but at the same time he was far from healthy. No loose style of clothing could hide how emaciated he was. He also stifled harsh coughs, which clawed their way out as extravagant wheezes.

As we prepared to ride to our cottage that afternoon, Fanny chased after us. We were nearing the stables. She threw a look over her shoulder back at the house. Then she let out a quick sigh that itself sounded like a plea. "Gentlemen, please say you will stay for supper tonight."

To my surprise, Davenport protested.

"Our man Cipaou wished to cook a special tiffin at our own modest table. We shall have to return or risk wounding his pride."

"Please, we will send a messenger to tell him. I have made mutton curry, a dish I learned from an East Indian cook in Fiji. You will like it. Louis will not talk so much of the island politics when guests are present. He does not eat when he is agitated, and the talk is not good for his health. There are rumblings of more interference by Herr Becker and the Germans against the natives who oppose the puppet king. The whole attitude of the Germans here is so excessively English."

"Of course we shall stay, if it is a help," Davenport said.

"Thank you," said Fanny, her face softening with gratitude—and, more so than any other as I look back, that was the moment we secured our places at Vailima.

"MY WHITE GENTLEMEN" was how Stevenson referred to us, while we were Fergins and Porter (Davenport's assumed name) to the rest of the family, and interchangeably White Chief to most of the Vailima natives. It was clear that Davenport's first hope—that Stevenson's isolation and his vanity as a writer would make him inclined to want to know another writer—had been misguided. Stevenson was vulnerable to our presence, but his vulnerability was of a different nature. It was precisely how seriously he took his life on the Samoan islands. He had not come to the island for an exotic escape into a kind of monastic writerly solitude; that much was now obvious. He was fully entrenched. He had brought his whole family, even his elderly mother. She was my favorite member of the household, and when she ventured down from her sewing machine to the ground floor, which was rare, the sunny old woman would never fail to speak in clever aphorisms. The novelist's whole life had been transplanted into Samoan soil. With help from his stepson, he even seemed to thrive on overseeing the very large staff of servants and dealing with the complexities of maintaining and improving the grounds of what he mischievously called his "plantation." As far as I could tell, he weeded as much as he wrote.

Because he cared so much about Samoan life, it made perfect sense that Stevenson would want to ensure Davenport portrayed the island in a favorable way for his supposed book of travel stories, and that resulted in more meals and more time. Davenport declined as many of the invitations that came to our cottage as he accepted. He explained to me that, once establishing our foothold, we must not appear overly inquisitive about the Stevensons or riveted by Vailima. Still, the more time we were there, the more clues Davenport gathered. Stevenson was actually quite open in talking about his writing. Hines had once told us that all whites were instant friends with each other in these lands of islanders, and perhaps that phenomenon contributed to Stevenson's willingness to share.

The novelist would stop in mid-conversation—mid-sentence, to be more precise—while walking, for example, down the paths that ran along Fanny's elaborate flower gardens, to dig out a piece of paper when he had an idea. He would then write a paragraph or a page right in front of us.

"Yes," he would mumble, "yes, just so!" Then, looking up at one of us with the wildness of creativity in his eyes, he would say, "One of you hold this, won't you?" He would pass over his ever-present cigarette, and Davenport or I would take it. We came to understand that the thing was meant to be preserved, however pitifully short, and there one of us would stand tending to the smoldering cigarette while Stevenson wrote in a mad dash.

On that occasion in the garden, it was Davenport tending to the cigarette. Stevenson, pausing from his scribbling, suddenly spoke of the virtues of their tobacco, which was called Three Castles.

"We are slaves to our brand, I'm afraid. They must be imported, like everything in Samoa. Do you know even the wood we used to build the house was brought from America? Trees all around us, but the natives know nothing of how to harvest wood and—this is crucial to understand, if you wish to grasp Samoa and its people for your travel book—do not want to know how to do it."

All of this while he was writing. It was as though the concentration came only at the moment of generating an idea, while the actual writing was a formality. There was a deep generosity that came across. Even while doing his own writing, he was trying to help the writing he believed Davenport was doing.

"It is quite foreign to you, isn't it, Mr. Porter?"

"What is, Tusitala?" replied Davenport.

"The idea of a man leaving behind civilization for what our esteemed literati back in Europe or America would look askance at. You come here to record the exotic, to see butlers with bare feet, precisely because you cannot believe it possible for a white man to belong here."

"I hadn't thought of it in that way."

"It is a hard and difficult place. But I am quite interested to see if you gentlemen will find, as I think you will, that this life is far better fun than people dream who fall asleep among the chimney stacks and telegraph wires. This is paradise, so close to heaven that to be really ill is almost impossible. This is the way it should be," he said, suddenly returning his pencil to his paper with brightened eyes. "Yes, this is what I wanted to say!"

Wherever we went with him around the grounds of the estate, Stevenson's shadow, John Chinaman, was usually behind us; I had heard one of the servants refer to him as a cook, though I had never seen him go toward the European-style kitchen with the natives who prepared the family meals. When Stevenson sat down in one of his writing fits, he would send John away on some chore. "He is a loyal fellow," was how Stevenson described him once, "and when I write he watches with disapproval, as though I might break my fingers doing it. He is the opposite of my publishers. They want a sequel to *Jekyll*, a sequel to *Treasure Island*, sequels to sequels! What they don't realize is that sequels are bound to disappoint those who have waited for them. I believe what I write now, Mr. Fergins, is in some ways my best work. I am—" he paused to shrug"—pretty sure."

But the most telling comment of all made by the Scottish novelist was on another occasion, looking at us with arched eyebrows and an air of confession. We were gathered in the library, while he was carelessly storing away some of those pages he had just composed in a fit. "What I am writing," said Stevenson, "will be my masterpiece, elusive until now." Mouthwatering as it was, it was not the talk of masterpieces that was so important to a bookaneer's ear. It was the other revelation. The novel was not finished yet—*will be*—and that meant Davenport had no choice but to wait before taking any action. It meant we would have to extend our presence in Samoa and at Vailima. Treading water could be the most dangerous part of a bookaneer's mission. It multiplied the chances for something to go wrong.

Of course, any comments Davenport or I heard from Stevenson about his novel were received casually, remembered verbatim, and entered at the first opportunity into my notebook. The trick was to give him opportunities to speak about it without ever being asked. Another afternoon, he asked us to help carry several bundles. The towering palms swayed above us and helped us along with a light breeze. The novelist carried a shovel under his arm as we entered the bush.

"I do not want you to get the wrong idea about the houseboys. They are awfully good on the whole, but Samoans rather enjoy discipline. They always look older than they are, which makes you forget they are not very mature. They are more like a set of well-behaved young ladies. That is why I hate to do this."

"What exactly are we doing, Tusitala?" Davenport interrupted him, growing a little anxious at the enigmatic errand. Stevenson was now tiring himself out digging a hole that began to take on the shape of a small grave.

He waved away our offers to help. "Burying that. Go ahead, my white gentlemen. Have a look for yourself."

Davenport and I both eyed the bundles we had carried into the woods. I opened one, half-imagining finding one of the severed heads we'd heard were valued by the natives. "Clothes," I announced.

"These are old clothes of mine and Lloyd's we no longer use. If my native boys find them, they'll start wearing them."

"Wouldn't that be better than burying them?" I asked.

"Oh, if a houseboy wants to wear a cast-off shirt over his lavalava, so be it. But European clothes do not suit their bodies. The scant covering and raw materials of their native style may look strange to our eyes, but their race developed that way for a good reason. Our clothes cling to them when wet, and do not protect them from the strong sun. They must be who they are, if they are to survive life and labor in the tropical climate. If they try to look European, which amuses them and some of the local whites, they die."

"That is rather bleak," I said.

He nodded and looked on with a cloudy gaze. "Sometimes I watch, as they are pushed from their lands, as whites introduce disease and opium and alcohol, and in a perspective of centuries I see their cases as ours, death coming in like a tide, and the day already numbered when there should be no more Samoans, and no more of any race whatever, and—here is a curious extension of my dream—no more literary works or readers."

Stevenson broke his own reverie by coughing and wheezing.

"It is just the smoking," he said, smiling unconvincingly between coughs. "You know my motto is 'Cigarettes without intermission, except when coughing or kissing.'"

"May I?" Davenport asked, taking the shovel from Stevenson's hands.

The novelist gave us more specifics about his book in progress, while Davenport deliberately slowed his digging. "The story begins about 1660 and ends in 1830, but perhaps I may even continue it to 1875 or so. Five, six generations, perhaps seven, figure therein. I can see it all. Some of the brevity of history, some of the detail of romance. *The Shovels of Newton French* will be the name. My finest novel yet written—mark my words, gentlemen, I will be remembered for this, if nothing else."

I saw the light in my companion's eye. The longer the work meant the more installments it could be cut up into for serialization, and that meant more money when Davenport sold it. Being so close to Davenport's side during a mission was highly illuminating for me. He presented himself to the household as solicitous, self-effacing, considerate, thoughtful. Though I knew he inhabited a role, it was still a pleasure to witness. Never had I felt myself more dedicated to the success of the bookaneer.

But the mission had its share of problems. Besides the fact that this behemoth of a book was not completed, and apparently expanding its scope by the day, the existing pages of the novel were stored sloppily in piles spread out across the estate. Paper is a rare commodity in Samoa, so even the smallest scraps could be used for a sentence or two. As far as we could tell, some of the novel was written on the backs of pages that had been discarded, or drafts of older manuscripts, or descriptions of Samoan civil wars, or alongside short poems Stevenson had jotted out, often in Samoan. It was a bookaneer's nightmare. It would be arduous, maybe impossible, for Davenport to assemble the pages himself once Stevenson finished writing—he would have to wait until Stevenson began to do it himself, or risk a situation similar to the notorious affair of '70, when Dickens expired with half a book in hand, pages scattered to the wind, publishers and legendary bookaneers in a perilous race for whatever remained.

Meanwhile, any searching was complicated by the presence of so many servants around the house. We grew accustomed to John China-man's distrust, which he directed at anyone who came close to Steven-son. Besides garrulous and generous Charlie, the other servants spoke to us in their limited English or not at all. Compared to our own is-lander, who served us at their cottage, and to the other native servants we encountered, the Vailima operatives were rather smooth and so-phisticated, the young women reserved and elegant; in fact, sometimes they seemed far more civilized than the Bohemian family employing them.

While we waited for Stevenson to complete his self-declared mas-terpiece, Davenport and I were picking up other pieces of information that he felt could prove useful. We rode all across the massive property of Vailima, creating a map of the egresses in case we needed to leave in a hurry. Davenport noted that he had identified only four separate streams, not five, which was what the name Vailima translated to mean; I could not find a fifth on my rides, either, and he directed me to keep looking whenever I was on the grounds, though I did not un-derstand the relevance. Meanwhile, Davenport discovered a list of ti-tles for unwritten novels composed on the flyleaf of a Bible (which Stevenson seemed to use as a sort of notebook). He studied and per-fected his mastery of reading Stevenson's handwriting as it was pro-duced with pencil and ink, careful and careless, sober and drunk, and familiarized himself with the various styles of Belle, to whom the nov-elist dictated when he was too weak to write. He had also found several short stories Stevenson had completed but never bothered or desired to publish. He did not want to risk provoking suspicion by taking any of these yet, but he noted the positions of these minor gems for later. There were also letters suggesting potential pilgrimages to Samoa from two minor literary lights back in England, James Barrie and Rudyard Kipling, and one quite popular one, Arthur Conan Doyle. I believe for a few moments Davenport hungrily envisioned an island crawling with productive authors, but subsequent correspondence we came across from those men indicated that each one's plan crumbled because of the expense and difficulty of the trip. Indeed, while doing what I believe New Yorkers like to call snooping, I found letter after letter from friends of the Stevensons who despaired at making the voyage to see him. And letters written by Stevenson to friends, often reproaching them for breaking promises to write, or visit him. Among the ludicrous ways he dated his missives, I noticed, "twenty-something of December" and "Friday—I think."

Davenport had been present when Charlie interrupted a music session to give Stevenson a message that Mr. Thomas, a local missionary, would be calling there the next day. We had heard Thomas, who we learned was a popular white missionary and occasional trader to these islands, referred to before.

"Our tobacco," Stevenson said, with the kind of exhaled relief men usually reserved for a hopeful diagnosis from a doctor. He had been perched on the edge of a table in his library, one leg crossed on the other, playing his flageolet. The whistling tune of the instrument in Stevenson's lips would sound lovely for a moment, and then shockingly off-key later ("the humidity," Stevenson would say, looking askance at the holes and keys). He put the flageolet aside at Charlie's tidings. "Thank goodness; our supply is nearly exhausted. John," he called for his Chinese shadow, who was standing inconspicuously in the doorway. "There you are, John. Have a meal ordered and prepared for Thomas tomorrow at two—Mr. Porter, Mr. Fergins, you ought to come. Are you religious men? I am not, but mother enjoys them. Besides, these missionaries are often surprisingly good company, and this mission has been here for so many years, he brings terribly good stories about island history."

"We should leave you to your writing for now," Davenport said, rising to his feet so the power of suggestion might spur him to complete the novel the bookaneer desired.

"In here? Heavens, I never write in here," he said, looking to the walls of books. "It's all so suitable for a literary man—drives every idea out of my head. Sometimes I come in here to look for some fact, but I generally seize the book and hurry off with it to my sanctum. People talk of *Robinson Crusoe* as the beginning of the modern novel, but Defoe based his book on the account of Alexander Selkirk, who stranded himself on an island purposely. That's how English literature was born, by marooning ourselves far away from everyone else."

Our attentions were diverted by the sounds of crashing surf that had filled the island for days all the way to the mountains; now, heavy winds were coming in. I stepped over piles of books, walking to the open window and peering down at the incredible view to the water.

"Mr. Fergins, the rain will roar like the blue sea. Yes, no doubt about it—the rains will be coming. But first will come the winds and more wind, until you can't take more, and pray for the rain."

I lifted my eyes to our host. I could sense the excitement from Davenport.

Stevenson glanced over at him with the full force of his piercing eyes, which in the dim light of the library looked almost black. Drumming out the sound of rain on the table, his long, tapered fingers made the sounds heavier and heavier. He put himself into a meditative state that was infectious.

"I always feared the sound of wind beyond everything. I do not love noise. I am like my grandfather in that, and my time in these islands has ingrained the sentiment. In my hell a gale would always blow. That reminds me of a chapter I've written for the final section of this novel."

Davenport asked if there was a storm in the book.

"Not a storm, Porter. The foreboding, some evil yet unknown that approaches us."

THE END OF THE MISSION could come even more easily, more quickly than my companion had yet dared to hope. How perfect for the purposes of the bookaneer: while Stevenson approached the conclusion of his book, the rainy season would soon throw down a curtain to keep him from being distracted by matters outside the house and to keep Belial or anyone else who might interfere far from the island. Davenport couldn't ask for a better development. Not that Davenport ever took anything for granted in one of his missions, something I observed in Samoa even more than I ever had in the past. The matter of Belial, for instance. Though there was still no sign of him, he would have been using an alias if he was on the island. Early in our stay, during one of our first visits to the village of Apia, Davenport made it known that he was looking to interview visitors to the island for their impressions to include in his travelogue, and would pay to hear of any new whites arriving. But there were none to speak of. We had very good reason to conclude that his rival bookaneer simply never made it, or that our informants back in Europe had been mistaken that he'd even tried.

One evening, we were back in the library, where Davenport was sipping from a goblet of beer, looking over the family's collection of books. He had been playing a hand of cards with Stevenson before the novelist stepped onto the verandah to give instruction to one of the houseboys, who was beginning preparations around the estate for the island's storms, which everyone anticipated landing in a few weeks. Browsing the shelves, Davenport located three and a half pages from what appeared to be an early draft of *Strange Case of Dr. Jekyll and*

Mr. Hyde, which had apparently been misplaced in a pile of newspaper clippings. His eyes went wide. It included characters not seen in the novel, and for that reason alone would be invaluable to collectors.

"What are you doing?" I asked, worried he was taking too long.

"Keep your eye on Stevenson. I knew these could be here." He had previously found clues to the existence of this original version. Now he could hardly resist devouring the pages for a moment. Then he pushed them back inside the clippings and the clippings between two books.

"More beer, White Chief?" It was Charlie, who had hurried into the room as Davenport turned his back to the bookshelf, displaying his endearing keenness both to practice his English and to make us feel at home.

"Thank you, I still have some," said Davenport.

"Have you seen?" the servant asked me excitedly. He pointed out a ceramic bowl and fork displayed on a table near where I was sitting.

"I hadn't noticed those, Charlie," I admitted. "What are they?"

"It is a brain bowl—and a cannibal fork! Used by the Solomon Islanders to eat their enemies."

I cringed at the thought and replaced the objects as he moved on to show Davenport a pistol gifted to the Stevensons by the son of Percy and Mary Shelley.

I found Charlie delightful. In addition to the charming orange dye in his hair, he had sparkling eyes and a wider build than most of his race. In physical stature, in fact, he was rather similar to me. His curiosity to learn about everything, too, flattered me as mirroring my own. He had a nice way of finishing his sentences in a quieter voice than where he began them. In answer to his questions, I told him about London, about newspapers, operas, streets divided into blocks and squares, and the underground rail system, which he seemed to take as a fairy tale.

Then there was Vao, the maiden who would chew and spit out our 'ava. Her name was spelled V-A-O but pronounced "Veeawoo."

She was a pretty eighteen-year-old, the prettiest of Vailima's female servants and, in fact, the prettiest girl we had seen among the generally handsome Samoan natives. Interestingly, her striking beauty did not leave her with an obvious air of superiority. If her looks alone did not make her easy enough to notice, she was, I should add, almost always trailed by the same dwarf we had seen at the 'ava ceremony, whose sole occupation seemed to be following her.

One morning, this young woman was setting the table for a family meal while I was in an armchair reading a book of poetry borrowed from Stevenson's library. Davenport was outside helping the novelist clear some brush and trying to draw out additional details about the progress of the novel, but I had become too hot and feared fainting if I did not go inside when it was nearly as hot. At least I had a book. For readers, books are a universal salve. When we are hot, we read to feel cooler; when we are cold, we read to warm up; tired, books wake us; anxious, they calm us.

"She doesn't favor white men," the dwarf said to me in English, poking me with his finger.

"Who?"

"Her."

I was doing my best to avoid looking at her uncovered bosom, so I merely murmured in response and tried to read more from *Lapsus Calami*.

"Her! Come on, look at her!"

I obliged him, then quickly looked away again. "You mean Vao?"

The dwarf pursed his lips with severe irritation. His head was big in proportion to his body, his face expressive and quick to redden. From my limited experience with little men and women who came to my bookstall, I would have guessed he was forty-five. "Where did you hear her name?"

"I've been told you can read most of the girls' names between their wrists and elbows, in their tattoos. Charlie taught me." I gestured at her long forearm, which had the three letters running down the inside in ornate script.

"Charlie thinks he's white and to prove it speaks too much. Don't look at her again."

"I was trying not to."

"Why don't you just go in another room while Vao goes about her work?"

"Cannot she decide if she wishes me to leave?" I rose to my feet. "My dear, would you like me to move?"

"Don't bother with sweet talk. Taller men have tried. She speaks no English," the dwarf barked at me.

"I can try it in native, but I'm afraid I might start a war." I thought for a moment that Vao smiled a little at my joke before she paused, wiped her neck with the back of her hand, and stood up straight as though to show us the full extent of her beauty. This time I had no choice but to look, before she moved to the next room. In the eyes of an old bachelor bookseller, accustomed to examining surfaces for any aberration, I could see right away that her feet pointed too far outward, to eleven o'clock and two o'clock, marring her grace slightly; that when her mouth opened the illusion of a docile maid was erased by sharp teeth not so different from the ones on her necklaces; and that her strong hands were slightly rigid. But the ordinary man would burn with lust for the sum of her all-consuming appearance and charm.

When I returned to my chair, the book I had been reading was missing. Looking for it in the next room, I found that a few of the younger houseboys had taken the book and were throwing it to each

other, then trying to make it fly, the pages wings. It was such an entirely uncertain object to them. Could a writer really survive in a land
where books, for all practical purposes, never existed and never really could? I could not decide whether I had been transported to a
time before literature was born, or had been offered a bleak window
into some outlandish future that was bookless, readerless. My instincts
are to stop any abuse of a book, but I was too fascinated to ask for
it back.

"Fool!" It was the dwarf, stepping into my view of the scene. His
face molded itself dramatically, and it now rearranged into a complete
picture of anger. "You fancy she takes a liking to you, I suppose."

"You're still talking to me about Vao? You'll have to excuse me." I'd
had enough of the fiery little man.

"She was only watching you to make sure you don't take anything
that doesn't belong to you. Take care, or you'll end up like the other
one who came here trying to claim what was not his."

I paused my step. "What other one do you mean?"

"Last month. The other white man. Arrested after sneaking around
the grounds one night. He rots in jail now like he deserves."

"Who was he?"

"Some thief." He seemed unsure of the details and had to strain to
remember. "Man named Banner, if that was really the scoundrel's
name. Probably one of the beachcombers who wander around looking
to find profit from our shores."

My mind turned at once to Belial, but I tried to hide the train of my
own thoughts from this perceptive pest. "Thieves prefer not to use
their names. Do you know exactly what it was he did?"

"No, there were errands to attend to in the village the day it happened. Most of us who work at Vailima mind our business, but my
business is to know what everyone is doing and why. There is nothing
that calls down Tusitala's wrath like an invader in Vailima, who seeks

what does not belong in his hands. Doubt not. The gods themselves would be no less forceful than Tusitala when he stomps out an offender."

He left me standing alone in the stomach-churning heat, consumed with this ominous vision of Stevenson grinding us down against his heel, with the old Samoan gods watching behind him, all the while wondering if I had just inadvertently located Davenport's enemy.

VII

CLOVER

Hail, King! Tomorrow thou shalt pass away.
Farewell! There is an isle of rest for thee.
ALFRED LORD TENNYSON

My luck has run against me again.
E. C. FERGINS

ake seats, take seats!"

Interrupted mid-thought, Mr. Fergins raised gently blinking eyes. From his throat came the sounds that older men make when silencing themselves, the way a venerable machine set to a heavy motion drags to a halt. He pinched his white spectacles at the end of his fingers as he polished them, and returned them over his ears with care. Looking across at me, he asked, "What's happened, Mr. Clover?"

"Take seats, all passengers, train going to start! Make haste!"

Disappointment gnawed at me while we listened to the conductor's cries as he stomped his way through the dining car, where the bookseller and I were seated. We overheard that the disabled train blocking our way was finally repaired, and suddenly each man and woman aboard our car was in an uproar to begin moving as quickly as possible. I guess I'd been imagining that every last soul on the train had been listening to the bookseller's tale just as I was, but how jarring to realize that nobody knew and nobody cared about the extraordinary lives of the bookaneers; there were so many ordinary and pressing things all around.

I straightened my apron and reached for my snow white waiter's coat, which I had folded neatly over the back of my chair. I wanted to beg Mr. Fergins for a promise to continue next time, but instead I said apologetically, "I kept you too long."

"I am due at the courthouse, aren't I? But I am always pushing a cart on this locomotive and scrambling down before it lumbers away, and you are made to be on your feet at all times. If nothing else, we have been reminded of the sublime comforts of sitting," the bookseller said before he left me a man famished.

I counted the days until Mr. Fergins returned to the train, but when I saw him again it was brief. I had to find another time and perhaps another place to satisfy my curiosity—to hear what happened when Pen Davenport encountered his rival Belial in the Samoan prison, how Belial managed to escape that prison (for I was certain he did), and if either bookaneer managed to take the prize of Robert Louis Stevenson's novel, and what stratagems they employed. I kept a sharp eye out whenever I happened to be in the sections of New York City where I had come across Mr. Fergins in the past. Still no luck. One occasion, I even found myself walking into the receiving room of his boardinghouse, but my entrance drew such an unwelcoming stare from the landlady that instead of asking for Mr. Fergins or leaving a card, I stood dumbfounded and turned on my heel as though I had the wrong address.

The bookseller's mention of his duties at the trial seemed to present the best opportunity to encounter him away from the railroad. I rode the omnibus to the courthouse. The court we had entered together three weeks earlier was once again thronged with people. After remaining among the eager spectators for almost an hour I couldn't see how any progress could have been made since the trial began. The judge would call the arguing lawyers to approach him in order to resolve some technicality of law, then direct them back to their tables, then summon them again for further discussions minutes later. I was surprised so many people were still in attendance for such endless repetition. Didn't they have anything more important to do? It was a hollow thought on my part, since I, too, thought there was nothing better to do with the little free time I had.

The accused, for his part, was sitting in the witness stand with his head bent forward. He seemed bored. His eyes followed the lawyers as they volleyed arguments. His head didn't move an inch; he just rolled his eyes in one direction and then the other, with the same enormous contempt for all involved, including his own representatives. His jaw was tight and clenched—and bruised.

The attorneys would emphasize words here and there apparently at random, spitting them out.

"Isn't it true, sir," said the prosecuting attorney, "that you were once among the class of persons known as 'bookaneers,' and in this capacity known by the name of Belial? If you look at this document, marked Exhibit A-6, estimating the amount of money authors were deprived of by this lot . . ."

"Your Honor," replied the defense, "must we *sit* here and listen to these insinuations against my unfortunate client?"

"Surely, Your Honor, the counsel to the accused does not object to a question intended to establish a very *simple* fact."

"Against a question that *imperils* the reputation of my client, I demand the protection of the court to silence the sharp and dangerous tongue of"—here the attorney for the defense pointed at the opposing lawyer—"this serpent."

All without a word from the prisoner, who did not seem to expect that he would ever be required to talk. Again it happened: the men scurried up to the judge's table to argue in quieter tones, then lurched back. When the court took its noon recess, the bookaneer was still in the witness seat, and the bailiff had to push spectators away. Women handed him scented letters and fruit; one man leaned into his face and stared, then went away without uttering a word. My eyes followed this odd bird walking to the back of the room, where he had an easel with a portrait in progress of the bookaneer, who, for some reason, was pictured in the unfinished canvas standing between a peacock and a human skull.

It was the man on trial, not the trial itself, not the lawyers, not the judge, that kept the audience enthralled. Just to look upon him in the flesh satisfied that crowd.

"He is a rare man," said my neighbor to the right. He was a small-boned and neatly dressed fellow who had big, watery eyes; thin, white hair; and a crisp mustache that hugged the tips of his lips and showed traces of auburn. "Belial has hardly aged a day since I first met him in . . . '56, I believe it was."

"You know the bookaneer personally?" I asked.

"Yes, of course I do. I acquired many a book from that titan, many that turned great profits. I had been one of the old publishers of this city for nearly forty years, before I relinquished my offices to men with their first beards. Oh, New York City is a different place than it was. You cannot buy even an old house in a decent neighborhood today for less than ten thousand dollars. Believe it, young man."

"I do," I assured him.

He explained that so many publishers and authors had heard tales of Belial without ever having seen him, or the other notorious bookaneers, that literary men and women had come as far as Boston and Philadelphia, and one even traveled from California to gawk at him. The book world was captivated.

"You must be rather distraught by his predicament."

He screwed up his face, his mustache now swallowing up his mouth. "What? How do you mean?"

"Only that a friend of yours—"

"No friend of mine!" he exclaimed. "If Belial met ten people, nine will be hypnotized by him into believing he is a righteous man. The tenth will be all alone on an island of truth. That man—I mean me—will know Belial is rotten to the core, as all bookaneers must be to do what they do. Yes, I dealt with him and with his brethren because we had no choice, but it was with deep loathing, believe it. I come here to watch him squirm."

"Isn't it hypocritical?"

"Explain, boy, or I will have you taken out of the courtroom by your ears." He seemed to notice for the first time that he was not just speaking to himself, and that I was not white.

I knew I had spoken too frankly, since I was hoping he could help me. "Very sorry, sir. I mean no offense."

"Ignorant! Then what do you mean?"

"Well, you say you were a book pirate yourself, so why condemn the bookaneers for the same thing?"

"I was no pirate, boy," he huffed. "I was a publisher. We have an obligation to the reader above all else to *let them read*."

He said these three words as though reciting a motto. I nodded my agreement, eager to move on. "Do you know a Mr. Fergins?"

"Come again?"

"He is a bookseller who has been helping to review the evidence in this case." I explained how the last time I was at the court he went into a room upstairs to study documents. "I remember the door was painted dark red, but I don't remember exactly where it was. You see, I thought I might find him here again today."

"A bookseller, did you say? No. I haven't heard of him. Do you know what the chief problem is these days with bookselling?"

I plagiarized the words of Pen Davenport. "I suppose that the greater portion of the population that learns to read, the more they revolt against having to pay to do so."

I don't think he intended for me to answer; he hadn't listened. "Booksellers think they are closer to the authors, and closer to God, than publishers, but no mistake about it, if the author is dragged down by any devil, it is by the bookseller who genuinely believes he is serving a just cause."

The publisher's attention was drawn away from me. Turning my head to the left, I was facing Belial himself, who was having his chains untangled as he was being led through the aisle.

"Afternoon, old friend," the pirating publisher said, saluting the prisoner. "Over here! It has been a long time. Fifty-six, wasn't it, that we met for the first time?" he asked. "A rare man," he repeated to me, holding his breath as we watched Belial (who had ignored him) disappear into the crowd. Despite his pronouncements about wanting to see the prisoner squirm, my neighbor seemed as enthralled and worshipful as the pretty young poetesses who had heard stories of the bookaneers of old.

Though I did not find Mr. Fergins in the courthouse that day, I still had some hope I would see him there and be able to entreat him for more of his tale; I went again the very next chance I had, this time arriving earlier, trying to match the time of day when I had met the bookseller there the month previous. On this occasion, however, the courtroom was empty, and from the smoking ashtrays it seemed to have been abandoned recently and in a hurry. I exited, wondering about this mysterious circumstance. There were noises of a commotion, and following the sounds brought me upstairs to the same crimson door where Mr. Fergins had once parted from me.

A dense cloud of smoke clogged the air. Scores of firemen in dark leather helmets were running to the spot and pouring water into the room, and steam was hissing from inside the room. The stench of burning—or of something already burnt—filled the air. A woman screamed.

I shielded my eyes from the stinging particles in the air. "What happened?" I asked one of the less panicked spectators, a tall man with enthusiastic expressions.

"There was a fire broke out in one of the evidence rooms," he said, shouting above the din. "Some unlucky bookseller saw the smoke coming out and rushed in to put it out—he's a hero. A fool, but he was a hero to the end, I say!"

"Do you mean to say he's died?"

"That's what I heard not a minute ago. Fergin was his name, I believe they said. Where are you going?"

I pushed past the man and right into the surging crowd of firemen and onlookers.

"Mr. Fergins! Mr. Fergins!" I cried.

I found a pair of spectacles on the floor, their white metal frame blackened and bent, with one lens cracked into shards.

There was a half circle of men closing over a prone form that I recognized at a glance. "Give him some air!" someone was shouting at me and others who were trying to get closer. "Some air!"

My heart dropped out of my throat when Mr. Fergins began gasping and coughing.

"Anyone know this man?"

"I know him!" I called out when arms and elbows tried to shove me away. *He is my one friend in this whole monstrous city*, I wanted to shout.

A lady who eyed me for a moment then commented that the fallen gentleman's watch chain and valuables should be secured. A man with a kindly voice called to me from behind to give Mr. Fergins air if I wanted him to survive.

The bookseller was rolled onto a stretcher and was trotted out of sight by three bearers. In the gallery of the courthouse more spectators loitered, having tumbled out of the courtrooms to see the commotion. There between a circle of blue police uniforms was Belial himself, his stiff mouth twitching, just for a moment, into a projection of malicious complacency.

I BECAME A CONSTANT OBJECT at the invalid's bedside. The first time I called to visit him after his injuries, Mrs. McGrath, the landlady who by now had seen me twice before, asked: "Who are you? Not a relative; if I have eyes I can see that well enough." But there was not exactly a clamor from people to help her look after her boarder, and she quickly tired of trying to chase me away. A nurse came for a few hours a day at first, and a doctor periodically visited. The Englishman was still a stranger in our country, as much a stranger in New York City as I ever was.

He had been lucky enough to escape any burns on his body, but he had inhaled too much smoke. He had trouble breathing and speaking, and slept for long periods during the day. His eyes had also been severely irritated by the smoke and ashes, and for several days he had to wear a bandage over one eye for four hours, then switch it to the other. I was sent on errands to retrieve his repaired spectacles and his suit after it was mended and cleaned. He gave me permission to read or dip into any of the books on his shelves.

There was a sadness to his book collection. Almost half of the books I looked at seemed to have been presented from one person—the author or someone else—to another as a gift. There were inscriptions, and names, and records of the book being given by beloved sisters, fathers, lovers. All the books had been cherished, at some time, before being sold to strangers.

I did my best to follow his directions in caring for his various plants and the creeping bookworms, which I was then charged with returning to the professor at Columbia College who had loaned them. A few book hunters visited in my presence and Mr. Fergins instructed me to retrieve volumes from his collection and to put away payments for them in a locked drawer. There was a large man in a big beaver hat who also appeared; I remembered him as the same man whom I saw speaking with Mr. Fergins on the steps of the courthouse. I was shelving a new shipment of books while the two men met in the bedroom. They spoke in whispers and, though I tried to listen, I could not hear much. It seemed they were talking of the trial, and the caller muttered about "the damned thief" and exclaimed his wish to "hang him high and dry." When I helped him back on with his coat, the visitor, carrying out a bundle of books, seemed disgruntled.

I wondered whether it was difficult for Mr. Fergins to part with volumes that he took such good care of. He laughed when I asked, relating the story of a man named Don Vincente, a monk and bookseller in Barcelona who coveted his own selection of books so much that he began to follow his customers home and murder them, taking back the books he had sold them. When asked at his trial why he would commit murder over books, he cried, "Books, books, books. Books are the glory of God!" The strangest thing about the story was that some histories of the incident insisted Don Vincente could hardly read. "Perhaps," mused Mr. Fergins when I asked how it was possible, "that was what drove him to such lengths. The books were just their outsides, just physical things, so that was all that was important to Don Vincente. I suppose he is the black mark on the history of my trade—but at least one cannot question his dedication."

One evening as I was preparing to exit the house, the landlady stopped me in the receiving room, which was dimly lit at this hour and smelled faintly of cinnamon.

"Well, I should think your visits are coming to an end about now," she said.

I was surprised as much by her words as by the fact that after ignoring me for so long she was now addressing me again. "Ma'am?"

She raised her voice as though I could not hear. "Certain young men, coming and going at all hours, it is frightening some of the ladies who board with me."

For a moment my mind stumbled, but then I remembered the reports I had seen in the newspaper just days earlier about a young lady in another part of the city who, when found in a state of undress in the middle of the night, had alleged two colored men had tried to abduct her from her chambers. I had noticed more wary and warning expressions since then.

"Ma'am, if I may . . ."

Her face was coloring red. "When I ask you a question, I suggest you jump to answer. Now, I shall ask you, young man, once more, how long you believe I ought to welcome you here."

"Mr. Clover will be welcomed by you however long I board here, Mrs. McGrath."

We turned and saw Mr. Fergins standing at the entrance to the receiving room, which was around the corner from his rooms. His body was bent over, one hand on the wall, while on the other side his weight was supported by his feeble umbrella. I had thought the bookseller was asleep when I'd slipped out of his room. He asked sternly if she understood him and waited until the landlady murmured that it was so. I hadn't felt so grateful since I had come to New York City.

Mr. Fergins worried that I was wasting all my free time in the two weeks since his accident tending to him. I was a young man, he would say. I suppose he was implying that my calendar should be filled with amusing adventures and romances. I did not want to say what I really thought: that I could see there was no one else who would be at his side, and anyway, with the cold weather curtailing my walks, I would be nowhere else but my dismal room.

One afternoon, I brought him some warm blueberry cake the land-lady's daughter had handed me with a shy smile when I entered.

As had become my habit, I sat in a chair by his bed reading to myself while he rested, sometimes sleeping, at other times sighing musically.

He sat up on the mass of pillows. "My luck has run against me again. Anyway, that's how I feel when I lie awake at night. But do you know, I'm beginning to feel stronger than I have in a long time."

He gestured for his spectacles case and I helped him put them on. "That is excellent to hear, Mr. Fergins." The truth was, I was concerned by his appearance. He was pale and seemed frailer.

"What are you reading?"

"I hope you don't mind me taking it down," I said, showing him the book in my lap. "All the talk of Stevenson—"

"*Kidnapped*," he said with a nod.

"I had read *Strange Case of Dr. Jekyll and Mr. Hyde*, and of course *Treasure Island*, but never this. What do you think of it?" I asked.

"*Strange Case*."

"What?"

"No 'the' in the title, except in misprinted or pirated copies. What do *you* think of *Kidnapped*, Mr. Clover?"

I closed it, as though examining the book's form would give me a better sense of its whole meaning. "Its story makes me think, no matter where you go, wherever you are taken by life's events, the one thing you cannot escape is family."

"You know something, Mr. Clover? You seem too preoccupied for a young man," he said, and for the moment I imagined those repaired spectacles gave him the power to read my thoughts.

"Mr. Fergins, I have not wanted to disturb you while you are recovering. However, I feel I ought to tell you that when I visited the court-house I asked someone—an ex-publisher—where I could find you."

"What did he look like?"

"A slight man with thinning white hair, a neatly groomed mustache, with an old-fashioned cravat."

"Chisholm. G. R. Chisholm."

"He is a friend?"

"Publishers do not have friends."

"He said that he didn't know your name."

"In my years of helping Pen Davenport, it became my obligation to know people who would never know me. But please, go on."

"Well, I mentioned to him you were sometimes reviewing evidence in Belial's trial."

He waited. "I see. Did Mr. Chisholm have something to say about it?"

"Oh, I think he was hardly listening to me once he saw I was colored. But when I looked up I saw that Belial was being led away by the bailiff near our seats, and it seemed to me the bookaneer was looking at me. He might well have heard what I was saying, heard me describing the room where the evidence was. I cannot help but fear that he had something to do with the fire that caused your suffering, and that because of what I said he knew where you'd be. Could he have managed such a thing from a jail cell?"

Mr. Fergins wore a brave and impassive face that prevented my guessing how my words affected him. Finally he replied, "Who can say with certainty what a great bookaneer *cannot* manage?"

"Would he have the motivation to try to harm you, to stop you from assisting the prosecution?" I could not miss my chance. "Mr. Fergins, if it would not exhaust you too terribly, perhaps you can tell me more about the bookaneers."

"Certainly," he said immediately. "There's a book that will illustrate a point, if you don't mind."

I followed his directions and retrieved a volume from his collection. I would not have even called it a book, but rather a loosely bound sheaf of old papers in a thick yellow hide.

"This," he started, taking hold of it as though it were a child, "is a handwritten copy of the *Royal Portrait*, better known by its Greek title, *Eikon Basilike*. Charles I is said to have dictated the book while he was in prison, only days before Cromwell beheaded him. This is a copy believed to be transcribed from the original pages by Sir Jeremy Whichcott. Sir Jeremy transcribed the first seventeen chapters and returned the book to the king's rooms when it became too dangerous."

"Then what you hold there is incomplete?" I asked.

"Yes. Oh, there are later printed copies of the whole *Eikon Basilike*, but this one means more to me because Sir Jeremy's position reminds me of the modern bookaneers. When everyone around a book, including the author, is helpless, that is when the bookaneer must step in to act. Of course, if it had been a true bookaneer, he would have been able to do more."

"You mean to save the king?"

He seemed amused by me. "To save more chapters. But I see your way of thinking. Yes, if a bookaneer had gotten ahold of it, and circulated the book sooner and to more people, perhaps there even would have been enough agitation to stop the execution, though, on the other hand, I suppose that would make us all very Catholic today. Pray be a good fellow and put it back in its place for me? Gentle with it."

"I notice it is an unusual sort of leather," I said, running my finger along the deteriorated yellow hide. "Sheepskin," I declared, gratified to show how much I had learned from our conversations about books.

"No, no. Didn't I say? Human skin."

"What?"

"Do be careful handling it. It's quite valuable."

I wanted to throw the thing out of sight but I juggled the horrible creation until it landed on a table. "Human skin! How is that possible? What are you doing with it?"

"Oh, there have been various examples of such a thing in the history of bookbinding," he said with a professorial air. "In this case, the binder was also a student at the local medical college and thought it fitting that a book written by a dead man should be covered by dead skin. It's rather a glorious thing, isn't it? I should like my own flesh to be put to such good use when I have died."

I stared at his face but could not tell from his expression whether he was joking. I washed my hands furiously at the basin, wishing I had turpentine.

"But you asked to hear more about the bookaneers, Mr. Clover. Have I ever mentioned to you the time Molasses, the sneakiest of the old bookaneers, got his greedy hands on Thackeray's last work? The look on Whiskey Bill's face when I told him what had happened . . . Well, never has a fellow, even a ginger-topped one, turned so red as a ruby! What neither of them knew, however, was that a craftier bookaneer from Krakow, by the unlikely name of Baby, already had a scheme to take it."

He stopped when he saw the disappointment form on my face as I took my usual place at his bedside. "Mr. Fergins, couldn't you say something about what happened after you and Pen Davenport found Belial in Samoa? Also, I have been wanting more details of Kitten's demise."

"Those tales have very dark turns, Mr. Clover."

"If Belial did try to harm you at the courthouse, Mr. Fergins, he might try again. I know it's awfully hard for you to ask for help, and I can be bashful about that, too. But I believe I can help you. I can even go to the police on your behalf. My mother's cousin is acquainted with important men in the department. But I must know more."

He seemed to be weighing in his mind what might come of not telling the rest of the story, and what could come if he did. "If you really wish it . . ." he said finally.

"I would not want to tire you out, of course," I added, though my eyes surely betrayed me.

"As one of the only female practitioners of bookaneering, certainly its most successful example, Kitten inspired extreme reactions from the other members of the trade. Many were hostile toward her presence, threatened by a woman's position among them. Others were intimidated, still others paternalistic. Almost every practitioner, to a man, was envious of Davenport for having earned her affections. To protect his relationship with her, he had to wall himself in. It created an isolated situation for him, especially once she was gone.

"But back to Samoa. Did I describe to you the way Robert Louis Stevenson's brown eyes, usually so genial, were always . . . what's the word I want . . . busy? Tulagi—that was Vao's dwarf. Yes. His warning to me, I believe that's near where we left off when we were on the train together. The rainy season coming. Davenport and I are about to make a quest to the mangrove swamp to visit jail. To find Belial and ensure he would not interfere with . . ." He paused, then spoke very slowly to me. "I will tell you what happened, Mr. Clover, but only so you understand why you must not involve yourself any deeper with Belial or the aftermath of the Samoa affair, no matter what happens to me. Do you promise that the rest of the story will appease your cravings?"

I raised my right hand and swore the same by God.

VIII

FERGINS

The bitterest tears shed over graves are for words left
unsaid and deeds left undone.
HARRIET BEECHER STOWE

You might as well join me.
ROBERT LOUIS STEVENSON

With the Stevenson household distracted by the anticipation of
having their tobacco replenished, I set off with Davenport the
following morning to investigate the dwarf's story about the white man
arrested at Vailima prior to our arrival. I sent Cipaou to the German
consul with a letter to arrange for our tour of the native prison, officially
an institution of Samoans but unofficially—like everything that was
part of the ruling regime—under the thumb of the Germans. In the
meantime, Davenport had asked Charlie and some other servants for
information and learned that the man in question, "Banner," had visited Vailima at least twice asking for work, but was told Stevenson only
hired natives as labor. Some of the servants later caught him trying to
break into the house. He remained locked up until the native authorities could sit in judgment.

"Is that how Belial would go about this?" I asked on our ride to the prison. Cipaou was ahead of us, showing us the way.

"Presenting oneself as a poor white beachcomber and laborer would be rather clever," Davenport said. "If hired, you would be on the grounds by rights, but ignored by the people who live there. Ingenious, really."

"It did not work, though."

"That is the problem with ingenuity."

Tale-Pui-Pui was the native name for the island's prison. There was a central passage running through the building with a number of cells on each side. In the courtyard, the guards, armed with rifles, sat talking with each other.

There were no bars on the cells—they were small rooms with doors that seemed to be left open. We were led through the humid, murky central passage. The guard who walked ahead of us told us about some of the prisoners, rebellious natives who had defied King Tamasese and the Germans' governing initiatives. There were about twenty or thirty prisoners altogether, I would estimate, and they seemed on the whole happy to see visitors, if only to break up the monotony of their days. Some stopped to speak with us. Justice operated quite slowly in Samoa. Some had been there for months, others for years, without so much as a trial. We reached a room at the end of the passage where we were told we could find the man we sought. At first, we could only see the prisoner's feet, callused and yellow, as he was lying flat on some coarse mats, very different from the fine material and brilliant colors of those in our own cottage or at Vailima. His arms blocked his face from the particles of dirt and grime blown into the prison through the window.

"Belial," Davenport called out in a voice that made me jump.

The man slowly lifted his head, which was rather bullet shaped with an open mouth full of drool. "Who are you?"

"No," Davenport whispered to me, disappointment and a little embarrassment in his voice. "It's not him."

"I said, who the plague are you?" The man whined rather than spoke. After his sentences he would make a loud noise through his nose and then pinch the bridge of it, as one who has taken too much snuff.

"Excuse the interruption, sir. Our mistake," I said.

"Tusitala sent you, didn't he?" The prisoner had light brown hair and a flabby face made more misshapen by a patchy beard. "Damn him down to hell."

Davenport paused and turned back to the man without any sign of understanding the question. "Who?"

"Stevenson. That Scotch scribbler. I wrote him asking for work and he wrote back promising it. Then he reneged, accused me of smelling like liquor. I lost the letter, but if I hadn't, it would prove his promise. He looked in my eyes and said I could not be trusted. I was just trying to get what was owed me, see!"

"I believe it," Davenport said. "Where do you come from?"

"New South Wales before this."

"Tusitala did not send us, but I can carry your message back to him," Davenport said. I knew he was trying to end the exchange without the man causing a scene that would call attention to us.

He sniffed harder. "He's no mere writer like he claims."

"What do you mean?" I asked.

"He's here to start a war, you know. To set this whole island on fire. I'm white, as you fellows are, you have to help me out! You can't leave me here like this!"

By that point, Davenport lost patience and the bullet-headed man started spitting furiously in our direction when we began our exit again. I felt rather confounded by the encounter, and my companion appeared unusually flustered.

"What do you think?" I asked as we walked the long passage to the gates of the prison.

"We've wasted time."

Our horses had to be kept back beyond the swampy land around the prison. As we walked, I flung open my umbrella to keep the wind off my face.

"Well," I commented, "at least you know Stevenson will not have made much progress completing the book in our absence, with all the preparations they are doing for the storm, and for the arrival of the missionary and their precious tobacco."

As I spoke, I noticed a group of natives following behind us; then there were natives to the left, to the right. I slowed and they slowed. I paused and swung around to Davenport, but he seemed to be in a mood of deep contemplation and had not noticed.

"Davenport, I think we are in some kind of trouble."

He followed my gaze.

Now a native called out an unfamiliar word at me, then another repeated the same word, pointing. I realized what had excited them.

"This?" I asked, twirling my umbrella.

The movement elicited a round of cheers; perhaps they had never seen an umbrella before, or at least not a striped one.

Davenport's contemplation suddenly broke, revealing his thoughts. "The tobacco," he said under his breath. "Cipaou, the horses!" he shouted to our man, who was waiting by some trees on more solid ground. He rushed to untie them.

"What's wrong?" I asked, alarmed by the change in the bookaneer's demeanor.

"Put that blasted thing away."

I folded the umbrella and the disappointed natives drifted away.

"The missionary," Davenport continued, "the one who is delivering the Stevensons' tobacco, this Father Thomas. He's expected at Vailima, isn't he?"

"Any minute," I said.

"What do you know of him?"

"He's from the Marist mission. Stevenson said he is one of the longest-serving missionaries."

"No, he said the mission is one of the longest continuously in operation. The man could be new there."

"What are you driving at?"

"What better way to the Stevensons' hearts than through their blasted tobacco?"

WE DISMOUNTED AT VAILIMA and hurried to the front verandah, where a narrow wagon had been pulled by a span of horses. In addition to a traveler's trunk, the wagon was piled high with crates that Stevenson's servants were unloading. The top of one of the crates had come loose and opened. There were the holy jars of tobacco. Underneath sat rifles and pistols. John quickly removed the open crate from my sight and said something to me in Chinese, which sounded like a stern warning—though I suppose even a comment on the weather would sound like a warning from John.

For the moment, my thoughts lingered on the contents of the shipment. I recalled the outlandish accusation that Banner had made against Stevenson. That he was no mere writer—that he was here to start a war. Davenport had believed Hines had been thinking something similar when his eyes landed on *Treasure Island* in the frigate's library. My thoughts on the matter were fleeting, for in the next moment we heard the voice of the new arrival, the missionary.

"It's Belial," Davenport whispered to me, then steeled himself as he turned around.

There he was, the bookaneer who kept himself on everyone's tongue while keeping himself out of view. Davenport's rival removed a white pith helmet. He did not have a hair out of place on his large head.

Belial's brow, nose, and chin sat at handsome angles, his eyes bright. He was tall enough for most people to have to look up to him, and his mouth was big and expressive. Everything jutted out prominently. His brow, his chin, his chest. His presence instantly commanded interest and deference. There was something about him that made it hard to believe he was the same individual described to me for years by Davenport and others as so ruthless and remorseless.

"Apologies, Tusitala, that I was away on business longer than I expected," the deliverer of the goods was saying in his perfect enunciation when we joined them.

"We can just thank the heavens that nobody had to face Barkis's wrath over an empty tobacco jar," Stevenson said. "Well, you understand how women are. By Jove, no, how can you? Show me the man who does! Thomas, may I present to you an Englishman and an American, recent arrivals to Upolu—Mr. Fergins and Mr. Porter—Mr. Porter, Father Thomas, a missionary we have all come to esteem and even like in his short time serving the people of our island."

"Talofa," Belial greeted us with a nod as we approached. "Tusitala, you know I always get on first rate with the natives on this beautiful island, but I do savor the opportunity to see white faces after these long months."

"Talofa," Davenport said.

"I trust you gentlemen have settled into our little metropolis," Belial said as he shook our hands. "Have you grown accustomed to picking the weevils off your bread yet?"

"Bread? Is that what it is?" Davenport joked.

The little show of friendliness was interrupted when Mount Vaea rumbled with the vibration of an earthquake. Stevenson enjoyed the concern in our faces. "Life is not so much what happens as what one waits for," he mused.

"I see Mrs. Stevenson has expanded her impressive garden with some tall corn since I last visited," Belial noted.

"I will take you on a tour of the latest crops, Mr. Thomas," Davenport said. "I gave Mrs. Stevenson a hand with some new plantings the other day."

"Thank you, Porter," Stevenson replied. "I'll bring more of the tobacco inside."

Davenport began to walk and Belial followed with a light step. I remained behind them by a few paces.

"Do you wish to yield the mission to me now or later?" Belial asked when we were out of Stevenson's hearing. "I'm amenable to either."

Davenport looked over at the native servant walking at Belial's elbow.

"You can talk openly in front of him. He knows only four words of English," Belial said. "It's a shame, really; the boy has a devilish sense of humor in his own tongue and would appreciate the strangeness of our situation. Is there anything in that little brown brain of yours, Samu? Go ahead," he suggested to Davenport as the native turned and nodded reverentially at his master, "test the brute for yourself if you don't believe me. Say whatever you like to him."

Davenport waved away the offer.

"You have been learning their language, I suspect."

"Trying to."

Belial nodded. "Its grammar is labyrinthine, but at least the alphabet resembles ours. Never was your strong suit—languages, I mean. How many were you speaking when we met in Zurich? Was it still only eight?"

"Understanding people's minds is just as important as their words, Belial."

Belial appeared amused. He threw a glance in my general direction.

"That's—" Davenport began.

"Fergins, your shadow, yes," Belial said, pleasing me very much, even though the bookaneers all kept informed of each other's associates and it reflected no actual personal interest in me. He stopped to examine me more closely. "Fergins, the bookseller and bibliomaniac. Is it true what they say about you?"

"What do they say?" I asked eagerly.

"That you know all there is to know about our profession."

I shrugged, since Davenport would not like me trying to impress him. "As much as anyone else, perhaps."

"Come, Mr. Fergins. Humility is too often self-deception disguised. Who was it who first coined the term 'bookaneer'?"

Davenport nodded permission to answer.

"There are several versions, actually, but the one I find most convincing involves a notoriously parsimonious publisher active in the 1820s and '30s. After he agreed to terms with a member of the earliest crop of agents to uncover closely guarded information about a serial novel starting in a rival magazine, he found out that the same fellow, two months earlier, had swiped a valuable manuscript out from under his own nose. 'Never again will I give a penny to these nasty bookaneers!' he was said to have groused. Whatever the veracity of this, the name spread with the anecdote."

"You forgot the best part, which is that the same publisher found need to hire a bookaneer again only a few months later." He turned back to my companion. "What next? I know you are not armed and so do not plan to assault me."

"Are you certain?" Davenport asked.

"The intelligence I've gathered indicates that you are—stupidly, if you permit my opinion—posing as a gentleman of letters writing about travel. Were the Subject to notice you with a dagger or pistol, or anything more than a bush knife, even by happenstance, you would risk exciting his curiosity and foreclose your access. It is ever more pressing to protect your identity for a mission than to protect your body."

Davenport tried to remain stone-faced, but could not hold back his irritation at the veracity of Belial's description.

"You know," Belial continued, "*I* am always unarmed. You remember my philosophy on that topic, I suspect, from the old days."

"The armed man is always more feared, and therefore less dangerous than the unarmed man."

"You have heard my philosophy, as well, Mr. Fergins." Belial nodded at my recital of his rule. "I have been in the South Seas for three months already, Davenport. I miss Christina dearly, of course, but it is worth it for the greater good of the mission. However comfortable you think you and Sancho Panza back there have become here, I am more so. You know, it is not a bad thing, playing the role of a missionary. Their missions are not so different from our missions, for what do we do as bookaneers but go among the heathen world and spread our higher purpose? I have become a veritable bishop in Upolu and at Vailima. I have fully prepared my groundwork for this triumph. For every ten facts you've learned, I have a hundred. If you even attempt a single move against me, your purpose will be instantly revealed."

"You may have been here first, but I can expose you just as quickly."

Belial gave an order to his man, who passed him a cutlass. "Thank you, Samu," Belial said in Samoan, then turned back to Davenport. He ran his finger along the sharp edge of the weapon. "I am never armed, as your Mr. Fergins correctly remembered. But the barbarians are— they must be, if not to protect themselves from the elements then from each other, or the runaway blacks in the forest."

"Runaways?" I asked.

"The cannibals," Belial clarified. "The Germans import them from the Solomon Islands to work their plantations, which cover thousands of acres. It is because of the profits from those lands that the Germans have so much more money and influence than the British or Americans. But sometimes the cannibals escape, so one must be leery. Look at me, schooling the two of you to my own detriment."

I could see Davenport ready to lunge for the deadly weapon but the other man put it down in the low neck of a tree.

"Please," Belial said, taking a step back.

Davenport gripped the handle of the blade lightly, anticipating a trick, then released it.

Belial watched him, ending his demonstration with a smug speech. "Exactly right. If either of us were to attack the other, we would be exposed. You would be exposed and the Subject will know you are not who you say you are. And I can see you have acclimated yourself just enough that I cannot easily rid myself of you without also provoking unhealthy curiosity in the Subject. So we have a sort of balance between us, you and I, am I understood? This may be the last mission remaining for our kind, Davenport. If you are anything like me, nothing would make you give it up." He extended his hand toward the other bookaneer. "Let us have honor enough to fulfill our mission. Let us call this what we know it must be: a truce. Your shadow shall be our witness."

"Had you been here ten years, it would make no difference to me. I will have what I came for."

"Well! I fancy you must be pleased I am here, then."

"Is that right?"

"It gives you the chance you have been waiting for. To try to prove you can surpass me as a bookaneer and justify sweet little Kitty's faith in you. Doesn't that satisfy you as much as any ugly amount of money?"

"I surpassed you years ago," Davenport said.

"You'll have to be able to control your emotions, all those feelings eating at your soul since she's gone. Do you think you're capable?"

My pulse raced at the mention of Kitten, hoping Davenport would not lose his composure.

"When I'm finished here, carrying Stevenson's masterpiece in my hands, you'll see what I am capable of."

"Tusitala," Belial said, correcting Davenport. "Tusitala's masterpiece. Take care you're not so reckless around him or this will be too easy for me. Could you ever have dreamed it? Delicious prospect." He passed the cutlass back to Samu. "If we are not going to kill each other today, let us return to work. I will give you one last piece of information about Tusitala, about why we must be here now."

"I know his health is grave."

Belial shook his head. "Oh, he is dying, yes—that is obvious, no matter what he says—but that is not what his time in Upolu is about. His deepest wish is that he were not a writer."

"Why do you say that?"

Belial ignored the question. "It is not when a man is at the end of his life, but when a man is at the end of his profession, that his soul shows itself. Tusitala's soul decays and withers, and all his regrets come out that he lived a life of words rather than bravery. He will do what he can to rectify that. You have been warned."

He and his native companion walked at a crisp pace back toward his wagon. The very march of his boots cried out that he had so much to do to outwit us that he could not spare another second.

DAVENPORT KEPT OUR PRESENCE around Vailima inconspicuous, coming and going with little notice or fanfare, but Belial's strategy was dramatically different. He'd interjected himself deeply into life at the estate. He had made himself noticeable and indispensable, an unorthodox choice for a man who was there to spy and plot. When "Pope

Thomas," as the servants called him, was on the grounds, the entire household knew. The conch shell would be blown to announce him, as though something was happening, like a meal or an earthquake.

Belial ministered regularly to four or five of the Stevensons' domestics. The previous missionary had been there for twenty years before retiring to England, Belial worming himself into the position at just the right time to pursue Stevenson's impending masterpiece. Among their beads and fish bones, the Samoans who'd converted to Catholicism also wore crucifixes around their necks to distinguish themselves from the Protestant converts, as well as from the savages who had not been taken by one of the white religions and still worshipped their own deities. Belial led group prayers in the mornings, clutching his big, polished cane to his heart; at other times he heard their private confessions, a clever way of learning about life at Vailima without ever asking. Vao was the only servant who seemed opposed to his popularity. I noticed when Belial came from one direction, the beautiful girl left the other way, then the diminutive attendant of hers, who would frown and puff to keep up with her quick steps, fire and smoke in his eyes for anyone who made the mistake of looking at her.

Belial also had an effect on the other Stevensons. Though not a Catholic, Stevenson's mother, Margaret, would sit with a look of utter joy across her face as she listened to his Bible discussions. Lloyd would consult with "Pope Thomas" about how to best manage a recalcitrant outside boy. Belle would blush and stammer and twirl her hair while telling him about her terrible ex-husband. He did not exactly flatter her, but his whole manner was flattering to women. She had so intently studied Davenport since our arrival, trying to decide whether she fancied him, but now forgot he was there. The household had changed with the return of the supposed missionary.

I was listening to Belial lead a prayer in the next room on one occasion when I noticed Charlie staring out a window over the grounds, his face tight and fearful.

"Charlie, what is the matter?" I asked.

"There," he said in a gasp.

It appeared the stout islander with the kind eyes was looking into the forest bordering Vailima. I could see nothing but the trees blowing in the wind.

"They're out there!" Charlie exclaimed, blinking rapidly. "In the bushes."

"Who?"

"My family."

Still I saw nothing and nobody. Charlie seemed more frightened every second. He clutched at the wooden crucifix hanging in the middle of his chest.

"Do you need help, Charlie? Charlie, can you hear me?"

"They must not find me. Tusitala is my family now; he is my chief, no other. They do not like the new God. If they find me here, Tusitala will—" Charlie stopped his sentence and took long strides out of the room before I could find out more.

Later, I ran across Stevenson in the fields. He was chopping away at the liana that grew across and over other vegetation and strangled the pathways. I suppose his body was set up rather badly. His chest, which was exposed in his loose garments, was flat as a board, but his limbs were so long they made it seem as though there would need to be a great effort to stay upright. I started to walk toward him to suggest he look in on Charlie, but something gave me pause. Watching the surprisingly powerful motion of the novelist's arm bringing the blade down on the vines, I thought about the servant's insinuation of Stevenson's potential for anger if he found out Charlie's family was looking for him.

"Fergins?" he asked, watching me watch him.

"Apologies, Tusitala, just wondering if you need a hand."

He waved my offer away and used the interruption to flick the sweat from his hair. "Our strangling enemy, this endless liana. Do you know something? When I ply the cutlass and make the equivalent of sixpence, idiot conscience applauds me. But if I sit in the house and make twenty pounds by writing, idiot conscience wails over my neglect and the day wasted. No, to come down covered with mud and drenched with sweat and rain after some hours in the bush. To change, rub down, and take a chair in the verandah, that makes for a quiet conscience."

The fact was, I had plenty to dwell on without becoming involved in Stevenson's dealings with his domestics. For one thing, Davenport was slamming doors on me and generally giving me the cold shoulder. I'm afraid he believed I was just as overly charmed by the newcomer as most of the household. To be perfectly honest, I had heard about Belial for so many years, had followed his exploits so closely as one of the top-notch bookaneers, that I could not help finding his presence fascinating.

Belial also seemed to read my interest as admiration. In a clear ploy to annoy his great rival, when we crossed paths at Vailima, he would wrap his meaty hand around my arm and regale me with stories of various predicaments encountered in spreading the word of God throughout the South Seas. Belial made an art of laughing when the person with him laughed, of smiling when the other person did, and then his laugh was the cause of the other's laugh, his smile the kindling for the other's.

Davenport would not admit to it, but he was eager to know my opinion on Belial and on Belial's power over even complete strangers. Even complete strangers, in the case of many of the Samoans, who did not speak English. I began to catalog what I saw as Belial's strengths for him—his refined face, his elegant company, his confident posture—

but Davenport could not listen. He grew especially warm with me one day when he found me using my umbrella as a walking stick.

"What on earth is that?" Davenport asked with absolute horror.

"What?"

"You know damn well. That . . . *umbrella*."

"Davenport," I said, cowed by his uncharacteristic tone. "It's nothing. I hurt my ankle the other day on the trails."

Davenport looked as though he might throw the umbrella and maybe me into the magma chamber of Mount Vaea. Belial was never seen without his golden-hued cane, though it was not clear whether he suffered from a physical limitation or it was an accessory; it made observers examine him all the more closely, one moment believing they could identify a limp or maybe a weak knee, sympathizing with him, stopping themselves out of politeness from asking, and then wondering again if any limp was there at all. Davenport suspected that however I injured myself I found the idea of imitating the great Belial appealing.

Of course, this was not so at all. Or perhaps there was truth in it. Perhaps the power of suggestion took hold of me without my knowing. I cannot say. I understand the intensity of my companion's feelings against Belial, especially after we learned more about what had happened with Kitten in the time before her death. But selfishly I could not help being tickled to think that here I was, Edgar Fergins, proprietor of the Hoxton Square Bookstall, dwelling on a remote island with the world's two greatest bookaneers in the battle to claim their ultimate prize.

Stevenson soon all but vanished once again from the public rooms at Vailima, and with his seclusion his work came to a halt. The last thing he said about his writing in our hearing was that he was broken down. "The orange is squeezed out, and I will do nothing as long as I can," he said in a sad, trancelike state. He was draped in a blue and white kimono from Japan that fit his skeletal frame like a scarecrow's coat. "Sometimes," he continued, "a man must wonder how anyone can be such an ass to enter the profession of letters instead of being apprenticed to a barber or keep a baked-potato stall." I could almost hear Davenport and Belial—who were on opposite ends of the great hall when Stevenson announced this—groan to themselves that the novel's completion would be postponed once more.

The novelist's spidery shoulders formed a slouch, and he slouched his way to his library and through the glass door at the end of that room, closing it behind him. The small sanctum, where we had seen him preside over his bedside court proceeding for the case of the stolen pig, was an enclosed portion of the upper verandah that contained little more than a bed and a table. I had been inside on only two occasions. The table could fold and unfold and swing over the bed. Two windows overlooked the majestic, luxuriant volcano. There were engravings of his ancestors in traditional Scotch dress along the plain walls. In one corner, there was a stand with several Colt repeating rifles. Opposite that, a small bookcase had editions of Stevenson's own titles. Above the bed was another bookcase with some more of his titles and a big book entitled *A Record of Remarkable Crimes and Criminals*, which I imagined him searching for ideas. Stevenson would write sitting up in the bed and tossing his pages onto the table, and when he could not write, he would lie there staring at the beams in the ceiling. We suspected he had fallen back into the latter state. We began to hear the frequent sad squealing of the flageolet. The sound of a man not writing.

There were new troubles to keep at bay in addition to the halt in Stevenson's progress. The dwarf who attended Vao continued his hostile stares and comments and had added Davenport as one of his targets. One damp afternoon, I was holding my reliable umbrella over Davenport on the lawn when we passed near the fierce little man, who was leaning against a tree, his legs in a sort of squatting position. His eyes were closed and he was mouthing something silently to himself. He paused and returned his usual glare.

"Is there some problem between us to address?" Davenport asked.

"No, White Chief. But Tulagi is not to be angered, be sure about it."

"Who is this Tulagi?" I was about to ask, before I understood the dwarf suffered from the trait, not uncommon among those Samoan natives who learned English later in their lives, of speaking of himself in third person.

"What reason have either of us given you not to trust us, Tulagi?" Davenport asked him.

Tulagi laughed hard. "You are a handsome man."

I looked over at Davenport. The tone of his skin had turned smooth and rich, a perfect parchment, during his time in the tropical sun. As with many who had come here from far away, his appearance had vastly improved.

"White men tend to infatuate themselves with my charge. Handsome white men think themselves entitled to be near Vao—to possess her, to seek pleasure from her, and to try to remove her from here."

"How is it that she is your concern?" Davenport asked.

"She is a *tapo*. Each village chooses their prettiest maiden to represent them to the island. It is my honor to have been appointed to protect her and guide her when she was just a girl."

"Well, I have business more important than stealing away your favorite little maiden, Tulagi."

"Making certain you do not try is Tulagi's business."

"Tell us, are you some kind of a mystagogue?"

"What is it you were whispering about, if you don't mind telling us?" I asked to soften Davenport's sarcasm.

Tulagi appeared to mind, but answered. "I am a memorizer."

"A what?"

"Tulagi is one of those chosen to keep our islands' history alive—to recite the stories of our past and practice them when not at my duties of looking after Vao."

"Why not write them down? Then they would never be forgotten. They would be safe."

"They are safer in my heart and my brain, than on pieces of paper that could be lost or burned or made false." He returned to whispering to himself and I listened to as much as I could before we moved on. From what I could gather, he was telling himself the story of the first whites who came to the island, and how the natives believed them by the color of their skin to be walking corpses. Just the fragment of this tale put me somewhat ill at ease, especially as Davenport continued to direct me to ride into the wild, overgrown portions of the property and the sunless virgin forests looking for the now almost-legendary fifth stream.

"What exactly is it you believe we will find once we locate the stream?" I asked on one of these tiring excursions.

Davenport seemed to relish my question, though a quick smirk straightened itself into a serious and profound answer, after he made sure none of the outside boys were close enough to hear. "Another way off the property, one where we cannot be followed. That is why we cannot simply ask the domestics. Another possibility is that the fifth stream may lead us to another outbuilding, where Stevenson piles up pages he is not ready to share."

"A kind of treasure chest of lost literature," I suggested.

It seemed fanciful, an idea worthy of a wine-and-cigar session at Pfaff's vault among a host of other bookaneers in the golden age of their trade. Still, I thoroughly searched my share of the grounds. The next time we were out surveying, we heard hoof falls approach. A horse and rider had started toward us and then stopped at a distance. It was Fanny Stevenson; she brought her horse to a halt about fifty feet away. I saluted her, but she did not return it. The encounter felt odd. I could not see her face very clearly, and as far as I could tell she seemed to be squinting at us in careful study. After a while, Lloyd and Belle appeared behind her on their horses and she turned around and cantered off with them.

The dark clouds had come closer and over the next twenty-four hours hovered in long clusters directly east. Cipaou—and the Vailima household, and for that matter everyone else on the island—was filled with dire, excited predictions about the rainy season. All this seemed to force Stevenson to emerge from his bout of isolation to oversee matters. The day he returned to the public rooms he looked dreadfully ill, his eyes hollow, his sticklike legs wobbly, his motions jerky. The household had spoken of his social moods alternating with his private ones, but seeing him like this led me to believe his encampments in the sanctum also served to conceal his worst spells of sickness. With his bare feet, one might have mistaken him, when lying down, for a dead body waiting to be prepared for burial.

In addition to the tasks related to the dangers of the rainy season, during our visits we witnessed regular callers to Vailima demanding one thing or another from the novelist. Chiefs representing the various villages of the island asked his counsel and advice on political matters, ranging from inter-village disputes over the marriage of a chief's daughter to the demands of one of the foreign consulates. We were at the house when one of the highest chiefs of the island came. Because of his status, we were all invited to take 'ava with him. He was there to ask Stevenson to reconcile two feuding chiefs by hosting a feast.

At the end of their conference, Stevenson asked the visitor what gift he would like from Vailima, for it was one of the most galling Samoan traditions, to the mind of an Englishman, anyway, that a distinguished visitor would not depart from your home without taking something with him. The chief asked for a revolver. Stevenson handed it to the chief's wife, another custom of the islands' gift giving. She proceeded to open the chamber and then empty the bullets on the floor. They seemed to enjoy the thing as though it were a novelty rather than a weapon. Then she pointed it at her husband's heart and pulled the trigger as he pretended to be shot. We all laughed at the morbid pantomime.

She kept pulling the trigger, eliciting more melodramatic reactions from the chief.

"No!" was shouted.

John Chinaman threw himself across the room and knocked the revolver away. It was then that I noticed what the mysterious servant had seen before any of us. There were only five bullets on the floor. When he rose to his feet amid confusion, he opened the chamber and showed us inside. Had she finished one more playful shot, the chief would have been shot in the heart.

We were all very somber after the embarrassed couple exited to think of the near tragedy that had occurred. When Davenport and I were making our own departure for the evening, I could hear Stevenson and Fanny in the great hall. They had recovered from the startling incident and were trading elaborately whimsical stories about what would have transpired had the chief been accidentally assassinated in their house. It was the happiest I ever heard the husband and wife during our time on island.

Stevenson had promised the chief to host the reconciliation feast as soon as the weather permitted, and that planned feast gave rise to another visit that could have threatened all our plans.

Belle told me that there had been some discord over a task, given to one of the servants, to secure a pig to roast for the feast. Charlie would usually do it, but because of his recent unsteady behavior, a servant named Eliga, whose English was less fluent, was sent on the assignment.

Instead of a pig, the servant brought home a boar. That was the sort of thing that became the talk of the house. I expected later to hear of Stevenson dressing down the native but instead he spoke to him quietly in the library and sent him on his way, livery securely in place. "Now, think of what I've said, Eliga," was Stevenson's parting message for him.

"Oh, I will, Master Tusitala," said Eliga, head bowed, hands cupped together and trembling. "My life is yours and I your servant until death."

I happened to be walking past Stevenson's sanctum while approaching Fanny at the time, and did not think of it again. After all, I was rather distracted. Fanny was unusually reserved with me, and the change in her demeanor was concerning enough to make me sweat as much as the humidity. She greeted me with a mumble and parted from me without much more than that.

A few days later, the conch announced a horseman, and Vailima's front door opened on Lionel Hines. I was in the great hall and my heart jumped. It was alarming to see our fellow passenger from the *Colossus* on Stevenson's estate, especially because I recalled him saying he did not know Stevenson personally. It meant something out of the ordinary had brought him. Davenport had still been tinkering with his plans for the mission while onboard the frigate. He had already been using the alias of Porter, but had told Hines he was a collector of primitive antiques, not a travel writer. It may sound like a trivial point, but it was the sort of thing that could be enough, if it came out, to plant a seed of suspicion in Stevenson—the sort of thing that could quickly unravel a bookaneer's mission.

While the visitor was busy fumbling for his handkerchief to display to Fanny, I rushed upstairs. I was out of view but that was not sufficient to feel safe. Davenport was in the stables, where Charlie had been taken to be cared for. Charlie had broken out into a fever and one native doctor after another, usually white haired and bent, came carrying palm-leaf baskets of exotic herbs and flowering plants. Davenport had been visiting the sick young man often—another way of contriving reasons for our calls to Vailima, I supposed, though it also seemed the bookaneer was genuinely moved by the native's plight. Davenport could be returning at any moment and would find himself face-to-face with the Australian. I rushed into the library and found a Bible and some writing paper. After copying some verses, I searched for one of the domestics. The first one to come was the beautiful maiden.

"Vao, could you please bring this to my friend? He is visiting Charlie in the stables." She stood blinking at me. I remembered myself. Here I was pleading to a girl who didn't speak English. While I was attempting to translate my request into rough Samoan, Tulagi appeared, steaming mad.

"Tulagi warned you against bothering her," said the dwarf.

"I am not. I need for this to be delivered to my companion."

"What is it?"

"It is a prayer to read to the ailing servant in the stables, Tulagi."

"Bring it yourself, then, if you care so much about Charlie's eternal soul," he growled.

I swallowed, unable to explain why I could not walk by Hines. Then the young woman took the paper and bowed to me; there was a deeper understanding of the situation behind her eyes that both made me feel great relief and worried me.

"Talofa," she said, and I returned the gesture.

I thought I saw her glance down at the message and wondered, for a moment, whether she could have noticed and perhaps even understood that I wrote certain words from the Psalm in a slightly larger hand, trying to convey the warning to stay out.

> *Lord, remember David, and all his afflictions:*
> *How he swore unto the Lord, and vowed unto the mighty God of*
> *Jacob;*
> *Surely I will NOT COME INTO the tabernacle of my HOUSE,*
> *nor go up into my bed;*
> *I will not give sleep to mine eyes, or slumber to mine eyelids,*
> *Until I find out a place for the Lord, an habitation for the mighty*
> *God of Jacob.*

The maiden's willingness did nothing to soften Tulagi, but he also did not prevent her from taking my message; he followed her, leaving me alone again. I took the opportunity to position myself on the mezzanine above the great hall, where I would not be seen but could listen. I could only hope the visit did not signal that Hines would be a new addition to Vailima society. I dared to lean over the banister just enough to see the two of them when Stevenson had emerged.

"Your card asking me here was most unexpected, I confess," said Hines after handing Stevenson a folded paper. It was clear from his voice that Hines, despite having run Stevenson down under his breath to us on the warship, was puffed up to have been invited. "I was actually at the British consul yesterday just after I got your card, and there was a wire coming in for you," he continued, "so I took the liberty of volunteering to deliver it. No whites really want to go this far into the interior, you know, but I must make constant visits to my properties, and always hunt for new potential plots. Savvy? If you ever think of selling this fine land—"

"I do not."

"Well, I hope there's some other service I might provide for you, Mr. Stevenson."

Stevenson glared at the man for using his "civilized" name but did not correct him. They were in chairs separated by a big Turkish rug, and, in addition to my eyes, two matching statues of Buddha on the stairs watched them.

Hines found a chair. Stevenson never just sat in a chair. He perched on the arm, or sat cross-legged against it, or, as he did now, positioned himself sideways like a bored child, bony legs dangling. There was a shift that came over Stevenson sometimes, something that possessed him, moved him from gangly European exile to imposing Samoan overseer. It was unspecific, intangible, but I had begun to recognize it when it happened.

"There *is* something you can help me with, Mr. Hines. It seems you sold a pig to one of my men, only the animal received was an old boar, too tough to be digested by human stomachs. When he returned to your house and asked you to correct the mistake, it is my understanding you laughed in his face."

Hines's cheeks reddened beyond his thick, curly beard. "I'm afraid it was your boy's mistake. Savvy? But if you had come to me yourself, of course, I would have rectified it at once and. . ."

The visitor lost his line of thought when his host yawned; it was a low-bred, gaping, animal yawn that could stop any speech mid-sentence. Stevenson locked his hands behind his head. "Was it my man's mistake for being brown rather than white, making him a mark to cheat?" he asked. He interrupted the stuttering umbrage from Hines: "Understand, Mr. Hines, that the men and women I employ at Vailima are not servants. They are ainga—family—I their chief, and if you cheat one of them you cheat me. The fraud against us is not to be repeated. Unlike men of your kind who come to wring coin out of the soil, glorified beachcombers, I have chosen this land as my land, the people as my people, to live and die with."

"Surely, we can come to some arrangement."

"It's my understanding that you require all native women who work for you to wear full dresses."

"Now, see here. If I help my brown boys and girls to be more civilized, I don't see how it's your business."

"Is your mind so base that you cannot see and admire what is beautiful in the form God Almighty has created? Do you not see that what you do on this beautiful island is pollute their minds and sully their modest thoughts?"

Hines, fidgeting like a marionette with the strings loose, offered to send a fresh pig over for the feast—a gift of hospitality from one white man to another, he said before he hurriedly gathered himself to exit. Stevenson did not make a move to see him out. The novelist closed his eyes as though he were going to take a nap. I was relieved, confident Hines would never be seen near Vailima again. I suppose I shouldn't have savored the moment as much as I did—as I leaned forward, my spectacles started to slip and, before I could catch them, fell from my face, drifting over the railing of the mezzanine.

They didn't break. But it might have been better if they had, so they would not be recognizable. They floated down and landed with a rattle in Hines's path. He noticed them right before his boot was about to crush them. He picked them up and studied them, before placing them back on the floor.

Davenport had received my message from Vao's hand and remained in the outbuilding until Hines was gone. Running down the stairs to retrieve my spectacles and make my exit, I nearly ran headlong into Fanny, who did not flinch from a possible collision. She stood stock-still, with the same hard glare I had seen her direct toward us in the fields.

"What is it you want here?"

I do not know how a person can be described both as almost whispering and almost yelling, but that is how I remember her words sounded. I was prepared to babble out an answer when she turned on her heel and went to check on her husband, who had broken down into a violent cough.

When I recounted these details later that day to Davenport, he seemed neither as concerned with Hines's visit nor as relieved at its outcome as I'd expected. Other things preoccupied him. The slow pace of Stevenson's writing, the novelist's untimely seclusion, my description of Fanny's sudden hostility and her peculiar question to me. And Belial, I suspected, more than anything. Not that Davenport would talk about any of it, lately less than ever. Instead, he was spending hours at a time in a laconic and expressionless state; he appeared suddenly plumper than he really was (this happened regularly with him, like phases of the moon). At Vailima, he had to play the part of the amiable visitor. When he was with me in our hut, he dropped all pretense and resembled one of the Stevensons' Buddhas.

Since Davenport's stony muteness in this period renders him rather resistant to all descriptions, I will return for a moment to an earlier point in time, and recount for you a conversation that occurred when he was in a more loquacious state. I had interrupted myself before— weren't you supposed to remind me, Mr. Clover?—when telling you of the time riding side by side when Davenport suddenly saw fit to finally answer a question of mine about whether he ever desired to be a writer. "Of course, every young man of a certain kind at a certain time in his life wishes to be a writer, often confusing eagerness and talent for reading with ability to write. You did not feel that way?"

"Who am I?" I replied. "It would never have crossed my mind."

"A born bookseller."

"How did your plans change?"

"About?"

I reminded him of the topic—his young self. "College," Davenport began, "was a bitter disappointment." At seventeen years old, he said, he knew with great passion what he did not want. He would not sit in a dusty chamber breathing the smoky air of a city street through a window while copying out legal documents. No, he would not share the destiny of other fellows who also had no fortunes to inherit. His would be a life of sophistication, a life of invitations into the best social circles and men of letters. He expected college to provide him with that.

Instead, Davenport explained to me, during his sophomore year he was accused of stealing. The matter had to do with a classmate, a rich bore named Halsey Alexander. The theft was that of a book, and the president of the faculty insisted Davenport confess. He did so, without coercion.

"Do you claim the book was yours?"

"No."

"Young man, I hope you understand the seriousness of this action. A student in our college is forbidden to steal. You must know that. Are you aware that it is a rare and priceless book? A family heirloom that belonged to his grandfather."

"Wait a minute there, just wait a minute. Professor, do you know where I found the book? It was propping open the window, the heavy pane crunching down the spine. Where I come from, books are rare treasures, and a book like this . . . Tell me honestly, do you think, sir, that Alexander deserves such a treasure?"

"Who do you think, young man, is in a position to judge that? A man from a family such as the Alexanders, or a man with an ancestry such as yours, a family of day laborers and wanderers?"

The president went on to insist that Davenport return the book at once and apologize for so basely insulting Alexander. Davenport handed over the book, shook the president's hand, and said he would not apologize were the earth to start orbiting Venus.

PREPARING FOR HIS DEPARTURE from Princeton, New Jersey, the latent ambition to be a writer increased by the minute. His departure, and its basis in the theft of a book, in retrospect pointed out his true destiny. The whole truth was, Davenport had no particular interest in book editions or in collecting books. His antagonism toward his classmate was against his ignorance and undeserved wealth.

Davenport would attain his goals not only for himself but also on behalf of anyone whose dreams had been buried.

"What in the land do you intend to do for funds?" Flowers, one of his college friends, had asked him when he announced his plan to go to Boston.

"Boston is an expensive place, Davenport," added in his roommate, Lank Bailey.

"See it this way, Davenport. Take a spot on the literary magazine here, make your name, then you'll find your place in Boston or New York later."

"That's a head on your shoulders, Flowers," Bailey said, applauding.

Davenport shook his head. He had not told them that the faculty had voted for him to leave for at least a year, and that he had decided he would never come back. "No, men. I shall not wait. Not a month, not a year, not another day. Writing, Lank, is about living—not living in luxury. Flowers, literature is about now. Its pulse comes from today, not yesterday or even tomorrow."

His fellow sophs stared glumly.

"Here, Lank, we merely kick our feet, hands in pockets, watching the active world move around us. I wish to move with it, from this point on."

"That's Emersonian enough," Bailey began. "See here, Davenport. If this is about what that fop Alexander said you did—"

"Not at all," Davenport interrupted, and waved all other objections away with his hand.

Once in Boston, Davenport waited patiently to hear when the stories he had sent ahead to *The Atlantic Monthly* would be published. After nearly a month, he received a letter from the editor.

He marched over to the famous bookshop that back then housed the magazine's offices. He described his business there to no fewer than four different people with vague positions of influence, and after what seemed to be an hour, he was ushered through a curtain to the messy chamber occupied by James T. Fields, the very man who had rejected his submissions. The big-bearded man was disarmingly enthusiastic as he explained the ways in which Davenport might tinker with his piece to make it more suitable for publication.

Before Davenport stepped out of the room, he saw something that sickened him. He was watching a man in an apron remove manuscripts from a large pile, glance through them, and discard them—all in a swift, almost unified motion. The apron made him look like a butcher and in the collegian's eyes he might have been covered in blood instead of ink. Davenport had felt reassured by what Fields had said to him and about his prospects, but now he realized it was a conversation the editor had ten times a week. He would never be published in *The Atlantic*. He knew all this the moment he laid eyes on the butcher.

Before he could think of it, Davenport watched himself as though from a distance, as his own fingers swiftly pulled some papers from a nearby desk and folded them neatly into the inside pocket of his raggedy coat. He felt unaccountably happier. His eyes turned to a small woman in a cream-colored bonnet, her eyes challenging him with their own accidental glance before she seemed to glide away.

He should have been contemplating the rote dismissal by the literary man and his own inexplicable theft, but instead he thought for hours about that face. Her eyes were certain, strong, wild. She seemed to be some mythological being whose gaze might transform you into some base animal, or disable your senses, or suit you in magical armor that would repel enemies.

In the days that followed his encounter at the publishing office, Davenport wandered. Gone was the sense of purpose and destiny he had brought to Boston. Every day he loitered in another place in this Athens of America. Every day he saw her. First, at the coffeehouse. Then inside the horse cars. And in the Common applauding a procession of Union soldiers who had returned home. She never looked at him directly, yet he was dismayed by the fact that she was everywhere. He lay awake at night. In those sleepless hours he came to believe that James T. Fields suspected him of his theft and had sent this pretty woman to spy on him before calling in the police.

Then a day passed without sight of her, and the fear flew right out of his mind. But still he could not sleep, and he walked the streets at night. To be a stranger in New York is to be like everyone else; to be a stranger in Boston is to feel what it is to be a stranger. It gives a man an unsubdued craving. He had worn out his only shoes. He stopped at a well-lit spot where he could study the face of some heroic and aloof soldier of the Revolution—he had not bothered to read the name on the base of the statue.

"You are a dull man."

He turned at the voice to see whom she was addressing. It would never have occurred to him that the words could have been directed at him; that was how far from dull he believed himself. Of course, it was the mythological woman from the publishing firm.

"You see me following you for days and instead of attempting to discover who I am, you try to escape. I suspect you escaped to Boston, too."

Davenport wanted to prove he knew more than she thought. "You were at Ticknor and Fields when I met with that cold-blooded liar, Mr. Fields. You believe I committed some wrong there, and hope that under your spell I will confess it."

"You fancy yourself important but you're not. You have never done anything in your life that would make you worthy of being followed. But that could change right now. I want you to do something for me."

"That's brash, miss." The truth was, the eighteen-year-old young man would have done anything she asked.

"Don't bother resenting the Boston literati. This city did not earn its place as a publishing center; it inherited it. That is why New York readies to overtake it, because it is craftier and more determined. I need a set of plates stolen from Houghton, *The Atlantic*'s printer."

"Why would you think I would help with such a thing?" He acted disgusted, though, for a reason he could not understand, he was not. Maybe because the writers printed in *The Atlantic* did not deserve to be, not like he did.

"The plates will be made and protected by the printers' devils. Women cannot be employed among those peculiar scum, which makes it difficult for me to gain entrance."

"But I can be one of the scum."

"You must be hired as a devil and then follow my instructions."

He shuffled his feet as though to get out of the trap she was setting.

"If you refuse, I will tell Fields about your theft."

He felt himself back in the president of the faculty's office. His outrage overtook him. "You haven't any evidence I ever stole anything. Nothing that would hold in a court of law."

She nodded and removed the proof sheet he had taken from the magazine offices.

"Where did you get that?" he asked.

"From your hotel room, Mr. Davenport. The room you are already behind four dollars on paying. This is your hand, is it not, in the margins, critiquing the poor quality of writing? You are very liberal in your exclamation marks. But I know something about you. You do not want to be a writer."

"Wait a minute. How are you so certain?" Her statement sent a nervous tremor through him.

She had an openmouthed grin. "Because you don't have to be. Writers must write and they suffer if they don't. Then they suffer if they do. It is no way to live, and if they could they would do something else, anything else. You can do something else—something that will give you far more control than those writers you admire." I ought to add that in person Kitten was just who she seemed to be; this was a peculiar trait for a woman who employed disguises and false identities from time to time in her profession, and I think people believed because, when it came to Kitten, you wanted to believe her. But there was no escaping the fact that she was going to take something in return for that faith; it was only a matter of when and how much.

"What is your name?" he asked with juvenile frustration. "I demand to know."

"I use one name in my temporary employment at the publishing firm. But in my profession, I have come to be known as Kitten."

"Kitten?" he repeated incredulously. "If I help you, Miss Kitten, then you return or destroy that paper and I am free of any further obligation," he said after taking a moment to think over the remarkable circumstance. "Then I will be free from playing your game any longer. Agreed?"

She agreed to terms, but perhaps both of them knew that his infatuation had begun: with her, with the new venture into which she was leading him. It would be several years before they would become romantically involved (exactly when is speculation, since Davenport would never talk about it directly), but the moment he took his first step away from the statue and toward her, their fates were interlocked.

IX

Our next visit brought a strange sight never seen at Vailima: the outside boys were standing around doing nothing. Davenport and I exchanged questioning glances. Dismounting before reaching the stables, we approached the cluster of young men. We could see now that they were staring across the property at Charlie. He was naked. Shouting. Swinging an ax. House servants had begun to creep out the front door, keeping a safe distance.

Stevenson came out on the verandah on the upper floor and looked at the scene with grave concern, first at the lunatic and then, angrily, at the rest of us who were standing around, as if to say, "Where are the men in this world?"

"What is he yelling?" Davenport asked.

"Pure nonsense," said Belial. He had come up from behind and was looking out between the two of us and listening to Charlie. "Something about . . . the devil being among us."

"Then he is not altogether insane."

"I never knew you to have a sense of humor, Davenport," Belial replied cheerfully. "Watch what is about to happen, Mr. Fergins. This is why your master will never win."

Belial ran toward Charlie. Slowing down at just the right spot, he stepped carefully around the naked native until he saw his opening and tackled him, sending the ax flying out of his hand. The rest of the servants converged on the fallen native and the heroic missionary. I looked up to the verandah and saw a satisfied expression on Stevenson's face, and, without turning to see, I could feel white rage coming from Davenport.

IT MAY BE SURPRISING to hear that the very first person in history I would classify as a bookaneer appeared long before the first copyright law, and managed to call down the ire of the most powerful man in the world. In 1514, Pope Leo X, an accomplished book collector, granted exclusive papal permission to a printer named Beroaldo to reproduce the works of Tacitus. The punishment for any who defied this order was excommunication. Hundreds of miles away in Milan, one Alesandro Manuziano began printing the same book of Tacitus before Beroaldo was finished—from what I can learn, probably having bribed one of Beroaldo's employees for the material. Manuziano only escaped excommunication through the intercession of friends. But the question isn't his punishment. The question is why Manuziano did it. There was profit to be made, yes, but one must also consider that the prohibition simply ate at his heart. I have not yet found a portrait of Manuziano, and I wonder if it would enlighten us as to what kind of man he was. Until I do, I cannot help but imagine this forerunner with the leathery but handsome face of Belial.

Belial's choice of roles at Vailima, as usual, resulted from an incisive calculation. By establishing himself as a missionary who traveled among the various Samoan and other South Sea islands, he had reason for leaving the island at regular intervals. At first, I could not understand why he would want this, before realizing it afforded him the opportunity to secure precious tobacco from busier harbors. But there was more to it. Stevenson, like many writers, grew tired of any one topic or person easily, as we had witnessed. But in the case of Belial, any periods of waning interest by Stevenson would be reduced by the would-be missionary's frequent trips off island.

Besides, whenever there was trouble at Vailima, Belial could step in because of his missionary collar. When Charlie ran amok, there was earnest Father Thomas to subdue him. When the poor servant was back in the stables, from that point on placed in restraints, it was Belial, as missionary, who prayed over him. The expression waiting just under the surface of Davenport's face increasingly became, to say it lightly, volcanic. Though I cautioned him to stay clear of Fanny until we could determine whether she had discovered something about us, he ignored me and again volunteered to help her tend to Charlie in order to keep one eye on Belial; in fact, Davenport was inside the stable almost as much as Fanny and the hoary natives they called doctors. I sat inside that dim, cramped wooden structure as much as I could bear. Stevenson was clearly troubled. His movements became jerkier and less even when something weighed on his mind. He announced he was going to a village some distance away from Vailima to procure more of the special herbs the doctors had ordered for the servant.

"Can these herbs be trusted to be effective?" Davenport asked.

"It's worth trying, and Jack is rather anxious to go for a ride, anyway," Stevenson said, gathering some supplies to lash onto his horse's saddle. "He is a bit of a dandy and likes to be seen by polite society."

"I will happily accompany you, Tusitala," Belial said.

"No. Charlie needs you. He has always been a young man of great faith in the Lord you preach."

"I do not like to think of you going on your own," Belial tried again.

"I *could* stand some company, and John Chinaman is occupied finishing some work on the west end of the property," Stevenson replied. He turned to us. "Perhaps my other white gentlemen. Mr. Fergins? Mr. Porter?"

This time Belial's usefulness worked to our benefit by keeping him tied to Vailima. We agreed to ride with Stevenson (to my surprise, Davenport seemed reluctant and almost teary-eyed leaving the suffering native's side in the stables). When Belial turned to wish us good luck a flicker of annoyance marred his composure. As we exited, Charlie moaned, his brow bubbling up with beads of hot sweat.

That day we rode along difficult paths. I wouldn't even consider half of them as having been cleared, and I know our horses would have agreed with me. The wilderness grew aggressively in Samoa as soon as there was a clearing made in it. I thought that either Stevenson or Stevenson's horse was sick and might collapse, the novelist's ride was so wobbly. But I realized this was simply the way wild Jack moved and, in fact, because the animal's body and legs shifted position so frequently it was perfectly suited to the uneven terrain.

We came alongside one village that appeared to have been destroyed by a fire in the recent past. In spots the putrid smell of burnt animals still lingered.

"What happened to this place, Tusitala?"

"The Germans ordered it set afire, Mr. Fergins," said Stevenson.

"The entire village?"

"Yes. The villagers here and a few other places had torn down a proclamation ordering them to swear fealty to Tamasese and renounce Mataafa, the former king."

Passing out of the ruins and through a small village farther down the same road, it was a relief to notice people occupying the huts, but a collective tension rose with our presence—natives with rifles were slowly coming out onto the verandahs.

"Soi fua," Davenport greeted a native man who passed our horses with a cold stare.

"Your Samoan comes along," said Stevenson.

"I am trying."

"That is what is important, to give a damn, as you Americans say. I used to admire the adventure books of Herman Melville until I realized how poorly he had mangled the names of the Marquesians and Tahitians," commented Stevenson. "He didn't even try for accuracy, as far I could tell. The romance of it mattered more than the real people."

Anxious to be free of this village, I spurred my horse to pick up the pace.

"What's the use of having eyes if we can't see the world we pass through?"

"Yes, Tusitala." I slowed my animal from a gallop to a trot, when what I really desired was a harum-scarum scamper.

Davenport knew what was on my mind. "They seem rather well armed here," he said.

"Where there are traders, there will be ammunition. Aphorism—by Tusitala."

"Perhaps they do not like foreigners in this village," I said, as a way of suggesting we go back or change our route.

"No, they don't. Certain foreigners, anyway," Stevenson answered me. "Then again, were I a Samoan, I like to think I would advocate the massacre of all white people for what they've done here."

"Tusitala!" I cried.

"They have seen white person after white person come and lie and manipulate them and rob them of their resources and lives. These particular villages are loyal to Tamasese, the sacred puppet who is beholden to the German consulate and their slave plantations. That is why they are suspicious of us. It is a widespread rumor that at Vailima we favor the position of the opposing rebels and their exiled king, Mataafa, and plan one day for his return."

"Isn't that the case?"

"Oh, yes, Mr. Fergins, most definitely. Rumors are usually best ignored but also are usually true, you know." By now our host sensed our nerves growing as more hostile faces of men with axes and rifles multiplied on all sides. He was never one to try to assuage fears during our time in Samoa; in fact, it seemed to me he was enjoying ours when he commented, "I guess the three of us will have to be the whole revolution, should it start today. But perhaps we ought to change the topic."

"Please," I urged.

My mistake. Stevenson went on to a point that I had hoped to avoid: "A man named Lionel Hines came to the house recently. Grotesque man."

"I'm sorry to hear you have any unpleasant callers," Davenport said, expertly skating around the fact we knew Hines. It seemed there was more on Stevenson's mind, and I wondered if bringing us out here, putting us in this vulnerable atmosphere, was more deliberate than it seemed. If Hines had said something about one of us that I hadn't been able to hear. . . I looked over and could tell Davenport's thoughts followed the same track. "Did the man say something to . . . cause you distress, Tusitala?"

"He did," he said, slowing down a little more. "Oh, that Hines is all wheels and no horse. But he carried a wire that he picked up for me from the British consul. It was a warning. There is a movement back in England to have me deported from Samoa."

"Whatever for?"

"As an appeasement to the Germans, Mr. Fergins. As I'm certain you've come to understand by now, they are the Gulliver among the Lilliputians here. The Germans have never liked what they call my interference on the island and their ambassadors in London have pressured the British parliament to do something about it. Me, caught in the talons of politics! Success in the political field appears to be nothing more than the organization of failure enlivened with defamation of character. It is awfully funny—no, I change my mind; it is sad. Nobody but these cursed liars could have so driven me. I cannot bear liars."

"What would happen if the measure passed the legislature?" I asked.

"Simply stated, I would have to leave Samoa immediately or be arrested. My family, also. Belle would surely be pleased, she is so anglified. She misses life in a city with its glamour and sameness. As for Fanny, well, when she feels well enough she adapts to island life quite a bit more than she will admit. She thinks she has followed me here, but sometimes I think she led us all. It is either gold or poison, to be here."

"There are worse punishments than returning to Scotland," Davenport said.

Stevenson threw back his head and made a slow murmuring sound. "If only I could secure a violent death."

"Pardon?"

"What a fine success!" Stevenson continued, spurring Jack into a canter as he lost himself in his thoughts. "I wish to die in my boots, you see, Mr. Porter. To be drowned, to be shot, to be thrown from this horse into a ditch, Mr. Fergins—aye, to be hanged, rather than pass through the slow dissolution of illnesses!"

"High heaven forbid, Tusitala!" It was startling to hear a man—a great man—talk about dying in such a cavalier way. This speechifying about his own death continued as we went through a poorly cut path through the bushes, until we came upon a sight that made him quiet and would have made me scream if I had not lost my ability to make any sound. Three stakes had been speared into the ground, a human head on each of them.

Stevenson removed his old yachting cap from his head. He was guiding Jack around the sight in a circle and studying it with a scientist's eye. "'Lord, what fools these mortals be,'" he said. Then he dismounted. "Fresh," he reported evenly.

I turned the head of my horse away. Davenport, jaw slack, actually inched his animal closer to the horrible display, though his boots were twitching, ready to spur away from it. "How on earth do you know that?" asked the bookaneer, swallowing hard. "How do you know the heads are fresh, Tusitala?"

"I have seen enough of them on the island to know. When war comes to Samoa, Mr. Porter, heads are taken. Those must not be more than a week or two old."

I forced myself to look again and tried to examine the horrible sight, but quickly concluded there was nothing to learn from their neutral, almost bored faces. The skin was very dark and the thick hair blown by the breeze. I had to choke down the breakfast rushing up my throat.

"But the Samoans are not in a war," I protested when I found my voice.

"Not at present, Mr. Fergins, no. The natives never want a war; it benefits no one but the white officials. But the foreign powers are always blowing the coals at each other. In fact, they say that when the next war comes, it will begin with the killing of all the whites. In any matter, those heads were not taken from Samoans; you can tell from the skin."

"Then who were these poor souls?"

"They are Solomon Islanders, Mr. Fergins. Men rounded up forcibly from a group of islands not far from here, past Fiji, to work on the German plantations."

"We've heard about them before," chimed in Davenport, "from Cipaou, our native man, and from Thomas."

"Cannibals, so it is said. It is funny to see the disgust and terror the Samoans have for cannibals, even as they will sever a head from its body."

"What happened to those three?"

"They must have escaped from the Germans, and been caught by the Samoans they control, the king's men. This is a warning. The Firm would have you believe it has almost never happened that their laborers—slaves, for all intents and purposes—have escaped."

"Is it untrue?" I asked.

"Past that deep valley"—Stevenson gestured—"across a very fast-moving river, and through the forest that borders it, there is a hive of fugitives from the Firm. These men must have been traveling to take shelter there when they were overtaken."

"So this warning . . ." Davenport began.

"Is for any other laborer who tries to escape and for men like me—us—to mind my own affairs."

Suddenly, Jack reared up with a terrible snort and began walking on his hind legs like a man. It was an unreal sight with the heads as audience.

"Your horse!" I called. "Tusitala, there's something wrong with your horse!"

"Oh, there's nothing wrong with Jack, Mr. Fergins." Stevenson took the reins and tugged twice. The animal gave a complaining whinny and planted his hooves back on the ground. "He was just bored because we were standing around too long."

"Bored? A horse?"

"Terribly so. You see," Stevenson explained as he returned to the saddle, "Jack was a circus horse in his prime. The circus came to Samoa but Jack didn't sail well, so the performers sold him before they folded up their tent and left the island. Sometimes he does his tightrope trick or his dancing for old time's sake." He patted the horse warmly. "You're safe," he cooed to the animal. "He is really quite converted, and is as steady as a doctor's cob. When he has to be fast, he is the fastest animal you have ever seen." The novelist began to hum a melody so silly I guessed it had to be a tune he had heard at Jack's old circus.

I was still hearing the ridiculous tune and seeing the horrible heads hours later at Vailima when we were seated at dinner. Belial said grace. I could not pay much attention to it nor to Fanny, though her discussion of a new plan for her garden—where she would put tomato seeds, and artichoke, and eggplant—was a welcome distraction.

"You were born to be in the garden, Barkis," Stevenson said.

Her hand froze before her cup reached her lips. "What do you mean to say, Louis?" she asked with a sidelong glance.

"Just that. You have the soul of a peasant," he said cheerfully, "not because you love working in the earth, but because you like to know it is your own earth that you are delving in."

"But you are not of a peasant soul. Only me. Is it so?"

The rest of the room, even the native servants, watched with dread as Stevenson sipped his 'ava and considered how to answer.

"Now, now, mother," Lloyd tried to interject with his meandering, lackadaisical calm, "what is it we're talking about here?"

"I am an artist," Stevenson answered his wife bluntly.

"It is a *lovely* garden, if I may interject," I tried, but I don't think anyone heard.

"Louis—" Lloyd tried again.

"Well, I suppose if I had the soul of an artist, instead of that of a peasant, the stupidity of possessions would have no power over me. You may be more right than you know."

"Barkis, my dear fellow, you misunderstand," he offered, a little late. "You know I think you are the most beautiful woman in the world."

Before any of us had more than a few bites of the first course of stewed beef and potatoes, the tension was broken by the sound of screaming.

"Can we not even sup in peace around here?" Belle said with a petulant toss of her fork. "If it is not arguing over some patches of brown grass, it's another loony islander to interrupt us."

"Quiet, Belle. That's Charlie," Fanny said.

The noises were coming from the stables. Davenport, unnerved from what we had already witnessed today, appeared ashen and turned whiter as the melancholy sounds continued. We all got up and walked in a line to the stables to investigate.

"Poor, poor Charlie," Stevenson said, leading us inside.

Inside the paddock the servant was bound to a makeshift bed at his ankles and wrists. He had become horribly gaunt and continued to perspire heavily even as Fanny rotated wet rags on his head and body. Two doctors, covered in more tattoos than the warriors, looked him over, chanting heathen songs, sprinkling some herbs into his mouth and ears, rubbing and kneading pungent arrowroot pulp into his skin. Belial placed himself next to them, delivering an urgent prayer. A few of the other servants were sitting nearby, heeding all of Fanny's instructions. Belle clutched her hands to her heart.

"I'm afraid we'll have no choice now but to keep Charlie restrained," Fanny said, her voice breaking. "We have had the best native doctor here three times to administer the herbs and other stronger medicines from the bush, but since the day he began acting like a lunatic Charlie's fever has not broken and he remains delirious. He is a danger to himself and to the others."

"I fear you will think we are a sort of imitation Wuthering Heights with all this drama."

"Not at all, Tusitala," Davenport assured him. "I only hope the boy recovers—and soon."

"I will not let a young man die in Vailima under my care," Fanny said, with tears in her eyes but with a robust voice. "Not in Vailima."

The noises that came from Charlie could be described only as yelps. Belle appeared faint at the dire condition of the man. She stumbled back and Davenport steadied her.

"Thank you," she whispered, folding herself into his arm.

"Your mother is right, Miss Strong. He will recover," Davenport said with the conviction of a promise.

That night, the conch sounded a mournful cry. Charlie had died, consumed by fever. His funeral out on the grounds was presided over by Belial. Even his big voice was nearly drowned out by the sobbing of the mourners from Vailima. Stevenson was bedridden for hours the next day, Fanny inconsolable. For all I felt over the loss of a young man with so much life in him, I was taken by the depth of sorrow in Davenport, a man who usually swallowed his emotions. He could hardly speak—this time not as a result of a stubborn or petulant mood, but because he was moved. Or so I thought. When he secluded himself in our dismal hut among the spiders and roaches and the howling wind beating at the shutters, I had a new thought. I began to suspect I had missed something.

"Davenport, I insist you tell me what's really happened."

"Damned fools," he said, banging his fist violently on one of the beams that supported our walls. He was sitting on the floor and his head was hanging low.

"You believe it was Belial," I said. "That's it, isn't it? That he caused this somehow? I do not know why I did not see it before. But no. No. I accept your great rivalry with him, but consider it with a clearer head. Would he do that to Charlie? Just to ingratiate himself further into the Stevensons' household by ministering to him, then by comforting them after he died? No, I do not believe it."

He raised his head toward me very slowly. His eyes were red with tears.

I realized at once what this was about, before he confessed.

"You're a fool to think Belial wouldn't do such a thing. But he did not. I did." He closed his eyes and let out a sigh from deep in his chest. "Charlie. Damned Charlie saw me searching through the papers in Stevenson's library, after I came across those original pages from *Jekyll and Hyde.* The damned dog was always sneaking up right behind us silent as Golgotha. You see how loyal the natives are to Stevenson. Charlie was likely to talk sooner or later, and Stevenson's slowed pace with his book meant there was more and more time for Charlie to reveal something that could sabotage us. I had to do *something.*"

"You gave Charlie the mixture you gave me onboard the ship, didn't you?"

He shook his head again. "No, a different one. Stronger. But still quite . . . well, harmless enough."

He gestured weakly toward a square leather case in his trunk. I opened it to find several rows of glass vials of powders and oily liquids. "I wasn't the first person you sedated, then."

"That case accompanies me on the most precarious missions, and I was well trained by an apothecary who had assisted Kitten and some of the finest bookaneers of old. My preference is to leave this untouched, and I have concealed it from you in the past because I knew you would disapprove. But there are, on occasion, people who need to be safely removed or kept temporarily quiet on a mission. Never before have I had a problem with these. Harmless as a blank shot. You must have known; you must have at least guessed I had some methods out of your view. Didn't you, Fergins?"

"Why is Charlie dead, if it's all so harmless?"

As usual when pushed, Davenport shifted blame. "Those damned herbal leaves and ointments from the island the witch doctors were giving him. The combination of those tinctures with what I gave him just seemed to make him sicker and sicker at every turn of their so-called treatments. I merely wanted him out of the way until Stevenson was finished writing—I thought if nosy Charlie fell ill briefly, Stevenson might send him away to his home village for a couple of weeks to recover, or at least would think him confused if he mentioned anything about seeing me dipping into his papers. What should have happened is they left him to get better himself, without their potions. Those so-called doctors concluded that a devil spirit had entered his head through his ears. Damned savage fools, this whole island is full of damned fools who never so much as laid their hands on a book!"

I had not seen him so distraught since Kitten's disappearance. I suppose I should have offered words of comfort, some wisdom of an older friend that could assuage his mind from the torment it inflicted on itself. But I could only think of poor, kindhearted Charlie, bound by sheets and straps, his hands and legs trembling uncontrollably, his oncoming death chilling his blood and ours. My thoughts then turned to the black dots that had overtaken my vision, to the collapse that had stolen the life from me for nearly two days aboard the *Colossus*. Charlie was me, unluckier.

The bookaneer was in shambles on the floor of our hut, actually pulling out his hair in thick handfuls. I heard him call my name out before I exited, but I did not pause to show that I heard him. I withheld even that. I walked out of the hut, and kept walking along the bank of the stream, though after a quarter of an hour I had only the light of the moon, and I was hearing strange noises in the bush, which I hoped were just the tree frogs and crickets. There was such a strong wind my spectacles were pinned hard against my face and filling with dust. I took them off and I closed my eyes, the soothing breath of the stream becoming the roar of the Thames, then our little winding stream again. Coming from nowhere, leading nowhere. Never had I felt so pried away from home. My life, so it seemed, was somewhere on the other side, the stream impassable.

Even after I heard a rider approaching, it took me a moment to consider how unusual that was out here, especially as night fell. By the time I had gathered myself, I watched the slow approach of a medium-sized black mare I had seen around Vailima, and a blurred figure riding sidesaddle. I fished my spectacles out from between the buttons of my vest. There was a lamp hanging from the saddle of the horse. Fanny Stevenson wore mourning black.

I helped the short but muscular woman down. I braced myself for the confrontation that had been waiting to occur for several days now, though I still did not know what had prompted it. Had Charlie somehow told her about Davenport's snooping while she was tending to him? Had she come to discover it through other means? Perhaps she had found something else: our true purpose in being in Samoa, or worse, Davenport's negligence and its role in Charlie's death.

There was no forthcoming recrimination, nor was there an explanation given for her appearing at our remote plot of land. Instead, she began peering around with her light with a surveyor's concentration. Though my anger toward Davenport still burned high, part of me hoped he had heard the approach and would come out to save me from saying the wrong thing.

"I have not been here before, Mr. Fergins," she finally said. "Do you have many birds flocking here? They say that the last dodo birds in the world are somewhere on these islands."

"I have seen some ducks, and a pigeon or two. Dodos?"

"Yes. It would be delightful to possess the last dodo on earth for a pet, though our cats might have a different opinion."

"Fanny, once again, if I may express to you my condolences about Charlie, and say how admirable your nursing of the poor fellow was."

She remained distracted by the flora and fauna illuminated by her lamp. "The lima beans started coming up today in my garden, and some of the cantaloupes are ready. I brought one for you and Mr. Porter. Here."

I accepted the gift she had carried in a saddlebag.

Her face tightened. "Mr. Fergins, you know that I welcomed your presence around Vailima from the time of your arrival. I have not been able to speak freely for fear of Louis hearing, but I have tried to warn you."

"Please go on, Fanny." Still worried I might place the mission in jeopardy, I glanced around furtively but there was no sign of Davenport. "Should we speak inside our cottage?"

I balanced the large melon on my hip and we began to walk side by side, but she guided me farther from the cottage. "No, let us stay outside. I cannot stay very long before I am missed. Besides, my warning is for you, and concerns Mr. Porter. I had one of our outside boys watching your cottage so I knew when I could speak to you alone. I am afraid for your safety."

"How do you mean?"

"When you first arrived with Mr. Porter, I understood you gentlemen were passing through. You know how rare visitors are out here, and can imagine why I was so anxious to find out the latest news from Britain and Europe from you. But then there came a change in his eyes."

"Tusitala's?" I asked.

Her own eyes flashed with urgency as she turned toward me. "Mr. Porter's. The island infected him. Just as it had my Louis long before you came."

"Do you mean to suggest some kind of tropical illness?"

She grabbed my wrist. "I mean something far more dangerous than fever, than the hurricanes or even the most warlike of the savages— well, I do not like to call them that—it is the effect of being here for too long on certain white men. How do I explain it? It . . . casts a spell . . ." She shook her head and tried again. "Returns a man to his primal state. Louis thinks my peasant soul comes out when I work on the land, but it is men who become drunk with dominion over the earth and soon are ready to sell their trousers and douse themselves in coconut oil. Their imagination grows out of proportion to real life. It is why Louis likes to write here, because he feels free of all constraints. But it is also what scares me down in my bones. You see it in the foreign consuls who seek power here, in the missionaries, and now in my husband and your friend. Vailima is no longer just a home we built for our family; it is an ancestral home—and we are the ancestors. Don't you see it forming in his eyes? In Mr. Porter's?"

I adjusted the fruit, which became heavier as I thought about her frantic questions.

"That melon—I brought the seeds with me to Samoa, you know. Look at it again, Mr. Fergins," she went on, her bushy eyebrows curling downward with impatience. I held it up and the lamplight went right through it, as though it were a round, fat telescope. My fingers touched the hollow, slimy middle of the melon.

"The rats have been eating through them. A rich and beautiful fruit from this infertile ground, but the core is eaten away by invisible forces."

She began hurrying back toward the tree where she had tied her horse. I shifted my balance and caught up with her. "I can assure you, Fanny, we have no plans to stay indefinitely. Mr. Porter's work, the book he wishes to write, simply takes time."

"I must go before I am missed. They say that after two months in Samoa, a white man will go mad. If you wish to save yourself, then see to it that you both leave this place quickly. You must promise me that." In her gaze and her imploring voice, I saw the stern mother in her, and understood how both of her grown children had trouble leaving her side.

THE NEXT THREE DAYS and nights Davenport barely said a word, and I must admit I did not try very hard to persuade him to break his silence. Of course, I told him of Fanny Stevenson's visit and my conversation with her, but he had so little to say in reply that this exchange deepened the chasm between us. The longer we avoided talking, the harder it was to try. What would you do about it, Mr. Clover?

—*About what, Mr. Fergins?*

If your friend were responsible for such a ... horrible ... wretched ... such a tragic death, how would you have proceeded?

—*I suppose I would have just the same thoughts as you. How could he still be a friend of mine after that? I would have marched right out the door and run away, very far away, as Mrs. Stevenson urged you to do.*

I told you the story enters dark places. So you would have jettisoned him altogether?

—*Yes, exactly. Why, I would have asked Cipaou to take me to the British consulate and make immediate arrangements to go home.*

I see what you mean, Mr. Clover. But here is what you overlook. He is already a friend; that cannot change in the blink of an eye. A man takes a wife "for better or for worse," and a friend comes with hardly less responsibility, sometimes more. Remember, I had agreed to assist in the success of this Samoan adventure, no matter what else happened. Sometimes, adversity requires increased commitment. Observing him in agony on the floor of our hut, I feared for what would happen to him.

I can recall other times over the years when I worried about his mental well-being a good deal. In the period after he lost Kitten, Davenport was adrift. He drank too much, he accepted missions that he would have never ordinarily considered from men who once upon a time would have made him turn up his nose. I remember one occasion in particular: he asked me to find out the location of a rather disreputable book reviewer, a man who dressed like a cheap poet and chewed tobacco like an American. A publisher had hired Davenport to pay this fellow a visit. It was Davenport's assignment to remind the reviewer that he had been paid to puff—to write a positive review, in layman's terms—a new book, after a rumor had been overheard that he was, in fact, composing a rather scathing one. This was the sort of mission usually only taken by one of the lowest class of bookaneers, the so-called barnacles. Davenport was so mastered by drink that I had to escort him to the address in a suburb of London or he wouldn't have found it. I heard a tumult inside and ran into the house. When the critic scoffed at Davenport's demand, the bookaneer struck him in the head, but it turned out the reviewer was also an Oxford pugilist. I had to pull the fellow off the bookaneer and peel my companion, bloodied, from the imitation Turkish rug.

I grew quite concerned about the health of the Samoan mission. We had not been back to Vailima since Charlie was buried and had no intelligence about what was happening there. And each day, as the death of Charlie began to seem more part of the past than of the present, the object of my sorrow began to shift from the lost servant to the despair of my companion. I carefully formulated a statement of reassurance that ran something like this: "It was not your intention, Davenport, to do the young native harm, and you mustn't blame yourself for doing what you had to do in the name of a mission." I hoped this might help him surrender those burdens he had brought upon himself, and allow him to move forward with what could still be accomplished. When I finally prepared to say this, it was no use; he spoke over me.

"Fergins, I am quite tired of so many delays," he said, a glimmer in his eye that had not been present since before the funeral. He was looking with intensity at the upper beams holding up our iron roof. He reached up and idly brushed his hand against it. He might have been studying the vaulted ceilings of an ancient cathedral. "Tired. Collect some fruit and prepare our trunks. We are finished with this place."

"Davenport? You want me to go out and collect fruit in the dark?"

He stepped onto the wooden plank that formed the threshold of our hut, outlined by the darkness, pushing his face against the onslaught of wind. "You can manage. I have already sent for Cipaou to deliver a farewell card to Stevenson. We're leaving first thing in the morning, as soon as Cipaou comes." He ducked his head as he moved inside and said no more.

That night, I lay awake thinking of what might happen next, when Davenport began to thrash . . . groan . . . cry out . . . even (so it sounded) weep. I did not have the heart when morning came to ask him what it was he had seen in his dreams. Later, while mired in disaster, he revealed to me that he had dreamt of Kitten in her final hours.

Whether by virtue of illness, death, incarceration, or the twilight of the profession itself, every bookaneer had a last mission, but it was rare that the mission brought about the end. Such was the unusual destiny of Kitten, a woman who believed destiny was a comfort for the weak minded. I remember hearing the first rumblings about her fateful endeavor during the summer of 1882. It was late at night and I was dog tired when Davenport finally entered the drawing room at the Hogarth Club, with its big chairs and long rugs. I was waiting to hand over a biographical listing he needed for an important negotiation in order to prove a contested item was not a forgery. But he hardly looked in my direction and had no interest in the document that was the product of hours in the damp closets of libraries and antiquarians' attics. He tilted back the strong drink I'd ordered him and snapped his fingers for the waiter to bring another before he slammed the empty glass to the table. In a few minutes he had produced more noise, without saying a word, than I had heard in the room during the previous two hours.

Davenport's moods were always unpredictable, but I knew something had gone wrong when he voluntarily started to talk about Kitten. He said that Kitten had been hired to go abroad and search out a series of manuscript pages that had been believed lost for more than sixty years. The facts seemed rather unremarkable in themselves and did not justify his agitation.

"She will receive market value for the pages? Then why—"

"From what she tells me, in fact, the offer made to her is generous, quite generous."

"In that case, what—"

Again he interrupted. "Never search for any kind of Holy Grail, Fergins. It is the sort of thing done by your onetime friend Whiskey Bill, who has been unable to forget the legends of Poe's lost novel, which is exactly why Bill is no more useful than a squeezed orange or a spent bullet."

"Well, if Kitten, who is as experienced as any bookaneer, judges it conducive—"

"She taught me that. Yes. Avoid the Holy Grail, the heroic journeys, the pursuit of a legend—that is not the life of the bookaneer, who must keep his eyes on the ground while other book people live by dreaming. A mission such as this could drag on and become a drain that ruins a bookaneer's fortunes."

I spoke quicker and completed a question. "Who has hired her for it, and what is it, exactly?"

"An anonymous collector. Shelley, that's what they're after, Fergins."

His personal concern for Kitten, which reached a near-hysterical pitch at the Hogarth that night, put away the canard that he could ever separate her professional life from his own. This is what you would not hear him say: "Without any good reason in particular, I have a feeling of dread about this." He never admitted a superstitious emotion. But I knew enough of Pen Davenport that it was exactly how his words sounded in my ears.

As for the object of her mission, it was indeed a bookaneer's version of a Holy Grail. It was something talked about for a long time but never proven to actually exist. The collector was pursuing Mary

Shelley's lost short story, sometimes referred to as a novelette, of *Frankenstein* she finished in the summer of 1816 before writing the novel itself, which would then be completed the following year. Short stories, notebooks, outlines, scribbles, even crude stick-figure drawings made in connection with an important work could command great prices—sometimes higher than pages of a finished manuscript—because these raw materials entered directly into the author's thoughts. A half-page list of potential titles Charles Dickens had scrawled out for his unfinished work, *The Mystery of Edwin Drood*, for instance, has been bought and sold in public—and purloined and copied and bartered in secret—more times than any other item related to that book.

Though an author such as Mrs. Shelley lived so much more recently than, say, Shakespeare or Dante, that does not diminish the value of materials related to her work. In fact, *Frankenstein* was such an unexpected and unprecedented success that the original documents were at best sloppily preserved and collected at the time, making their later recovery more difficult and their value dearer. Frankenstein's creature, as a literary creation, stood alone in its originality, one of the reasons for that novel's incredibly enduring popularity. To find Mary Shelley's story that originated it would rate with the top two or three discoveries by any bookaneer, certainly in modern times, maybe in history.

The novelette was presumed destroyed by bibliographers until some pages of the late Mrs. Shelley's diary rediscovered in the late 1860s in the drawer of a discarded desk suggested it could be extant. The collector who'd hired Kitten had come into possession of a fresh clue where to search. Armed with this information, Kitten left England less than a week after I heard about it from Davenport. Bookaneers did not tell their own tales, but from what I understood her expedition was less eventful than Davenport had expected. She was gone only two and a half months, all told, and by all accounts met with great success. She found Shelley's novelette. And when the intermediaries for the collector received the novelette from her, as promised they passed the enormous payment on to the victorious bookaneer. All of this transpired without complications. I remember seeing Kitten at a distance during the period after her return to London; perhaps it was my imagination, but she seemed buoyant.

That was the beginning of the end.

I had to leave for some travels to conduct some business at Davenport's behest, and when I returned to London he was in as wretched a state as I had seen in the ten years I'd known the man.

He didn't stop moving as I tried to talk with him, and I could not follow his broken line of discussion. "Mark this, Fergins . . . someone has lured her into a scrape. . . . Someone has done it!"

He went up and down his rooms, pacing, I thought, until I realized he was plucking up clothes, maps, and scraps of writing paper. I recognized these scraps: they had been accumulated over many years, and written on them were the locations of trusted men and women in every quarter of the world.

"Calm yourself, Davenport, please. If we can just talk about this calmly, I am certain . . . If you could just stand still and explain . . ."

"Calmly! She's missing. Kitten—she's gone missing!"

"On a confidential mission," I suggested.

"I'm not a fool, Fergins. I know when she is on a mission. She has been lured into something, I promise you. She was so distracted by her mission for the Shelley papers that she must not have noticed some trouble was brewing against her." There was a whistle that rose up from below the window. Davenport glanced down to the street, then took my hand and gave it a hard, affectionate squeeze, as unexpected as a slap in the face. "I've pinned some instructions for you on the wall next to the fireplace, Fergins. Mind my affairs for a while. You are the only man I trust in London. I do not have time to answer any of your questions but one: I am going to find Kitten and bring her home."

"But go where? Davenport, you cannot simply walk out the door without so much as a . . ."

I listened to his footsteps on the stairs as long as they could be heard. Just like that, he was gone, and the circumstances of Kitten's disappearance still a mystery to me.

X

⸻◆◇◆⸻

The morning we unceremoniously left our cottage with nothing more than half a biscuit and coffee in my stomach, I was exhausted, having spent more than an hour gathering fruit before going to sleep and then lying awake wondering about the nightmares that ravaged Davenport. I was so hungry and groggy, I nearly nodded off as I followed in the hoof steps of Cipaou's and Davenport's horses. I had to tie my spectacles behind my head to keep them from being blown off. I tried a few times to ask Davenport where we were going, having to wait until the narrow paths widened enough to fit next to his horse, and even then I had to shout over the gusts.

"I told you," he said, shouting back (having to raise his voice made him angry), "that I am tired. We are going to Apia, and I want no discussion."

"So the mission will be aborted? Left to Belial to complete?" I asked, offended by the idea. "We have come so far. A shrug? Is that your response?"

There is not much more of this conversation to report, because the ride was increasingly slow and tedious due to the trees and branches that were tossed around by the shrieking wind. Our horses lowered their heads and stretched themselves out. The horizon was an eerie movement of black and purple, as if the night had never fully made space for day. Finally, Cipaou blocked our way with his horse, and after Davenport demanded an explanation, the loyal Samoan announced the tempest was so dangerous that we had to return to the cottage. I expected bullheaded Davenport, if only because he had engineered this ride, might argue, but he pulled his horse back and complied. Maybe he was relieved to retreat; maybe after he'd had a chance to think he knew we had come too far to throw away his mission. This was rather perfect for Davenport. It gave him a way to retract his decision without admitting he was wrong.

By the time we were finally approaching the cottage again, my eyelids were heavy, my limbs numb, and this time I actually fell asleep on horseback. I would have tumbled right to the ground if the shout of Cipaou had not woken me. I shook myself but remained in a state of dreamlike confusion: there was our plot of land, but the cottage had vanished. Once we came closer, we found the wind had blown the little place over into a pile of ruins. This ridiculous ride, this petulant whim of Davenport's, had probably saved our lives. It had happened again: his instincts were right even when all of the reasons were wrong.

"The devil has visited this house!" Cipaou cried.

Cipaou was distressed about the discovery but even more distressed about the prospects of finding other shelter before the wind became so strong the horses would refuse to continue, and before the rains fell. We crossed the stream that formed the border of the property, and after another hour came upon some of Stevenson's outside boys collecting his cows, which had scattered. Cipaou spoke with these young men and then returned to us.

"Vailima is the closest shelter safe for white men. Come, follow me!"

Our attempted flight to Apia had brought us all the way back to Vailima, where the outside boys immediately stabled our horses and rushed us to the front door as though expecting us. Stevenson watched all of it with his face pressed against the window and came to greet us.

"I received your card saying that you planned to leave the island," he said, mulling the notion over with a curious expression. Even so, he did not seem surprised to have us on his doorstep.

"I'm afraid we didn't go very far, after all," Davenport said. "Our hut could not withstand the winds."

"Nor would you have gone much farther until the first storm comes and goes," Stevenson said flatly. "My white gentlemen," he said, this time the phrase a gentle critique of our inexperience, "as soon as my boys returned with the tidings that your hut tumbled down, I have had them on the ready for your arrival."

The skies were shrieking against the windows with heavy gusts, as though to say that we had arrived just in time.

"We will not inconvenience you long. I understand the Germans have a few vacant houses available on the other side of the island. As soon as we can, we will ride that way. I know they are involved in rather shady activities on their plantation, Tusitala, but I'm afraid we must rely on their generosity."

"Generosity!"

The novelist was outraged by Davenport applying that word to his political rivals on the island. In no time at all, Stevenson was giving orders to various servants for us to stay at the house and to accommodate Cipaou, though our servant declined, insisting on continuing to ride toward his own family. Fanny passed by on her way to another part of the house and, hearing the news of our staying on, gave a nod. She did not say anything, and I had to imagine she felt insulted that her warnings had been ignored.

I did not have time to ponder the state of mind of the novelist's wife very long before Belial entered from the other side of the room. He was pristine as ever in his priestly collar and frock and a somber expression of concern.

"I'm afraid there is still so much grief over poor Charlie," the faux missionary said, crossing himself. "I have been spending more and more time among our dusky brothers and sisters here because of it. Why, I'm practically living here as of late."

"Can you imagine," Stevenson said to Belial, "that our friends were considering taking shelter with the Germans?"

Belial puckered his lips in a show of measured thought. "You know, Tusitala, that I must remain neutral in my mission."

"How unfortunate for you, Father Thomas. Mr. Porter. Mr. Fergins. You will stay right here through the storm. No protests. I command it. There is plenty of space, and my boys are already untying your belongings from your horses. You are part of Vailima, and this home is your home now."

Davenport's eyes traveled from Belial to Stevenson and back. "We're grateful, Tusitala."

When we were alone and walking to the other side of the house to our rooms, I grabbed Davenport's arm. I wanted to scream at him but forced a whisper: "You planned this."

"Go on."

"You dismantled the foundations of our cottage while I was out picking up coconuts and breadfruit. You knew we needed to stay at Vailima, but without making it seem to be our choice. And you threatened to take lodgings from the Germans, knowing how that would rankle in Stevenson's mind." I kicked myself for believing that the mission had been aborted—in fact, it was the opposite. Davenport's maneuver had pushed us into the next phase. I had a mixture of admiration and astonishment that he would destroy our home in order to create the most believable scenario.

"*Hines's* cottage, you meant," he whispered back. "Not ours, not really. You should be happy for his loss."

"I do not wish him ill, in particular," I said. "I am just a bookseller. I do not have enemies."

"You underestimate yourself, only fools have no enemies. Fergins, soon will come the triumph you've been waiting to witness."

He was right, much to my frustration. I had been waiting. Not only since our passage to Samoa, but it was the kind of moment I had longed for since I began to assist the bookaneers. I would never have acknowledged it, but I was consumed with fresh enthusiasm.

So began our eventful residence at Vailima. The household was awakened at daybreak each morning by the sounding of the conch shell. Our presence—and Davenport's proximity to Stevenson just when his book would be finished—seemed to unnerve Belial, who as a result showed up with an even greater frequency. Belle was tickled by all the excitement of the storm, fulfilling Lloyd's observation that the potential for trouble woke her senses. Fanny, meanwhile, remained conspicuous in her absence from the public rooms. Stevenson's spirits, though, were fully revived by having houseguests, despite the worrisome weather, which kept that very umbrella now hanging behind you on my coat rack, at my side at all times. He took us on long walks through the house and around the grounds while preparing for the storm. On one of these dark, cloud-covered expeditions, we were walking through the garden. We were supposed to be looking for any weak spots in the red roof above that would have to be reinforced, but our host was spending most of the time discussing his favorite nuances of the Samoan language.

"Alovao: it is the gem of the Samoan dictionary," Stevenson was saying. "It means to avoid guests, for in Samoa there are always guests on their way, but literally it means 'to hide in the wood.' Hold on there.

Did you hear something, too?" His narrow face perked up in the fashion of a hound dog's. A brief, piercing noise from somewhere in the house surprised all three of us.

We all ran inside to find the source. Davenport could run much faster than either of us. The commotion having ceased, Stevenson split from us and tried a different direction. Knowing Davenport always possessed a keener-than-ordinary sense of hearing, I followed him into another section of the house, where we traced a loud, bellowing voice.

Belial was there, holding out a copy of the Bible. He seemed flustered and was crying out: "I am the way and the truth and the life. No one comes to the Father except through me!"

Vao was on the other side of the Bible, tiptoeing away from the fiery recitation, her bare feet deftly avoiding a pool of red on the floor. I feared it was her blood, but feared more it could be Belial's, as violence by any Samoan against a white man could only end with a native's death. But as we came closer I could see it was wine.

Tulagi was tugging at Belial's coattails with his small hands. "Stay away from the girl or be sorry you ever laid eyes on Tulagi!" he shouted, his attempts at restraining futile.

"Be gone, little man!" Belial shouted. He gripped his cane and swung, hitting the dwarf on the backside and sending him to the floor. Vao threw herself on the cane and wrested it away.

Undaunted, Belial swiped my umbrella out of my hands and once again began hitting the dwarf, over and over, splattering blood of the poor man; he raised his arm higher. Tulagi cringed and curled into a ball to prepare himself. Davenport caught the umbrella from behind and stopped what may have been a death blow.

"I suggest that whatever is the matter, end this presently, Father Thomas," he said with the almost preternatural calmness that still managed to impress me after many years.

"This is not your concern, Mr. *Porter*. Am I understood?"

His eyes blazed. It was not Davenport's interference with the beating that seemed to provoke him. Rather, it was the fact that Vao took cover behind my companion and placed her arm into his, her hand into his, her strong fingers interlocked in his. Davenport might have been just as taken aback at the native beauty's touch as Belial must have been, but any surprise he felt was hidden.

Tulagi broke the staring match between the bookaneers by using his last ounce of strength to shout up at them. "Go on, now! Go away, now, Pope Thomas! Tulagi commands it!"

"The work of a missionary is not easy among the savages," Belial said to us, as he straightened the top half of his suit before exiting the room. He licked his lips, a slow, rather disgusting gesture that I'd later notice he did often but I only marked now for the first time. He dropped my umbrella, freshly speckled with blood, two of its metal ribs broken and its spine bent from the impact. "I merely asked the young woman for help choosing a necktie for morning prayers and in her primitive way she reacted poorly, as you see. Worry not, my white brothers. I will not judge your misunderstanding." He turned again to look at Vao before he left, his eyes traveling from her face down to her bosom. "Cover yourself up, harlot, if you hope to escape the wrath of the Lord."

"What happened in here?" I asked the two natives after Belial was gone. Davenport had bent down to check on Tulagi, but the dwarf slapped him away, then proceeded to pull on his leg to raise himself to his feet.

"Fortunate Tulagi found you when he did," Tulagi said to Vao in Samoan. "'What happened?'" he repeated my question. He seemed to be dizzy from his beating but would not let any of us inspect his wounds more closely. "Why, I found that missionary trying to convert Vao to his religion—her, the *tapo* of her village, Tulagi's charge, daughter of one of the greatest chiefs of Samoa, a man who would have been king, if this were still a just place!"

"The daughter of a chief," Davenport repeated the words to himself.

Vao was still holding on to him, with no apparent intention of letting go. The dwarf interrupted this tableau, which must have seemed as dangerous to him as it did to me, pulling her away and out the door. Just then, Stevenson caught up to us. He was winded from running and the exertion had brought on a coughing fit.

"What is it? What had happened?"

"Nothing important, Tusitala," Davenport answered without hesitation or a hint of deception. "Just a broken wineglass."

Stevenson examined the scene with a deliberate look. "Well," he said, "I suppose the storm has set all our teeth on edge. That reminds me, my white gentlemen. I must ride out to the consulate to send some responses about this deportation business before the rains land. There was a yacht that sank in the Pacific a few weeks ago, and you may want to write out a message to wire your relations or they are liable to read about it in the papers and think you were on it."

"Excellent idea," said Davenport. "My aunt in Chicago believes every worthwhile tragedy must involve a member of our family."

I HAD TO LAUGH inside when Davenport left with Stevenson to send their telegrams—not only to think of a confused woman in Chicago named Porter handed a message from a nephew she never heard of but also because as long as I could remember, Davenport hated telegrams on principle. If they did not contain bad news, he'd insist, they contained something offensively mundane. "If you are ever in trouble, Fergins," he once commented with aristocratic irritation when I had to make a stop at a Paris hotel's telegraph office, "throw a rock through my window."

Yet, the first thing I heard about Davenport's search for Kitten back in London in 1882 came in the form of a wired message:

Come as soon as possible. Hotel de Ville. Geneva.

Though it was unsigned, I had helped Davenport for more than ten years by that time; I would have known a message from him by the rhythm of its words. It had been almost a month since he had left me standing in his hotel room to watch out the window as he climbed into a hackney coach. I was surprised that his path would go through Geneva, as I had reason to believe Kitten had already been there when looking for the Mary Shelley story, and that great mission of hers had been over and done with before her return to London and subsequent disappearance.

Geneva had a part in the fascinating history of Shelley's novel. It was during a summer trip there with her husband, the poet Percival, when she dreamt her inspiration for *Frankenstein*. She was eighteen.

Unlike Davenport, who, I'd teased, was born with the ocean's temper, I have never felt myself a natural traveler, especially with long distances involved. But there was no hesitation on my part after I read the message. A series of steamers and trains brought me to the Continent and into Switzerland. I was driven right to the hotel named in the telegram, but did not find the bookaneer signed in under any of his usual aliases. I waited, knowing nothing of Geneva or where else to look; this made me appreciate Davenport's own challenge to find a woman who could have been anywhere on earth, a woman whose profession depended on her being able to go anywhere and become part of the scenery.

I fell asleep in a comfortable chair in the corner of the sitting room by a hearty fire. Then I heard Davenport's voice chastise me. At first I thought I dreamt it.

"Asleep. Asleep!"

I stirred, catching my breath and emitting a loud noise through my nose. He was standing over me in an ankle-length, loose-fitting coat.

"Sorry, Davenport."

"Fast asleep, at a time like this." The bookaneer swept off his beaver hat; he looked as though he had not been sleeping, his unshaven face swollen around his eyes and cheeks, his eyes red, his hair hanging in loose, disheveled knots. He had a series of scratches along his neck that suggested he had been in a scrape recently.

"I did not find what name you were under with the clerk," I said, mounting a mild defense and changing the subject.

"I do not lodge here; I just come for some of my meals and my mail. I was here for a while when I arrived in Geneva but—never mind, we must go. I mustn't leave her alone too long."

I waited until we were outside on the lawn to speak further. "Then you found her! Thank goodness," I said with relief.

"Found whom?"

"Kitten."

"No," he said. He gave instructions to a waiting coach driver and the span of horses whisked us away from the hotel.

Cologny is a beautiful village high up among the lakes and mountains near Geneva, with charming cottages and hotels well placed for the most delightful views and the homes nestled in between. But instead of the surroundings I studied Davenport, trying to glean from his face whom we could be going to see and what any of this had to do with Kitten's disappearance. I could think of only one scenario that made sense: he had found a woman who knew what had happened to Kitten, and was keeping her locked away until she would agree to tell him what he needed to know, or maybe as ransom against another person who withheld information. I did not relish the notion of having any kind of prisoner and was eager to ask if this was it, but his gaze and brain were fixed on the mountains, and he sniffed and rubbed his eyes as though suffering through a cold.

We rode for almost an hour. After taking smaller, winding roads along one of the lakes, we were released from the coach at a path that disappeared into an overgrown garden. This led us to a cottage that had also been hidden from view. The house was of a charming design typical of the old style, but had been left in an apparent state of disrepair. It seemed the height of odd timing to me that Davenport in his haste would pause to light one of his beloved cigars before we entered, but I was mistaken. Shutters and musty curtains were drawn closed inside, and Davenport was lighting our way with a match.

At the door to the last room, he stood on a chair and unfastened a series of latches. Inside, there was a single dim lamp burning; I could make out a bed, dresser, and table with a pitcher and a basin of water.

"Light stings her eyes," Davenport said in a whisper, "so I keep it low."

Only then did I notice the small figure of a woman crouched in the corner of the room, shivering. Davenport picked up a blanket from the floor and draped it over her. Then the light caught her doughy face as he tried to lift her up and she revolted against his touch. She scratched and shrieked, kicked and screamed. I jumped in to help restrain her. Her pupils were contracted, her hair long and wild, her pulse racing.

She finally stopped struggling after fifteen minutes, and as Davenport settled her under the bedclothes, I stumbled out of the room into the dark hall. I was having trouble getting my breath back in those stale quarters. Outside, dark clouds were drifting overhead, and the slight sunlight that broke through rescued my senses. I found myself at the bottom of a hill, facing a larger house situated beyond this one. It struck me: I had seen all of this before.

I wheeled around when the door opened.

"She sleeps again," announced Davenport, whose feet crunched the gravel behind me. His shoulders slumped, his head was down, his expression abashed.

"You told me back at the hotel that you hadn't found Kitten!" I was trembling with confusion and fear. I was shouting.

He did not look up at me. "You saw her, Fergins. No. I did not find Kitten. I found a . . . a body deprived of a soul, a being abandoned by its maker. That is not the woman I have loved for eighteen years."

That was the only time he ever said it to me.

"That house up there on the hill—I have seen it in illustrations. That's Villa Diodati, isn't it?"

Davenport slowly nodded his head. Villa Diodati had once been the summer cottage of Lord Byron. He named it after the family who had lived there long before him, patrons of the great John Milton. The often-heretical Byron savored the connection with the Christian poet and loved to invite friends to visit. It was there, so close to the cottage where we were standing, that young Mary Shelley first began to invent the story of a medical student who experiments with animating a corpse, a trifle to entertain Byron and his friends; she became so preoccupied with the idea, she saw it in her nightmares. That meant the cottage we had just exited had to be the Maison Chappuis, rented by the Shelleys that summer more than sixty-five years before. I asked him if it was so and he swallowed hard.

"Kitten was a sight to behold after she came back to London with the Shelley story. Had you noticed?" he asked me with wide-eyed curiosity. "She was flush with the success. Watching her . . . well, she was stepping on clouds. It was every bookaneer's dream, to do what she had, to improve the knowledge of literature and be showered in money for it."

His words caught in his throat. He dropped his head again, and I realized his haggard appearance did not come from sickness or a lack

of sleep alone. His red and puffy eyes and cheeks, his runny nose—
he had been crying.

"She had been through Germany and here in Geneva before she
completed her mission." He went on with his explanation. "After
she returned to London, I didn't really spend time with her. She would
refuse to reply to my notes, would usually not be at home when I called
on her. Her problems sleeping multiplied until she was no longer sleeping at all. Other missions came her way, some that she said she would
accept, but then it was as though she would forget all about them. I
came to believe, Fergins, that she must have seen something in the
Shelley papers—something that suggested more to be found, something even bigger and better than what she had sold to the anonymous
collector. After she disappeared, her trail led me back to Geneva, and I
knew she had to be here to track this other Shelley discovery."

"What was it?" He raised an eyebrow to my question, and I could
see he was curious to hear my own guess, so I tried my best. "Something else about *Frankenstein*. Another discarded draft. A different beginning or ending. Or, no, nothing of Mary's at all. A piece of writing
of Percy Shelley's that could have been mixed in unnoticed with some
Mary Shelley material—why, could it be? The final section of his 'Triumph of Life' that he was writing before he drowned?"

"I do not know. Any of those are possibilities. I couldn't find out
the details, and as you can tell she has not been in any condition to tell
me very much. Here is what I could gather about what happened here:
While Kitten was searching for whatever it is she sought, she must
have sustained some kind of injury—probably from crawling around
one of these damned abandoned houses littering these mountains. I
have come to believe she was prescribed a mixture of opiates by a local
doctor. Soon, she must have been drowning herself in it. I found her
not in her right mind, wandering in and out of this cottage, which I

have been told was allowed to deteriorate more than ten years ago, though was once fine enough, as you remembered, for Percy Shelley to rent for himself and Mary to be close to Byron. I have been able to keep her inside here, where she seems calmest, and have brought some doctors around, but we must get her well enough to return to London as soon as possible to receive proper care. I do not want her reputation damaged. We must keep this between us. I need your help to do that, Fergins."

"You can count on it."

Over the next two weeks, I became a nurse to Kitten, relieving Davenport at regular intervals. I had heard of Kitten's past troubles with opium, but had understood that she had left the compulsion behind long ago when she achieved success as a bookaneer, a combination of not being able to afford any distraction and not needing it. This period of watching over her in Maison Chappuis was the most concentrated time I spent with the profession's most celebrated woman. For the first time in my eyes, she looked her fifty-two years. Not only had she visibly aged, but unhealthily; she was delicate and gaunt. She was shrinking out of existence.

I'd pass a warm towel along her brow and caress her hollow cheeks.

"She saw him here."

I asked her what she meant.

Her voice was small, a croak. "Shelley. She saw the creature, that glorious thing, when she looked upon these very mountains, across that peaceful lake, she saw it waiting, when others saw nothing but the scenery. She was Mary Godwin then. But called herself Mrs. Shelley to everyone she met. She knew."

Despite her general stupor and her gnawing hunger for opium, I was impressed by how well Kitten could tell a story, even if it was not wholly coherent. She talked of other missions, as well, though most often of the *Frankenstein* novelette she had been so proud of procuring.

There was sometimes an air of confusion. She would speak of looking upon the mountains and scenery as though her eyes were on them, even though she was confined to a dark chamber. She could not answer questions about what she was looking for that brought her back to Geneva.

Another time, she said: "He cannot understand."

Her eyelids were fluttering and she was shivering badly. I thought she might be imagining scenes from Mary Shelley's time in Cologny again, surrounded by Byron and Percy Shelley and other men whose reputations in literature were secure when hers was in its infancy.

"Who? Who does not?"

"He does not understand that I need to do this, and he never did." Then her eerie ice blue eyes opened and she exhaled.

"I read it all to her," she said after I frowned and nodded; then she was asleep.

I heard her repeat this phrase, "I read it for her," or "I read it all to her," or something to that effect, numerous times.

Sometimes I began to ask too many questions, and I'd give pause when she'd move her hand—bony, more so every day, and ice cold—to mine.

I had never seen someone cry herself to sleep, but that is what our poor opium eater did more than once.

Another moment I remember as happening a day or so later. I was trying to brush the tangles from her hair, which had become wiry but brittle. I tried to be as gentle as possible, but if too gentle the tangles would worsen. Then she said: "Belial." The word was carried on a gasp. I asked her to repeat, to explain what she wanted to say about him, but this time there was nothing more.

Davenport sent me out to gather the belongings Kitten had left at scattered hotels and boardinghouses around Geneva where she had lodged. Most of what I found was inconsequential. There was one item—a well-worn edition of *Frankenstein*—that caught my bibliographical interest. It was French, and from the early 1820s; if my memory served, it was the third French translation of the novel ever published. I hoped it might lead us to find out why she had returned to Geneva, what she was searching for, but that was not to be. I showed it to Kitten and she embraced it tightly, but never said anything about it.

Davenport did not want to leave her alone for any long period. He and I would sit in the small dining room and eat cheeses, some too soft and strangely colored for my conventional taste, and crusty bread purchased from the market on the other side of the lake. I learned more about Kitten in a matter of days than I had in years previous. Trivial facts about her that Davenport mentioned intrigued me. She had suffered her insomnia for many years. She had long had a problem of crying frequently and suddenly, sometimes without knowing why. This shed new light for me on his feelings for her, on the memories I had of him running to be by her side. I had imagined him as the young puppy following at the heels of his overbearing mistress. But he was protecting her, guarding her from her nightmares, even as she was guiding him in the profession. He also spoke of her struggles with opium in the past, long before either of us had known her. The fact that these epochs had preceded him in her life made him positively jealous of them, beyond the dangers with which they had once threatened her—and now threatened again.

I thought of telling him about her spontaneous cry of their elusive rival's name, but he was so generally distraught, I could not add another item of sadness and confusion to the catalog. The last thing he'd want to hear was Belial's name. Besides, she had not been speaking very fluently.

The longer we stayed, the less I could conceive of moving the poor creature to try to get her back to London, but Davenport remained insistent. When she would be screaming and begging for her opium, throwing plates and lamps, scratching off patches of our skin, he would curse himself. "If I had been there to prevent her from falling, she would never be in this state. If only I had been here to warn the doctor against plying her with opium." He had convinced himself more than ever that she must have suffered an accident—through the floor of an old attic or stair tread, he believed—and that was what had put her on the opium track. Bringing her back to London became a way of redeeming this failing. But the self-recriminations would have no relief. The Swiss doctor attending her confirmed that her body had reached an impossible position that nobody could reverse: it could neither go on with opium nor go on without it. All we could do was wait for the inevitable. She died in that cottage one early morning, a few minutes after three a.m., the fourteenth day of May, 1882.

At first, Davenport showed no change or release in emotion. After her body was taken away, his knees began to buckle and he convulsed with sobs. I caught him before he could fall, and he sobbed into my shoulder for a half hour as I tried in vain to comfort him. Then he pushed me away, embarrassed by his grief. The push was so forceful I fell backward into the wall.

We never found any evidence of what she was searching for that would have brought her back to Geneva, and no further Shelley papers of any significance have been uncovered in those cottages or elsewhere since. When I helped Davenport clean out her rooms back in London after our return, we discovered a half dozen vials of opium.

"Davenport, it means you do not have to blame yourself. She had begun using opium before her final journey. Her fate had nothing to do with you not being in Cologny to prevent her from an injury." I thought this would be a great relief, and was dumbfounded that he didn't care.

Davenport glanced down at the black crepe around his arm, then back at me. "Fancy that," he said. Later that day, while smoking a cigar in the dark, he asked: "Which should haunt me less, Fergins, believing I could have saved her or knowing I could not?"

THE NIGHT AFTER we walked in on Belial's assault of Vao and Tulagi, I scrubbed and scrubbed but could not get the bloodstains out of the fabric of my umbrella. I did not want Stevenson to notice it and ask questions, so I kept it tucked away among my belongings.

As we expected, residing at Vailima gave us the time and luxury Davenport had been longing for to explore more thoroughly. He assigned me the completion of our inventory of Stevenson's library—it was part of his standard analysis of a subject, though in this case I think there was an added element of plain curiosity on the bookaneer's part. Even for a man who had encountered most of the celebrated literati on both sides of the Atlantic, it was difficult not to be intensely interested in everything to do with Stevenson the man. The novelist was so entirely singular that learning more about him became a way of trying to prove to yourself he was of the same species.

A man's library opens up his character to the world. There were some penny dreadfuls that were on a shelf hidden behind the door. Then there were shelves of travel books, with a vast selection of volumes chronicling Pacific Ocean adventure, which confirmed the wisdom of Davenport's disguise as a travel writer; near that was an impressive collection of modern poetry. There was a French history that I noticed had a passage Stevenson marked, which translated as "I know my tongue has caused me a lot of trouble, but also sometimes lots of pleasure." There was a small set of classical texts, some in translation and others in their original languages, several with the pages uncut. I note that without meaning to criticize. The biggest secret kept by the literary world I occupy is that the best way for a book to become successful is to be unread. There is a book that is prestigious to own, to show to friends, and it is printed and purchased, printed and collected, until people forget to read it, but no matter—it must be in every family library to make it a complete one, and nobody knows enough to ever argue against it.

Two walls of shelves were filled with Bibles—more than 150 varieties by my count. We had not seen any evidence that Stevenson was a particularly religious man; if anything he seemed indifferent or hostile toward his mother's Christian pronouncements. He welcomed the missionaries for the purpose of social company and guiding the natives, not for improving his own spiritual nature. "The religious man has the need for only one Holy Book even as he wants only one God," Davenport said to me as I began to catalog the books, "but the literary man can never have enough of them."

After studying and admiring several rare editions among the collection, I noticed one Bible published more recently. I examined it at length. Why it caught my eye, I could not explain at first. There was a lurking sense of familiarity. It was the same edition that Whiskey Bill had had at his bedside—his deathbed, as it turned out. In my hours sitting beside him at the asylum, I had seen at a glance that Bill's was well read, the pages thumbed and marked at intervals and the spine strained.

Stevenson's copy of the same edition, in contrast, was fresh and stiff. It was a rather macabre and whimsical project that I'd had, as I thumbed through the pages and wondered in vain what last words Bill had read before his death. I rather liked the idea—admittedly a romantic one—that Bill, that every bookaneer who ever walked the earth, should be reading from a book when death sets him free.

I was ready to put away the Bible and commit my attention to the rest of my inventory when my eye struck on a verse of Revelation, or rather the footnote by Mr. Randolph Hawkins, the editor of this edition, to a particular verse about the "beast out of the abyss." Hawkins's scholarly exegesis suggested the beast due to emerge at the end of the world is Belial, one of the angels who fell with Lucifer and, according to Milton, one who could not be subdued even by Lucifer himself.

The words with their new significance echoed in my mind and the room seemed to shake with them: *Beware the beast, Penrose Davenport, beware the beast. . . .*

The beast.

The beast was Belial all along.

XI

Whiskey Bill had known Belial would be on the island. At first a perverse pleasure dawned on me, because if my conjecture was correct, it meant *Davenport* had been right about Bill leading him into a trap, though not in the way he had originally expected. Confirming the genius of Davenport's instinct was something perhaps much more important to me than it ever was to him. It must have amused the old hairless man, a sort of last chuckle of a frustrated life, knowing he was sending two of his brethren into a sort of final, mortal battle. Here was Whiskey Bill's ultimate role: the Instigator. I remembered what he had muttered to me from his bed. "And he gathered them together into a place called Armageddon." It was a lesser legacy than he dreamed about, maybe, but it was the best one he could produce given the time he had left.

Upon first connecting the Bible's passage and note about Belial as the beast, I got up from the chair and ran outside. I still had the book with me. When I realized this, I tossed it away, as though it could curse me. Instantly I regretted my action—it was a Holy Bible, after all, and it was Stevenson's. But after a frustrating search I could not find where the woods had swallowed it up, and I fretted to myself that it could only be a bad omen, which I then had to reassure myself I didn't believe in.

Davenport listened to my theory but neither his eyes nor his general expression evinced any signs of life.

"Don't you hear what I told you, Davenport?" I said with frustration. I was speaking in quiet but urgent tones on one of the verandahs. "I think Whiskey Bill sent Belial—he knew that it would come down to the two of you."

"What difference does it really make if so?" he asked after considering my conclusion. Then he added, as though a kindness, "I suppose you are after praise for your clever thinking."

Perhaps the truth did not make a difference in what actions we should take at this point, but it certainly seemed as though it *should*. I stated as much, but could not satisfy him. We retired to our own rooms without speaking more about it.

In fact, my discovery that Bill had pulled the wool over his eyes shot deeply to Davenport's core, though in typical fashion he could never say that to me. But he did something more telling. He acted on it, heatedly, even recklessly.

"You convinced that ginger-hackled rascal to send me here," were Davenport's words when he confronted Belial the next morning. He had found the faux missionary, white pith helmet on his head, planting flags in the ground, helping to mark the less sturdy trees that the native servants would cut now that the first storm was finally set to land. A light rainfall, which had begun overnight, pattered against the tops of the leaves and into the grass.

"Are you talking about Whiskey Bill? Why would I want you—or any bookaneer—slithering your way onto this paradise and bothering me?"

"Pray spare me the posing, Pope Thomas. If you didn't convince Bill to send me, then he sent you."

"He wrote me a letter, Davenport," Belial admitted. "With the spelling of a child and the mind of a woman. He did give me information about Samoa and Stevenson, and after I had the chance to examine it, it proved correct. Has his health improved? Whiskey Bill's, I mean."

"He's deader than George the First."

Belial nodded his head somberly.

"Why would he have wanted us both to come after this book?"

"Davenport," he said with sudden and unexpected enthusiasm, "there is something I found over there that I think you ought to see."

Knowing he probably should not, Davenport shadowed Belial deep into the woods. When I daydream of the golden age of the bookaneers, I sometimes think of this tableau, of two great enemies pushing through to the edge of the known world. Belial used his long cane to point out a spot in the bush. Davenport moved closer cautiously. Within a tight web of harsh vines and thorns, a nest of human bones on the ground appeared untouched. Crossed over the bones was a long stick, which on closer inspection revealed itself as an elaborately carved spear.

"What do you see?"

"A skeleton."

"Notice what is strange." Belial said this as a master would while waiting for his pupil to catch fire.

Davenport stared until the horror of the oddity presented itself. His face darkened. "There are two skulls—but only one skeleton."

"Right you are! Can you tell what happened? Come closer. You see, this skull has a bullet hole in the front." Belial used his cane again to demonstrate. "This," he continued, indicating the full skeleton, "was the body of a heroic warrior. He killed his prey, probably a chief or a son of a chief of a rival faction, and then cut off his head, which brings us the second skull. The whole practice is gruesome to our sensibilities, yes, but remember it is their way, just as your American Indians scalp. All races have their eccentricities about killing each other. He was bringing his trophy back to his village but he had been injured, or was injured during his return journey, and fell here, dying quietly and out of sight. Clutching his spear to his chest with one arm and the head of his rival with his other."

"How old are these bones?"

"That is hard to say but I would guess ten or fifteen years, back to the battles between the forces of Laupepa and Talavou, two great chieftains from the time, which would have occurred on what is now Tusitala's land. I am thinking of making a sketch of it to bring back to Christina. My doubting other half will not believe many of the scenes I have witnessed here. This, well, this is a dilemma. Do you think they should be buried together? Would you bury a skull without its body?" Belial's big eyes flashed. He straightened his priestly collar and took a few steps until he had a view of the estate below. "I'd see it all burned to the ground before we are done."

"What nonsense are you talking about?"

"Vailima. Reduced to ashes. There is something that suits me about that."

"Stevenson's manuscript. That is the mission. That alone."

"You know I have done what I do for the common people who would otherwise be abused and excluded by the publishers. What we do—you and I—provides more access where there would be less. Men such as the two of us do what the ordinary person is not equipped to accomplish. I am the Prometheus, but instead of fire I hold creativity in my hand. If this is to be the last mission of our race of men, I should as soon leave nothing behind—just flames and bones, the past charred and punished. You and I are no different from those two warriors. We have done much, but the world will not let us leave any mark."

"You can spout gibberish and high ideals about common people all you want, Belial. Remember, I know you. The only thing that makes your blood flow is power and the only thing that thrills you once you hold that power is destruction. What happened between you and the girl?"

Belial frowned in his lofty manner, blinking himself out from his vision. "You must know what it is that makes you want to protect the Samoan girl," he said, with his typical way of presuming more knowledge about another person than that person. "Kitty. You see her in Vao! Not Kitten as you knew her, no, not that woman who enlisted you into this life as the price of winning her approval; but a different Kitty, one from long before, a poor girl from the outskirts of Paris without wiles, a Philistine at heart, craving a better life, when you could have steered her, possessed her, saved her, or so you imagine, if only time and place were different. Even when I first knew her, she had been an actress, spy, and a budding bookaneer. She was ruined before you met her."

"Take care how you speak."

Belial ignored his warning and continued to pontificate. "The young women of Samoa are just old women trapped into young bodies, waiting for age. But not Vao. She is different, not simply because of her pure beauty, which is even more irresistible to whites than to her own kind. Vao refuses to marry. She is fierce in determination to be different and better than those around her; she is content to be alone because of it, and aims to change—she is an actress, too, who could betray or love you just as easily. A seductress."

"Are you saying Vao tried to seduce you before Mr. Fergins and I found you in that room?" Davenport asked with an angry laugh.

Belial shook his head slowly. "You see the most superficial part of the picture, and only that. Just as you did when you watched helplessly while indomitable Kitty left behind everything—left you behind—to chase down Mary Shelley's nightmares."

Had he been in possession of his usual steadiness, Davenport would have walked away. Here was the topic that could unmoor him. He knew that better than anyone. He felt his clothes soak through from the rain as his heart was careening to a dangerous tempo. "You know nothing about that."

"I know it all," said Belial, his tone free of any boast.

Davenport had to raise his usual chalky voice to speak over the pounding rain. "You were after the Shelley papers, too. She beat you to them, didn't she? That is why you still resent her."

"Wrong. True, she got them before I did. But those documents went straight from her hands and into mine."

It was as though the earth had opened up below Davenport's feet. Later, he would say it seemed an eternity passed before his mind would stop spinning long enough for him to speak again. "No. It was an anonymous collector who paid her. . . ." Davenport stopped.

"Anonymous," Belial confirmed with a proud grin.

"You sent her after them. You paid her for them? Why would you do that?"

"Kitty was my greatest competition, and nothing I tried all those years slowed her down. She would not have stopped until she was considered the best bookaneer."

"The more you speak the less I believe you. If your aim was to surpass her, then why let her have the rare glory of one of the great missions in our profession?"

"Because over time I came to realize there was one way to weaken her, and only one: turn her ambition against her. Let her have the highest achievement imaginable in her career. She was a woman who thrived on improving herself. Did you ever notice what happens to a person like that when they reach the summit of the mountain? When there is nowhere else to go but down the other side? They do not descend—they tumble and fall, or jump. I knew she would become bored, distracted, maybe wander into listlessness."

"And opium."

A twitch of regret narrowed Belial's mouth. "No, I could not know that would happen."

The question that had been plaguing Davenport for nine years came out. "Why did she go back to Geneva once the mission was already completed?"

"Isn't it obvious?" Belial asked, in his demeaning way of being deeply surprised at another's lack of knowledge.

"She was looking for something else, something new. There had been another mission she came upon after the Shelley novelette, wasn't there?"

"Don't I make myself understood to you, Davenport? *Nothing* new was worthwhile to her anymore. The novelette would have been the ultimate mission for most bookaneers. I not only handed it to her; I made certain the whole thing would be rather easy. Once it was over, she could think of nothing else. Any other mission, any other spot on earth, was just a reminder, a kind of emptiness, because she knew she would never be close to that other feeling again. She wasn't returning to Cologny looking for something new—quite wrong thinking, Davenport. She was clinging by a fingernail to the last great thing she had accomplished, the greatest thing she ever could reasonably expect to do."

"A bookaneer without her trade is a farmer without land. It was Kitten who told me that. You stripped her bare. You left her rudderless."

"How did I put it a minute ago? Yes, to quote myself: 'All races have their eccentricities about killing each other.' But I shan't take so much credit, certainly not for her death. Really, Davenport, it was you two who were engaged in a depraved relationship. A woman with a man almost half her age. That damaged her, made her feel as though she had to remain young and noticeable forever. An unnatural state for a woman."

"You pushed her into the hole."

Belial stuck his powerful chest out. "All I did was clear the field a bit. Made a profit, too."

"I want that Shelley novelette back. It cost her life and I won't permit it to be passed around for money. Tell me where it is."

"Certainly. I sold it to a wealthy Russian, a man who liked to dress like a peasant, and apparently took some perverse pleasure in destroying manuscripts."

Davenport cringed. His head was spinning madly. "Not long after that, you were also involved in seeing Molasses arrested, spoon-feeding evidence to the police."

"Who says that?"

"Whiskey Bill was a nuisance, never skilled enough to risk your crown, so you left him to destroy himself, and for the most part he complied. Kitten, Molasses, those were your closest competitors for years. And me. But you never tried to push me out."

"You wish I had?" A mocking laugh.

"Why do I deserve the sorry fate of being your last rival? If you were intent on clearing out the competition, why leave me alone?"

"I didn't think I had to do more." He let out a sigh that broke through as unusually sincere. "When I heard what happened to Kitty, I was certain you would fold up, that you would leave our line without any effort on my part. You may think me devious, Davenport, and maybe sometimes I have had to be. But I do try to be efficient. One fell swoop. Still, you proved me wrong. You persisted—your soul cleaved in half, perhaps, but persisted nevertheless."

"What you did to Kitten . . . What were you after that was worth that?"

"The same thing as you, the same as she. The same as anyone who has ever been doubted or told to go away. To prove myself better."

Davenport grabbed Belial's arm and leaned into his face. "I haven't gone away."

"You're right, Davenport." He acted as though he did not even feel the other man's grip. "I thought you would fall to pieces like a poorly bound book. But no. You are more like me than I ever knew." He slipped his arm out and turned his back, hands in his trouser pockets.

"You've made a mistake this time, Belial. I have you by the throat." Davenport's voice lost its usual hush completely, the words roaring out with the rage he could no longer contain on Kitten's behalf.

Belial slowed down his pace to listen, but did not turn around.

"Assaulting Vao. Let us pretend the young girl's word would not be trusted. There were witnesses. The dwarf, for one, and me, and Mr. Fergins. You've no doubt seen Tusitala angry. If the chief of Vailima hears that the trusted missionary was attempting to force his will on one of his beloved servants, you'll be thrown out of his sight, probably put in jail to rot. Then you can say all you want to Tusitala about me. At that point, nothing you say would be believed and I would be the only one left close enough to him to get the manuscript."

"You wouldn't be trying to break our truce, would you, my friend?" He seemed morally troubled by the idea.

"I'll warn you one time. Stay away from Vao."

Coconuts torn from trees by the wind flew overhead. Both men looked up at the sky. Now it was Davenport who turned and began walking away. The last glimpse he had of Belial showed his features contorted with uncharacteristic ire. I did not hear any of these particulars until late that night, hours after a bloody, soaked Davenport collapsed at the doorstep of Vailima.

"THE SKY WAS FILLED with branches and coconuts used like missiles by the wind in a war of divine forces. We both fled as the downpour started. The water became torrents around us. I'm afraid his foot got caught in a spontaneous mudslide. Poor Mr. Porter—he truly tumbled.

Never saw a man fall so hard, so suddenly." Belial was telling the story to the rapt household after some of the servants helped him carry Davenport inside.

"Please. I'm well enough," Davenport said, struggling not to show any discomfort and to shoo away the solicitous natives (and me). There were cuts and abrasions all over his body from his fall, but the pain seemed to me to be concentrated in his right leg.

"How did you ever get back, you poor idiot?" Belle asked, taking his hand. Her eyes were wide and wet.

"Father Thomas found me, and helped me, thank heavens," Davenport said, and I would venture to say never had my companion wanted to chew and swallow his own words so much.

Belial's grin, inimitable as always, could not have been contained if his life depended on it.

After the mud was washed off him, Davenport was carried to his room and tended to by Vao, who cleaned and bandaged his leg, and Belle, who mostly sat and blinked at him. I had followed them in. He screamed in pain when Belle poured what she said was perchloride of iron on the deepest gash.

"Imagine the luck," he said to me after we were alone, "that he would be the only man there to rescue me."

Davenport refused to follow Stevenson's recommendation (command, really) to rest and stay in bed, but he grimaced with pain when he tried just to walk around the room. He claimed he was not tired, simply angry, then passed into sleep in an instant.

From the moment Davenport first told me the details of his confrontation and the fascinating revelations about Kitten's Shelley mission of 1882, my mind returned to Geneva and would not leave it. I was once again in that cottage in the shadow of Lord Byron's, hearing the word from the weak lips of Kitten, the cry of "Belial." When Davenport woke, I was there by his side and I unburdened myself. "I must tell you something, my friend," I said, preparing myself for his fury that I had not told him nearly ten years ago.

He slowly moved his face toward me and forced his eyes to stay open.

I blurted out my confession: "It's about Kitten. When we were in that cottage outside Geneva caring for her in her final weeks, she said his name. Belial's. She didn't say anything else about him. Forgive me. I should have mentioned it to you."

To my surprise, he did not have the reaction I'd expected. In fact, there was hardly a reaction at all. He rolled his head away from me. "I knew that she said his name. I already knew that. I heard her say Belial, too, once or twice. Much of what she said had no connection to anything in particular, you know, when she was in that state. I also did not think much about it when I heard it."

"Now, what do you think she meant?"

"It is impossible to be sure, Fergins, but now that I know more I believe maybe she came to realize who it was that had led her to the *Frankenstein* novelette. To conclude who would have had the motivation to take her purpose away while at the very same time appearing to reward her. She understood."

He fell asleep and slept another hour or so. I could have been mistaken, but his thoughts stamped a slight grin on his face that remained as he slept. He was pleased, you see, despite all that had happened to Kitten, that she was so sharp-thinking even in the end to have identified the hidden culprit. He worshipped at the temple of her intellect and I believe it was a comfort to him to know that she left our world with it still shining.

Stevenson and Belle looked in on him later in the morning. I stood up to greet our hosts and give the latest report on Davenport's condition.

"Poor fellow," Belle said, shaking her head as she kneaded his cheeks. "He looks rather pallid, doesn't he?"

"You talk about me as though I were part of a waxworks display, Miss Strong."

She laughed from the bottom of her stomach. "You know you are a perfectly unusual man, Mr. Porter," she said.

Davenport was about to respond when Belial appeared in the doorway, which made Belle jump.

"I beg your pardon for startling you, Miss Strong. Haven't you told them your good tidings, Tusitala?" asked Belial, chuckling a little with anticipation.

Stevenson gave a shrug. "I think Mr. Porter is rather occupied enough with his recovery to care one way or the other what I am doing, Father Thomas."

"Nonsense!" Belial said, beaming and holding his gaze on Davenport. It was astounding that even in the company of Stevenson—one of the most beloved writers of the modern age—Belial carried himself as though he were the most important man in the room. "It will cheer him up while he recovers. You see, Mr. Porter, our esteemed friend here is nearly finished with his novel."

"By the end of the week." Stevenson gave up, confirming the news with childish giddiness and crossed fingers. He seemed weightless as he moved across the room to a window. "I've been averaging two pages a day. I calculate that makes me only half the man Sir Walter Scott was for pages by the day, yet I still will try my best."

"Do not overtask yourself," Davenport urged. "For your health, Tusitala, you must also rest."

"There is no stopping now, Mr. Porter. I feel it all ready to froth whenever the spigot is turned. I shall rest when I am in the grave—or perhaps if we make it to Italy one day. I hope you'll excuse me if my visits to your room are infrequent during your recuperation, Mr. Porter.

Pray give it no thought. Your every need will be attended to in the meantime by my family and my family of natives, and I know Mr. Fergins will inform us if there is anything you need."

"Congratulations, Tusitala," Davenport said, and I echoed the sentiment.

Stevenson waved this away.

"Shame that you won't be up and around in time to celebrate, Porter," Belial said to Davenport. "But I know you will have plenty of time with Tusitala once you are better. Plenty of time for leisure once the storms have passed and you've finally gotten back on your feet. It looks as though I will have to be moving on to business at some of the other islands."

"Of course you will," Davenport said.

"But I will wait until I have a chance to congratulate Tusitala on a completed book."

"Again, of course you will."

"Gentlemen, if you'll excuse me, I am late for a prayer circle with some of the pious young brown men and women. We will pray for your health, too, Mr. Porter. I am going to give a sermon on a Biblical figure close to my heart."

"Who is that?" I quizzed him.

"An obscure character by the name of Belial. He is interpreted as a minion of the devil by some scholars, but that is wrong. It is ignorance. The name means, literally speaking, 'one who cannot be yoked,' and it is really every one of us who takes control of our own destiny while others blow in the wind. We may be punished for it, but we would never do it another way. We are all Belials."

Stevenson watched Belial saunter out of the room, then broke into his own chuckle. "Missionaries. They are always so anxious that we believe in one truth or another. That is their entire calling, I suppose." He noticed the anxiety I could not hide from my face and he pulled at one of the loose end of his straggly mustache. "Mr. Fergins, are you unwell?"

"I only fear Mr. Porter may not be in a position to finish his own book that brought him here, before we will have to return. With such an injury to recover from."

Stevenson took my hand. "Remember, Mr. Fergins, that there is always a sunny side, if you look for it. And another thing, don't worry. I have learned one thing in this life. It does not matter much what you accomplish. The only thing that really counts is that you tried."

"I tried," Davenport said sadly. "Yes, Tusitala, I tried."

AN INCAPACITATED DAVENPORT could never outmaneuver and outrun Belial. The fact is, by the time Stevenson and Belial left the room, I was already in a panic, and as my nerves grew Davenport's steadied.

"There is nowhere for Belial to go as long as these heavy rains continue," Davenport tried to assure me after we listened to their footsteps descend the stairs. "There's that on our side."

The incessant rain pelted the roof above us. I was pacing the floor. I spun around to look at him, my eyes wider after taking in his statement. I was at my wit's end with his calmness. "Forgive me for violating the rules of bookaneers' assistants and questioning you. The whole mission hangs in the balance, and you will hope for thunder and lightning? We will rely on the barometer as our weapon?"

He blinked lazily and rolled his shoulders back with a sigh. "What plan would you prefer, Fergins?"

I had to admit I could not think of anything better. Every time I alluded to the urgency of the situation his passivity increased. By the end of the day, his leg was causing him greater discomfort and we spoke less of the impending crisis of Stevenson completing the book and more about his pain. I confess a bit of irrational impatience toward Davenport over his injury, and annoyance at the fact that Vao had to be sent for repeatedly to change his bandages, breaking up our deliberations.

All the hurricane shutters were in use in the house and Vailima was as safe as possible, but airless and dark. The atmosphere was suffocating and had a way of dividing the human mind against itself. By this point, it seemed to me there were only two possible paths to success that remained for Davenport's mission: we either had to find a way to hinder Stevenson's writing, or a way to prevent Belial from being inside Vailima once the book was finished. Our lone advantage was that we were ensconced inside the house, however limited by Davenport's condition, while the other bookaneer, though having essentially free access to the estate at all times, had to go back and forth to the Marist mission to keep up appearances.

Consumed by unriddling our predicament, I could hardly sleep. *If the bookaneer requires assistance on a mission, the assistant must never question anything that may occur.* Davenport's rule kept repeating itself in my ears, but using the freewheeling logic that comes to man only in the middle of the night in the middle of a roaring storm, I convinced myself I was not questioning what had occurred, but what *would* occur, and so shook off all restraints. I put on my dressing gown and stepped quietly and quickly through the hall back to Davenport's door, ready to wake him up if I had to, in order to settle once and for all on a successful revision of our plans.

I cannot say what it was that prevented my knocking. I rolled my fingers into a fist but something stayed my hand. Had I heard some slight sound, a tapered breath, an unfamiliar sigh, warning me away?

I wrapped my arms around my chest as though to protect myself from a biting wind, and turned away. Before I was able to go very far, I heard the creak of Davenport's door opening. I told myself not to look back but I could not stop. I watched as she stepped out and closed the door behind her. Vao was not holding any bandages or medical supplies. Her skin was shiny as always from the oil the natives covered themselves in; framed by my candlelight in that dark hall she actually glowed. Her big brown eyes met mine and she showed surprise, but no shame, no concern; no, there was a hint of elation and intrepidness. She remained still and I could not help doing the same—out of some instinct of politeness not to turn my back on a lady, or from a desire to communicate some thought, again at the time I could not have really said what it was. The entire experience was so novel, I could not guide my face and body to an appropriate response. "He rescued me from the Beast. Now I will rescue him," I imagined her saying, but she did not say a word in any language, much less in English. I felt myself floating over the scene, looking down and wishing to take her by the arm to remove her before anyone else realized what had happened.

My chin thrust downward, my lips retreated into my head in an embarrassed smile, and with that I turned on my heel and began the walk to my chamber. I did not hear her walking and wondered why. Then I saw. Tulagi had come. In a primitive woven robe of green and brown, he looked like a kind of magical elf, and his breathing was labored as though he had come from far away after a long search. His eyes then searched and found mine. His strong, soulful face crumbling, I was certain the dwarf was about to break into sobs. I opened my door and returned to bed, not wanting to see more.

I kept my distance from Davenport the next day. Tulagi must have been doing the same to Vao, for I saw her several times around the house but did not see the diminutive shadow usually extending from her own. The worst of the rain had left us but the winds remained mighty and dangerous, and occasional lightning, thunder, and showers still fell. Except for some of the outside boys who had to make necessary excursions for the welfare of the livestock or horses, we were all confined to the house.

I did happen to cross paths with Tulagi. It was that evening. He was smoking tobacco wrapped in a banana leaf, looking out at the black sky on one of the verandahs. All of it added up to a sight. For one thing, we were told to stay away from the verandahs for the duration of the storm, and for another the natives were not known for smoking cigarettes. He suddenly appeared to me to be a different sort of man; perhaps it was the lighting produced by the tropical sky, but he was neither native nor white in my eyes—not the garden elf, this time, but a sort of other-worldly and oracular entity. Suddenly, his mission to protect Vao seemed the most worthy in the world to me. It did not occur to me to wonder why he was not overseeing her now. I fell into a spirit of cama-raderie.

"Good evening, Tulagi," I said, struggling against the rainy gusts.

He whispered back, but I could not hear, could not make out whether it was English or Samoan.

I moved closer and asked him to repeat himself, but then I realized he was not paying any mind to me; he was once again reciting the island's history to himself.

"Then the god of heaven sent down his daughter, Turi, in the form of a bird. She could find nothing but ocean so she returned to her father and told him so. He sent her back and she flew until she found some land in the water. So she returned to her father and told him so. He sent her back with a plant, which she put into the earth. The plant grew and grew, and when she had returned, it was swarming with maggots, and when she returned again, the maggots had become men and women."

If it had not seemed as though it would be a rude thing, I would have sat next to him and listened. He seemed to disappear into the peculiar myths, most of which had been banned by the missionaries in favor of Christian doctrine. As he spoke, he became as big as the god of heaven and as lofty as the bird flying from land to sea and back again. There was a tranquility coming from this man as he repeated the stories to himself, maybe because there was nothing of all the madness involved in the rest of the world of stories as I knew it: the search for customers, the impatience of readers, the brittle egos of authors, the publishers' and the bookaneers' jousts over profits. Here was a man and a story.

When his eyes met mine he repeated: "The plant grew and grew, and when she had returned, it was swarming with maggots, and when she returned again, the maggots had become men and women."

How unreal the memory seems when I think about what was to unfold only hours later.

Half the house was woken by the shouts of the outside boys; one of them, raising the hurricane shutters, had seen a small child running through the fields with a torch. Even with the downpour having passed, the property was littered with dangers, fallen trees and branches, sliding mud and overfilled streams, not to mention the violent winds. Two of the servants searched, thinking it might be the child of one of the runaway cannibals, and instead found a small broken body at the rocky bottom of a deep ditch.

Davenport and I came out a few hours after the discovery, the bookaneer leaning his body on my arm. Vao had collapsed on the ground nearby, her face hidden in her hands and the rest of her lit dramatically by the torches held nearby as different members of the household took turns to comfort her. Davenport—perhaps to protect her, perhaps because he could not bear it—did not go near her. Stevenson watched over all of it, stricken.

"The poor man must have fallen!" moaned Belle, who tried to comfort her wailing mother, and Stevenson sighed. But there was nothing for Tulagi to trip over near the ditch, and no good reason for him to have been outside in the first place. He was far enough toward the middle that he had to have made as big a leap as his short legs could manage. I leaned out over the ditch as far as I could without risking my life. I needed to see him. The dwarf's body looked like a girl's doll, twisted out of its form.

"This will distract Stevenson from his writing," I whispered to Davenport, then gasped at myself. "I'm sorry. That was an awful thing to say."

Whispered Davenport, "You always wanted to know what it was like to think like a bookaneer."

XII

⸺◦◦◦⸺

Vailima was abuzz at dawn with news. First, the burial. Though many things in Samoa were done at a leisurely pace, burial of the dead was not among them. The humidity would not allow delay. Tulagi's body was wrapped in decorative mats and we all sat on the ground, men on one side and women on the other, as Belial delivered yet another eulogy. After his speech, the women filled the open grave with smooth black pebbles gathered from the ocean into baskets. As the company of mourners dispersed, I began to hear whispers. Only once we were all back inside could I understand what else happened overnight.

Stevenson had been up all night after the tragedy, but he had not been grieving mindlessly; I know this because there came the announcement we originally had been waiting for so long to hear, and now dreaded. His masterpiece was finished. *Finished*. It was whispered and repeated among the household, the staff and servants, in Samoan and in English, by those family members who depended on his books and those natives who never saw a book outside the Vailima library and the writer's sanctum.

With the storm subsided, visitors to the house were coming and going one after another on various business and personal errands that had been delayed. Mail was distributed, brought in a trunk from a merchant ship that had come in just at the tail end of the storm.

I was on my way to find Davenport when I was stopped on the stairs by John Chinaman. He greeted me with his usual glare of belligerence and handed me several letters.

At first I could not understand how there could be letters with my name on them, then remembered that Davenport had left word with the post office in London that I could be reached in Samoa, and separately told various associates of his that he could be reached through me. I tucked them under my vest for later and continued on, eyeing Belial, who was conducting a prayer circle in memory of Tulagi. The natives sat in a semicircle around him with heads bowed, and he held his hands high like a tableau of Christ with his disciples. John, meanwhile, gathered up an entire trunkful of letters that I guessed were for Stevenson.

"Davenport!" I called when I found him in the great hall practicing putting weight on his bad leg. "Haven't you heard?"

"What is that?" he asked, looking at the bulge in my vest.

"Oh, letters. Just arrived on a merchant ship of some kind. John Chinaman was carrying a whole trunk of them to Stevenson."

"Let's see."

"Here." I switched to a whisper. "Davenport, forget those, he's finished! Did you hear what I said?"

He ignored me.

"Belial is inside the house. If Tulagi had not died, perhaps he would not be here already, but he is." My words sounded accusatory, though I had not intended that, but it hardly mattered. He had entered into a haze of distraction that could forfeit the mission.

The bookaneer shot me a brief and meaningful glance. "I'm afraid this concerns you, Fergins."

He had been going through the letters and handed one back to me. I could not help but wonder if his dalliances with the native girl had put him in this mental fog. "Davenport, are you even listening to what I'm saying? Everything hangs in the balance."

I looked down at the letter and read: it was from Johnson, the man charged with watching over my bookstall. There had been a rut of bad times in London and worse luck, it said. All the bookstalls in London had been affected. He'd even had to dismiss the boys who helped guard the stalls, which in turn led to a rash of thefts by other boys (including one former guard). That had made everything even worse. There simply was no money left to pay expenses—he had closed the stall temporarily. Worse still, as it was a term of my lease not to leave the space idle for more than four days, a fact unknown to Johnson, it had been repossessed. My bookstall was gone. And I was thousands of miles away. *I'm awful sorry, I am, Brother Bookseller,* Johnson wrote in a postscript, as if he thought of regretting it only at the very end.

"He should have tried expanding the inventory," Davenport said. "I suppose it had to happen sometime. Doomed calling."

It was a doomed calling, and my life. I read the letter again and I wanted to deny it, to rip it up, burn it. I wanted to shout down Davenport's unmovable fatalism. But I knew we were at a crossroads that required my attention. I carefully folded the letter up. There was nothing to do about the stall, and something had to be done here and now. I collected myself. We had come for a purpose and if it was to be fulfilled, this was the time.

"Davenport, never mind about that, not right now. But Stevenson is *finished*. Belial is here, the storm has passed on to the next island. Davenport, please, attention!"

The idea struck me right then. I dropped the letter I was still holding. This got his attention.

"Fergins, what's wrong?"

I had to catch my breath before I could find the right words. "The mail, Davenport. It just got here."

"I suppose it is rather much to take in about your bookstall."

"Whiskey Bill."

Now I had his interest.

"I'd rather listen to your piano playing than have to talk about that swindler."

"Bill imagined setting up a kind of Bookaneer Armageddon, yes? He convinced both you and Belial to come here, knowing you would try to rip each other's hearts open. He wrote you to come to the asylum; he wrote Belial about Samoa. What if he wrote to Stevenson, too?"

"Why would he do that?"

"In my study of the field, Davenport, every bookaneer lives with the inner belief that his talents are unique, and he can hardly suffer the mere existence of his fellow bookaneers because it threatens that belief. I see him in my mind's eye with his wobbly hand over the chessboard I set up for him at the asylum. He had his own game in mind. This was a final ploy by Bill to ensure his rivals destroyed. He set a trap, turning the author against the final two bookaneers, to determine which would be the last."

"If he was trying to do that," Davenport said, "the mail that just came in . . ." he did not finish the thought.

I helped: "Could have a letter in it to Stevenson revealing every-thing."

"Go up to his library and go through the letters that John car-ried up."

I shook my head. "Not me."

"I cannot," he replied. "I cannot move fast enough to avoid being caught. You know Bill's handwriting. You could recognize it at a glance, couldn't you?"

"Yes, of course. But if I was discovered digging through the letters—"

"You invent an excuse. What's worse than him reading a letter from Bill, Fergins? Nothing is worse than that. If that were to happen, our entire mission evaporates, and nothing else matters."

"How could I manage it?"

The plan was hatched. I was to contrive a reason to go to the library. Find the trunk of mail I had seen John Chinaman carry up. Search for any letters with handwriting that could belong to Whiskey Bill. Bring said mail to Davenport to examine and destroy. Somehow, avoid Belial and all servants along the way.

Keeping these instructions in my head, I started for the second floor of the house. A climb up a flight of stairs had never before seemed to take so long, as if each tread tilted up and away from me, the walls shaking and trembling like a runaway train, my mind dark as a tunnel. I headed for the library, eyes down at my feet except to look for anyone who might be watching my path. My heart thumped; my excursion became more momentous and life altering with each step I took. "This, my dear Fergins, this alone, could save my mission from disaster," Davenport had said to me before we separated, encircling a hand around my wrist like my oldest friend or a policeman making an arrest.

A few seconds later, as measured out by the big clock by the stairwell, I was inside the Stevensons' library. There was the trunk I had seen the Chinese servant carrying. It was resting on the floor in one corner of the room. I had my moment. Here, now, I was to become a . . . the word *bookaneer* retreated from me. It would take much more than this. I thought about the advice Davenport had given me. I walked to the nearest shelves as though to reach for a book, then I dropped to my knees in a quick motion. Opening the lid with one hand, I readied my other hand to dig through the mail.

It was empty. The room swallowed me whole.

"It is so, so lovely."

The voice came from Fanny Stevenson, sitting in a deep armchair facing away from me. She wore a brown gown with yellow flowers stitched into it, and her toes rested on the windowsill. The mistress of the house was so compact she had been completely concealed by the back of the chair.

"Fanny," I said, trying to determine how much I needed to explain.

She continued looking out the window. I realized she wasn't watching me at all. I had disturbed her reverie.

"It is all so, so lovely," she said, then with a birdlike motion she finally glanced at me. "Mr. Fergins, I have made a mistake."

"Fanny?"

"Oh, a terrible mistake," she said with a warm smile. "I should never have told you to leave this place. It is the loveliest spot in the world sometimes. The South Pacific can have everything you ever dreamed of, or everything you ever feared coming to pass. We mean to live our lives in Samoa and leave our bones here. Do you know, I was out walking yesterday? The air was soft and warm from the storms, and filled with the most delicious fragrance. These perfumes of the tropical forests are wonderful. When I am pulling weeds, it often happens that a puff of the sweetest scents blows back at me and all is well again. It does not seem possible that we have not been here longer than we actually have. Everything looks so settled, as though we have been here for many, many years."

She threw open the window. No action imaginable could have been any more absurd. The awful winds howled and rushed in and nearly knocked her over, pushing pencils, papers, and books off the table behind her. Lloyd rushed in and steadied his mother while I forced the window closed.

"It's all so lovely, so, so lovely," she was repeating through tears but still with a smile.

"Mother, let us take you to bed to rest. Yes, that's it, come with me," Lloyd said, waiting until she had recovered herself and was walking on her own toward the door. "I'm very sorry," he said, turning to me with the dutiful face characteristic of a grown man whose mother was becoming a burden. "Sometimes she will rant against this place; other times she will seem ready to throw herself into Mount Vaea to stay forever. When she is caught between the two feelings is when she goes to pieces. It is very hard for her, because when Louis makes up his mind there is nothing to do, and all she wants to do is keep him happy. It has become her . . . calling, so to speak."

"We all must have one," I replied.

I could hear Davenport's shouts from downstairs and I tried to ignore them. It meant I was taking too long. He was trying to draw as many of the servants to him—and away from me—as possible by acting as though he had reinjured himself.

When mother and son were both gone, I looked everywhere I could think for any sign of the mail, under the pretense of cleaning the mess blown around by the storm. I rushed to the glass doors that led to Stevenson's sanctum. My legs were moving faster than my brain, but I was imagining a scenario of what must have happened. John had brought the mail to Stevenson's desk, then removed the empty trunk to the library, for it would not fit inside the narrow sanctum without being a hazard for the novelist to trip over.

The doors to the sanctum were closed. I knocked lightly, then made a few bolder taps. Nobody called to come in or go away, so I held my breath and stepped inside. There were stacks of mail on the bed and the floor. My eyes took these in before landing on Stevenson, almost invisible, tucked under multiple blankets, propped against pillows. He looked up from a letter he was reading, but his wide-set eyes, as ever, seemed to absorb everything at once, while mine scrambled for crumbs.

Me: "Tusitala."

Him: "Mr. Fergins, I have here a most interesting letter from abroad. You might as well join me."

XIII

By the time I had returned to Davenport, I could hardly keep from talking over my own sentences, there was so much I needed to say—I suppose the same is true as I recount the story to you now. I told him how the letter had been written on the other side of a page ripped from a book, which, as it turned out, was a page from a Bible. Whiskey Bill's Bible.

"As best I can remember, Davenport," I said, "the letter began like this." I recited:

> *My dear Mr. Stephenson* (I interrupted myself here to explain to Davenport that any letter spelling Stevenson with "ph" was usually torn up without reading any further, but for some reason the novelist made an exception), *justly celebrated author, sir,*
>
> *I write to warn you of two visitors to expect to Samoa, or who have already arrived by the time you receive this letter depending on the speed of the mails to no man's land. I speak of one man called Belial and another named Penrose (Pen, to friends, like me) Davenport. They will both enter your life, separately, in ways that might seem natural but are in actuality highly calculated. Belial will likely come to you first, is a man standing six feet one or two inches in height, and*

seeming taller than a man with greater height, teeth like diamonds in the sun, his hair like a clump of pretty seaweed, and his voice like the thunder and trumpets that might greet the day of judgment. Davenport? Well, he is the one somewhere near you intent on being intent, always tormenting himself about one trivial thing or another as if he were Christ himself, and who has a face as serious as a dead German, as Heine says. Make no mistake. He is as scheming, in his way, as the other one. I'll wait a moment while you wonder who they are, for of course they come with false names and purposes.

Davenport might've brought his inseparable caddie, his shadow, if you will, though a rounder and shorter and balder shadow. A whistling, book-lugging fool. Second thought, I'd wager he was wise enough to leave disloyal old Fergins the bookseller behind this time, like a train needing to move faster would unhook its rusty caboose.

Finished? Know everyone we're talking about? Excellent. These two snakes come from the line of men and women known as Bookaneers—a brave and necessary and dying breed, alas—and they come to you to steal your latest masterpiece for the sake of profit and glory. The high seas of literature swarm with plunderers. Certainly, if I could have I would have been there, too, and I would have been so honored, sir, so much so I cannot tell you. Not since Lord Byron nearly became King of Greece, had he not had the misfortune of dying instead, has a literary man exiled himself so grandly as you. If I had come, I would have presented myself as a doctor with the newest cures from Europe, to try to tempt you in your state as an invalid, but those fools might not have thought of that. Feed them to the cannibals, if you permit suggestions.

Your servant,
William Perkins Richmond

*P.S. In your position as an esteemed author, if you should
ever be made privy to the whereabouts of a novel called* Life
of an Artist at Home and Abroad, *supposedly once printed
anonymously in a French newspaper, written by Edgar Poe
but wrongly attributed to Eugene Sue before being lost forever
and forgotten, please order a copy to be left on my grave, and
from the spirit-world I should be thankful.*

"We have to get out of here!" I cried after finishing. "Stevenson knows all. He knows who you really are. We have to leave now!"

"Belial." Davenport cringed while grabbing his leg. "Where is Belial?"

I shook my head. "Stevenson called John Chinaman into his sanctum after reading the letter to me and ordered him to immediately protect the manuscript and hunt for Belial. That is when I slipped out of the room."

For the second time since our arrival in Samoa, the first being the death of Charlie, I saw what I would describe as absolute fear reflected in the deep green of Davenport's eyes. "What does he plan to do, Fergins?"

"I couldn't say. Stevenson fell into one of his uncanny fits—you know how he does. He was speaking so quickly in Samoan, I could hardly understand any of it. Are you well enough to move, Davenport?"

I tried to help him but he remained on the bed. I knew he understood he had no choice and minutes, maybe seconds, to act. Yet he could not help groping for some other way out than flight. He knew, as I knew, that the moment he rose from that bed and snuck out of the room, this mission was lost. That his career, in essence, was over. That he could never match Kitten's achievement nor—in some profound way—reverse its consequences to her.

"Davenport. Now is the time. All is up; he knows everything. We haven't another moment to spare. We must get away from Vailima and to the American consulate to beg for protection."

He nodded. The nod itself seemed to cause him as much pain as his mangled leg. After he accepted my hand, I pulled him to his feet.

His leg was leaden, dragging behind him. We progressed slowly to the door. I opened it and Stevenson was waiting on the other side, holding a cigarette out in one hand, inspecting us, first him and then me. His wide-set eyes had a kind of mesmerizing effect.

The novelist put the cigarette back to his mouth. "Look at me, I almost forgot to smoke just then."

"I suppose there is nothing I can say to satisfy you, Tusitala," Davenport spoke quietly, the respectful tone of a truehearted soldier captured in war. "Whiskey Bill seems to have made certain of that."

"I see your co-adventurer has already relayed news of the letter. There is something you can do. It will not help you much, but I still recommend complying. You can satisfy my curiosities. Did you ever steal from me before, in this storied so-called vocation of yours, Mr. Davenport?"

Davenport took a few unsteady steps back into the room. "It's not so simple as that."

"Grown men, hunting books like pheasants in the wild. Lord in heaven! Now, did you steal from me before you came here or not?"

"Not really."

"Indirectly, then?" Stevenson's question really did seem to contain more curiosity than anger, as if speaking about someone other than himself.

"You will remember a map you drew to be printed in *Treasure Island*."

"I ought to; it took a great amount of my time and strength. My publisher lost it, after all that, and engaged an illustrator to do the far inferior one printed in the book."

"The publisher did not lose it," Davenport said.

"*You*—"

"No, I was not involved in taking it, but it passed through my hands sometime later, and I commend you on the quality. There was another mission I was involved in. I need not tell you, of all people, the prelude," Davenport continued. "The autumn of '88 your *Strange Case of Dr. Jekyll and Mr. Hyde* was whispered about in the streets of London. Those who blamed it—and the stage version of your novel then underway—for unleashing the murders in Whitechapel feared an army of Rippers would emerge in London. All from the influence of your slim book. I believe you were in San Francisco with Mrs. Stevenson at the time, so it was said."

Stevenson gave a guttural agreement.

"There were publishers seeking to capitalize on the frenzy, who ordered shipments of pirated editions of your novel to sell. I was engaged to protect the shipment from another bookaneer hired by a consortium of committees trying to keep them away from the public."

Another grunt.

"Do you think it possible, Tusitala?" I ventured into the exchange. "For a book about a changeable man actually to change a man into something he is not?"

"What is your opinion, Mr. Davenport?" Stevenson asked, still fixated on the bookaneer.

"I once believed books could start wars or end them," he began, phrases from a speech I had heard him make about his profession more than once. This time his voice broke off.

"I suppose you believe books made you into the criminal being you are today."

"The laws of your land and mine left creative works made outside its borders unprotected. That was not our doing. There was chaos and confusion. We were needed because we were able to do what nobody else could—not authors, not publishers, not lawmakers—to control the chaos. So the literary world relied on us and resented us for it, named us bookaneers, began to shout that we were criminals, to write poems and books against so-called pirates, until the laws finally started to change and now we are about to be left to wither and die in order to purify the rest of you. Did a book make me into this? No, Tusitala, I made many books into what they've become."

"Well, you might be surprised that I should *not* be inclined to thank you for protecting my 'slim book,' as you call *Jekyll and Hyde*, from destruction by the amateur society of censors. In fact, I would have been happy to see the copies destroyed, not only because the piratical publishers selling them were stealing from me. It is a thing I have often thought over—the problem of what to do with one's talents. Some writers touch the heart; I suppose I tend to clutch at the throat. *Jekyll and Hyde* was the worst thing I ever wrote. My brightest failure."

I tried to assess if this was one of his momentary fancies. "That book made you rich," I blurted out.

"And was that one of your responsibilities, Mr. Fergins? To know how much money every book made every author?"

"To the penny," I admitted.

"You are wrong, Mr. Fergins. It did not make me rich. It made me richer. Financed our voyage here and, indeed, some of the construction of this house. Wealth beyond a certain point is only useful for two things, if you ask me: a yacht and a string quartet. The fact remains, and I repeat, *Jekyll and Hyde* is the worst thing I ever wrote. But you and Mr. Davenport would not understand. For you gentlemen, it's only about money."

I felt myself blush and would have tried to defend against the accusation, but my companion reacted as you might expect, by fighting back.

"As it has been for you authors from the moment when man stopped telling their stories for pleasure and honor, and began to forget it was the readers who made them what they were." After a moment, he added, "You were able to intercept Belial. Please. Tell me that at least that one consolation remains for me."

"Thomas—the man you gentlemen and Whiskey Bill call Belial— is gone, my manuscript spirited away with him. It seems he entered the house and disappeared shortly before I read the letter I shared with Mr. Fergins. I had just collected the pages all together. I suppose we will never see him again. He is a man with luck on his side."

"Damn his luck. Send some of the natives to track him down before he leaves the island. I will pay the expenses and more. Do what you want with me, but do not let that man get off this island!" Davenport's throat sounded hoarse and tight, his words unspooling wildly. Pleading was not part of his nature. It was heartbreaking. "Please, Tusitala—"

"I am one of the foremost men of letters of the day, and you and that false missionary come here to steal the labors of my brain?" Stevenson interrupted, then swallowed down his fury. "You know, I liked you down to the soles of your boots. I did." His eyes darkened and he could not stand still—shifting from the bed to the table to the door and all along the perimeter like an animal circling his prey. "In the future I would recommend you employing a different false identity."

"Tusitala?"

"A real author would never introduce himself as an 'author,' Mr. Davenport. Why, if we had to walk around calling ourselves authors, remarking upon meeting a new acquaintance—'Greetings, I'm an author. And you?'—we'd never consent to write in the first place. When I used to be asked my business, I would answer only: 'I sling ink.' Lord, I should have known from that very first meeting . . ." The novelist finished by murmuring under his breath, "Bookaneers!" Then, with a dark laugh to himself, he shouted an order in Samoan to someone unseen and stalked out through the door.

"Tusitala! Please! Stevenson!" begged Davenport. I held him back from trying to follow, seeing at once it was fruitless.

Stevenson only glanced back with a glare at the sound of his name, then continued on.

Stationed in a chair in the hall was one of Stevenson's larger Samoan men, a rifle slung over his shoulder with a strap.

There was a thump from inside the room. I turned back to find my companion had fallen to the floor against the wall. He did not move from that spot for the next three or four hours. During the night, our guard was relieved by a tall, strapping Samoan named Sao, who looked in on us. Davenport seemed to take a little interest in this new arrival. Neither of us knew Sao, but had seen him doing his grueling work on the grounds chopping through encroaching liana with a bush knife in the impossible task of trying to keep paths clear of the ever-growing forest. He wielded an ax with grace. His legs were covered in tattoos that represented battles fought. Davenport called for assistance from Sao several times toward the end of the night shift, and Sao came in a state of utter exhaustion. Later, I could hear the Samoan curse his relief guard, the carefree and handsome Laefoele, for arriving fifteen minutes late, at least that was what I surmised from the part of the conversation I could translate. Davenport, I would discover, understood it all very well.

I FELT A TUG on my shoulder the next night. Raising my head, the reality of our situation pushed out the sweet oblivion of sleep. I had been sleeping on the floor, without even a mat beneath me. Davenport gestured for me to come with him. To my surprise, I saw he had opened the door very slightly. Now he pushed it farther open. An even greater surprise, there was no apparent reaction to this, so he peered around the edge of the door, holding his breath as he did. Sao, who once again was our night guard, was slouched in his chair asleep and nobody else was in sight. Davenport gestured that I hurry; I shook my head and mouthed a protest. But he already had started his dangerous path, leaving me to either obey or be left alone.

Davenport dragged his uncooperative leg as quietly as he could and I remained so close behind I was almost touching him. We passed the guard's chair without a stir from the dog-tired Samoan. Davenport later told me he had been tempted to grab Sao's rifle, which rested loosely on the man's lap, but judged it too risky. We did not know the exact time of night, but it was late enough that the rest of the house would be asleep—except perhaps for Laefoele, the relief guard, wherever he was. Possibly on his way.

A loose floorboard emitted a sound under our feet. A soft creak, no louder than a sigh. I willed myself not to look back, as though the glance itself would alert Sao. But I could not help it, and as I turned my head, I knew what was about to happen. Sao looked first at the open door and then at us.

Forgetting, it seemed, that he had a lethal weapon at his fingertips with which to shoot us down, Sao lowered his head and charged Davenport. The bookaneer watched this unfold with his usual composure, and easily dodged the runner. Sao smashed right through the stair railing. He toppled over the side and held one of the broken posts, dangling from the edge of the top floor, below him a long drop to the lower level.

Davenport grabbed one of his hands and I clasped the other. We heaved.

"Hold on to us," Davenport said, struggling with his weight. I lost my grip on the other hand, which was slick with sweat, then the hand Davenport gripped began to slip, but Davenport was able to grab on to Sao's long, thick hair and pull with better leverage. When Sao was safely back at the top, he remained on the floor, catching his breath and shaking off the scare.

"Thank to you, White Chiefs," he said in English. "Thank to you, you save Sao—"

Davenport interrupted the speech by pummeling the back of Sao's head with the butt of the rifle, which the man had dropped. "Apologies," Davenport muttered as he stepped around the unconscious lump on the floor to close the door to our former prison. He gestured again for me, but my jaw and mind were slack, frozen by the scene as my companion strained to pull Sao into the chair. Though I was urging him to hurry, I had an idea why he would slow our progress to get Sao into position. If the relief guard thought Sao was asleep, we could win a few extra minutes for our escape before the room was entered.

I helped Davenport down the back stairs of the house. He was extremely winded from the confrontation with Sao. It struck me with a fresh jolt of fear just how weak his injuries had left him, worsened by these last sedentary days at Vailima. We found a lit torch outside the ground floor and Davenport swept it up, staggering and groaning into the night.

It was steamy and windless, but the air on my face and mouth refreshed me. Davenport was visibly relieved to find no signs of pursuers from the house. He was emboldened. But as he took a few more steps onto the grounds, his head swiveled upward. I followed the line of his gaze.

There, on the second-story verandah, the long figure of a man was wrapped into the hammock. I knew that some nights the novelist found relief from his physical ailments by sleeping in the hammock. I could see in the dim blue mushroom-shaped lamps of the verandah that there was a conch shell beside the hammock, alongside the ever-present supply of extra tobacco. A cat was curled up by his feet.

The netted cradle rocked Stevenson and the cat back and forth. After trading whispers, neither Davenport nor I could say whether the man above us was asleep or awake. The long face was covered in shadows. Thunder from the retreating storms rolled through the mountain. Davenport started scrambling across the grounds toward the paddock and I did the same. Sao, Laefoele, Stevenson: the ways to be caught were multiplying at a rapid rate. When we were close enough to the paddock for our eyes to memorize the path beyond, Davenport extinguished our torch under his boot. The blinding darkness that swept around us immediately made the decision seem like a bad one. The hammock still rocked back and forth in a blue glow, now the only light we could see. Stevenson's head had turned slightly, facing us. For all the gold in the world I still could not say whether the novelist was awake, though the fact that he was not moving from his hammock in spite of our flight suggested he slept soundly. Then I noticed that Stevenson's long toes curled and then stretched, curled and stretched again, scratching the cat's back. Davenport perceived this at the same time I did, and launched into the best run he could manage. Stevenson had been watching us all along, toying with us.

When Davenport emerged from the paddock climbing on a horse, his aches seemed to recede; the creature's strength became his own. He reached down to me.

"What are you waiting for, Fergins?"

"Not Jack."

"What?"

"We can't take Jack! He's Tusitala's favorite! It will kill him."

"It is the best animal on this rotting terrain, and our best chance; now take my hand!"

The hammock was empty and the next noise was the sound of a

conch being blown. The slightest differences in the shell's notes could call the family to dinner or announce that the island was at war, but neither of us had mastered the sounds enough to guess their meanings. Then we heard shouts in Samoan, including one deep, angry voice I recognized as Sao's, amid the din of general chaos we had just unleashed.

I never before noticed how tall Jack was. I was struggling to climb up behind Davenport, and slipped down into a cloud of dust.

"Go without me," I urged.

He was determined to wait, but I had hit the ground hard. When we heard hoof-falls I yelled again for him to go, and Davenport finally set himself on the animal and galloped away. A few moments later, I heard Jack snorting and whinnying, the sounds moving back toward me. The clouds covering the moon had begun to fall away. There were silhouettes of Samoans everywhere I looked. Axes, rifles, and knives were at the ready.

WE SPENT THE REST of the night in the same room from which we had originally escaped, this time with two guards at all times who were, I assume, exhorted by Stevenson to stay more vigilant, or at least awake. We made no further attempts to flee. The next morning we were escorted by John Chinaman and two young Samoans into Stevenson's sanctum, where the master of the house was sitting up in the bed, not so different from the position I now take telling you the story. The bed was covered in mosquito netting. His flageolet was disassembled into many pieces, spread out on the quilt in front of him.

"I have just discovered what is wrong with me, my white gentlemen," Stevenson said, looking at his reflection in a small mirror. He contorted his face a couple of times, then turned to the profile. "I look like a Pole."

Davenport and I glanced at each other, unsure if the novelist waited for a response.

Stevenson put down the mirror and waved his hand over the segments of his musical instrument. "Seventeen separate members, you see, my white gentlemen, and most of these have to be fitted on their individual springs as fine as needles. Sometimes two at once, with the springs showing different ways." His rage seemed to have dissipated, at least outwardly.

I looked again at Davenport, whose eyebrow was now raised and taut as he was nodding in agreement.

"Tell us just one thing, if you would," the bookaneer said. "About the other stream."

Stevenson squinted.

"We only found four," Davenport explained. "*Vai* means water and *lima* means five. We looked everywhere we could. Where is the fifth stream and where does it lead?"

The novelist shrugged. "There are only four. 'Vailima' sounded better than the Samoan word for 'four streams.'"

Davenport smiled his gratitude for the explanation, then tried to build on the exchange with a confidential tone. "Perhaps we can still work out an arrangement, Tusitala."

"Do you know what the traditional punishment for deception in Samoa is, Mr. Porter?" Stevenson said, now looking right at him. "Apologies, I mean Davenport. It is this: You are cast off alone in a canoe in the middle of the ocean. If you are lucky, you die at sea rather than make land on one of the cannibal islands."

"Is that your intention for us?" I asked, swallowing hard.

"I forced Mr. Fergins to accompany me," Davenport said. "He deserves no punishment."

Stevenson opened his mouth, then closed it before he started again. "Do you know what angers me most? The truth should have occurred to me. After all, where would one meet a man as agreeable as you, but in fiction? A man who would volunteer to hold my cigarette after only knowing me a few weeks." He twisted two pieces of the flageolet together. "I have been disappointed in so many friendships I supposed I tricked myself into having high hopes. Has any author ever fought back against you bookaneers?"

"Some."

"Have any succeeded? Have you literary Robin Hoods and Rob Roys ever been vanquished by a mere scribbler?"

"That remains to be seen," answered Davenport.

"You made a grave mistake this time, taking on one of your 'missions' of greed against what may be the only author on earth who has his own little militia"—another piece of the musical instrument was fitted and twisted in—"armed up to my teeth. When I deal with literary pirates, I do it with gloves off. You know, I suspect there is more that drives your conquests, Mr. Davenport. Love for a woman, perhaps, hindered or lost long ago. Is that so?"

Davenport's eyes popped.

"What are they still doing here?" It was Fanny, who had just walked in. Her lips trembled after she spoke.

"Never mind, Barkis, I am taking care of it."

"Taking care! You told me these men came to steal from you. This is no house; it's an asylum, where our family has come; one by one, to lose their minds, and everyone else looks in on us to make certain it happens!" She was in tears. Lloyd trailed a few steps behind her. "No, don't take me away! These men must be judged! You"—she pointed right at me—"you were supposed to help convince Louis to take us all back home! Now we are all doomed!"

Lloyd could not manage to pacify his mother at all. But Stevenson extended his hand through the netting and reached hers.

"Teacher, tender comrade, wife,

A fellow farer true through life,

Heart whole and soul free,

The August father gave to me."

Her hysteria settled down to a low sob as he recited and she squeezed his hand. Lloyd managed to lead her away into another room, leaving us to resume our quiet confrontation.

Davenport, as though he were in the position to make demands, said, "Let us be done with the games. What will you do? What will happen now?"

Stevenson turned his head away without answering. Then he said, almost reassuringly, "Whenever I think of you, I will damn you until the air is blue, and when you think of me, you will damn me until the air is blue, and everything will be all right in the world. Tell me, what happens to 'bookaneers' when they must finally leave the little bubble of literary life?"

"I suppose they usually disappear from sight."

"Then you shall be no different. Men, you are now retired from your business. I suppose I know nothing, except that men are fools and hypocrites, and I know less of them than I was fond enough to fancy." At a signal from Stevenson, John led us out of the room and through the house as Stevenson began to play a slow, tortured tune in a minor key.

Davenport spoke in Chinese (he later translated the conversation for me). "I will pay you generously to help us."

"You can speak my tongue," John answered back in Chinese in utter surprise.

"My profession has brought me many places," Davenport continued smoothly in the other man's tongue. "I know you wish to go away from here, to go home. Back to your own people. Where you will not be demeaned any longer as 'John Chinaman.' Help us to find Father Thomas and get off the island safely, and I could help you. I will send you money and find your passage."

John grabbed Davenport by the throat. They had to be separated by native servants. We were then pulled and pushed until we were outside, where we were both thrust into the same empty stall of the paddock inside which Charlie had died in the midst of hallucination and mental anguish. Davenport looked as though he had been dropped into hell, kneeling to examine the ropes and leather straps that had held Charlie down. After a few hours, we heard a commotion outside, and I pressed my face against a slot between two boards.

"What, Fergins?"

I tried to think how best I could tell him what I saw: an entire regiment of Samoan soldiers gathering outside, with a litter that had an iron cage on top, tied to two horses.

XIV

"O*le Fale Puipei.*" That was the inscription over the entrance to the Apian jail, built on the edge of the island's most miserable swamp. Perhaps I will find a satisfactory translation of this motto one day. Maybe it was some antiquated form of the language that did not match the words as I learned them. "In the Talons of Hope." Understand, Mr. Clover, that might not be what it means, but that is what it *should* mean.

We had been there one time before, to visit the man who had tried to steal from Stevenson and whom I had first suspected was Belial. Now that we were the prisoners with that same wretched Banner in a chamber near those we were put in, it seemed the whole place might have been erected for those whom Robert Louis Stevenson perceived to have wronged him at one point or another.

There is a little room in the back of the jail used for interviews. We were taken there separately for interrogations by the authorities. They were not so interested in the bookaneer's mission and purpose, for after all there were no books on this island except those brought by whites, and certainly the whole notion of stealing one was rather fanciful in the realm of crimes on the island. Instead, it was the issue of presenting ourselves with false identities that appalled their sensibilities. It was the terrible crime, as Stevenson had warned us, they called deception, something bookaneers practiced before eating breakfast.

"What is your friend's name? Davenport? He called himself Porter, no? You said his name was Porter? But you knew his name? You knew he was Davenport, and called him Porter?"

The issue of what Davenport was called provided endless fascination and distress to the magistrate. There was one official of the prison, a perplexed and angry man, who scowled and sighed at my every answer. Meanwhile, there was a representative from the German consulate, a commissioner or deputy commissioner of some sort, who observed it all with a cold indifference.

On the walls of my cell were carvings and chalk drawings, of ships and sea monsters, of dancing women and dead animals. There was one particularly elaborate and well-done drawing that drew my eye. It showed a very tall figure of a giant or a god, surrounded by smaller men. As I studied it the giant started to look like Davenport, then Belial, then Stevenson.

Davenport and I were held in adjacent cells and could communicate between the thin walls. The fact was, our doors were usually unlocked, leaving us free to move up and down the passage. The guards armed with rifles usually remained in the courtyard in front of the building, and other native guards, who appeared to have only knives, brought us food. Banner laughed and spit at us, screamed that we got what we deserved for not helping him. But he was lonely, and soon enough he just wanted to talk with us.

Belle came to visit us—I should say instead to visit Davenport. She was dressed in a picnic dress of white and crimson with braided trim around the collar and sleeves, and also wore an enthusiastic grin, which popped into a big smile, as she spoke to him. She seemed entirely taken with the fact that he had turned out to be a criminal.

"Whatever will you do, Mr. Porter—Davenport?" she asked.

He and I were on a bench in the central passage, and she sat on one opposite from us. "It appears I haven't much choice in what I do, Miss Strong," he said mechanically.

"Do you mean"—she lowered her voice to a whisper and almost giggled her question—"you will escape?"

Both of us were too amazed to respond.

"Louis will not tell us very much about what you did or tried to do," she continued, too excited to wait for an answer to her earlier question. "I told him I was going to the village for supplies to make some new dresses. Do not worry. Neither Vao nor I will ever breathe a word of this visit or of your plans."

"Vao?" Davenport echoed.

"Yes, the most prized of our house girls. She accompanied me here and listens to what I tell her to do, so don't worry about her either. You know of her?"

"She was the dwarf's charge," I said, hoping to defuse the tension that came from Davenport's sudden animation.

Belle rolled her eyes. "He was always the funniest little creature. Since Tulagi jumped into that ditch we have hardly known what to do with her. I caught her trying on one of my dresses yesterday. She was seen drinking alcohol from our cabinets by one of our houseboys, and some food that had gone missing she had apparently eaten in one sitting. If it were not for our feeling sympathy for her because of the dwarf's death, she would have had to be dismissed. I am trying to keep her busy so it will not come to that."

Davenport interrupted before she had finished. "Was it Vao's idea to come here, or yours?"

Her head tilted in a gesture of suspicion at the question. "Who do you think makes the decisions, Mr. Davenport, me or the brown girls who serve Vailima?"

Davenport had lost patience for her. "Just please tell me where she is."

"Waiting outside. You greet my visit with lassitude and apathy, yet your eyes dance at the mention of the little native girl. Do you fancy her?"

"You misunderstand," Davenport said, though in fact the young woman had been astute. "I just need to speak to her—"

She was seething, her cheeks streaked red, reminding me of her mother during her first outburst toward me. "Perhaps you do belong in here, after all," she said, and there ended the visit.

Davenport continued to be sullen and quiet after ruining any chance that Belle might help. Having known him for so many years, I was inclined to assume he was plotting—that he would hatch some victory from the darkest and lowest point of his adventures. I thought back to a time he sent for me while authorities in Dublin were questioning him and, once I arrived at the police station, rather a nervous wreck, the confidence in his eyes that it was an amusing and merely temporary problem (he was right). But when we were able to come together in the central passage of the Samoan prison and I looked closely—the rare moments his eyes met mine—I knew how different it was this time. I had never seen him like this. He was overcome.

I told him he should not have waited for me so long when I fell from the horse at Vailima. Perhaps he could have escaped Stevenson's men.

"Could I?" His words were muffled, his mouth covered by the palm of his hand. He had not shaved since his injury and his coarse beard had been growing again, and with the latest crop of whiskers his whole face seemed to be cast in shadows. "Had I known, Fergins, that it would be an author who would vanquish me—why, I think I would have enjoyed the devilishness of it all. No, there would have been no escape this time, not with an army of islanders after me. Kitten was right."

"What do you mean?"

"She once told me that when the last bookaneer appeared, he would leave grinning, and so our business would end." He was speaking to me, but it was almost a trancelike state from which the words emerged. "She thought I would be her legacy. She thought it would be me."

I was confused. "Who?"

"The last bookaneer. She said I could be the best because I was heartless. She meant it as praise, Fergins. That unlike all the authors whose books we chased, I had learned to separate the sentiment from the ambition. I tried, I always tried to be what she thought I was. . . ." Then he hung his head. *Overcome.*

It was so rare for him to speak of Kitten that whenever he did, I hardly ever responded. After her death, I had held on to that French edition of *Frankenstein* I mentioned earlier, the one she had left behind at a hotel near Geneva during her opium haze. Even if Davenport would seldom discuss her, my time with Kitten on Lake Geneva left me wanting to try to understand her better. Though she had not been able to tell me anything about it, a secondhand book reveals much to the keeper of a bookstall. From the types of cracks in the spine and the edges of pages, I can tell at a glance a book that has been well read from a book that has been abused. I believe it was the litterateur Charles Lamb who told Coleridge that books are not just the words on the page, but the blots and the dog-eared corners, the buttery thumbprints and pipe ash we leave on them. I knew a bookseller who by habit marked his page with his wire-rimmed spectacles, dozens of his spectacles being found for years after his death in libraries across London. Books are written over with names, dates, romantic and business propositions, gift dedications; the pages could be pressed onto flowers, keys, notes. A book can unfold moments or generations, if you know how to see it. Most people, of course, do not. How odd it must be to go through life believing that a book is a book.

In the case of this particular edition of Shelley's novel, it was one of the first translations to be printed after the young Englishwoman's story became such a sensation. In France, unlike in many other countries, people will go without food in order to own a book they enjoy. The French publishers were fragmented by regions in the early 1820s. The whole world was smaller then, and there was no better example of it than in books. Booksellers and publishers in the olden days were one and the same. You would meet an author in person, print and bind his book, and sell it to your friends and neighbors. Though the bookseller who printed it was no longer in existence, I easily identified the area of France where it most likely had been first sold. I could also determine almost immediately it'd had at least two different owners, judging from the different ways pages had been held and marked, and some writing on two different places on the flyleaf—the first line of writing was crossed out too thoroughly to read; another appeared to be the name Loui.

I thought about that book as Davenport finished speaking about Kitten's wishes for his career.

"If you could have overtaken Belial this time, what would you have said to him?" I asked, in part to relieve him of the topic of Kitten.

He smirked to himself, I suppose thinking of an answer, but had no intention of telling it to me. We stood there in silence.

Without a conversation, the flow of my memories continued: Whenever I was traveling near France after Kitten's death, I brought her book with me as well as a list of all the aliases I had heard associated with Kitten, gradually narrowing them down through defunct directories to determine her birth name. Because it seemed to have had two owners with no familial resemblance in handwriting, I suspected this *Frankenstein* had been a secondhand purchase before landing in Kitten's hands.

When I was satisfied I had identified her surname and its proper branch, I was able to discover several people who remembered Kitten's family, which had moved away long ago. One old lady had a vivid memory of Kitten's mother, whose name, Louisa, matched the one on the flyleaf. She did not recognize the edition of the book but did remember her fondness for *Frankenstein*, describing it as an obsession. "It was her favorite story—she said it was the only book other than the Bible that she read beginning to end, and her Bible she would throw at her children's heads or use to beat them. She was a mean woman, had three or four sons and the one girl, who had to steal to feed herself. But that book, she loved. Why, that witch even begged her daughter to read the book to her when she was ill—imagine, a dying woman coughing blood onto her pillow, asking a fifteen-year-old girl to read such a disgusting story out loud. I'd spit on her if I saw her living again. A detestable picture!" She spit right on the book.

I was very moved by the image of Kitten as a young woman whose mother only appreciated her through this book. One of my earliest memories is of my own mother singing to me. Nothing sophisticated, Irish peasant songs she had heard from her grandmother. Over the years, I found the words to these songs printed in various obscure books, and when my mother had long forgotten the songs herself, I would sing them to her, and I believe that brought her some happiness, or at least the memory of happiness.

No doubt Belial had been right when he told Davenport that giving Kitten such an enormous success as the Shelley novelette hollowed her ambitions. But I believed there had been something more, and that Belial, as Belial did, flattered himself to think he knew the whole story. There are some who would never want to look at a book again associated with such a bleak past as her mother's abuse of her, but to Kitten her mother's copy of Shelley's novel had become a talisman. It was impossible to ask her now, but it seemed to me that perhaps she sought some peace from that mission. Mary Shelley had once said that writing *Frankenstein* made her cross from childhood into life; I think Kitten believed that finding the long-lost Shelley document, the supposed key to the creation of *Frankenstein*, would have finally given her dominion over the bedlam of her childhood. This is just my speculation. I cannot really say what was in Kitten's mind, other than to repeat the scattered, incomplete comments she made in her final weeks. Do our professional accomplishments ever really act as salve to personal grief?

I'd tried speaking to Davenport about Kitten's copy of *Frankenstein* after I discovered its provenance, and I asked him again in the corridor of the Samoan prison. I had no more success trying to engage him about it than I'd had years before. But he did tell me about his nightmares, about his visions of Kitten dying, about the fact that he thought success in the Samoan mission might finally banish these visitations from his dreams.

That night, a prison guard came and woke me from a deep sleep. He began leading me away. He did not respond to any English, and in my stupor I could not manage sufficient Samoan to question him.

"They are releasing you," said Banner, who had come into the passage to see what was happening.

"Davenport, do you hear that?" I called. "We are freed."

The bookaneer rushed to the doorway of his chamber. The guard gestured at him to return to his place.

"Not him," Banner continued, punctuating his declaration with his usual snort. "The brown fellow says because you used your true name, you will not face charges of deceit. Your grumpy friend must stay in this dismal hole with the rest of us."

I dug my heels into the clay floor. "I won't go either."

"You some kind of martyr?" Banner asked, his hollow eyes widening.

"You must go," the bookaneer said with a stoic air.

"What about you? The mission?"

"You complete the mission."

"What do you mean?" He might have been speaking Samoan himself.

Davenport grabbed my shoulders. "Fergins, listen. I do not know when we'll next meet, so remember my instructions exactly. Leave the jail with the guard. If there has not yet been a ship to sail from here, you can still find him."

"Belial? How could I—"

"Find him, do what you must to take the manuscript from him."

"How on earth could *I*—"

"Quiet! For once in your life be quiet!" he shouted, his eyes red and wet. He dried them with the back of his sleeve. His hands, gripping my shoulders again, shook me and drifted toward each other so if he squeezed, he would have strangled me. "Do whatever you must, for God's sake, Fergins! Surprise will be your best stratagem, since he will not expect you. This is my last chance to see Belial defeated."

"But you will not see it if you are in here."

The guard physically dragging me away, I shouted in protest against him and against the bookaneer's plan but all to no avail. The sinking feeling that had begun to form in the pit of my stomach settled in as I lost my view of Davenport. I laugh now, but not because I find the memories humorous, Mr. Clover. I only laugh at my slightly younger self because I could not know how entirely alone I was about to become.

I WAS SO STARTLED by my release from incarceration and separation from my only companion on the island, I did not pay attention to the odd timing of it all. I was being taken away *in the middle of the night.* I had been placed facing backward on a waiting horse, sitting behind one of the guards already in the saddle. The time of night was not the only queer thing. I was taken not toward the beach, where I would have expected to be handed off to the British consulate, but somewhere else, far from the prison, with no explanation or response to my many questions. At several points, it seemed we were going straight up inclines and the sides of cliffs. I tried to whistle away the anxiety. The angry official who had attended my interrogation was riding ahead of our party, and when we stopped in the dark interior of the island jungle, he was the one to come to me.

To my surprise, he spoke English well. He had not been perplexed at my words, as I had thought, during my interrogation. He had been perplexed by the fact that the line of questioning resolved itself against Davenport and not me.

"If it were my decision, you would stay in prison until you rot away, as your friend will," he said to me now. "But our orders are to release you."

"I thank you for it," I said in my most docile voice. I looked around in the dim light of torches, confused at what was happening to me.

He snickered at my note of appreciation. "A white man can rot in the heart of our island as well as any prison."

"No," I said, my chest pounding away, "you don't understand. . . ."

They had brought me all this way to discard me. I was pulled down from the saddle. The men turned their horses around in unison and then galloped off into the night.

IT SURPRISES ME as much as anything else does when thinking about surviving in the wilderness of Samoa, how long I was convinced I was being followed. Who would have bothered to pursue me? The prison guards who discarded me under the cover of darkness? Native assassins hired by Belial? If they really had been after me, I don't doubt they would have taken me quickly and easily were it not for a fresh deluge of rain, which covered my tracks. Any pursuit beyond that had to be in my mind alone, and in the vast silence and loneliness my mind was spinning.

In the dark interior, the dead wood all over the forest floor seemed phosphorescent. The glow seemed to come from below the earth, as though from the flames of hell. It only took a few minutes out there alone to believe with all my heart in the ghost stories of the natives.

There was a cave. I don't know how I found it when I think back to the thickness of that terrain. I remember I could not even see its entrance at first, feeling the formations of rocks with my fingers through the walls of liana wrapping around me. The cave was big enough to become my temporary shelter while more storms fell. I took stock of the little I had with me. One of the guards, in a fit of compassion, had dropped a burlap sack we had with us when we were taken from Vailima. Davenport had saved pieces of biscuits and other food scraps from Vailima in anticipation of our attempted escape. Among other fairly useless items was my slender umbrella. To supplement the paltry food in the sack, there was the usual plentiful fruit in the portion of forest close to the cave. Here were more berries than coconuts and bananas, making it harder to quell my hunger.

It was hard to know day from night out there because the jungle, which was all around, was so dark; hard to know how much time had passed. I would spend hours building a fire, keeping the swarms of flying insects at bay, and then count the sparks until it would burn itself out and I would be assaulted by their buzzing. One morning, something new woke me. My eyes opened on a tall, dark shape standing over me, outlined in firelight. I reached for my umbrella, which I had been keeping by my side. Then I jumped to my feet poised to defend myself.

The stranger held a sharpened spear slightly behind his body and to his side. He easily could have skewered me while I slept, so I calculated that my best chance was to avoid appearing threatening. I slowly placed the umbrella by my feet.

The man was a head taller than I was, at least. His skin was much darker than that of the Samoans I had met—a deep chocolate color instead of reddish brown—and his muscular arms and bare chest were glistening with sweat and blood. He spoke a few words, and I did not recognize any of them. I had improved greatly in Samoan since our arrival, yet I couldn't place the sounds that came from this man's mouth.

I put up my hands in the universal sign that I meant no harm— at least that's how I hoped the stranger would interpret it. His gray loincloth appeared strangely European, unlike the usual lavalavas of the natives, which were made of bark. Then I remembered seeing the same gray cloth on a group of laborers from the German Firm who were being taken to a boat on the beach in Apia. Those men had been the Firm's plantation slaves. The ones whose escaped comrades' heads we had seen exhibited on stakes while riding with Stevenson.

Cannibals.

He took a step closer to me and I stumbled back over an uneven rock formation. I gasped as the cannibal dashed toward me. He caught me and stopped my fall.

WE COULD NOT UNDERSTAND each other except through the occasional very simple exchange, but he was sharp as a needle in knowing what I was trying to say. I had enough clues to feel certain the young man was indeed a runaway from the German Firm and he, in turn, must have guessed that I was also a displaced soul of some sort. This vague connection tied us together. As we spent more time together, I was able to conclude that the islander was no more than sixteen years old, though, remembering Stevenson's maxim—they grow fast in the South Seas—a Western eye would take him to be closer to your age, Mr. Clover, eighteen or nineteen. His natural timidity, genuine eagerness, and a quick enthusiasm suggested his true age. Our tutoring sessions involved pointing—at a plant, a piece of fruit, a lava rock, the moon, the sun—and saying the words in our respective language. The runaway pointed to himself and said what sounded to me like "*No-bo-lo.*"

We stayed together when we went out looking for food and supplies. When we climbed to higher elevations, Nobolo pointed out at the violently choppy ocean beyond the island and I interpreted this to mean he wanted to leave the island to return to his homeland. I pointed toward the Apia shore and Nobolo seemed to understand where I needed to go. The rains had slowed down after the first few days but until they stopped, and until the treacherous mountain paths dried, the safest thing was to stay where we were—we had a brook for water, we had discovered decent supplies of fruit along a belt of trees, even some clumps of oranges, and the cave was suitable for sleeping and sheltering both of us.

I had cuts on my legs and arms from wandering through the bush, and the insects were relentless trying to savage me. Nobolo brought hollowed sticks of rainwater and cleaned my wounds with a careful, precise hand.

When the rain stopped, the mist was high and soupy. We went hunting together, moving single-file through the thickly wooded, slippery paths. Nobolo had carved a spear for me that looked like his own. The clearer sky and drier earth gave me a feeling of freedom and I sensed that Nobolo was also infused with a new spirit.

We also spent time drawing in the mud and sand outside the cave. We were sketching maps and the path we would take together and marking where I would ultimately separate from my companion, a fellow I had come to believe was as loyal as Crusoe's man, Friday. Losing Nobolo was a prospect that I found quite sad, in defiance of any piece of logic I might muster. Having Nobolo nearby, I realized, reminded me somehow of my life before this, when I accompanied Davenport through the great cities in the world. Neither of us knew the island well enough to dictate the plan with full confidence, but between the two of us we possessed a passing amount of information about where we sought to end up and where we ought not to go. Nobolo needed to stay clear of the German plantation and its masters, while I needed to avoid any sighting by Belial.

The maps made communication with Nobolo easier; more challenging was deciding when to set off on our journey. I felt we had to start at night, so that at the height of the midday heat we would not be locked into a part of the island where water was scarce and sometimes dangerous to find.

One night before we were to begin, we roasted a pig over a flame and ate more than we had since living on rations inside the cave. Then, Nobolo brought over a knife he had been carving out of cherrywood and animal bone, and gestured toward his hair. I understood that he did not want his hair to get caught or pulled in the brush during our long journey to come and I agreed to cut it.

As I neared the end of butchering his hair, there was a slight rustle outside the cave. Both of us receded into the blackness to listen. Then there was the light of a torch, held high and in front by one who moved with a slow and purposeful step. I peered into the light, first making out the staring eyes and then a face.

Before I could speak, Nobolo caught sight of the tip of the rifle and was thrown into a panic. He launched into a run and disappeared into the darkness outside.

I tried to catch him as he burst out of the cave but he was quick as a spark. "She isn't here for you!" My cries went unheeded, unheard or simply not comprehended. Another companion was gone.

XV

As soon as Vao entered, the setting seemed to change: no longer stranded, I felt all that had happened back in Vailima return to the atmosphere. She looked around before she lowered the rifle. She offered some basic information about how she had found me: Having traveled between several villages after leaving Tale-Pui-Pui with Belle, she had overheard that a white prisoner was about to be released and decided to find out whether it was one of us. As soon as she and Belle had returned to Vailima, she rode back to the prison again on her own. When the guards would not tell her anything, she demanded to see the officials at the prison and eventually discovered where they had brought me in the bush, and from there began tracking my movements. She went on with her explanation, retracing her steps that led to the mouth of this cave, but I could hardly concentrate on any of her words, because the language mesmerized me. English.

"How on earth did you learn to speak so flawlessly since I saw you?" I interrupted, realizing even as I spoke that it was foolish. She could not have mastered a language so quickly. We had been keeping our secrets, and she had been keeping her own.

"When my father was one of the leading chiefs, and I a little girl, I was given tutors. Mostly men from the religious missions, they taught me in the languages of all the foreigners who come to the island: German, English, French, Spanish."

"I never heard a word of English come from your mouth at Vailima."

"I never speak it in front of white men, or they will not leave me alone." It was not just the language that was startling, but the heat of her emotions—anger, confusion, loneliness—within the words she spoke, emotions I had not been able to hear in her Samoan. "There have been many attempts to take me since I was quite little."

"That is why Tulagi was always with you?"

"When a village chooses a *tapo*, she is assigned a guardian, usually a dwarf or a hunchback, since they cannot start families or fight in our wars. My father was the chief of one of the villages burned to the ground by the Germans for not accepting Tamasese, the king installed by the power of the Firm. Father did not survive the flames, but Tulagi did, and he swore he would protect me until the day when I was married, when my husband assumes the responsibility. Except I never agreed to the potential marriages. Tulagi was unusual, for though he was impatient with my refusals, he respected my decisions. Now with Tulagi wandering the spirit realms looking for rest, everything left of my birthright has been taken from me."

I was careful with my next question for her. "That is why you have come here?"

"I have come for vengeance against the man who led Tulagi to his death."

I held my breath, expecting her to speak against Davenport—and perhaps, by extension, me. She may not have come to rescue me at all, but to exterminate me, and here I was trapped, at her mercy.

Before my fear revealed itself she went on: "The man you call Belial. From the moment he stepped foot on Tusitala's grounds calling himself a missionary, I saw the devil in him. His humiliation of Tulagi, beating him in front of you, ripped Tulagi's heart in two."

She returned my stare and I tried to shake away any outward sign of confusion. It was the sight of Davenport leaving her chambers—not

Belial's earlier attempt to seduce her, and his ruthless beating of Tulagi—that finally dragged Tulagi down to despair. I resolved I could never tell her.

—Wait a minute, Mr. Fergins. Wait. How did you come to know the true cause of Tulagi's suicide?

Well, I did not know, Mr. Clover. Nobody can really know what had been in Tulagi's mind and heart that day. You are absolutely right to wonder about that. But if you saw Tulagi's face as I had, after he watched her emerge from Davenport's chambers, you might think the same way I do.

—Then why did you not tell Vao what you suspected?

I felt myself prohibited *personali objectione*, as the lawyers say, from telling her. To reveal it to her could place me in danger, because a grudge against Pen Davenport would probably have fallen on me, too. She might have believed leaving me there to die would give the dwarf peace in the spirit world. I had to keep quiet about it, you see.

—Forgive me, but I do not think that is the only reason. You saw she could serve you, no different than Cipaou served you and Mr. Davenport, or Charlie served Mr. Stevenson. Isn't that right, Mr. Fergins? It benefited you to ensure that she believed it was Belial's fault, because it meant she would help you hunt for him—so you could find the manuscript—using knowledge of the island that only a native has.

Good fellow! You see it clearly enough. And, don't forget, it was to her advantage for *her* purposes that I knew Belial better than she did.

I asked her: "You will help me find him, then?"

"I will and when we do, I will take his head."

There is something immense about watching a person—a woman, especially—you have seen speaking in one language speak in a different tongue. When she spoke Samoan, it was soft and warm, yet in English she was imperious. She seemed not only transformed but transformative, as though by being in her presence you crossed boundaries, geographical and metaphysical. I speak lyrically of the sensation, but that is how I recall it struck me as she sat cross-legged in the cave as if some ancient goddess. There was a beauty to her speaking English that was independent of her physical attractiveness, and I had to wonder if Davenport had the same experience in his time alone with her. Speaking of her beauty, I had taken this long on the island to appreciate just how radiant she was. Perhaps this is one thing that distinguishes a bachelor from gentlemen who marry—by the point at which we truly recognize a lady's charms, the time for a natural courtship has passed.

She was made an even more striking vision by her changed appearance since I had last seen her. She was wearing a ceremonial costume, draped in animal skins and multicolored leaves, her hair lined with small purple flowers and pinned back in a cocoon. This, I gathered, Samoan women used as a warrior garb.

She had already done some investigation that eased my mind. None of the larger ships had departed from port, and the waters remained too rough from the ongoing storms for Belial to have hired a canoe or other smaller ship without great risk to his life. Vao had also stopped in several villages along the way to my shelter. While some tribes were strictly loyal to the king and would not speak to a member of a tribe that was not, there were still many who had common cause with the rebels and felt affection toward a former *tapo*. Through these exchanges, she learned that Belial had traded information he had about Stevenson, a supporter of the exiled chief Mataafa, the king's greatest enemy and threat, in exchange for the king's protection and sanctuary.

After remaining the night in the cave, we had an early start looking for clues to where Belial had been concealed. There is a strange fact about a place as rainy as Upolu. The ground does not seem to absorb the raindrops, so that long after a storm has vanished there are still torrents of water rushing down the island toward the coast. Streams that were usually ankle-deep became powerful rivers. We went on foot down one treacherous precipice after another, each one seeming to end at the horizon, until we finally reached the place where she had tied her horse. I shared Vao's horse but the animal was not strong enough for the two of us and began to rebel under our combined weight, at one point stopping in protest and stomping, and other times audibly groaning; we would not have been able to go much farther but for the fact that we reached the outskirts of a small village outpost. There I bartered my downtrodden umbrella and some kava root we had collected along the way in exchange for another animal. Much like the other natives who had seen the object, my trading partners grasped for the umbrella with awe on their faces and, in spite of its wear, seemed pleased by the multicolored stripes as they took turns twirling it. Without this second horse, the young woman would have had to go without me, and I would have been left to plod through the fickle elements of the island until means were presented to allow me to try to find her again—a risky proposition to body and soul, as you have seen, which is the reason to this day I call that umbrella a lifesaver.

The hurricane had scattered giant branches and tree trunks the size and girth of temple pillars that slowed our progress. After another night in the mountains, with two crashing waterfalls in my ears as I tried to sleep, I watched the clouds dissolve and the mountaintops above light up orange and purple with the new day.

Vao built a temporary abode for us out of banana leaves. We had simple meals collected from the surrounding forest: breadfruit and pigeon cooked *fa'a Samoa*, that is to say wrapped in banana leaves and cooked over hot stones. I told her about prison and she spoke more of Tulagi, more about her life at Vailima.

"He is our chief and our father," she said of Stevenson, with a glow to her cheeks. "Tusitala sheltered me and Tulagi after my village was burned, but now it is time that I left," and there she paused, fear and exhilaration in the treble of her voice. "I cannot always be protected:

first my father, then Tulagi and Tusitala and, one day, a husband. This is all Tulagi wanted, was for me to marry, but every time I tried, every time I tried to tell him. . . This time, I must protect myself. I must finish Belial for myself."

"Why didn't you just tell Tusitala that Belial tried assaulting you?" I asked.

"I knew Pope Thomas—Belial—was a conniving man. For a smile from him my people bow at his feet. I tried to arrange that Tusitala would find Belial trying to force himself on me, but you came instead."

"You mean you *did* try to seduce Belial?"

"He had taken every opportunity he could to lean in close to me and brush against me every time he was at Vailima. I did nothing to invite that. I did lure him to me that day, hoping Tusitala would hear me and catch him in the act and have him expelled from Vailima, yes." Seeing my expression, she gave me a wise half smile, amused by a white man's shock. "But Tusitala had gone outside, and Tulagi was closer to the room than I thought he was, and then it all went wrong."

Her little smile disappeared, replaced by a quivering lip. Davenport must have heard all of this from her, too, when they were alone together, and I could envision a grin curving onto his face, as he would have admired her resourcefulness. I understood the weight of her guilt at her own actions, as much as Belial's beastly behavior, drove her determination to punish Belial—then again, the extent and weight of our guilt drives so much of what we do.

In one corner was the banana leaf I used as a bed; in the other, Vao's. Though as far as I could tell she never slept, but sat, once again cross-legged, staring. She said nothing was wrong, but I knew, in addition to mourning Tulagi, she worried how we were to succeed. The fact is, the little information we had was too flimsy for us to ever hope to find Belial among the vast places he could be hidden on the island—

we wished we were simply looking for a needle in a haystack, but the fugitive bookaneer was a needle in a flaming haystack. Still, a flicker of faith rekindled in me as I listened to the incessant murmur of one of the nearby streams. We had moved closer to Apia and, I hoped, to my ultimate goal. I could leave nothing to chance.

I was woken by music. Beams of light were spreading over me, and through my heavy lids I saw Vao was not there. I pushed myself up and went outside, where I found her on the edge of the stream playing a kind of improvised pipe made of a hollow stick of bamboo. She seemed at peace.

"It is beautiful."

"I only like to play music when the birds are singing; that is why I wake up with them," she replied. "My father would never allow a bird or any animal to be injured. He was called 'the bird chief.'"

"If we find Belial . . ." I began, trying to think how to remind her delicately that a confrontation could become violent.

She stared up into the sky. "He is lower than the smallest animal or insect, lower than any brute, for he sings only false notes. Tulagi would tell me that I must free my mind from thoughts of revenge."

"Perhaps he would have been right."

"As a woman, I am to inspire and support the men in their fights, but not fight my own, just as a dwarf he was never to be a soldier, never to be a husband, no matter how much a woman—"

Here she ended her comments abruptly and she played her pipe to hide fresh tears.

"My dear," I said, gasping. "Forgive me. I never realized."

She had loved Tulagi and, not allowed to, had to live through the torments of being presented one candidate after another for marriage by him. There it was. Had this driven her into the arms of Davenport, or had she been trying to show herself there could be a man for her other than the dwarf who had held her heart for so long—instead breaking his into pieces?

IF, MR. CLOVER, you happen to find yourself in the South Seas one day, you might notice the way many of the islands of importance divide themselves naturally into the places the whites plant themselves and those places the natives live, from which they observe the whites. Most of the white settlers and officials seem content in this. But the Germans in Samoa were an exception. They were never willing to keep their distance. The German consulate buildings and the German Commercial and Trading Firm, together referred to simply as the Firm, occupied almost 150,000 acres of land on Upolu, making it the largest portion of land controlled by a foreign entity in Samoa.

The coat of arms, a picture of a soaring eagle, greeted us when we rode up to the consulate the next day. German guards in bright blue jackets stood outside the door watching our every move. There was a moment when we simultaneously took deep breaths.

"We do not have many choices left," I reassured her about what we were there to do.

She gathered herself. "I trust in you, Chief Fergins. I only wish I did not have to step foot on their so-called property. Their greed to have the lands my people deserve is what killed so many, including my father."

The government building was rather plain and not very large, at least in the shadow of the commercial structure. After we sat for a while staring at the whitewashed walls, we were greeted by a peculiar bureaucrat whose sloppy smile directed itself nowhere in particular.

"First thing in the morning, so much business to be done," he said, his interest in us flagging immediately. "I do apologize if you have been waiting. If you please follow me."

The first man left us in a private room, then a new and less friendly arrival introduced himself as Becker, the consul, and asked our business.

"We wish some information about a friend of ours who is missing," I said.

"I see," Becker said in a neutral voice.

"The Marist missionary, Thomas."

"I have met him on occasion. But as to his location, I'm afraid I cannot help. This island has many places where a man can disappear." His English was fluent but the words were rocked uncomfortably by sharp Germanic pronunciation.

I looked at Vao and nodded. She removed a pouch, pinching her eyes closed with distaste as a mixture of American and British coins slid out from it. It did not add up to very much, perhaps twenty American dollars in all, but it was what Vao had been able to bring with her from Vailima.

The consul made a clucking noise in his throat. "I am afraid my hands are tied," he said ambiguously, never denying he knew where Belial could be found.

"Herr Becker, I know the Firm watches all that happens on these islands, and this is of some importance," I said. His laconic expression did not change. I looked away from Vao as I continued: "Perhaps there is something else to trade. Information for information. It concerns the Solomon Islanders who escaped your plantation. The ones who still have their heads."

You appear shocked, Mr. Clover, at my ruthless tactic in my dialogue with the consul. But do not forget I had been in the presence of Whiskey Bill and Davenport many times over the years in negotiations such as this where securely held information was extracted using quiet aggression.

"What are you doing?" Vao hissed at me.

"I'm afraid you have been misled," Becker said.

"Oh?" I replied.

"Our consulate, like those of our American and British friends, is a resource to the native islanders. We are merely observers here."

"It was my understanding that you burn down houses that do not accept the king you chose."

Becker shook his head and offered an expression approximating compassion. "Houses! They are not houses. They are merely native huts, Mr. Fergins, no more substantial than the trees. The village I believe you speak of could have incited the king's followers into violence against the villagers. We protected them."

"Very well. I wonder if you wish to know information on the location of the camp of cannibals who escaped from your plantation."

"Traitor! Vile traitor!" Vao shouted at me. "This is your plan to get what you need? To lead those runaways to massacre?"

"Please, Vao, they are not your people. You must stay quiet while I do business."

"What is the meaning of this girl's outburst?" Becker demanded, pointing at her.

"I am the daughter of a man you murdered, sir," she replied vociferously in German, "in your attempt to prop up the marionette Tamasese, a devil who traded his soul and his island for power and riches. You believe you control our land because you amass warships and money. No. It is part of nature and does not belong to you. Who else will you betray for what you want, Chief Fergins?" she turned back to me, much to the other man's apparent relief. "Tusitala? Me? After I rescued you from the mountains and brought you safely to the beach."

I kept my eyes locked straight ahead: "I am sorry."

When she had begun screaming, the consul had clapped for his guards, who now came in and held her back. She struggled against them, and broke free long enough to land an elbow against my cheek.

"Off this man, you savage harlot!" Becker yelled.

I watched as the fiery girl was carried out.

The consul, wiping sweat from his face, folded his hands and rubbed his thumbs together in a performance of casualness. "Unfortunate that some of these brown women debase themselves, even the pretty ones, by trying to fight like their native brothers. It is, as I say, our role to improve the position of the natives any way we can. They will learn how to act more like we do. I will tell you about these runaways you spoke of. We give them the opportunity to lead lives here of hard work and productivity. Alas, sometimes they succumb to nostalgia for their heathen lands. Some of these, unfortunately, present a danger to the peaceful inhabitants of the island and we would certainly be a willing party to their capture alongside the native authorities."

I sat silently, still looking in the direction of where Vao was taken away.

"Never mind her. You wish to share what you know?" Becker pressed. "Perhaps to sketch a map?"

"I hardly know the island well enough," I said, shoving away some paper Becker brought over.

"How is it you would come upon the location of such savages, then?"

"An accident. I came to know Robert Louis Stevenson—Tusitala, as he is called here. While riding with him, he happened to tell me where the cannibals could be found."

Becker propped up a contemptuous smile, though just barely a smile, by jutting his large front teeth over his bottom lip. "Mmhmm," he murmured. "Herr Stevenson thinks he can be like a character in one of his sensational tales who leads men to glory by revealing secrets. Tell me, though, if you have become so friendly with Herr Stevenson—"

"We have had some differences over a mutual friend that left me aggrieved, and have led me here," I interrupted him.

He rose at his chair and waited for me to do the same. "Yes, I heard that Herr Stevenson, or shall we call him the Chief Justice of Vailima, even had you placed in that awful prison. Please, follow me, Herr Fergins."

I pretended to deliberate on my decision, as I smiled widely on the inside.

VAO WAS NOT HELD for questioning for very long. "They merely asked some questions about my intentions toward the king," she told me when we reunited. She laughed and called them "a dull lot." It took me some hours working with a charcoal pencil on a piece of paper to re-create what I had discovered in the consulate. The consul had promised me he would find out where Belial was, which of course I knew would not happen. More important, they had brought me into a long room filled with maps for me to show them where the runaway group congregated.

Vao had informed me of this room the night before, as we designed the scheme. She had said: "It is a room believed to be highly guarded in the consul. It is said in there they keep details of their plans, inch by inch, to control all Samoa and force the natives and the other foreign powers under their thumb."

As we had planned, I refused to show them anything on the maps until they agreed to all my conditions. This included a request for a lucrative official position in the German commercial firm, as preposterous a demand by a British bookseller as if I had asked to be made a Samoan chief. When they excused themselves to debate my terms, I examined the maps displayed around the room. Everything was marked in German, but fortunately it has long been one of my best languages because of its importance in collecting philosophical and scientific texts. As soon as I had examined everything in reach, I put them on a wild goose chase for the cannibals.

With the charcoal and paper, and Vao's help with geography, I sketched the locales to the best of my recollection.

"I hope I didn't catch your jaw too hard," Vao said as I worked on the map, examining my chin.

I felt myself turn beet red at her touch, and shrugged a little. "It needed to be convincing. I know Tulagi would be proud of you."

I did not mean to sadden or embarrass her, and though she blushed, I believe the thought of Tulagi's delight in her brought her comfort. With her further assistance, I marked the locations that seemed to match those places on the Germans' maps that had appeared to indicate the isolated outposts and hiding places controlled by the Tamasese government. With what Vao had already discovered, we concluded that the information Belial traded on Stevenson must have gained him sanctuary in one of these places.

We rode off as soon as we could gather our belongings; one of the spots on our list was a remote encampment that had been completely blocked off early on in the storm, eliminating it as a possibility. There was one locality we concluded was farther from the harbor than Belial would be willing to go. Another one was a cavern high up on one of Upolu's lush, treacherous mountains. We stopped at the foot of it and squinted up through the mist, then went around from another side. We could see hints of life: small fires that were lit on the outer ledges that contained entrances.

"He's been in there," Vao said.

"Someone looks like they have. How do you know it is him?" I asked.

She smiled at my ignorance. "Because no Samoan would enter, not without a man like him, anyway."

"I don't understand."

"You see, Chief Fergins, the caves are filled with the banished spirits of our former gods, the ones forced out by the Christian religions brought by white missionaries. They have long since turned into *aitu*, demonic ghosts. That is why you will see no caves on maps made by us. But if a white man is inside the cave, the devils will be kept safely at bay. So if there are Samoans inside those caverns, then so is a white man."

Vao's description of the aitus made me remember Tulagi, streaks of lightning in the sky creating a glow across his face, reciting the history of the island to himself. She became quiet and contemplative, maybe carried away by her own memories of her champion.

We waited many hours without progress until a soldier passed along the way alone, returning from some chore, and Vao called after him. He was armed with a blade, but Vao's beauty stopped him in his tracks, and gave her time to explain that she was a *tapo* and daughter of a deceased chief, and had some questions. He seemed to recognize her, or at least her dialect, and he invited us to walk with him.

This was the story the soldier told us.

A week or so after the worst of the last hurricane had ended, one of Tamasese's advisers was working to repair a broken fence in a remote parcel of his land when he was approached by a bedraggled white man, pulling a leather satchel alongside him. It seemed he had been walking through the bush for miles. As frightening as was his entire aspect, the adviser said the man's eyes were the most fearsome trait about him—dark and deadly.

This adviser sent for a buggy and the man was transported to the king's village. Once the man was recognized as Thomas, the powerful Marist missionary, word was immediately brought to Tamasese. Belial asked for sanctuary from enemies, and in return he would provide information on various enemies of the king's whom he had come into contact with as a missionary.

The missionary was sequestered as he had requested, taken from the king's palace to these secret caverns. He announced the rules to all soldiers who guarded him: Samoans were not to speak to him without their heads bowed; they were never to look into his eyes. When one native was slow to understand this request, and asked Belial if he could bring him anything to eat, Belial took a riding whip and slashed him across the neck and back until the whip unraveled.

The king at once began asking the new white chief advice on various political issues. It was said that their new white premier decided to write a codification of laws for the king—he called those the Heathen Codes—while he lingered in the caves. He began suggesting new laws for the king's followers to abide by regarding women's clothes (there should be more) and dancing (there should be none). Belial seemed very content and rarely went above the surface.

"Sometimes, he spoke to himself down there, but not just words," said the soldier regarding Belial. "Almost a chant, and sometimes he dances."

"Then he is still inside there?" I asked him, after Vao translated his words for me.

The soldier ignored me, justifiably appalled by my twopenny Samoan, so Vao repeated my question.

The soldier shook his head with relief. "When we brought news of a white man released from Tale-Pui-Pui, and that one had visited the German consul to find out where he was, he demanded to be carried to another location. Carried, I mean, on a litter decorated with flowers of his choosing—it took six of us eight hours."

WE WERE ON HIS TRAIL—and yet still he eluded us. The soldier told us where he believed Belial had ultimately been taken after being carried by the soldiers. So we rode on. But our guess was that Belial was moving every couple of days to stay ahead of us. I kept a close eye on Vao to try to observe whether her resolve had wavered. Hers were the eyes of youth—easily swayed toward excitement and despair. She was becoming more determined even as our joint quest increasingly seemed hopeless.

I did not find any hesitation on her part, but her earlier talk of needing to be free and liberated from her keepers gave way to looking to me for commands and direction. The truth was, she had always had a protector and with or without her rifle and warrior costumes and her command of languages, part of her had not learned what to do without one.

The next section of jungle where we found ourselves was so thick it was pitch-black. I could hardly see in front of my face. Despite the covering of trees, there was no shelter from the fierce heat, and the mud baked in the high temperatures and oozed with noxious gases. My eyes stung, my other senses rebelling in equal measure.

When we reached a slight clearing in the trees, I was more relieved than I would have admitted. But in the bush, relief is transitory. The ground was bubbling and sinking in; the horse bucked and I was thrown forward. I had to keep leaping until I was on rocky but solid surface inside an even smaller clearing, strangled above and on all sides by heavier woods. But I had lost Vao, and my heart sank. I began calling for her.

Then I heard the first sets of noises. They sounded like short bursts of air, or low menacing whispers. I was almost certain they were human sounds even though they were unlike any I'd heard. I could not go back through the sinking ground, but this clearing offered no room to hide from an attack.

Then there was a shout. A word. Not Samoan. I still could not see anything through walls and walls of trees and vines. I tilted my head back very slowly, dreading what I might find and whether—whatever it was—it could be the last thing I'd see. There was the point of a blade inches from my face, held there by a man perched in an impossible position in one of the trees. I started to reach for a cutlass given to me by Vao, before noticing that the trees were filled with men and boys, each armed with deadly, handmade weapons. Their skin was darker than that of Samoans. All the men were physically powerful, statuesque, and poised for a strike.

I knew these were the feared and famed runaways—men and boys like Nobolo—escaped from the plantations of the Firm. To challenge this posse would be suicide.

I was marched into a different part of the woods and made to stand for what might have been hours, until my knees were about to buckle. A newcomer, who carried an ornate spear, seemed to be the group's leader. His bleached hair glowed with light even in the absence of sun. I went quietly in defeat as I was forced onward. In sight came a small village of mud huts with brown grass roofs that were barely distinguishable from their surroundings. Another white man, wrists tied behind his back, was pushed into our path.

"Hines!"

His face, streaked with mud, turned toward me with an expression of horror. "How on earth do you know me? Who are you?"

I realized only then how the time surviving in the mountains and wilderness must have changed me. I had lost twelve or fifteen pounds, my face was drawn and haggard, my skin as darkened by sun and dirt as a shriveled Egyptian mummy. "Edgar Fergins. From our passage together on the man-of-war. How did you get here?"

"I was on one of my excursions to negotiate a deal for land, until these black devils grabbed me. Why, you're the blasted bookworm!"

"I cannot understand you, Hines. You risk your life in order to try to trick natives into selling or trading for land?"

"Of course you can't understand! You have a damned poor brain for business. The Firm will pay through the clouds for those lands once they've gotten this whole place under their fist."

"I suppose you put up a fight, which is why they tied you."

"You'd better try to do the same. Savvy? We're both about to be stewed, chopped, and cooked by these flesh eaters unless we do something, you damn fool!"

"Rope or not, we'd have no chance by fighting," I replied.

"You keen on becoming dinner, is that it?"

I gave a little shrug of contempt to my adversary from the *Colossus*. There had been no sign of Vao. Even if she had seen what happened to me, she would be powerless against this ferocious group. I had one prayer left: that Nobolo had reached the cannibal village by now and would see me and protect me. But my heart sank again as we were steered ahead and I could make out a pair of the runaways digging in the ground. A fire nearby suggested this was their current camp. There was a body next to them. The body of my former companion.

"What is it? What's wrong?" Hines could sense my grief and fear.

I ran ahead and flung myself down at the side of the body, cradling the head and hair I had so recently trimmed with my own hands. Nobolo had a hole in his chest, in his heart. I was dragged away, now my wrists tied, before being brought back to the procession.

"They're out for blood," I said to Hines, recovering my composure long enough to explain.

"What?"

"The Germans shot down one of the runaways from their labor farm," I said. "Back there. His name is Nobolo."

"How could you possibly know the name of one of these cockroaches? Anyway, one less black pig to contend with."

"It didn't make sense that the runaways would stray from their encampment where they are safe," I said with a burst of realization, ignoring his crudeness. "They must have sent their men out to look for who could have killed Nobolo."

"You mean they captured us because they think we did that? That we killed their friend?" Hines asked, gasping in horror.

I didn't bother to give him an answer, but the obvious one occurred to me: *Why shouldn't they?* For all the runaways knew, this wretched merchant and I were among those nameless white overseers who kidnapped their people from distant island tribes, enslaved them, hunted down those who dared run as examples to the rest. I fought the onslaught of emotions, of fear and anger at these dark strangers, but the anger didn't hold. Why should they show any mercy to white men, who had shown them nothing like it?

Behind the large open fire were more mud huts. Two men, older than the others, sat there and warmed up some bowls, the same kind of "brain bowls" displayed in the Stevensons' library. Hines sobbed and his whole body became slack as he sloppily panted for air and babbled.

"I saw them," he shouted, turning his anger toward me. "Your spectacles."

"What are you going on about?"

"At Vailima. On the frigate you acted like you knew nothing about Stevenson, but a man doesn't simply walk up to Vailima and let himself in the front door. You hid something from me. You and that somber friend of yours, you came here for some mischief. Didn't you? You'd better get me out of this situation or I'll see to it that everyone here and in England knows you are a sneak and a blackguard! I'll ruin you! Savvy?"

"I suppose you think I would allow that," I said tersely.

"What the devil would a blasted bookworm do about it?"

When we reached the destination, the sound of hoof falls perked up all of us, islanders and whites alike. A horse broke through the indistinct shapes of the forest. Vao sat atop.

"We've been found." Hines began to laugh with the same touch of mania as his sobbing. "Saved. We're saved, bookworm, old boy, our hides are saved! Over here!"

He was screaming. I could see the runaways become tense with anticipation. "Hines, be quiet!"

He was hollering now, losing control. "Kill these damn darkies, in the name of God! Kill every last savage!"

I watched as the fool's mouth creaked open but this time no more sounds emerged, just a stream of dark red. A spear pierced through his throat, the runaway who had thrust it in waiting a moment before withdrawing it. Hines collapsed without another sound and I watched the life wriggle out of him, knowing I was next. Two of the fast-moving cannibals pulled the merchant's body away by the ankles and though I could not see, I heard the moist crashes of the axes as they hacked through flesh. I averted my eyes and cried out for mercy for myself. I had a thought: *They want to make an example, to warn whomever comes to stay away.*

Terror overcame me. I tried not to see, not to look at the freshly cut head as it was placed upright on the same bloodied spear that had felled the man. Yet, I admit, when I recall these events, though I am still filled with utter revulsion, I never did pause to mourn my former tormenter. We are born to be susceptible to savagery when we have nothing else.

The hoof falls grew closer. The runaways still seemed startled by the appearance of the beautiful Samoan atop the horse, but regained their senses and began to approach with weapons readied to take her. She would be no match.

"Don't fight them, Vao," I shouted.

Next came more sounds of horses and a larger steed, Stevenson sitting tall, followed by John Chinaman and two of the best native warriors from Vailima, Sao and Laefoele. The latter two had faces painted for war, with black streaks under the eyes and across their cheeks. But the newcomers all appeared either unarmed or only lightly armed, and would be easily overtaken.

"Vao, get them all away!" I called out. "Ride now and save yourselves! Ride, Tusitala!" I cried out my admonitions again and again at the top of my lungs until my captors muzzled me.

"Tusitala" was repeated and murmured around the makeshift village of runaways. Soon, the hand across my mouth came free. The light-haired cannibal leader moved to the front, his eyes bright, and repeated, forcefully, that one word, which in his mouth became a wish, a demand: Tusitala!

Stevenson remained in the saddle on Jack and began speaking the runaways' language. He spoke fluently and, as it seemed to my ears, eloquently.

I watched the watchers held spellbound. In that tide of words that I could not recognize or understand, I saw Stevenson, perhaps for the first time, as the natives had seen him all along. Not as a writer, not as author or novelist. Tusitala: the teller of tales. I could finally believe in that Tusitala, as though I had received from above the brief and radiant gift to believe in a prophet or oracle. I understood, too, what kept Tusitala here. In the South Seas, in this land unencumbered by the powerful and suffocating printed page, the novelist had not forsaken what he had once been; he had finally become himself, even if it cost him everything else he'd ever had.

After Stevenson finished, the cannibals untied me and pushed me into the circle of my rescuers.

"Let us return to Vailima," Stevenson said.

John Chinaman came over, his tanned face appearing flushed in the torchlight. He lifted his bandana and wiped his forehead. Though he was speaking Chinese, it became clear by his gestures that he objected to the idea of me coming back with them. Stevenson's eyes caught mine for a moment.

"He has been officially ruled a free man when released from jail," Stevenson reminded his attendant. But after another round of argument from the usually obedient fellow, Stevenson relented: "Very well. Then he will not come back with us. Take him to Apia, John, but from there he may do as he'd like. He is not a prisoner of ours or the island's. Vao," he said, turning to her and frowning, "no more adventures of vengeance for you. The war clouds are moving over the island fast, and a bloody battle is expected any day. You are to come back home with us."

"Tusitala," she said, bowing her head and seeming to be a much younger girl again.

"Tusitala," I called out to him, knowing it could be my last time ever speaking with him. "What was it you said to the cannibals?"

"Do you think a man jogging to his club in London has so much to interest him? Can you still not conceive of why this place is awful fun?" Stevenson remarked as he looked around the dark, unforgiving woods, holding up his long fingers to the sky. He came around to answering my question. "I told them a yarn about you, Mr. Fergins."

No answer could have surprised me more. "Me?"

"Yes, about you and Mr. Davenport, and your expedition, and imprisonment, and the machinations of Belial."

"But they wouldn't know the first thing about such matters."

"Of course, you are right, they do not care about Davenport, or you, or me for that matter. Do they care how many novels I have published, how many pages written, or how many copies sold or stolen by literary pirates? No, they would have heard about me as they hear of the various spirits and demons of the island. Would they care about Belial the high and mighty bookaneer? Would they care whether Davenport ever achieved the pinnacle of his calling? No, you are right, they would not. But they would understand—deep in their veins—the desire for your revenge against a man who took something away that you believed belonged to you. To tell a story of vengeance that is yet to be satisfied is to forge a connection with them, to bring to boil what simmers always in their blood, and to draw them into your sphere, which would otherwise be a foreign and unknowable thing. Do you know why they eat other men? They eat other men because they believe the spirits of their enemies occupy them, and it is the only way to chase those away— but if they think they begin to understand you, they will not eat you. Usually." The last word was added with a deep but hoarse tone, a primeval growl I only ever heard in my life from Robert Louis Stevenson.

XVI

The Chinese servant was a brisk, controlled rider. The passage to the beach felt even longer than it was because of the distrust and anger I could sense from him as I sat behind him in the saddle. Though the island had altered his dress and even the tint of his skin, there was something about the way he rode that remained different than that of the natives and Europeans—something that harkened to faraway lands.

Lloyd Osbourne traveled alongside us on his horse and treated the ride as he seemed to treat everything he did—half pleasure and half inconvenience. We slowed down several times to wait for him to catch up, each halt accompanied by a snort from John that mixed with those of the impatient animal beneath our hips.

Other things weighed down my mind despite the reprieve from the cannibals delivered by Stevenson: Nobolo's murder, the horrific sight and sounds of Hines's brutal demise, the abrupt loss of Vao's companionship, Davenport's imprisonment, the lost hope of ever finding Belial.

The final time the horses took on water, we were perched on a hill overlooking the village of Apia. It was dawn on a foggy morning. We saw a troop of natives with tall headdresses, their faces covered in black war paint, while from somewhere in the bush, war drums pounded.

"Is it true that if war comes, this time the whites will all be killed?" I asked.

"Hopefully not, selfishly speaking," Lloyd said, after thinking about it for a moment.

There were sounds of another approaching party below. John removed a spyglass and, extending it, watched with interest before passing the lens to Lloyd. I asked if I could have a look and was given the instrument by Lloyd, whose smile seemed to bear no grudges about what had happened in Vailima. I removed my spectacles and pressed my eye against the instrument. I could make out a group of two dozen Chinese men marched across a road by armed natives. They were not chained, but were being kept in a controlled formation. Two Europeans headed the group. John began to roll a fresh smoke in the style of Stevenson, as though dangling a reminder over me that he remained part of Vailima while my place had been permanently forfeited. I studied his reaction to the strange vision below.

"Wherever there are merchants, there are men in chains, metaphorical or otherwise," Lloyd philosophized, modifying one of Stevenson's axioms about arms and ammunition. "Aphorism: Lloyd Osbourne."

John could see I was waiting for his thoughts.

He turned toward me, his usual look of harsh scrutiny softened. It is hard to represent for you the broken and frustrated way he spoke in English, for anything more than a few words was obviously a great effort for him, and a challenge to understand. In fact, it made me feel honored that he used so much energy to address me. He explained that when he was eight years old he was sold to a French merchant, and brought to the Marquesas Islands as a plantation slave. He was later forced to be a soldier in the civil wars there. He continued: One day, he escaped his enslavement in a rickety boat and would have drowned if he had not been picked up by the ship Stevenson sailed in. "He ask me if I wished to be cook. I offer my services as servant for life."

"In return for rescuing you?"

"Tusitala not rescue me. He was just passenger. No, not for rescue. He did not order, did not try to purchase or demand. He asked me, with . . ." He bobbed his head and ground his teeth together until he found the right word. "Respect. I am called John Chinaman so that real name not heard-over and repeated to someone who might encounter my former master. Heard-over by traders like men there." He gestured toward the party in the valley below us sloping into the village. "Tusitala remarkable man. Man dedicate himself to write is a man of courage because he rely on his mind, nothing more. That you not understand."

"Those men," I replied, spurred to a new thought. "The Chinese ones being moved. Have they been sold into labor here?"

"No, not likely," Lloyd chimed in. "The Germans do not like having such light-skinned men perform their labor for them. They would have been brought from one of the outer islands, and probably taken here only for transport from our harbor to another island, or perhaps to America for railroad work. What do you make of that?"

I rose to my feet from the rocks where we were sitting.

"What is it?" Lloyd asked me, noticing a change had come over me.

"The harbor."

Those men, I knew, must have been on their way to some kind of vessel, and one big enough to take them all together and to travel far. Chinese laborers would not be transported on a man-of-war, which meant it had to be a merchant ship. We had heard of one coming in with the mails. If it was ready to sail now, Belial already would be on it. I was certain of it. I would be on it, too.

THE HASTILY CONSTRUCTED BERTHS on the lower deck of a merchant vessel are not made with the comfort of man (or beast) in mind.

They represent a calculation of maximum profit, in this case for human chattel. How I longed for that humble berth on the *Colossus* that once seemed to me a coffin.

A formless mattress, spitting out the shavings with which it was stuffed, fitted into a kind of netted hammock that was attached to two hooks in the beams of the ceiling. A small box nailed to the floor in which to keep belongings, with the end of my misshapen umbrella hooked to it. That was all. My so-called bed swayed with every awful motion of the ship. There were four other men in my berth, Chinese members of the group we had observed on our way to the beach. We each had a pot, spoon, and a cup that we kept in our respective boxes and brought with us to the mess for our mealtime rations, though our stomachs were usually too unwell for eating, for they rolled and pitched as much as the vessel. The Chinese passengers may have been just as miserable and sick, but at least they could converse with each other about it.

I have seen you cast your eyes on my coat rack, Mr. Clover, remembering I had parted with my umbrella under desperate circumstances and wondering how it appears here in New York and, in my narrative, on the merchant vessel. I will explain. Shortly before the vessel launched, I heard cries of "White Chief! White Chief!" There was the unexpected sight of a Samoan waving around my umbrella and running toward the ship. He explained to me that the chief of the village where I had traded the thing had been informed by an elder that the umbrella was an object of bad luck, due to its stripes, or perhaps its bloodstains, I could not make out the reason. The chief had ordered that I be found because according to the superstitions of this particular village, a talisman of ill fortune could not simply be discarded; it had to be reunited with its original owner. Much frantic searching ensued until this representative of the tribe discovered me on the beach hurriedly preparing for my passage. It was a relief to them and a small stroke of luck for me, as I now opened and closed its ribs to create a bit of breeze when I felt I was suffocating belowdecks. When you are reduced to nothing, you make use of everything.

Each lurch and pull of the ship sent my stomach reeling and my heart with it. I had used every last cent of the funds that had been restored to me in my belongings returned by the prison officials to arrange my passage inside the depths of the vessel. I was lucky to be able to afford even steerage. If my berth was the cloud, I reminded myself that the silver lining would be that the more time I spent down below, the better hidden I was from the sight of Belial, if he really was onboard at all. By the time I had reached the ship in Apia's port, there had been no time to confirm his presence—I had to trust instinct alone, in the incorrigible style of Davenport, and arrange my passage or remain behind on the island.

I carved a little calendar from a loose square of wood and crossed off each passing day of this horrid journey with an X.

After the first few nights the sea and my stomach grew calmer and I wandered with caution. I came across a big brown trunk in stowage that *could* have been the one I saw in Belial's wagon during our first encounter with him. It was unlocked and filled with some out-of-season clothes and nothing more. No hidden compartments. Little to go on. Still, it was just enough for me to keep faith he really might be on the ship.

Had Davenport been there and demanded to know my plan, I would have been able to lay it out in a very logical fashion. First step, I would have said, was to confirm the Subject's presence; then locate his stateroom; then identify to a reliable degree what times he was dining with the officers (where else would Belial dine?), before infiltrating and searching his chambers. Not as laden with natural impulse as

Davenport might have orchestrated, but it was efficient and sensible, which was my life in a nutshell. But none of it mattered.

As my cot rocked me through the fourth night of fitful sleep and terrifying movements, I was jolted awake by the sound of music. It was beautiful humming—an aria from an opera that had been staged in London a few months before our departure. I had attended one of the first performances. I could not begin to imagine how one of my poor Chinese steerage mates had learned this tune, or why he would be rehearsing it in this floating dungeon. Thoughts and memories crashed together in the manner of a confused dream. I felt around for my spectacles, hanging on a nail protruding from the boards on the wall. Then I groped in the dark for a lantern and turned the gas up. It gradually illuminated the craggy, remarkable face of Belial, grinning expressively. He was sitting at the edge of one of the other passengers' cots, with the prone man pinned underneath peering up at the formidable stranger. From one of the other hammocks emerged a string of curses in Chinese.

"How did you know that I was here?" I asked, a question I had been imagining I would hear from Belial's lips before the voyage was finished.

His humming stopped and he bestowed upon me a munificent nod. "With our dear friend Davenport so unjustly detained, I supposed the only move he had left would be to charge the king with his pawn."

"I am a pawn, you mean. And you are the king."

"You understand me. I supposed you sufficiently intelligent to find the first large ship to sail after the storms fully cleared, and correctly presume I would be sailing on it, and if so that you would attempt to conceal yourself from me, and of course to sail in steerage would be the best way to do so, if an affront to your good English sensibilities. I might have waited for you to show yourself. But to be honest, I tire of all the games just as Davenport did. Tell me, bookseller, how do you sleep in here, swinging like a man hanged?" He passed a sad glance around the crowded berth, and a disgusted look at the confused man on whose arm he was still sitting. "Look what Davenport has done to you."

"What do you mean, what he has done to me?"

"Surely you are sufficiently intelligent to see . . . Well, no matter. He has lost his final gambit. It must be a sweet relief for you, in a way."

"Relief?"

"You do not have to struggle to help fulfill his potential for him any longer. That is too much a burden for any man, even—no, especially— Pen Davenport himself." Then, with increasing pity and a strangely uncaring solicitude, he whispered, "Look at yourself."

I needed no mirror to know what he beheld. I was unshaven, my hair unwashed and greasy, my once-pristine and polished spectacles stretched, blackened, and scratched. I was almost touched by the note of sympathy in his words. I welled with emotion and could not convince my tongue to work.

"You are lost, dear man," he concluded, in his Pope Thomas voice, which, after all, was just a natural part of him. I had known him only in his missionary role, but it now occurred to me it had reflected the bookaneer's natural disposition.

Belial invited me to take breakfast with him on the upper deck. Liberated from the tough salt pork and vinegary bread of the lower mess chest, I gratefully ate the finer servings of fruit and meat, and it seemed to give Belial pleasure to watch, chin at rest on his knuckles. After the meal, we walked the length of the ship. I took in the raw, fresh air with the eagerness of a starved man.

"Did you *really* believe in your heart you would come here and filch Stevenson's manuscript from *me*?" he asked. He seemed genuinely curious but also completely unthreatened.

"I suppose."

He gave a heavy, rolling laugh while he patted my arm with the affection a victorious politician might grant his opponent. "Is there anything less natural than taking a stroll on a ship? It is as if the earth were flat, and in every direction you will eventually drop into nowhere. I despise it. We never should have been at each other's throats, Mr. Fergins. Davenport got in the way of what could have been a friendship between us. You have been one of the greatest appreciators of our profession. Where did you rate me as a bookaneer?"

It was the second time in my life I had heard a variation of that question. "Quite at the top. Indeed, with Davenport's failure in Samoa, I suppose you will be seen as rather untouched in your position."

"Thank you! It is an honor to hear so from your lips, and Christina will be tickled pink to hear of your praise. Think of this, you have been witness to the last and greatest of the bookaneers. You will have that story to tell in the future to those with brains enough to listen. What will you do when you go home?"

"How do you mean?"

"My informants wrote me that your bookstall in London is shuttered."

"Perhaps I will not go home," I said with a windy sigh, acknowledging the fate of my life's work. "Not yet, anyway. I cannot bear to go back to Hoxton Square—well, I can stay with my brother and his wife in Slough, where we were raised; there is plenty of space and my nieces humor my reading habits. Or I can do something temporary when we make port in New York, perhaps, until I feel ready to go back. Perhaps a traveling book cart."

"A fine idea. Gothamites are as aggressive about reading as about all their sport. Or, as my Christina says, the people of New York are as fine as they are rich."

Most of my waking time on the ship was spent with Belial. The Chinese men were passed along to their buyers at a small port island where we made a brief stop for the purpose. Belial convinced the officers to move me into a comfortable berth on an upper deck. Though he did not say as much, I knew Belial would not want to make himself too conspicuous to the captain or the officers during a mission, and so he limited his society with them; his intrinsic need for adulation and interest kept bringing him back to me, and the fact that I knew who he was and what he was doing allowed him to talk freely. And talk and talk and talk. He spoke frequently about his wife, which in his mouth really somehow seemed fantastical, just as Davenport had warned me. I asked him if they had children and he said four daughters. "Alas, no sons to carry on my work, but, then again, there is nothing left to carry." There were not many opportunities to interject my questions and thoughts because of his fluid and winding elocution, but at least, unlike with Davenport, I never felt obligated to keep up both sides of a conversation. Belial lectured, pontificated, boasted, and brayed. He would ask, "Do you know what I'm thinking?" and, after having to reluctantly admit I did not, he would not tell me the thought until a half hour later. From afar, this tendency in him seemed utterly obnoxious, but after being taken into his confidence I noticed that something changed. I could not help but feel enthusiastic to be the object of his general attention, even when he was especially self-important and obnoxious. The secret of despots and tyrants is that people enjoy dining with them.

We took our meals together; lounged and played cards in the common rooms together; sat on deck chairs on sunny days. He even told me his given name: Benjamin Lott. I only called him that once because in a feral voice he said, "Belial." The weather, which had been mild, turned harsh and Belial began to appear less often. Strangely, I was not seasick even as we dipped and sloped. A new feeling settled over me. Now that I was suddenly without Belial's frequent company, I was eager to talk to someone, anyone; the first mate had grown comfortable with me, a sailor thirty or thirty-one years old with a square jawline and half-moon eyes. I began to tell him stories from my stay in Samoa—without names, of course—stories about a white genius making his life among island natives as a sort of king or chief. He urged me to go on, and though I felt an indescribable and unexpected itch to tell every detail, even to confess why I had gone there in the first place, I knew I should not, and made an excuse to return to my berth. That was how close I came to throwing away discretion for the temporary glow of friendship.

When the sky grew wild, the ship had to tack and change course, and Belial appeared at my door with a tired, twitchy air. His head was covered with an oilskin hood used to keep dry above deck. I had not yet seen him look so distracted.

"The calendar," he demanded.

"What?"

"I saw you scraping one out. The damned calendar you were carving from wood!" He stomped his boot against the floorboards as he spoke. His eyes bulged and his substantial lips and chin quivered.

"Oh. There." My voice sounded meek and defeated in my own ears.

"Thank you," he said with relief. I watched him carefully as he rummaged where I'd pointed, under my mattress, until he found it. "Have you been checking off the days?"

"Yes, since the very beginning of the voyage. There is little else to do at night." Indeed, by this point I had read each of the few books in the ship's library twice through, all but one of which I had read in the past (the downside of being a bookseller, at least the kind who reads).

We conferred about how long the vessel would be delayed, according to the members of the crew we had each consulted. "Let us put the worst case forward," he said, studying my calendar, "and add four full days to our journey—why, that would return us to New York City on the twenty-seventh of June."

"I believe that's correct."

"Splendid!" He checked the calendar again and found the same result, which expelled the tension from his face and voice. "Time to spare. Splendid indeed. You know, Fergins, I've been meaning to ask you. Would you like to read it?" He leaned forward with a smile that showed all his teeth. "Stevenson's novel."

"Truly?"

"This will be an historic moment for me as a bookaneer. The last book I can bring to the public before the wrongheaded changes in law set in. There is one thing more I'd like to do, something I've never done. I'd like to watch the pleasure I bring to a reader, the very first reader of the thing. I want it to be you."

"You mean you'd want to watch me while I read the book?"

"Exactly," he replied with haughty triumph. "Who else will read it on a ship like this? A sailor? I want to read the surprise and gratitude in your face as you become the first man on earth to bear witness to Stevenson's final masterpiece. You saw that the poor exile does not have long in this world. I know you cannot resist such an offer. Not you, of all people. You cannot turn down serving an immortal part in the history of literature."

After the initial dramatic surprise of his offer waned, I turned the idea over in my head. Then, you may not believe it, you may believe I am reporting someone else's words, but I flattened my hands together and said: "I will decline, but thank you."

It was as though I had struck the man. "Did you understand what I said to you?"

I explained myself the best I could at the time, knowing how quickly the bookaneer could be enraged. "I came to Samoa with Pen Davenport to help him with his mission and to chronicle his final success. He failed, of course, and in his failure, I also failed. If I read the novel before the rest of the world, I would do so with the sneaking knowledge that I did not earn it—in fact, that I earned no privilege like it."

He held his gaze on me for another moment before dropping his chin in thought, then giving a heavy nod, as though in mourning for me. "You *are* an honorable man, Mr. Fergins. I am thankful that we have become such fast friends, and I know Christina would adore making a big feast for you. Do you like a brace of grouse, fried with truffles and butter? Of course you do. That is what it shall be."

My racing heart slowed. I knew I was never going to meet his wife and eat grouse alongside his four daughters, yet the offer to do so felt generous beyond description. I had a sudden feeling as though I had betrayed Davenport, my lost master, by engendering such feelings of friendship from his rival. I thought back to what Davenport had once asked me in the smoking room of the Garrick Club, so many worlds removed from the strangling jungle and the swamp-bound prison of Upolu, through the more civilized suffocating air of his cigars. If he and Belial had both offered me a place beside them, what would I do?

Belial popped his lips, as he did when he seemed to have a thought that impressed him. "You said you came to chronicle Davenport's mission to Samoa."

"Yes," I answered, "though that plan became waylaid by, well, all the complications, in many cases because of you."

"You must have come to finally realize what poor Davenport's biggest flaw was."

"I have not stopped to think about it."

"He was a professed misanthrope, yet he had this need to know that people recognized him and knew him as a great bookaneer."

"You speak as if he were not still alive."

"Take his missions, for instance. When he was not on a mission, he was rather lethargic and sluggish, lying around in hotels and brothels and concert halls for weeks at a time. But when he was on a mission, he was bigger than life. When he secured a prize, for instance, a manuscript or proofs to sell, he marched in plain view to the publisher to sell it."

"So?"

"You see, he disappeared at the wrong time. The time to disappear, utterly and completely, without a trace, is as soon as one has a prize, and if you think nothing of the literati, then they will think of nothing but you."

I nodded.

"There is more for you to learn and witness if you'd wish," he said, the familiar self-satisfied grin on his face. "I mean it's not over, our journey, even when we reach port. They will be after the thing, you know."

"Who? You mean bookaneers? But they—" I stopped myself. I knew why he had been so urgently concerned with the calendar, and I understood the relief that possessed him after examining the dates. On July 1, the new copyright laws would finally be in effect.

"You needn't shy away from talking about it. Speaking of the death of our profession is like eulogizing an old friend. True, as you consider, that most of the bookaneers have run for the hills before now. It is the barnacles I speak of—the lowest of our line—they are minor fellows and rather ordinary, that is true, but with all this time they would have heard of our mission and be expecting my return. These bottom-feeders are without vision or philosophy but possess certain skills—in gathering intelligence, in smuggling. If you wish, you may accompany me off the ship and watch me scrape them away."

In the depth of his vanity, I saw traces of Davenport. It should have been no surprise, at the end of this, that I found these two men possessed twin souls, however differently expressed, separated into enemies by the cosmos. I accepted Belial's invitation to be by his side when we disembarked.

He was right about the so-called barnacles waiting for him. When we arrived in New York, having switched from the merchant ship to a packet in the tiny port of Halifax, he sent his trunk up with one of the porters who came onboard; the trunk disappeared before we reached the docks. Belial was carrying a bundle of papers in a valise; I turned and saw him jostled as we entered the crowds. After a passing few seconds in which my view was blocked, when the crowds cleared a bit, his valise was gone. He gave me a meaningful look free of any concern. I knew the papers inside the valise were actually worthless ledgers that had been left in his berth by a businessman on a previous voyage. More jostling and every item *from the inside pockets of his coat* had been removed in a flash. Meanwhile I had not been able to identify a single one of the barnacles among the crowds, as though these bandits were invisible and operated by black magic.

A sculpture of the look on Belial's face as we walked down the street—the creased eyebrows, the wide black nostrils, the tight pucker in his mouth—would seem to say, "Is that all you can manage, you fools?"

"You see, my dear Fergins, that barnacles are merely that. Thieves. Pickpockets and launderers. A true bookaneer is another breed altogether, one the world will now be emptier without. You may write that in your chronicle, if you like, but attribute it to me."

I abandoned any written chronicle long before this, but didn't want to bruise his ego. "Of course. But where is the manuscript?" I whispered.

He had, as far as I could tell, run out of any places to hide it. His golden cane might have been hollow but was too narrow. Then I noticed I had to look higher up to meet his face than in the past. His boots. They were wider around than necessary and much taller.

We were separated as we entered another throng of people crossing the street. Then, just as his trunk and the valise had vanished, the man himself vanished from my sight.

I NEXT ENCOUNTERED BELIAL less than two hours later. In the entrance to the building occupied by the publishing house known as Charles Scribner's Sons is their bookstore, to use one of your most unfortunate Americanisms, with galleries of volumes arranged by theme and glass cases of the most expensive editions. By the time I arrived, I had only to wait for fifteen minutes before Belial also appeared. I rushed to his side. "Good afternoon," I called out. I was still short on breath. I had hurried through the crowded streets, down to an underground train, up the steps outside the four-story building, and inside the spacious elevator, which floated like a slow rocket to the third floor, where the publishing offices were located.

"What the deuce are you doing here?" he demanded. "How did you know where . . ." he stopped himself because the answer was obvious. From the years at Davenport's side I knew which of the New York publishers would pay the most for a Stevenson novel, according to its history and finances; Scribner's not only was a well-known book publisher that had published Stevenson before, but it also had its own monthly magazine that would benefit from serializing a new book. Belial would start here and, were the terms offered not lucrative enough, would move on to the next publishing firm.

Belial had also come straight there, but in a less hurried manner, befitting his philosophy of dignity. His leisurely pace served to make a point.

"I wanted to see it. To be a witness," I began. "You yourself said our journey was not over."

His eyes burned into me, causing me to stumble backward, nearly falling over some furniture and into a bronze sculpture of an Amazonian woman locked in battle with a leaping tiger. "I do not understand you. I give you the chance to be the first reader of this historic addition to literature, and you reject me. You, a lowly peddler!"

"Peddler?"

"Our journey together ended when I left you in the streets. Do you have brains enough left in your head to understand? I *left* you behind, left you with the empty-handed barnacles. Now you pop up again. You little pig. You dare make yourself a pest to me. You were nothing but an amusement while I was trapped on that ship. Did you invade Whiskey Bill's life like this, too, and Davenport's?"

"No . . ." I tried to protest.

He held the thick manuscript in front of me, then pushed it against my spectacles until the metal pinched the skin around my eyes. I asked him to stop, with no effect. The spear of the sculpture's female warrior pinched my back.

"Do you really think this is how you'll finish your friend Davenport's story? By taking this from me? What will you do in order to accomplish it, shoot me for it, stab me?"

"Of course not! You said—"

"Go on, try to take it! Try! No, coward, you cannot. If you ever speak to me again, if you even look at me, I'll tear you in half, am I understood?"

I was completely startled by the degree of his anger, even though I had seen it before directed to others. By this point, some publishing clerks, a male and two young females, had come from their desks to stare at the spectacle. "Belial, please," I said with quiet embarrassment. "I really just supposed you would expect me to guess where you were going. . . . After all, you spoke of the chess pieces, of our roles in the match, the pawn and king, and I thought—"

"You were the pawn!" He pointed at my head with his cane and I thought of poor Tulagi, bent over with the life bleeding out of him.

I suppose I must have appeared greatly cowed by the memory of the deceased dwarf's pain, for Belial suddenly seemed satisfied with himself. His well-slimed tongue smacked his lips. Perhaps you notice that when I am happy, I chatter; when anxious or scared, still I chatter. It would be obvious to you, as a reasonable and assiduous young man, that I should have said no more in the face of this volatility. But I could not help it: "There was one last thing, though, something I thought about, Belial, after we parted, that might be of some help and importance to you—"

In one grand movement his broad back was turned on me and he marched away through the main door of the office, closing it in my face. I tried to make my suit look a little more decent, though it was wrinkled and had patches of sweat at odd angles, like streams coming to a common crossing. There was loud noise from outside, like a series of gunshots, but my attention was too consumed for the moment by what had just happened. I dropped myself onto a bench against the wall.

Only a few minutes later the same door opened again, revealing Belial. This time there was another man directly behind him. I could not yet see who he was because of the shadows thrown by the doorway.

"I know you asked that I not speak to you for a while, but, as I was saying, I realized there is one other thing I need to tell you," I said to the bookaneer, as though he had returned in order to complete our conversation, or to apologize. "The dates. I believe while we were at sea we might have miscalculated."

Now he stepped forward, closer to where I stood, or rather was pushed forward. The man behind him was a New York City policeman and his brown-gloved hand was encircling Belial's arm. Then yet another man, whom I can only describe as grimly mirthful, walked out behind the other two, holding the big manuscript under his arm.

"How dare you manhandle me! Do you know who I am?" Belial shouted, rearing back.

The policeman cracked his baton against Belial's face. "Don't care who you are, but you'll learn to talk with respect to one of our city's attorneys."

The sounds from outside the windows fronting Broadway were renewed, sounds of missiles and rockets, popping and fizzing, sending pools of bright light over us. More pistols firing. Now the air smelled of gunpowder.

"Starting earlier and earlier, every year," the attorney grumbled to his companion. "It's not even five o'clock, is it?"

"True enough, sir," the policeman said.

"Full of patriotic feelings, as long as they can be noisy about it. Isn't that the way?"

"True, indeed."

"Show me the warrant," Belial was demanding of the two men. "Show it to me!" Blood trickled from his mouth onto his battered jaw.

The attorney had been searching through his papers and held one out for Belial. "Here you are, Mr. Lott."

"It is the fourth," Belial said to himself, reading from the paper. "Today is July fourth." Then he turned to me. "*You* made me believe I had more time. You wanted to avenge Davenport's failure, however you could, even if it meant throwing away the result of this entire mission."

"No, it's not true!"

I kept protesting as he was led away.

Within four months there would begin the trial you've visited where men and women alike would line up to glance at this specimen of the legendary breed. A bookaneer, snared and captive, a sight never before beheld and, I'd venture to say you've seen and heard enough to agree, a sight as sad as any imaginable. It makes me think of the great jaguar I saw one summer in a Paris zoo, pacing with his bounding steps, nowhere to leap.

What I remember most about this historic moment is watching the bookaneer as the bright, artificial lights filled the room and the noises from outside repeated themselves—*rat-tat-tat-boom, rat-tat-tat-boom*. As he turned to look at me over his shoulder, the expression on Belial's comely face grew darker and helpless, and the grand inner rage—you saw it for yourself in court—took hold. But I still believe, perhaps from naïveté or idealism, he knew his accusations against me were false and that his rage stemmed from realizing his general error. Had he envisioned me burning to death in that evidence room? Judge for yourself. Belial had already known before that day at Scribner's the bookaneers were finished—he had even come to accept it—but I think he did not realize that the world was not finished with the bookaneers; as recompense for the glory and excitement they had seized for years for themselves, all that life would be wrung out of him now. I still hear it all around me.

Rat-tat-tat.

Rat-tat-tat.

Rat-tat.

XVII

CLOVER

*We were not meaning to deceive, most of us were as honorable and as
ignorant as the youth themselves; but that does not acquit us of failings such
as stupidity and jealousy, the two black spots in human nature which,
more than love of money, are at the root of all evil.*

J. M. BARRIE

No, friend, no. This is Samoa.

LLOYD OSBOURNE

When Mr. Fergins was describing to me Belial's arrest, he became so enthusiastic he even tried to imitate the sounds of
fireworks that had filled the air that day from the publisher's office;
"Rat-tat-tat!" Then the bookseller stopped. His head fell back onto his
pillows. He appeared to be short of breath before breaking into harsh
coughs. I was convinced that my greed to possess the whole story for
myself had overtaxed him.

I poured him more water (I had filled the pitcher at the side of his
bed during pauses and interruptions). The tired man's face turned red
and he croaked a thank-you. Even when the coughing subsided, his
throat plagued him, as if (as he described it) someone's hands were
squeezed around it. I pleaded with him to try to remain still and

searched for another blanket, as his rooms were drafty in the winter; before I could finish draping the blanket over him, he was asleep. For a horrible moment I feared that the act of telling the story had driven the life out of him. I did not move a muscle until I saw him breathing steadily.

Imagine a railway waiter; now imagine a railway waiter inside the august reading room at the Astor Library, reading up on the laws of copyright. Now add the stares directed at me. That was how I spent my two free afternoons the following week. I also began following the trial of the bookaneer Belial as closely as an outsider to law and to the case could. I read the short courtroom summaries published in the newspaper, which would be left on the seats of the train, and when possible, I would visit the court sessions myself, though I continued to find these technical and fruitless.

I knew Mr. Fergins would disapprove. He would worry I was breaking my promise to put the whole story out of my mind once he finished telling it. But, after all, I was just learning, just observing.

In speaking to some of those spectators who attended the case religiously, I learned more of the background that had led to the man's arrest. One of the prominent New York judges had, in an earlier position as an alderman, argued that copyright theft should be a criminal offense because it was an affront to the greatest tool possessed by mankind: the brain. This judge, a man named Salisbury, was half-English and had detested the theft of British literature by American publishers as an immoral example to the nation's youth. Although criminal provisions were not included in the new copyright legislation that was based on the international agreement signed at Berne, Judge Salisbury convinced the city's prosecutors to concoct a complicated bundle of charges tied with the new treaty to make an example of this notorious literary pirate: possession of stolen goods, fraud, unlawful importation of cargo, attempted larceny against the publishing firm. Copyright was just the beginning. The case of *New York v. Lott* would herald the start of this new era in protecting authors.

But the defense counsel was astute and the criminal charges could not be maintained, especially after the fire that nearly killed Mr. Fergins—the cause of which remained undiscovered—also destroyed or badly damaged almost half the evidence against the prisoner. Belial was released by the court after months of useless hearings and motions. In the six months since the July arrest, various authors and publishers had brought private suits against the bookaneer in civil court. But none of the other cases ever moved forward because after he was freed from the nearby Tombs he vanished from the jurisdiction. His disappearance, mentioned only in passing in the *New York Evening World*, came as no surprise to me. Though I had never exchanged a word with the notorious bookaneer, I almost felt I knew him through my visits and through the honest, spectacled eyes of Mr. Fergins. I was even a little gratified that the fellow had acted just as I expected.

I swore to myself I would not pester Mr. Fergins for further information after he seemed to have become so worn out. Just a few days after New Year's, Mr. Fergins began reappearing on our train route. The first day of his return I was stacking dishes and did not have the chance to speak with him at any length before he had to go. He did tell me that he felt much better; in fact he said he had "never felt stronger." The next occasion when we were both present, his time was monopolized by a loud bibliophile who was lecturing him about the flaws of various editions in his cart. We barely exchanged greetings. I decided to call on him at his boardinghouse. Finding him out, I left a note, and I could not help myself, despite promises to myself and to him: in a postscript I included only one of the many queries I was itching to ask.

"Was it Samoan," asked my note, "that the bookaneer spoke to you that first day at the courthouse?"

The note sent to me in return read simply: "My dear Mr. Clover. Perhaps! Cordially and gratefully yours, as always, E. C. Fergins."

Then he was gone.

I STILL HAD SO MUCH to ask about Davenport, about Belial, about Vao and Stevenson . . . If only I had taken note of the postmark on Mr. Fergins's letter in response to my note asking about the bookaneer speaking Samoan, maybe I could have found him. It never occurred to me to save it, for I fully expected to see him soon. But Mr. Fergins never again stepped aboard our train. After three weeks of worrying about his health, I made the trek again to the bookseller's rooms, slipping and gliding across sidewalks encrusted with ice. The rooms were empty. Not a single book or even a pamphlet left behind. The landlady would not say where he had gone. Maybe she did not know. I paused at the street door before exiting. There, in an otherwise empty iron stand, was the gaily striped umbrella of Mr. Fergins's, the one that had been with him in Samoa; I picked it up, studied the dark crimson spotting on its wings, chilled to think of its source. I let it fall freely down into the stand with a clang, annoying the old lady one last time.

Remembering those last, brief meetings on the train, I began to wonder if the bookseller had been avoiding me. Our eyes had met as usual, he had whistled and smiled as usual, but there had been distance and hesitation in his demeanor. Toward the end of his narration of the Stevenson affair, he had recounted telling Belial that his time in New York would be temporary. He had never intended on staying here forever. Still, I never expected him to vanish.

One day, a few weeks after discovering his departure, I was walking by the courthouse. I recognized one of the men outside. He had a beaver hat, a distinctive set of lines around his eyes, as though someone had painted them, and a full, flabby chin; he had that air of importance seen around a courthouse. I had seen him while I was helping Mr. Fergins during his long convalescence, and before that glimpsed him with Mr. Fergins on these same steps. He was walking with a purposeful and rapid stride in the direction of a waiting carriage. I took a deep breath before I followed him.

"Excuse me, sir," I said, and had to test my resolve when he gave no reply and I had to repeat it in a louder voice.

"'Your honor,' boy!" he roared, then kept walking after a sidelong glance at me.

"Your honor, very sorry," I said, trying to keep up. "Your honor, excuse the interruption, if I could speak with you for a moment—"

"What could *you* possibly have to speak with me about?"

"It's about Edgar Fergins. You called on him at his boardinghouse when I was there."

He slowed down, then stopped, jiggled his chin and made a noise of agreement at me. "That bookseller is a fortunate man."

"Because he recovered from his injuries?"

"Thank goodness. But I meant he is fortunate to return to London. A much more cultivated place for a bookman. Some of the finest editions in my collection came from my time in London society."

"Are you Justice Salisbury?" I asked after listening to his accent and remembering the Anglophile judge I had heard about, the one who first hatched Belial's arrest as an example to all copyright thieves.

"Indeed I answer to that name," he said, so proud of the fact he did not seem to wonder how I knew. "Do not tell me your name, boy. I have an appointment and I haven't the time to hear it."

"Did you help arrange for Mr. Fergins to review evidence in the case of the great book pirate that was later dismissed?"

"Do you see this courthouse?" I nodded that I indeed saw the massive, three-story building that overshadowed the entire park. He went on: "The funds that were raised to build this very building were also used to line the pockets of city officials, friends of mine in many cases, some of whom still rot for it in the Tombs for their foolish corruption. But what of those so-called bookaneers? They stole a much rarer resource than money; they stole the creative ideas plucked right out of the best minds on both sides of the Atlantic—scoundrels like that man we had in chains and, from what we learned, even some depraved women made a practice of it, a virtual profession of dishonesty. Yet, nobody saw fit to punish them, not even to try. I tried, hand to God, I tried. I have contributed to the most humbling of tasks, rebuilding a bridge connecting two great lands. Did we fail to secure justice? I shall answer it this way. When I have the honor to be Senator Salisbury, I will proudly declare I tried to give one of those pirates what he deserved."

After his speech, he continued on his way without a farewell. He may have been half-English, but he was all New Yorker.

I shouldn't blame Mr. Fergins's departure for the fact that the romance of the railroad was lost to me, especially since so many train routes had already been permanently unhooking their restaurant cars to save money. Maybe I have a better way to put it, which is this: once reading books lost a little romance, so did living in New York City and, in some related way, so did being a railroader. I suppose Mr. Fergins's story had a part in my moving on from this era of life, though at the time the reverse seemed true. It seemed as though Mr. Fergins, having found in me a willing recipient for his narrative, had finally freed himself from the memory he carried around of those events and had been able to return to his humdrum but contented existence in London without another thought.

I cannot remember ever conceiving of a book as a piece of property before meeting Mr. Fergins. Or if I ever had stopped to think such a thing, it was that the book I held in my hands belonged to *me*, or to Mr. Fergins, who had loaned it to me, or to my father, or a public library. I suppose it might have occurred to me that the book belonged to the author, too, but this would have seemed remote, something that mattered only in the past. Now I understood that intellectual property, as it was called in the language of the law, was always in danger and the reason began with my own impressions. It had seemed natural and right that the contents, the ideas should belong to me as much as to their creator, and in a nutshell that explained the whole existence and history of the bookaneers.

I had trouble looking at a book the same way I had before Mr. Fergins told me his incredible tales. He once said to me that books can make you do things without your realizing. For example, he said, when a book describes someone opening his mouth slightly and licking the outlines of his lips, you cannot help but touch your tongue to your own lips. If it is a bit more specific, say, describing the tongue running along each tooth under your upper lip, your own tongue will perform the act involuntarily sooner or later. A trivial example, of course, but he cautioned me that the pages of a book can influence our thinking and our actions in ways we never comprehend, and that the world of publishing has always been well aware of it. I have revered books, but now I never read a page without sensing the various demons fighting for control of the words, control of me. There were times when I cursed myself for it, and cursed Mr. Fergins for peeling the ink from the page and showing me what lay between.

A new book cart, smaller and creakier, appeared on the train before the winter was out. The vendor's New York accent seemed strange and modern when expecting Mr. Fergins's lively and soothing English. This impostor's cart never made a stop, never even slowed down, unless a paying customer snapped fingers or waved a hand. This made Mr. Fergins's removal from my life sting more.

Another few months went by. There used to be a small bookstore in the city, not far from where I was enjoying what passed for outdoors in that metropolis. In the window, I noticed the name Robert Louis Stevenson on a book under a placard announcing, "Newly Published!" I picked it up straightaway, expecting that Stevenson's masterpiece, the source of the battle between the two greatest bookaneers, had finally been published, and would give me some answers. As I held it in my hands, Belial's face, his proud and repulsive scowl, appeared in my mind. But this was no novel at all. It was called *A Footnote to History*, a long essay of sorts on Samoa. I could only read a few pages in the store before the glare of the bookseller paralyzed me. Mr. Fergins told me a bookseller can determine almost immediately whether one who enters his store can afford to buy a book or not, and, as usual, I fell into the latter category. Before I returned it to the table, I happened to notice the name of the publisher, Charles Scribner's Sons of New York—the same firm where Belial had been taken by the police.

That summer marked my last run on the New York Central and Hudson River Railroad before I joined the merchant navy, where I would remain in service for more than five years. The first two years I sailed the African and Asian continents, and I suppose it could be said that the experience changed and hardened me, but no more or less than any other man; after a brief sojourn on my own, I shipped with another vessel, which went through the South Seas.

There is so much to see when touring new places, I've found it interesting to notice what I remember and what is soon forgotten. What stays in my memory about my first passage through the South Seas are colors. Because of the volcanic coral below, the ocean waters take on a variety of colors depending on the spot, as though a rainbow dripped into the water. As we hove to, the giant black hull of our ship seemed an unwanted conqueror of all that beauty, the seabirds crying out at us. All the ships and buildings that could be seen on land from the sea were of European or American styles; only in the interior of the islands would I see what the native houses were like. Naturally, when I found myself in that amazing part of the world I began thinking again of the events as told to me by Mr. Fergins. The details were as fresh in my mind as if they had happened last week and happened to me; indeed, they were more real than some of my own adventures. When I had the opportunity to visit Samoa, with a little free time on my hands, I could not resist. I hired a guide and asked to go to Vailima.

Upolu was quiet. I saw scorched ground and from a distance I spied severed human heads on stakes—brown and white heads alike, and three of the heads appeared to be taken from women—but judging from the degree of decomposition, these horrific remnants of war must have been baking in the sun for a long time. My guide said that after an unusually dry season, famine had struck the island and the war halted. I had learned from Stevenson's book on Samoa (which I eventually read during my travels) that the island could have famine or it could have war, but it could not sustain both.

Vailima was as desolate as the island itself. Most of the livestock I'd heard described by Mr. Fergins wandered free or were gone altogether; two lonely horses grazed in the humid afternoon air near the paddock. One was a black mare with a lump on her knee. I recognized the other one as the novelist's unmistakable piebald circus animal, Jack. His mane was filled with flowers. Jack raised his head with a faint snort and blinked out at me with handsome but vacant eyes; I could picture him rearing on his hind legs and dancing. Instead he just chewed his grass and, tiring of me, lowered his head again. After a time, the tall, slender figure of a man approached and my heart beat fast with anticipation. He was wearing a straw hat and dark sun spectacles and was barefoot.

As he came closer, I recognized Lloyd Osbourne from Mr. Fergins's descriptions as a sturdy man with a juvenile face. He seemed sluggish in general, an impression made stronger by the striped cotton clothes that looked like pajamas, but he appeared equal to having visitors, even a stranger. He led the way inside to the great hall. There was the piano—now covered in layers of dust, like much of the furniture in the house—that Pen Davenport had once ordered Mr. Fergins to play.

"You can play?" Mr. Osbourne said in a tone between a question and a statement.

"My father's church had an organ and he used to teach me when the chapel was empty. I only know some very stiff church music, unfortunately," I said, running my fingers just above the keys, thinking of the bookseller nervously coaxing out Stevenson on Davenport's command.

We were joined by a native girl, no older than fourteen, who sat on the floor and mixed a drink in a sliced coconut shell.

"Have you had 'ava?" my host asked.

"I've heard about it from—" I stopped short. ". . . some of the sailors."

"Chewed root mixed with water, and strained. Oh, it takes some getting used to. But it's authentic, at least, more than can be said for the tinned beef and religions we've managed to introduce to the islanders. 'Ava is made in a rather grotesque fashion in the young girls' mouths, but one gets used to anything. Just stay away from green root."

"Oh?"

"The green 'ava root is stronger, and has a positively awful effect in nonnatives, so much that they cannot move their legs for twenty hours or so. The natives giggle about it, but you wouldn't if you ever drank it."

"Thank you," I said, as the shell came to me.

"My stepfather is over there," Mr. Osbourne said. I followed his gaze to a window that opened onto a view of the volcanic mountain rising above us. "We had a great ceremony with some of the local chiefs who helped carry his body up."

"What happened?" I asked, taking a small sip of the pungent beverage. "Forgive me for not knowing, Mr. Osbourne. I have been at sea and we see newspapers infrequently."

"Why, it was about a year ago from this past December. He wrote hard all day, *another* new novel he judged his best work—about a father who is a judge and a son who is a lawyer in Edinburgh—he always thought a new book would be his best. We had our 'ava as usual. He actually mentioned how well he was feeling, and that he was thinking of making a lecture tour of America as Dickens once did. He was talking and talking on the verandah, as buoyant as you please, when he suddenly dropped to his knees. We brought him to that green chair and later our little brass bedstead was carried down here. I took the fastest horse we had—Louis's fearless old circus creature, Jack—and went to fetch the doctor. When I jumped off, the doctor got on and Jack brought him back as though the animal knew what was happening and what was needed. I refuse to give Jack up for any price, for I think he is extraordinary, and the native boys who pass drape him in flowers as a reward for how he tried to save Louis. But, in any event, Louis never recovered consciousness. '*Tofa!*' whispered the Samoans all around the house. *Sleep.*"

"So much for a violent death," I said with a pang of unexpected sorrow.

Mr. Osbourne did not hear my quiet aside or ignored it. "You will find which path to take up when you are closer, now that we have marked it. I can tell you the inscription on the grave, but most want to read it for themselves when they reach the summit. You are a pilgrim, are you not, Mr. Clover?"

He shuffled to a chair and sank into it as I tried to think how to answer. "An American reader, traveling here to see Louis's grave?" he tried again, a touch of annoyance in his voice. "Oh, we have all kinds— acclaimed literati, political gentlemen of high standing, single women, Negroes, men who know not a word of English—nothing surprises me anymore. So many always said they *meant* to visit while he lived here, yet it's once he was in the ground that the visitors finally come for

Louis. He would not have liked to hear me call him that, you know. They called him by a savage name here and"—he chuckled—"he took to it after a while."

"Tusitala." This prompted a second look from the writer's stepson, and I moved the conversation hastily along. "Where is the rest of your family, Mr. Osbourne, if I may ask?"

His sister, Belle, had left the island almost immediately after Stevenson's death, and his mother departed from Samoa a few weeks later. Fanny returned to America, which, Mr. Osbourne said, she acknowledged as her true home. Stevenson had given a purse of gold to Ah Fu, the real name of John Chinaman, in case he ever wanted to return to his family in China, which he did only after the novelist's death. All but a few of the remaining servants removed to their own villages or joined the various warring factions. Mr. Osbourne stayed on to finish clearing out the estate. As I looked around, the scenes Mr. Fergins described to me four and a half years earlier came to life—the quiet infiltration by Davenport and Belial that had gone so wrong.

"What will become of Vailima?"

"Indeed, Mr. Clover," Mr. Osbourne said, then gave what Mr. Fergins had called a philosophical shrug. "My sister and mother prayed so hard to leave this island, prayed that Louis, a man who never changed his mind, would decide to go back to England or Scotland. This was rather a grand place once, and I even find myself a little reluctant to close it up and go. What a world this was! Louis may not have always been happy here, but I am sure of one thing: he was happier here than he would have been in any place in the world. Maybe one would not think a stepson could judge best."

"Do you recall a visitor to your house called Penrose Davenport?" I asked. "Or Thomas, the missionary?"

He seemed irritated that I had let his lofty comment float away in favor of my eager change of topic. I tried to make up for it by adding something personal. "I, also, have a stepfather, actually. I was ten when my mother married, and soon after I was told the white minister at the same church where my mother worked was my father. Maybe I had secretly known before; it's hard to really remember. I had two fathers after that, I suppose, but could not really call either one father."

He sat up straighter, closing his eyes and nodding before blowing another cloud from his cigarette and taking a long drink from a glass of beer that must have been near the boiling point, as it had been in the room before my arrival. "Who was it you're talking about? Davenport?"

"An American. It was some five years ago he would have arrived here. You might remember him by the name he originally gave: Porter."

"No, friend, no. This is Samoa. You cannot expect me to remember such things after so many have passed through here. Why, what white man in the South Seas doesn't go by a false name at one time or another? I wouldn't bet a single shilling your name is Clover."

"It certainly is."

"Even 'Tusitala' was a disguise of sorts for Louis," he went on, then sighed when he saw I still waited for him to give real consideration to the question. "There are four steamers a month that make port at Apia when it's not the rainy season, and back then there was an endless parade of strangers and visitors trying to stake claims to the island. And the missions, trying to collect as many souls as possible. Well, there were the Methodists, the Wesleyans, the Marists. Perhaps I do recall something of the missionary you mention. There have been so many who came through here, I probably could not remember half the names. They all liked Louis, and he usually liked them. Missionaries enjoy knowing men who have no religion. Fancy that! Thomas left rather hurriedly, if we are thinking of the same man. I tried to stay uninvolved in most of my stepfather's business and political dealings; it seemed to have a way of making me his partner, and I always wanted to feel I was his son. I spent my time overseeing the outside boys. As for Davenport . . . Porter, did you say he was called at first?"

"He was arrested when it was discovered he planned to steal some papers from your stepfather. You must remember. I heard about the affair from another visitor you might recollect, Mr. Fergins."

Mr. Osbourne rubbed his long chin and then began to make another cigarette. We were facing the barren fireplace that had cost Stevenson so much to construct. "The name Fergins sounds somewhat familiar, but my memory is very poor when it comes to remembering names. If you had their portraits to guide me . . . Porter, yes. Some of it comes back to me a little. I remember watching the pair of men being carried away by soldiers in a litter with iron bars around it. I cannot give you very many particulars, though, or tell you whatever became of the poor fellows. We've gone through so many wars here, so many coups d'état, it's a wonder we haven't all been tossed into the prison at one time or another. I find I remember such useless things sometimes. What do you make of that? I seem to remember the man's eyes—this Mr. Porter, I mean. Sleepy green eyes. Rather a handsome man, in a funny sort of way, no doubt my sister must have harassed him. Is that the fellow?"

I said it was, though of course I had never met the man outside my mind's eye.

"Yes, I remember those catlike eyes, but nothing about what happened after he was taken away. You can inquire at the prison to see their records, if they even keep any, which they probably don't since, I'll remind you again, this is *Samoa*. I think you have the other name wrong. Fergin, I believe it was, there was no 's' at the end. I helped bring him to Apia. Fergin was always reading one book or another he'd borrow from Louis's library. Do you know that once, in this very room, Louis laid down the copy of *Don Quixote* he was reading, and told me, in words that linger still in my ears, that it was the saddest book he had ever read. I asked him what he meant. He said, 'That's what I am—just another Don Quixote.'"

When I was riding away from Vailima, I looked back and noticed a swirling line of white smoke coming out of the chimney.

Three days remained of my furlough on the islands. Most of the men had taken canoes to one of the islands known to be filled with ritual dancing, feasts, and friendly girls. After speaking to Mr. Osbourne my purpose became fixed. I would find out what had happened to Davenport after his imprisonment in Samoa. That had been one of the questions I most regretted not having asked when I still had the chance.

Nobody at the Upolu prison had any distinct impressions of the man as I described him. One guard I interviewed thought certain the American had been in the prison for only six weeks, while another prison official believed the bookaneer had suffered confinement for years before deportation was arranged by the consulate. In any case, the prison had been through two fires and a dynamite explosion in an attempt to release political prisoners, and, as Mr. Osbourne predicted, there were no written records kept there. I could gain no reliable information about when he was released, or the bookaneer's whereabouts after leaving Samoa, if he did make it off the island safely. The men at the consul knew nothing more than the prison officials. My search seemed pointless until, back in the village of Apia, I heard a rumor.

It was said a white man of great ability and mystery who had been in Samoa had sailed to the nearby sovereign island of Tonga, and became a sort of informal adviser to the king there, after which he was granted control of his own small, sparsely populated island on the edge of the kingdom. I asked several Samoans and some foreigners who had been there for a long time whether this man was still on the Tongan island, and whether he and Pen Davenport might be one and the same.

"I do not know his white name, and I doubt it is remembered by anyone," said a Chinese man who owned one of three new restaurants in the village. "He is called Fa'amoemoeopu," said a fisherman, whose words my hunchbacked guide translated slowly in my ear. The name, I was told, meant "one who does not forget words." "It is said Fa'amoemoeopu was in Tale-Pui-Pui once, years ago."

"That's the prison?" I asked. I brightened up. Perhaps Davenport himself could finally give me the answers Mr. Fergins had not, if I could persuade him to talk to me.

"I saw him once." This came from a gray-haired Samoan woman whose excellent English brought her odd jobs for the American consulate.

"You did?"

"Not in person, no," she admitted. "I saw a portrait brought back from Tonga. He will not allow most men to see his face and it is covered by a bushy beard. But he has many followers and admirers who serve him, as I understand it. He is like you," she said after a moment of studying me.

"What do you mean?"

She grinned. "You could be his son."

I was not sure what she meant. Since to these natives my coffee-colored skin seemed more white than black, it could have simply meant Fa'amoemoeopu was a white man and the native woman thought I was also, or a close enough approximation.

By this point, there was not enough time left in the furlough to go to Tonga. In the months that followed, as we continued our route through the South Seas, Davenport—the exile, the secret white king of the natives—flourished in my imagination. His calling taken away from him, his rival having vanquished him, he would have refused to return to a world desolate and empty. The bookaneer would have a new purpose and a new source of power. As I became increasingly fascinated by these notions, I determined to return one day to investigate them. Then, there was a stroke of bad luck that proved a godsend to my curiosity. On our return voyage, the rains came and lasted a week; our ship had leaks and required repairs so we returned to anchor near the nineteenth parallel south latitude—not very far from Tonga. While repairs were being made, one of the masts was found to be rotted, which would require another week, at least. Being stranded let me solve the mystery of Pen Davenport sooner than I'd hoped.

THE CRESCENT-SHAPED ISLET in question was so small no map or chart shows it. The few histories of it I have found suggest it was discovered by Captain Bligh a few weeks before the infamous mutiny against him. I had to travel two days with no more than four hours' sleep in order to secure my transportation. The islet was part of a chain of land masses that formed a tail of the 150 islands that comprise Tonga. It had very little fertile land and was rocky even where verdant. I could see almost nowhere to land, the edges skirted with coral reefs and rough-breaking water even at mid- and low tide. I had been told that the small number of natives who settled there served as lookouts in the event enemies of Tonga tried to approach. This was confirmed as soon as we coasted through the early gloom of dawn into a treacherous and narrow opening in the rocks, the closest thing the isle had to a harbor. A group of watchful islanders appeared on the beach with spears out.

The natives who rowed my vessel stopped suddenly, some distance from shore. I was about to demand to know why they halted our progress. Then I noticed a rope drawn across the harbor's opening that would have capsized us. My escorts offered a series of elaborate gestures to our greeters to indicate that I wanted to visit and that I was coming in peace. The island guardians kept their eyes on me while my escorts conveyed the purpose of the tired, weather-beaten foreigner seated in the middle of the canoe: to meet the half-legendary Fa'amoemoeopu.

The rope was soon lowered but their continued skepticism toward my visit was palpable once I stood on the beach. All my pockets and cuffs were searched. Then I was asked to remove my boots and they led me farther ashore. The sand felt surprisingly solid between my toes. I was brought up a hill alone to a hut to wait, wait, and wait, and I could only hope the guides and oarsmen I had hired from the Cook Islands would not grow impatient enough to strand me. I pressed my fingers to my temples. Hanging from the rafters, there were palm-leaf baskets filled with colorful birds, whose squawking made any attempt to think or rest impossible.

New places and experiences don't frighten me. I was not the boy who once boarded a train to flee my small village. Indeed, if I was ever to return to New York City after my wandering years, I do not think I would be belittled by it. Neither was I so impressed as I once was by newness for its own sake. I could hardly remember all the places I sailed, and the journeying had only left me more restless. Still, there was something different about this. It seemed I had not merely reached another spot on the map of the world, but rather was seeking entrance into the secret life of a man who did not wish to be found. The truth dawned on me. My life could be at the mercy of Pen Davenport, this white dictator who had long ago traded civilization for raw power.

"If you please," said a tall bejeweled native who entered the hut with a silent step and spoke with a stern voice, but managed to convey enough kindness toward me to give me a little comfort. He left a tray that had a bowl of cold orange soup, some mango and pineapple, and some white grubs wrapped in leaves. I thanked him and I devoured almost all (leaving behind the grubs, which I feared might still be living). The tall native returned and gestured for me to follow.

I walked behind him up a steep hill to a larger structure, a building with a verandah and some enclosed rooms, though the roof and beams were still of the native style and I had to duck my head under the eaves upon entering. Once inside, I was brought into a chamber that I suppose could be called a parlor, though it had no chairs—just the mats on the floor in the style of so many of the islands in the area.

There was a white man lying on a mat on the floor, stretching his feet into the air. Chickens were pecking at the ground around him. He wore a loose-fitting native gown, the bland color of bamboo, while around his head a garland of satiny red and purple leaves marked him as a person of authority. His radiant face, revealed in the glow of the strong sunset coming through the windows, was covered by a full white beard.

"Fa'amoemoeopu?"

"My dear Mr. Clover, what a pleasure," said Mr. Fergins, a single tear creeping down his cheek.

"BUT I DON'T UNDERSTAND," I said after an exchange of mutually surprised greetings. "I expected to find Pen Davenport. . . ."

"Look at me, weeping like a schoolboy to meet an old friend," Mr. Fergins said, sniffing and drying his eyes. "Davenport?" He pronounced it as though he had not heard or spoken the name in a long time.

"From the descriptions I heard of Fa'amoemoeopu, a white man who had been in the prison on Upolu . . ." Even as I said it I recalled that the bookseller had been confined, however briefly, in the prison alongside Davenport. "Never mind. What could have possibly brought you back here after you returned to London?"

"What could have . . . ?" he again echoed my words. He polished his spectacles with the tail of his gown and, returning them over his eyes, blinked out at me with the look of a trapped animal. To observe him was to think that more than four years had passed since I had last seen him. He appeared different. I do not mean he looked as though he'd aged so much. True, the top of his head was now completely bald and his remaining hair whitened along with his new beard, but on the whole the bookseller, who at this point had to be nearing sixty, looked far heartier and more alive than the last time I had seen him. Perhaps it was the light, so much more natural and forgiving in this tropical setting than in the confines of a train car or the distracted haze inside any room in New York City. He seemed a man remade.

As I continued to wait for an answer, the details of the story he had told me on the stalled train and in his boardinghouse swirled in my mind, reordering themselves into something that had a new and fuller meaning. He was still examining me, expecting me to answer my own question—something, I thought, Pen Davenport himself might do.

"It was you," were the words that came out of my mouth, and suddenly I was trying to fathom my own realization.

"What? What do you mean?"

"What happened to Belial and Davenport . . . You did it. . . . You did it all. . . . You were the one."

"You always managed to impress me."

"If I impressed you so much, then why did you lie to me?"

"Lie? I did nothing of the sort, Mr. Clover." He seemed genuinely distressed by the charge. "Everything I told you was true. There were certain omissions, I suppose. Why, stories never can include every detail—it would be dangerous for all involved. Things *must* be left out."

"Tell me the rest of what happened when you were in Samoa."

"Mr. Clover, it was such a long time ago."

"You said stories must begin somewhere. Well, they must end somewhere else. Tell me how you turned the events against Davenport," I demanded, and he seemed to know that I had no intention of repeating myself.

"When we realized Whiskey Bill had sent both Davenport and Belial on the mission, and suspected that he might have written Stevenson in the latest mail to sabotage them both, I went upstairs to Stevenson's little sanctum, as I related to you from my sickbed in New York. 'Tusitala,' I called out to him. I found him there opening his mail, just as I described it to you. 'Mr. Fergins,' you'll recall he replied, 'I have here a most interesting letter from abroad. You might as well join me.' Only . . . there was nothing there from Whiskey Bill. He was showing me an amusing letter from a man in Wales who claimed that Stevenson stole the idea for *The Black Arrow* from him. That's when I interrupted and told Stevenson everything about us. Everything. I told him the truth about why the man they knew as Porter—Davenport— was really there, I told him who Belial was, too. Even about Kitten, and about the lives and times of the bookaneers.

" 'You mean you men have all come here, clear across the globe to Samoa, to steal my book?' Stevenson replied to me. 'Did you think I would stand for it?'

"I asked him to hold his fire. I said I had an idea to make things right. I began to tell him the intricacies of a plan. Then I added, 'You'll need my help with this design, because even with Davenport out of the way, Belial has to be dealt with.' "

Incredulous at what I was hearing, I interrupted. "Wait a minute. You mean to say you were the one to arrange for Davenport to be imprisoned?" I asked the bookseller.

"Yes, Mr. Clover, I arranged it with Stevenson, and I went along to the prison, so Davenport would not suspect my part."

"But Belial still got the manuscript," I pointed out.

"Of course he did! That was part of our design!" Mr. Fergins said, and emitted a joyful laugh. "It was essential to make sure he took it without any problems. You see, I knew that by the time we reached America the word would have circulated about our adventures, and every bookaneer left in the world would be trying to take the manuscript. They would be the bottom-feeders, the 'barnacles,' who would not mind the laws until they were in jail. But even if they were lesser lights than the top-notch bookaneers, they were still far too skillful for me to handle. I needed Belial to transport the manuscript in order to get it past them. Nobody but a bookaneer of the finest caliber could have managed it."

"But then you had to find a way to get it away from him once he was in America."

"A bit like taking a bone from a starved dog."

"The calendar—wasn't that it, Mr. Fergins? You tricked Belial into walking into that publisher's office, didn't you, by providing an incorrect calendar on the ship and making sure he wouldn't realize it was already after the first of July. Is that it?"

"When I was first in the South Seas," he said with a glimmer of pride in his eyes, "I noticed how there was almost no sense of the passage of time, usually hardly anyone even knew the date. Sometimes they didn't know the year! Time really does seem unsure of itself here, as though washed out by the tide tick by tick. With the copyright laws changing and paving the way for other charges, I suspected that if I could make Belial think we had arrived just a few days before we actually did, then the manuscript could be confiscated as soon we got past that final and crudest rung of literary thieves. I knew Judge Salisbury— now Senator Salisbury—a man who had bought books from my stand and who had traveled to London to deliver a lecture he called 'The Wrongs of Copyright,' was hungry to put a literary pirate on a whipping post to use for his campaign for the United State Senate. While I was at the German consulate with Vao, after she was carried out, I used their telegraph desk to wire Salisbury, telling him the publishing firms where I suspected Belial would try to sell the book upon arrival. His men were waiting at the offices of each important publisher the day our ship came in, with policemen ready to make the arrest."

"That is how you knew Salisbury would arrange with the judge presiding over the case for you to review the pages at the courthouse."

"Yes, he was in my debt. All was well for me, because I needed time to prepare it for publication. Meanwhile, Stevenson wired Scribner's. Everything was set."

I felt myself riding a wave of suspicion that I was misled again. "No—that can't be right. The novel you spoke of, *The Shovels of Newton French*, was never published. I tried to find it over the years with absolutely no luck."

He was nodding before I finished. "When Stevenson and I were planning that day what would happen, I talked about how I would help bring *Newton French*, his masterpiece, to light.

"'That? Really?' Stevenson gave me a humorless laugh under his breath. Then he said, 'Well, that book. The more I think about it, the less I like the blasted thing.'

"'It is your masterpiece. You said it was the masterpiece you had been missing from your career. I heard you say it!'

"'I write two or three novels at a time, Fergins, with two or three more in mind at all times. They come cheaply, and you must serenade them while writing, but all novels are disappointments as soon as they leave your hands. Think of this fact: my reputation will always rest in good part on *Treasure Island*—*Treasure Island*, for goodness sake!—a book for boys written with considerably less labor and originality, and probably more than the usual unconscious plagiarism, than anything else I've written. I do not think it will live beyond me, though I believe *Kidnapped* might. But that thing I've just finished? Why, I've burned far better books that that.'

"He was carried to his bedroom after a fit of coughing during this conversation, and I was bid to follow a few minutes later. 'Fifteen drops of laudanum, Fergins, that is all it usually takes.' The novelist spit into a silver bowl, where I could see saliva swirled with blood. 'Pay no attention; I have proven myself incapable of dying. You were correct that I was writing my masterpiece. It was *not* that foolish novel I was referring to.'

"I waited, holding my breath.

"'Samoa saved me,' Stevenson added in a very serious tone.

"I asked him rather bluntly what that had to do with anything. The novelist blinked like a man who has stood out in the sun after a long sleep. 'Fergins,' he finally replied, 'when I lived in Edinburgh with its icy winds and conventions, I spent much of the day lying on my back just how you see me now. How little our friends in Europe know of the ease they might find here in Samoa. Half the ills of mankind can be shaken off without a doctor or medicine here. It was Mark Twain who first told me about the enchantment of the balmy atmosphere of the South Seas—said it would take a dead man out of his grave, and, you know how Twain caricatures things, but he was right. I know what I look like to you, like an old skeleton, but I have become a healthy old skeleton. Now, were I to be deported—that would be a death sentence for me. The German powers that seek my removal must be repelled. My very life, not to mention the future life of the island, depends upon it.'

"'Then this masterpiece . . .'

"'There,' Stevenson said, looking at the pillow beside him on the bed, where a thick manuscript rested. It was in rough shape, the edges bent and folded, spotted with tobacco marks, the strained handwriting scribbled almost end to end, the very narrow borders of the paper filled with marginalia and notes. It was an incredible sight.

"It was the same novel he had just said should be burned, *The Shovels of Newton French*. Freshly confused, I was about to ask him again what it all meant, when I remembered how Davenport had found those original pages from *Strange Case of Jekyll and Hyde*—the very ones that led to Charlie's death—that had been used as scraps for other writing. I flipped the novel over and found on the backs of some of the pages, scattered among other meaningless and discarded writings, an entirely different narrative. I asked him if this was another novel.

"'*Here* is my masterpiece, Fergins. The most important thing I have ever written, that in which everything else I have tried culminates. It is no novel, heavens no. A comprehensive chronicle of the turmoil and the injustices of the foreign intervention in Samoa.'

"I scanned the pages, which contained dense descriptions of the islands' political and military conflicts. I remembered Davenport had come across similar scribblings during his first searches at Vailima but never gave them a second thought. It had some potential titles written in a list, including *A Footnote to History*. I looked back up at Stevenson and he continued explaining to me:

"'I have been writing it at the same time, Fergins, and with writing paper so rare and dear on the island, I had to conserve my materials and use the backs of my silly novel's pages. It may be found unwelcome to that great, hulking bullering whale—I mean the public. Nor is it likely to make me any friends; in fact, other dangerous enemies will follow. Still, I must not stand and slouch but do my best. Without my name, perhaps five people would read this. A few hundred people may read this because of my name only. But that is all I need, for those will be the right people, among them statesmen. To have your work read, that is one thing, and I am used to it. To have it read by the right people—well, to modern authors that is positively utopian! There will be no money to be made, and yet there is something far more than that this book will bring to life. The pages in your hands will open the eyes of the Americans, whose hands are not immaculate but are the cleanest of the three powers, to send their forces to counter the Germans who have enslaved and terrorized the islanders.'

"'You *are* trying to start a war,' I replied, unconsciously echoing the words of the embittered prisoner, Banner.

"'Not so. If the German Firm continues its way of overthrowing inconvenient monarchs and oppressing the other consuls, they will be the ones to let loose the dogs of war. I am trying to stop the island from being destroyed, Mr. Fergins. We haven't much time left before we need Belial to play his part in fulfilling your plan. He must think he has stolen this free and clear, and once he makes it past the other thieves—what did you call that lowest class of scum? The barnacles of the bookaneers—and is arrested in New York, you find a way to copy the Samoa pages from this pile to bring to the publishing house of Scribner's,' he urged. 'As soon as I am well enough, I will ride to the British consulate and telegraph a lawyer I know in Washington so the proper copyright will be registered the moment the law changes on the first of July, before you reach American soil. If the book is to help this island, this scheme must come to pass soon. If they will not publish it, I will pay for it to be printed myself. The best part is, any of your bookaneers still in business whom you encounter before the change in law will not even know what they look for. Even Belial will not know what he has in his own hands. This is what I relish about Samoa: you can be in a new conspiracy every day. Oh, and make sure to burn *Newton French*, won't you? I don't want to risk making money from it.'

"'You were working on this all along, knowing this was what mattered, and meanwhile Belial and Davenport chased each other around the island going after a novel that had no consequence to you. This was hiding right in the center of the maelstrom.'

"'Unchecked, the island will come to war again; before that to many bankruptcies and profiteering, and after that, as usual, to famine. Here, under the microscope, we can see all history at work. I find it is no fun to meddle in politics, but there comes a day where a man says: *this can go on no longer.*'"

Though Mr. Fergins was quoting Stevenson's words, the bookseller said the phrase with such conviction and clarity, he might have announced his own maxim for life.

I interrupted: "Then the letter you recited to Davenport in which Whiskey Bill revealed everything to Stevenson . . ."

"A fiction, Mr. Clover. I invented it as I was 'reciting' it to Davenport!" Mr. Fergins said with a gleeful smile. "When I saw Davenport was convinced by it, I knew my entire plan could succeed."

There were, he pointed out, certain real and unforeseeable obstacles: His release from prison was quickly arranged by Stevenson, but they had not anticipated the vengeful guards would drop him into the bush. Then there was Vao, discovering him in the mountains—though her help was crucial to return him to Apia, the bookseller now had to find a way to distract her from completing her sworn vendetta against Belial, whom she hated more than ever because of Tulagi's death, since Mr. Fergins and Stevenson needed Belial to get safely off the island with the manuscript. It was like walking across a tightrope. Had Mr. Fergins tried to divert her by telling her Davenport had contributed to Tulagi's woes, it might have taken her off Belial's trail, but she might not have been inclined to help a friend of Davenport's escape the bush. Meanwhile, Stevenson had promised to tell no one else at Vailima of their secret plan, and after the rescue from the cannibals the novelist abetted him by escorting away Vao and charging John Chinaman and Lloyd with bringing Mr. Fergins to the beach.

Mr. Fergins went on to explain to me how events transpired while he was operating his temporary book cart in New York. Judge Salisbury had Mr. Fergins assigned to authenticate the manuscript as having been written by Robert Louis Stevenson. As Mr. Fergins spent hours at a time examining the manuscript in a room at the courthouse, the bookseller carefully identified and copied the pages on Samoan history that were interspersed on the opposite side of the novel's pages. He later brought the transcribed copy to Scribner's as planned.

"That little book was published and brought new attention to Samoa, just as Stevenson intended," Mr. Fergins said. "The American presence was bolstered. Consuls were removed and replaced. Extraordinary, what a little volume no thicker than a penny's worth of gingerbread could do!"

"Yet the wars did not end."

"No, new men brought fresh arrogance and old hostilities remained. I'm afraid war continues in Samoa, as awful as before," Mr. Fergins said. "Perhaps it is a good thing Stevenson did not live to see it. He had his hopes that the book might change things once and for all but, in truth, every writer believes that about everything he writes."

"And the novel that you all once believed would be his masterpiece? *The Shovels of Newman French?*"

"*Newton French.* Burned. Just as Stevenson wished," he said with satisfaction. "Once I had the transcriptions I needed."

"The fire in the evidence room. You . . . you weren't caught in it. You didn't rush in to put it out, nor were you trapped there by some shadowy confederates of Belial. You started the fire yourself!" I cried.

"Well, naturally, but I did try to put it out, too. It got out of hand, I admit, and spread faster than I imagined. The sensation of burning those pages, the only copy of the work of a master, stopped me cold and was a feeling like none other I had experienced before. It quite literally almost killed me. I certainly did not think I would inhale so much smoke so quickly." He paused, and seemed embarrassed. "I am eternally grateful to you for nursing me to health, Mr. Clover, whatever the cause."

"Whatever the cause, you say! *You* were the cause! Besides, even if you honored Stevenson's wishes, you hurt the case against Belial."

"That prosecution"—the bookseller stopped and shrugged—"never had a chance. Salisbury knew it as well as anybody. He just wanted to have keelhauled a literary pirate so he could campaign on the idea that he was the champion of authors. People hate the idea of politicians, you see, but love the idea of authors, at least until they meet one. Fire or no fire, Belial eventually would have been released. I just needed it to drag along until I had completed my transcriptions to bring to Scribner."

"Where did Belial go after the case against him ended?"

"From all I heard, after he fled New York he decided to start a new life as a poet. Apparently, it was what he'd always dreamed of doing. But his jaw had been broken in two places by the policeman during the arrest, and it made it hard for him to talk at length, and almost impossible to be understood by an audience at recitations of his verse. He was a diminished man. He never stopped running, and did not stay in any one place for more than a few weeks. He had plenty of money, too, for he had saved and invested it over the years. His problem was not financial. It was a gap that opened between reality and his self-importance. Once he had been touched by the law, Belial thought everyone was trying to follow him, even long after he had become, in actuality, a forgotten man. The poems I saw of his were rather nicely composed, actually, if limited to obvious themes, sailing on rudderless ships in the night, that kind of thing. He ended up getting his throat cut in a fight with some men he accused of following him into a poetry recital in Hong Kong."

"As soon as Belial heard the fireworks outside the office of Scribner's," I said, "he knew you had done him in. It *was* Samoan, wasn't it? What Belial said to you when we met him in the courtroom." When

Mr. Fergins nodded, I knew I had finally cracked through the ice. I had unearthed a blatant lie.

He could tell what I was thinking. "I did tell you the truth, Mr. Clover, when I told you I did not know what he said to me that day in court. I could only assume he was threatening me. He believed I was vengeful and had orchestrated this on behalf of Davenport. Of course, that was not the reason. I vow I did *not* know what he said when you first asked me, but I do now. Since I returned to the South Seas, I've had time to study their languages much more fully. One night, in a dream, I remembered part of what Belial had said to me that day. It was: 'Ou te le malama lama.'" The bookseller appeared crestfallen as he recited these words. "It means, 'I do not understand.'

"You must see the pathos of it, Mr. Clover. He was the greatest bookaneer of our day. I rather hate to think of him so . . . bewildered."

"It was you," I repeated, fighting back a flash of anger. "*You* were the last bookaneer. Not Davenport or Belial, but you. You took it away from them."

He laughed. "Who am I?"

"You're as disloyal as you dare. Whiskey Bill was right about you. Why did you do it? Belial might have deserved to be tricked, but why betray your closest friend? Why did you decide to arrange for Belial to bring the pages to New York instead of letting Davenport succeed? If what you say now is true, you did not even stand to profit from any of this."

He straightened his spectacles and looked away. "I should think the why of this would be the most obvious part," he said, mumbling his words with a tone of disappointment.

"So it is, Mr. Fergins." I was ready to meet his challenge. "Davenport brought you to Samoa without your consent, and in the process you lost your bookstall, the one place, as you've said, that was really your home. He never respected you and that showed in how he treated you. What he did to Charlie was the same thing he had done to you, only the poison killed this time—you could not forgive him for that, and for contributing to Tulagi's despair and self-murder by corrupting Vao out of—well, some kind of perverse bitterness that Kitten had been taken away from him by Belial."

Anger flashed in his eyes as I cataloged Davenport's actions, but that passed, quickly replaced by surprise. "Say again? I did this for Davenport! For his own good!"

"What?"

He furrowed his brow and then began to pace up and down the chamber. "Yes, naturally, Mr. Clover. Think of it. Once Davenport's foot and leg were badly injured in the storm, I knew Belial would defeat him. It was a matter of hours once Stevenson finished the book. What could a hobbled and stubborn bookaneer do against an able-bodied one? The only way to avoid this, to preserve the legacy of this final mission, was to use Belial to our advantage—to allow him to take the manuscript but then upend him. However, I knew Davenport as a man too vain to allow Belial's triumph, especially after his discovery that Belial had been responsible for seducing Kitten into her final, fatal mission. When I realized this, I vowed to remove the mission from him altogether, from both of them. In the process, I would also do right by Stevenson, who had been kind to us. I saved Davenport's most important mission the only way I could, by tricking him out of it. I saved his legacy, and that of all bookaneers!"

"Do you think Davenport sees it that way? What does Frankenstein think of his monster?"

Mr. Fergins lowered himself back onto the mat on the floor, folding his chin into his hands and sighing wistfully.

This seemed to perplex him, so I tried a different line of questioning: "Where is he? Where did Davenport go from here?"

"He was held in Tale-Pui-Pui for about a month before being

released. Soon after leaving the prison he found passage back to London. I saw him frequently in that period after I left New York and went back to England. He even stayed in my rooms for a while. 'You, my dear Fergins, are my greatest friend in the whole world, or at least in London,' he'd say with rare affection and his usual obliviously insulting tone. He never did suspect that I had been the one to deceive him, and though I do not know if he would have sympathized with my reasons, I'm not certain he would have cared by that point. There was nothing behind his eyes anymore, and now he lies beneath the earth.

"When a great author dies, it is cried out by the newspapers and the newsboys who sell them. But when a bookaneer left us, what memorial did he ever have? Davenport was unmoored, perhaps not so different from how Belial himself became after turning poet. Davenport drank and drank. Unlike Belial, Davenport had never been able to keep a penny in his pocket, especially after Kitten's death. He owed a large sum of money to an infamous printer in Paris, and when he did not profit from the Samoan affair he could not pay his debt. He eventually had to work for the man in France, delivering messages and packages. When he could be found, I ought to say. I heard from one French binder that Davenport disappeared for seven days straight once on a binge. One day he was asleep in the woods, and when he woke, not knowing where he was, he tried to cross a frozen lake, but he fell in and drowned. Ovid once wrote that suppressed grief suffocates and multiplies its strength." He was silent for a long time. "I warned you not to involve yourself in the story I would tell you, that it would lead to dark passages. Mr. Clover, why dwell on any of it now?" His expression cleared itself of concern and I saw the face of eager, open friendliness I remembered, though I could hardly enjoy it.

"How is it you came to be on this storm-blasted little island, of all places on earth?"

"Now, that's a sensible topic. When I was first on Upolu with Davenport, I had overheard that the King of Tonga was seeking to devise and print a constitution that could be shown to interlopers in order to prove Tonga was free and self-ruled, and prevent the foreign powers that had fragmented so many nations in the South Seas. When I was back in London without my bookstall and without even the occupation of helping Davenport, I did not know what to do, but I knew what I would not do. I would not be left with nothing. I would not feel myself wither and fade away. I began to corresponded with the King of Tonga and made my arrangement with him. I would help write and print his constitution, in return for his financing my own ambitions here."

He was about to continue, but the tall native returned and whispered something in the bookseller's ear. Mr. Fergins nodded. He turned back to me, saying, "Rest, Mr. Clover. You have had a tiring expedition here. I must tend to some business, and then will return."

I wanted to ask exactly what ambitions and what business he had on this island, but he and the other man were already resuming their conversation in the soft language of this region, and exited. I followed at a distance, as quietly as possible. I heard them leave the building and so found an open window where I could look for them. They were standing outside with a dark-skinned man, dressed in ragged clothes, balanced on a wooden crutch to compensate for a missing leg. He had a simple haversack with him. Mr. Fergins raised his right arm in the fashion of an oath taker and the crippled man did the same. I could hear the bookseller say: "I am the keeper . . ." but he spoke the rest of his statement in a whisper, or maybe it was the strong southeast winds that prevented me from hearing what else he said. The other man seemed to repeat the saying.

I returned to the parlor and laid my head down on a white mat to wait.

My skin and hair stuck to the woven surface of the mat. It was dark outside the windows, but the darkness was starting to lift. A palm leaf of food was on a shelf in the corner of the room. A pig lay on its side and snored rhythmically. Realizing I had slept the night, I jumped to my feet. Outside, I found an older native man cooking over a stone fire pit. I explained to him that it was urgent I return to the shore and see if the guides I had hired were still there. He did not seem to understand a word, but took his leave to fetch someone at an unhurried pace. A few minutes later, Mr. Fergins appeared, once again in a formless suit that looked like a sack, decorated with a string of shells around his neck, and a crown of leaves.

"Do not worry at all, my dear friend," he said, interrupting me as I stated my concerns. "I took care of everything. When we found that you had fallen into such a deep sleep, I had one of my boys release your vessel and explain that I would arrange for your transportation whenever you needed to go. I hope you feel better rested?"

I said I did.

"Good fellow. It is such a rare pleasure to have a visitor here. Please"—he gestured—"have your breakfast and I will show you what I've been doing."

"Is that . . . ?" I began, staring at the selection before me as a native unwrapped a palm leaf from it.

"Turtle. Baked in its shell," said my host proudly. "Some gannet's eggs and some nuts."

Being around him was like being around a young boy. After breakfast, we went to a quiet lagoon, where he plunged in for a morning bath with a giant splash. I tried again to ask about what business he was conducting on the island, but his reply was that such things could wait. After bathing, we gathered crabs into a basket for an afternoon meal, and continued on our way. He was almost galloping.

The island was of such a narrow and curving shape, and had so many glittering rock and coral formations around it, we were always near some shoreline. But the breakers did not create the usual rhythmic, back-and-forth flow of the ocean. Instead, the noise of the waves was constant, like the engines of the trains where I used to dwell.

Unlike the terrain in Samoa, there were no mountains here. It was mostly low and flat, with some small hills throughout. When we gained enough ground to have a new view of one of the inlets, Mr. Fergins pointed out a surprising sight: a warship, rusty but upright and armed, basking in the light.

"My understanding was that there are no foreign powers here," I said. "I thought that is what you made their constitution to prevent."

"The frigate belongs to no foreign nation."

"Then who?"

"Me!" he exclaimed.

I tried to assess whether this was one of his little jokes. "You are serious, Mr. Fergins."

"Indeed. This was the German ship wrecked at Apia years ago in a hurricane. Since the Germans did not want to spend money to repair it, I convinced the King of Tonga to negotiate for us to tow it in and work on it. We still have some final repairs to make, but we are getting closer."

"What will you do with a warship?"

"Well," he said, seeming to think hard, "nothing *personally*. But one never knows what you will need to protect your own property. Come, we'll walk through the village."

We passed a massive stone formation, with twenty- or thirty-foot slabs covered in moss and creepers placed perpendicularly on top of pillars of similar sizes. What they meant, and how they were placed that way, explained my host, the modern generation of natives could not say. I followed as we climbed up a steep path, through a dusty hamlet of small huts and one larger, a wooden church painted white. I was still overflowing with questions from the day before.

"Can you tell me what happened to Vao?" I asked.

"Only what I've heard. That she eventually married a great warrior of a nearby village and dedicated herself to the local wars against the king and his German allies who had ordered her village burned."

"I had the impression that you had fallen in love with her when she helped you after your release from the jail."

He paused for a moment, shaking his soft, silky beard of the last few drops of water while he looked me over. "Me? Do not be ridiculous! I have told you my life before this was about books; my heart and head were stacked with them from floor to ceiling. There was no room for love. Vao was a dear girl but never the same after her misbegotten liaison with Davenport. After her quest for vengeance against Belial, I think the darker matters consumed her, and that beautiful young girl, the girl who had loved Tulagi so desperately, was gone forever."

It seemed to me he had misjudged the native girl entirely, that she had not been corrupted out of some state of purity, but had long been enveloped in grief for her father, waiting for her first opportunity to break free to fight the injustices, and might have felt an understanding from Davenport from his own grief over not saving Kitten. It made me wonder what else he might have understood incorrectly, and what I might have learned if I could have heard the same story from the lips of Vao herself, or from Davenport or even Belial.

He continued, ready to move on. "Here is what I am very excited for you to see."

As we came out of the bush into the beating sun, I heard a strange murmur, as though a thousand butterflies and flowers around us whispered a secret into the air at the same moment. There beyond a field stood a massive house, four times the size of the building where I had spent the night, with giant windows and long verandahs running on the upper and lower levels. It was like another Vailima. Such an unexpected place to encounter on this tiny, forsaken island.

Two natives escorted us inside. I was so distracted I only vaguely noticed that the helpful pair of men were extreme opposites: one tiny, the other nearly a giant. The first man was hardly the size of one of the other's legs. The house—if that is what it was—was built on an elevation and commanded remarkable views of the ocean breaking against the borders of the islands nearby. The interior of the palace, painted yellow and white, was filled with long tables with a peculiar variety of men and women sitting and reading books—dwarves, hunchbacks, old men and women with elephantiasis in a limb or severe trembling in a hand, one-eyed men, a young lady with a cleft palate, persons with limbs too long or too short. They were all natives, but the tints of their skin suggested they were assembled from a range of island populations rather than a single race. Those who were not seated were making their way from one part of the place to another. Occasionally one of these occupants would pass by us, whispering to themselves. I recognized some lines being spoken from books I had read—*The Odyssey, Gulliver's Travels*, a passage from an adventure tale by Dumas, even something from Stevenson himself. Each speaker bowed their heads at Mr. Fergins, keeping their eyes averted. The cacophony of whispers drifted through the house and, added to the heat and the jolt of recent revelations, left me dizzy.

"What on earth is going on in this place, Mr. Fergins? Have you made yourself some kind of despot?"

"Poor Tulagi. He was the hero in all this, Mr. Clover—a guardian angel of all that is worth protection. These dwarves—along with hunchbacks and the others you see who have come together here—are considered useless in society on these islands because they cannot partake in battle and other ordinary obligations, but I have recruited them all for a great endeavor. They work hard to prove they are capable since others no longer believe they are, or never believed it."

I wiped the perspiration from my head and eyes. "What endeavor are you talking about, and whose palace is this?"

"Isn't it marvelous? I ordered it erected!" His wolflike laugh flickered again. "As I say, the King of Tonga has been very grateful for all my assistance. I came back, Mr. Clover, because these South Sea islands may be the last place in the world where books have yet to exist. Do you see now? We can start anew with all of it. This time, we can do *better.* So much better."

I could hardly fathom what he was prattling on about. He did not seem to require a response though, and continued as we passed through an arch onto a grand staircase.

"Think of what you are witnessing here, Mr. Clover. I am creating a true Republic of Letters, a living Library of Alexandria! When I heard Vao speak English so perfectly, I realized in that moment that the natives of these islands were sponges, ready to soak in alien languages and knowledge on a vast scale—and in a purer way than we ever can—just as they had done with our religions, believing in them with directness and simplicity. Books are only as strong and as weak as pieces of paper, ready to be engulfed by all the elements around us. They are bound to disappear into dust. But people—well, you will recall how I was so struck by Tulagi, that little man carrying around the history of his islands on his sturdy shoulders like Atlas taking the world upon his back. That is what gave me the first germ of my idea. Here, I use the money provided by the Tongan government to train natives from dozens of South Sea islands in all the world's civilized languages, and then each one memorizes one of the great books. Fortunately, the churches here and at many other islands have already taught English to some of the natives, and made them familiar, generally, with higher sorts of morals."

We walked through another reading room, filled with carpets and silk hangings. My guide paused to lean in and listen to a younger man, missing one arm, reading aloud the moment in the tale of Sir Gawain when the green knight calls on Gawain to cut off his head. The bookseller, delighted, gestured for me to listen.

Gawain gripped his axe and raised it on high, the left foot he set forward on the floor, and let the blow fall lightly on the bare neck.

I pulled Mr. Fergins aside. "Where did these books come from? I thought there were hardly any to be found in this part of the world."

"I had my collection transported here," he replied, then showed a moment's hesitation. "Come with me, if you wish. I'll show you."

He led me to another staircase, from which we returned down below. There seemed to be two types of people inhabiting this mansion, the memorizers and the servants. Though it was difficult to tell them apart, since they were all South Sea natives of one kind or another and they all bowed and, it seemed to me, very nearly wept to encounter Mr. Fergins in the flesh. I continued to feel light-headed and had to steady myself at several points as we climbed through a hatch and down a ladder into a kind of basement story, which was supported by huge pillars of stone.

"Don't you see what you are doing here?" I asked as we descended. "I don't think you do. These people you have gathered together are outcasts. That's what they are. You have taken vagabonds and outcasts who are desperate for something more than what they are offered by their people, and you tempt them with the promise that these stories— stories that are not even their own—will make them ascend into a life of meaning, a life of happiness."

He thought about this and then gave a low whistle. "Why, Mr. Clover, that is a remarkable formulation. Yes. I must remember that. Promise that stories will make them ascend into a life of meaning. That is exactly what literature has done from the beginning of time!"

Behind a heavy door was a kind of library that was more like a dungeon. The floor was slippery, the walls slimy. The air seemed to have a film of dust in it. There were books everywhere.

"There," said Mr. Fergins.

"Why, you've practically buried them down here."

He nodded thoughtfully, pushing his spectacles up his nose until they seemed to stick to his face. But he seemed unwilling to look directly at his once-beloved volumes. "I'm afraid there is no choice but to store them away, for each memorizer must be restricted to a single book, in order to maintain their knowledge of it, and the temptation to find more books from my library would be too great."

"You've gone mad. This is mad. These books will shrivel away in this crypt. It is too humid. You might as well burn them!"

He gasped. "I would never do that, Mr. Clover." He ran a finger gently across the spines of the books.

"I won't allow it," I cried out. I began to grab books from the shelves. Soon I was cradling a large pile of them, some of them practically disintegrating in my arms. "I will take them back myself—back where they belong."

He picked up a bell and rang it.

"Call for your giants and criminals, and whomever you have tricked into being here, Mr. Fergins. I am taking these with me." But my fanciful rescue stopped as my head felt lighter and my vision blurred.

I could hear the former bookseller whistle for help and a moment later I was being carried away. I let my eyes creep closed. When I opened them again, I was inside a room propped up on some pillows on a sofa. Across from me, there was a young girl with cocoa-colored skin and big eyes, fanning me with a large feather. Her hair was twisted up above her head and my eyes were drawn to the brightly colored seashells that formed a rainbow from one ear to the other.

"Methought a serpent eat my heart away, and you sat smiling at his cruel prey."

The words sent a chilling sensation through me and made me blush, then I shook off my dizzy spell, remembering reading those same words in one of Shakespeare's sonnets. As I tried to regain my strength, I looked around. There were the usual woven mats on the floor, a stone washing stand, a glazed bookcase.

Mr. Fergins came inside the room and I satisfied him that I was not going to faint again.

He said, gravely, "Milton said that to kill a man is to kill a reasonable creature, but to destroy a book is to kill reason itself."

"Then why condemn books to that dungeon?" My voice was hoarse and trembling.

"To clear the way. Think of it like this: we will usher in a new age, free of all the shadows that have fallen on literature in the past. Call me quixotic, but this will revolutionize the literary inheritance we leave behind. These islands will be the New World for literature— an Eden of stories. Pilgrims will travel from all corners of the globe to this spot right here, to bask in a living literature, to witness what we have created. One day, I foresee new authors coming here; they will fill these empty halls and occupy these islands and tell their stories to my growing army. Sixty years ago, Emerson tried to make a utopia of storytellers in Concord, but man's natural selfishness ruined it. Not this time. We are not condemning the books; we are releasing them from their dead skin. No need for the likes of publishers or dealers or lawyers or censors or bookaneers as in the prehistoric era of books—just living, breathing, walking stories free to grow and prosper."

"The natives in this house will not live forever."

"Each memorizer will pass on his or her book to another memorizer, who will in turn do the same. Those who hear a story from the lips of one of my memorizers will never forget, just as I did not forget poor Tulagi's words that, unconsciously, became part of me. Oh, the once-great Library of Alexandria burnt to the ground, but the human soul will live on."

I was frozen in astonishment as he gesticulated joyfully and broke into his howling laughs now and again.

"Ah, here we are. Thank you."

Another native girl, as pretty as the first, came in with an open coconut shell, filled with a strong-smelling liquid inside it. "Fa'amoemoeopu," she bashfully greeted Mr. Fergins, then turned and held her coconut bowl out to me. The brew was bright green.

"Our own version of the 'ava they have in Samoa," said Mr. Fergins cheerfully. "Have you had any before? This will make you feel all better, by and by, Mr. Clover."

"Thank you."

"Why don't you stay?"

"Another night here?"

"That is not what I mean. Not just a night."

I looked over the room again—the washing stand, the pile of mats—this was a bedroom. It was to be my room. I turned again to the glazed case and this time noticed there was a single book inside, the glass too cloudy to make out any identifying marks on the book, showing only the reflection of my own sorrow-stricken face.

"There's plenty of room here, my friend. You would be very comfortable, would never want for anything. I have received letters from people around the world who have heard rumors about what is happening and beg to join us. But the composition must be just right. Yes, you must stay. It is decided."

The eyes of both beauties remained fixed on me. The two natives who had carried me, a blur of feathers, tattoos, hatchets, and rifles, stood in the far corners of the room, also seeming to await my answer. Mr. Fergins perched on his chair, his smile wide, watching as he waited—waited for me to drink, answer, join.

I looked down at the mucusy brew, which was bubbling over the coconut shell and dripping in warm strands down my fingers. I shivered, thinking of how I slept the previous night, after my meal, as though I was never going to wake again.

Mr. Fergins began to move his right hand and I thought he might take me by the shoulder to try to convince me. But instead he held his hand high. "Repeat after me, if you please. I am the keeper of the story—"

"I am awfully sorry, Fa'amoemoeopu," I stopped him. "But I cannot stay here now. I am signed on to help with this voyage once our ship finishes repairs. I cannot leave the other men shorthanded. I will come back when it is completed."

"You always were a good and honest soul," Mr. Fergins said. "Very well. Promise you will return?"

"I promise," I said, carefully placing down the shell and rising to my feet.

After he arranged for my departure, he bid me farewell at the shore with talks of our next reunion, his eyes becoming moist again. I don't doubt I left that speck of earth not a moment too soon.

I sailed far away, and when that ship ran its course, I joined another, and sailed again, all the while telling myself to forget my encounter with the last bookaneer.

Before the canoe had pushed off from the shore of Mr. Fergins's island to take me to Mangaia, I had been prepared to ask one last thing. I wanted to know why he never said good-bye to me before he left New York City. With this childish question forming on my tongue, I realized that, more than anything else, this was what I had wanted to know all along. If he had said good-bye, had written me a simple card once he'd arrived in London, I might have put aside the story he had told instead of dwelling on its mysteries for all these years. But as I phrased that final question to myself, it sounded pathetic and wistful, and I could not speak. In New York, Mr. Fergins had seen me for my interest in reading instead of the color of my skin, and at that time in my life I would have followed him to the end of the world. Now he had brought me there.

I never heard anything about Edgar Fergins again and, even though I endured a number of passages through the South Seas over my years at the mast and later as a captain, I would never return to that island colony to see what became of him. I have presumed he died years ago, orphaning that ragtag settlement. But, for all I know, he remains there, a little ancient man amassing hunchbacks from exotic islands and dreaming of a living state of literature. Sometimes, in my nightmares, I see myself trapped among them in that palace, babbling to myself for eternity, like a man hypnotized.

Today, I am still the reader I was in my youth. Every book I pick up, I pause to wonder whether it was the one behind the glass, the one intended to transform me. I also wonder about other things. Whether his tropical experiment really was the result of a sort of madness that had seized him, or whether it was the rational end of a man with a passion for stories who refused to feel his soul disappear with the end of his calling. I think of Don Vincente, the Spanish bookseller who stalked and killed his customers. He could not bear a life apart from his books, and Mr. Fergins could not die before seeing his own books come to life.

But I try not to think of how I saw him last. It makes me feel too great a loss. I like to think of him with both his hands clamped on one of mine in the giant train shed in New York, just after I'd help him down with his green cart filled with colorful books of all sizes, being careful not to rattle the cargo.

THE END.

THE STORY BEHIND *THE LAST BOOKANEER*

When Robert Louis Stevenson moved his family to Samoa, he indeed styled himself as a kind of chief of Vailima. As much as possible, the characteristics and details of the Stevenson family and the natives associated with them derive from history. As shown in this novel, Stevenson's role in island politics, particularly his opposition to the German consular and commercial activities, provoked both respect and animosity. Of her stepfather's various tangles, Belle Strong later remembered that authorities "attempted to deport him from the island, to close his mouth by regulation, to post spies about his house and involve him in the illicit importation of arms and fixed ammunition." Toward the end of his life, Stevenson believed his book on the Samoan situation, *A Footnote to History*, would have an impact, and to some extent it did—placing a magnifying glass on the actions of the German Firm and prodding the American and British governments to make changes in the leadership of their sometimes corrupt and complacent consulates. But the conflicts and civil wars still escalated.

In 1900, the Germans would claim Vailima as the residence of their colonial governor. It is currently a museum and still the only house in Samoa with a fireplace. One of Stevenson's short stories, completed in Vailima, became the first original piece of literature ever printed in Samoan.

Stevenson's hand-drawn map for *Treasure Island* really was lost, though it is my invention to suggest a bookaneer swiped it. Still, Stevenson, like all popular authors of his day, was affected by literary piracy throughout his career, and was keenly aware of that. "I have lost a great deal of money through the piracy of my works in America," he wrote, "and should consider it quite fair to use any means to defeat the lower class of American publishers, who calmly appropriate one's works as soon as they are issued." Rudyard Kipling, a younger contemporary of Stevenson's, who at one point planned to visit Vailima, merged the two senses of *pirate* when he put the situation this way (paraphrased in the letter recited by Fergins): "The high seas of literature are unprotected, and those who traffic in them must run their chance of being plundered." Stevenson's writing habits also set up a uniquely vulnerable scenario, with a British visitor to Vailima later recalling how the novelist's compositions often "were flung on the floor or allowed to drop into the waste paper basket; indeed a rummager in this sun-baked little room might have culled many riches from the scraps of paper carelessly flung aside and forgotten." At the time of his death, he left behind several unfinished and abandoned novels, including one of those mentioned here, *The Shovels of Newton French*.

Did bookaneers really exist? A few years ago, I stumbled on a stray detail indicating that nineteenth-century publishers would hire agents to obtain valuable manuscripts that were fair game under the laws. Because of their shadowy place in history, I could not find much else about this group, but I was intrigued. Building on this fragment of legal and publishing history, I tried imagining more fully these freelance literary bounty hunters—the history of their profession, what they might be called on to do, who they were, their backgrounds, how their lives would bring them to this unusual profession and how the profession would shape their personal lives. As far as historical fiction goes, it fit one of my ideals: a bit of gray-area history that cannot be explored very far without the help of fiction. In this case, it seemed to me to call for informed speculation—what I'd refer to as research-based fiction—plus plenty of imagination. I applied the term *bookaneer*, one I had noticed had been used in a generic sense in the nineteenth century about literary piracy (the earliest use I find is in 1837 by poet Thomas Hood). I cast a few bookaneers in supporting roles in an earlier novel, *The Last Dickens*, in which we encounter Pen's mentor-lover, Kitten, and hear about Whiskey Bill.

I realized I wanted to see more of these and other bookaneers, and reader feedback on this front encouraged me. This led me to create Pen Davenport and his assistant Edgar C. Fergins, whom I decided to follow on a journey that would test them professionally and personally. I envisioned my fictional characters crossing paths with a number of prominent authors in history, but my compass pointed them to Stevenson. I had been fascinated by Stevenson's time in Samoa. It was intriguing and mysterious to his contemporaries to think of a European author at the far reaches of the known world, and I had to imagine it would have been an irresistible quest for my bookaneers—a kind of moment of destiny for both sides in the (still raging) battle over creative property.

ACKNOWLEDGMENTS

This novel features some underhanded, nefarious members of the publishing field, but luckily there are none on this list. From the earliest version of the story, Suzanne Gluck and Ann Godoff guided my creative goals with insight and respect. I'd like to thank all the others who helped from William Morris Endeavor Entertainment, especially Eve Attermann, Raffaella De Angelis, Tracy Fisher, Ashley Fox, Samantha Frank, Alicia Gordon, Clio Seraphim, and Elizabeth Sheinkman; and from Penguin Press, especially Matthew Boyd, Emily Graff, Sofia Groopman, Darren Haggar, Sarah Hutson, Juli Kiyan, Kym Surridge, Claire Vaccaro, and Veronica Windholz, as well as Stuart Williams and his colleagues at Harvill Secker. Gabriella Gage helped my research get off the ground. I owe thanks to my usual readers and encouragers for key feedback and moral support: especially Kevin Birmingham, Joseph Gangemi, Benjamin Cavell, Scott Weinger, Marsha Helmstadter, Ian Pearl, Susan Pearl, and Warren Pearl, and, of course, my wife, the ideal partner and my ideal reader, and my children, whose pecking at the keyboard is responsible for all mistakes (and anything avant-garde).